SECRETS LIES & OBSESSION

Copyright © 2024

Edited: Eden Northover

Cover Design: Alex Perkins

All rights reserved.

ISBN: 9798334235427

For Charlie the cat, who sat beside me during all the planning, writing, and edits for this series.

CHAPTER ONE
A Direct Warning

Before Emily unfolded the unmarked letter, she stole a glance over her shoulder to scan the empty street outside her window. The neighbourhood remained tranquil, as pristine as always. She swiftly closed the blinds and returned to her spot in the kitchen, gripping the letter and memorising the words. *'You may think you have made friends here, but remember, you have enemies as well.'* Her heart pounded.

Just then, Theo strolled in, scratching his head. He yawned, oblivious to the threatening letter clutched in Emily's hands. What should she do? She pondered her options before discreetly folding the letter and slipping it into her back pocket. She didn't want to alarm Theo. After all, he had only recently settled in with her and was finally beginning to sleep through the night. It had taken a few months to get this far, since he arrived on her door step.

Emily's phone flashed again, and she reached for it. Multiple missed calls and messages from Rose. "Hey, is everything okay?" Theo asked, wrapping his arm around Emily's shoulder.

She nodded and took a step back. "I'm fine. Did you sleep well? Is Gran still asleep?"

Theo furrowed his brow, though clearly decided not to push further. He nodded and made his way to the bathroom until the sound of the shower drowned out the silent morning. Before Emily could contemplate the letter further, a persistent thudding sounded from the front door. Emily's hands tightened into balls, her nails pinching against her palms. Could it be them—the ones who sent the letter? Yet when Emily peered through the peephole, it was Rose who waited, her usually well-groomed hair damp and her face devoid of make-up. Emily swung open the door and ushered her in, pleased to deal with a more mundane problem.

Upon closer examination, it soon became apparent the issue was likely not mundane at all. It seemed serious. Rose's heavy breathing filled the room, momentarily overpowering the sound of the shower. She entered, feet moving unsteady as a deer on ice. Rose shut the door behind her, her gaze sweeping the room until settling on the bathroom door upstairs. "Who's that? Upstairs."

"It's just Theo. Come on, let's talk over here," Emily guided Rose toward the kitchen island. "What's the matter? You never leave the house without drying your hair first."

Rose was rather dishevelled. Not only was her hair unfinished, but a few buttons were undone on her shirt.

"Who have you told? Who?" Rose demanded, a sense of urgency in her voice.

"Calm down. Told who what?" Emily tried to maintain composure while watching Rose, who sighed; she had aged ten years since Emily had last seen her. "I received a letter this morning."

Emily's hand instinctively tightened around the letter concealed in her back pocket. But this was Rose, after all. The letter could be anything. An unpaid bill or misdelivered letter. Emily glanced across Rose's features again and it became clear. It had to be bad, had to be the same person. What were the odds that two separate letters would arrive at the same time? "What did it say?" Emily whispered, but Rose seemed blank. "What did the letter say, Rose?"

"It's about George. They claim to know that we were there when he died," Rose whispered, her voice trembling. "How the hell does anyone know about that? Who have you told?"

"Me? No one. Why would I?" Emily whispered.

Rose began pacing the kitchen, her voice growing louder. "Someone must have talked, Emily. Only you and I knew about George, and I can assure you, it wasn't me blabbering about my dead husband." Emily followed Rose's movements, desperate to regain control of the situation and lower Rose's voice. She contemplated retrieving the letter from her pocket, but it didn't mention George and would only add to Rose's distress. She wracked her brain, trying to recall any potential leaks. They had been certain that no one else knew. The police had accepted their account, and Florence and Ava were privy only to the bare minimum of what had occurred. It had been well over a year now. If the police knew something, if *anyone* else knew something it would have come out then. So why now was someone sending threats?

When she glanced back at Rose, the same anxious expression from that fateful night marred her features. They believed they had gotten away with it while watching George take his last breath before their eyes. Rose didn't deserve for the past to be dredged up again, and a murder charge was the last thing Emily wanted with the weight of a possible money laundering case hanging over her, too.

"Who do you think sent it?" Emily asked, trying to steer the conversation towards a more rational path.

Shrugging, Rose replied, "I have no idea. If you've told no one, well, I guess it could be anyone, couldn't it? But why threaten us now?"

Emily poured herself a glass of water, desperately seeking a respite from the mounting tension. "How much do Ava and Florence know? Did you share more with them than we had agreed?"

"Of course not. All they knew was to support the story that I wasn't home when George fell. That's it."

"And you haven't confided in Ava further?"

"Why would I? Just because she's my sister? I wouldn't even divulge my password to Ava, let alone involve her in a cover-up for murder." Rose crossed her arms with a defiant lift of her chin.

"Do you have the letter? Did they demand anything else? Money?" asked Emily, desperate for any clue that might shed light on their tormentor.

Rose chuckled dryly. "No. No ransom or anything of the sort. The letter said something like, *'I know more happened the night George died, and your recent relationships aren't as trustworthy as you might think. Be cautious about trusting your closest friend.'* Or something. I didn't have time to memorise it."

Emily replayed the words of the letter sitting in her pocket. Both had a similar threat. Warning of trust and friendship. They could be from the same person, but even so, no names jumped out in her mind.

"Well, perhaps that's a silver lining. No evidence, just

vague threats. It'll be our word against theirs," Emily suggested with optimism.

Rose bit her lip. "But they didn't ask for anything. There's bound to be more letters on the way. Some kind of demand."

A voice from upstairs interrupted their conversation. "Em, care to join me up here? Cynthia is still sound asleep, and the water is delightful."

Emily felt her cheeks flush when Rose glanced at her. She feigned a smile, silently pleading with Rose not to delve further, but with a cautious tone, Rose said, "Emily, dear. You and your friend Theo. Exactly how *close* have you gotten recently?"

Emily held out her hand before Rose could say anything further. "Before you even suggest it, Rose—no. I haven't breathed a word to him. This has nothing to do with Theo or whatever we do behind closed doors."

"Well, I suggest you give it some thought. Because if this gets out, we can bid farewell to the rest of our years."

Ever since the police had launched their investigation into Emily's art sales in the summer, the image of iron bars had haunted her thoughts. The freezing of her bank accounts was bad enough, but the prospect of spending the rest of her life in a cell was a terrifying notion. She wouldn't be able to handle the harsh realities of prison, and the thought of Rose enduring the same fate was even more unbearable. It seemed unjust that even in death, George continued to control Rose's life.

As Theo descended the staircase, gratefully clad in a towel, Rose and Emily's attention shifted to the commotion outside. Blue lights. Wailing sirens. An unsettling symphony grew louder with each passing moment. Exchanging a knowing glance, they silently stepped out into the open. As the police approached Beechwood Close, Rose clung to

Emily's hand, seeking solace in their shared uncertainty.

"What's going to happen to us?" Rose's voice trembled.

Emily shook her head, her gaze fixed on the distant sirens. "I don't know."

"Will we be alright?" Rose pressed, her desperation evident.

A tight knot formed in Emily's stomach, constricting her words. "I don't know," she replied, her tone devoid of the certainty she knew Rose craved. They stood together, bracing for whatever fate had in store.

CHAPTER TWO
Hidden Depths

The tranquil lake within Beechwood Close had a strange impact on Ava. It reminded her of her late husband, who often sought refuge there during his private walks to clear his head. Memories from years ago still haunted her: Nick strolling through these woods with Katherine, conspiring in the night. During the darker times of Ava's marriage, she found herself walking along this very path and felt like a fraud as she strolled beside Florence now, especially when, not long ago, she would meet Florence's husband Oscar here.

They continued strolling along the dusty path, surrounded by trees, the leaves crinkling in the breeze. The sounds of nature were soothing to some. Ava couldn't help but glance at the metal bench when they passed it—the last place she had spoken to Oscar on that fateful night, gazing out at the lake, planning for a future that would never materialise.

A year later, the fellow widows strode side by side; their situations both unthinkable and unbelievable. The past year had been harsh on them both, and Ava marvelled at how well Florence seemed to cope. She wouldn't blame her friend for turning to drink again. Truth be told, Ava would probably join her.

When they finally reached the bench, Florence crouched down to retrieve a stone and toss it into the lake. It sank with a thud, creating ripples that disrupted its mirror-like reflection.

"So, what was the reason for bringing me out here? You know I rarely exercise if I can help it," Ava said, trying to keep the mood light.

Florence turned back to Ava before slumping down beside her. Having known Florence for years, Ava knew when her friend was struggling. Her eyes were like empty pools, and Ava could tell her smile was feigned.

"I needed some time away from the house. My parents are smothering me. Lucas is hovering around them like they are the second coming, and all Olivia is concerned about is how swollen her legs are getting from the pregnancy," Florence said. She picked up another stone and flung it into the lake. "If Oscar were still here, I'd kill him myself for leaving me with this mess to deal with alone."

Ava chuckled, wrapping an arm around Florence. Ava remembered well what Florence's parents could be like. Oscar and her had many after sex chats about them. How smothering they could be, how Florence could never do anything right in their eyes. How he was never quite good enough as a husband or father. "It's not all bad. At least Mike isn't around anymore. Plus, you have me, a couple of widows with an entire future ahead of us."

Florence turned her gaze back to the lake, seemingly lost in its depths. Ava tried her best to put herself in Florence's shoes. A child barley old enough to cook her own meals, sitting there with a child on the way. The idea of a baby in the house at her age made Ava's face crumble. Her friend was taking it well though, or as well as could be expected. Ava wasn't so sure she'd be able to continue on the way Florence has been. "You haven't mentioned Nick much. How have you been, back at home without him?"

Ava raised a brow and hesitated. Life without Nick was hardly different. In fact, she felt freer than ever, but she couldn't share that with Florence—not yet. No matter how long they had been friends, it was still too sensitive a subject.

Ava tried to deflect the conversation. "With Katherine around, I've been so busy that I haven't thought much about it."

"I counted five different men coming and going from your place last week," Florence teased.

Ava couldn't ignore how her home had gradually transformed into a makeshift brothel since Katherine moved in, just a few months ago. In truth, it had felt like years. Men of all kinds would arrive at various times throughout the day, timidly passing her window and making their way to the annex at the back where Katherine awaited them. Some visits were brief, lasting only a few minutes, while others extended for hours.

"I wouldn't mind, you know," Ava said, a touch of longing in her voice. "At least she's having fun. But they don't even look at me—not a single glance! They have a better option right in front of them, but they don't even realise it." She sighed. At least when Nick was alive, he'd look at her, arrive home with gifts. Now with him gone, Ava found herself longing for something, anything in the long evenings that was no longer there. "How long should a widow wait after their husband dies? You and Doctor Mike moved on rather quickly, although perhaps he isn't the best example..."

Florence rolled her eyes. "You don't want to follow my lead,. It's been one disaster after another."

"More than one disaster? Do tell." Ava turned to face Florence directly, catching her friend's eye. When Florence quickly averted her gaze, Ava knew she had struck a nerve. "Come on, spit it out. You're hiding something, aren't you? Tell me."

"Ava, no." Florence stood and approached the water's edge.

"I knew there was something going on. Even after Mike left, you had a spring in your step," Ava said, determined to unearth the truth. "Come on, I promise I won't tell anyone."

"It's really nothing," Florence insisted, yet the reluctance in her voice gave her away.

Ava sensed there was more to the story. Florence was keeping something under wraps, and Ava's curiosity was getting the better of her. Was it an affair with a married man, or perhaps someone younger? What other reason could there be for Florence's secrecy? Ava pulled her face straight, the first signs of a smile had graced her lips, but for the moment she needed to keep her cards close to her chest. The idea of a secret, pulled on her, allowed a moment to fill her recently empty life. She didn't know if that was sad to admit, but she needed something.

"I promise. It'll stay between us. Just give me something to keep my mind occupied," Ava implored.

"It's private, Ava." Florence focused only on the water.

"Fine. I'll just ask your mother," Ava said, her eyes twinkling mischievously. "I'm sure she'd be more than willing to spill the gossip."

Florence spun, eyes wide. "Please don't mention this to her."

A smile crept onto Ava's lips. "My silence can be bought."

Taking a deep breath, Florence relented. "Fine. But this stays strictly between us."

"Of course," Ava assured her, leaning forward with anticipation. This was so unlike Florence, who was always the dependable and level-headed one of the group. The prospect of a juicy secret had piqued Ava's curiosity.

"It's me and Regina."

Ava scrunched up her face, waiting for Florence to say more. What did Florence's secret man have to do with Regina? she thought. "What? Does she have a brother?" Ava asked.

Florence ran her hands through her hair and crouched to throw another stone into the lake. "No, Ava. It's not about someone else. It's about me *and* Regina. *We're* the secret."

The realisation hit Ava like a lightning bolt. *Of course*. It had been right in front of her all along. Regina had been living with Florence for months, and the two of them barely spent any time apart. When Ava turned to Florence to crack a lighthearted joke, a tear rolled down her friend's cheek. Ava stood and enveloped Florence in a comforting embrace. Ava couldn't work out the tears. They should be ones of joy, happiness, but her face told a different story. Why was Florence keeping such a huge thing secret? "Flo, come on. This is fabulous news," she reassured her, gently wiping away the tear. "We all know men are trash. Am I a little upset and slightly annoyed that you didn't fancy me? Yes, but I'm thrilled for you. This gives you such an edge. Some real character-building stuff here, Flo. No one can say you are the boring one now, can they?"

Ava held Florence tighter, a mix of emotions filling the

silence until a gurgling from the water interrupted their embrace. Bubbles rose to the lake's surface, and the two women drew apart, turning to it. A splash erupted, and a dark suitcase—or some sort of large bag—began floating towards them. They exchanged puzzled glances. "What the hell is that?" Ava exclaimed.

Florence and Ava circled the lake for a closer look. Ava recoiled at the overwhelming stench, but Florence leaned closer to the mysterious object. Stretching on her toes, she peered intently at it until her face turned deathly pale. The repulsive odour must have proved too much for Florence, who hunched over and vomited on the ground. "Call the police," she said between gags.

The putrid smell reached Ava, too, as she leaned over to comfort Florence. When she glanced at the object again, her heart sank. Beneath the sludge and grime was a black suitcase, with torn fabric revealing what looked like a skull. Overwhelmed, Ava turned away from it before pulling out her phone. "Police? My friend and I have found a body. Yes, a body. It's in the small lake beside Beechwood Close."

They waited in silence. Florence's revelation suddenly felt inconsequential to this. The discovery of a body submerged in the depths of the lake had shattered any sense of normalcy. Ava's thoughts raced, landing on Nick and the countless nights he spent here with Katherine in the past. She closed her eyes and fervently prayed he had nothing to do with this horrifying find. Wrapping her arm around Florence again, they sat and waited as the sound of sirens grew louder, filling the street—a sound that the residents of Beechwood Close had become all too accustomed to.

CHAPTER THREE
Suspicious Minds

More police officers arrived and flooded the close, joining the worried neighbours spilling out of their houses onto the street. Emily passed by Edna, her beady eyes already surveying the scene. Rose clung to Emily's hand as they walked toward the lake. Amidst the commotion was a glimmer of relief when Emily noticed the ambulance. They weren't there for her and Rose, after all.

Navigating through the gathering crowd, Emily caught sight of Florence conversing with a police officer, while Ava perched on a rock, engaged in conversation with another. Aware of the curious gazes following their every step, Emily and Rose proceeded toward the crime scene. Police tape had been placed, cornering off a section of the lake. Police men and woman stood guard, keeping people back. Thoughts swirled in Emily's mind—had one of their neighbours sent the letters? Had someone from the close seen them that night? As the officer left Florence, Emily reined in her imagination and draped a gentle arm around her friend.

"What the hell is going on?" asked Emily. "Are you two okay?"

Ava joined the growing circle then.

"We're absolutely fine," Ava said before Florence could utter a word. "It was quite a shock. I've already had to recount the story three times. Haven't I, Flo?" Florence nodded, crossing her arms.

Cynthia and Edna hobbled over to join them, dressed in matching cardigans. They shuffled forward, leaning on their walking sticks, while Larry followed a few steps behind, struggling to catch up. He had been living with Edna for a month now, and though Cynthia wouldn't admit it, Emily sensed her jealousy. Ava seemed to wait until a suitable-sized crowd had gathered before speaking up. "I won't beat around the bush. Florence and I stumbled upon a body emerging from the lake."

The crowd gasped, and the hushed murmurs grew louder. "A body? Are you sure?" Edna pushed her way forward until pausing at Ava's side. "Here?"

"Believe me, Edna, the smell was unmistakable. The police have already taken it away. Judging by its condition, it wasn't a recent occurrence, so we can all sleep soundly, knowing it wasn't someone we know from here," Ava assured them.

Cynthia stood beside Edna, her face laced with lines as she narrowed her brows. "We can't be certain of that. The killer might still be lurking; any one of us could be next." She turned to face Larry. "You better fix the lock on Edna's back door. We wouldn't want her to fall victim next, would we?" Larry grinned, but Emily noticed Edna give the back of his leg a stern whack with her stick.

"Are we safe here? Maybe we should all find temporary places to stay," Rose piped up, folding her trembling hands behind her back.

"The police assured us we are unlikely to be in any danger," Florence interjected. "As Ava mentioned, the body wasn't... fresh. Whoever committed this act is long gone. I believe we should allow the police to do their job and not spread rumours or gossip." Florence aimed a pointed glance at Cynthia just as Ava stepped forward, elevating herself above the crowd. She stood on the small rock she had perched on earlier.

"Flo is absolutely right. This community has been plagued by so much gossip and rumours lately. How about we organise a fundraiser for the victim? Next week, everyone can come to my place. We can raise funds to support the family of the deceased."

Emily had to stop herself from laughing. Ava never seemed to miss an opportunity to make everything about her. This fundraiser was more about attempting to raise her own status than offering any real help. Edna muttered under her breath, "A fundraiser for someone you don't even know? Come on, Ava, get real."

Ava's composure wavered. Emily had always been impressed by Ava's ability to handle herself and her unique way of controlling the crowds, but since Nick's passing, it appeared her facade had faltered slightly. As the crowd gradually dispersed, Ava stepped down from the rock and retreated from the spotlight, her cheeks flushed from embarrassment.

Emily welcomed the tranquillity back inside her home. It was still quite early, and her head throbbed as she glanced outside to where her grandmother gossiped with the neighbours. Emily couldn't summon the energy to care much about it, and while it felt terrible to admit, it was the truth. A cold case murder from years ago was the last thing she had time for. She needed to stay focused on the present. She reached behind her to where the note still burned a hole in her back pocket. Theo was busy in the kitchen, preparing breakfast. He wore a pair of chinos and a button-up shirt—a sight that still felt unfamiliar to Emily.

Emily had purposefully left Theo behind. After university, they mutually ended their relationship to pursue separate paths. It was only when Rose needed help with her book launch that Theo reentered Emily's thoughts. Taking a seat at the breakfast bar, Emily was greeted by the enticing aroma of grilled fish. Theo was an excellent cook—he always had been, yet now it felt like having a professional chef in the house.

"The rice will be ready in a second if you want to grab a few plates," he said, lifting the lid of the wicker basket with the rice inside.

"Another one of your family recipes?" Emily asked. Theo was always so proud of his heritage. Fish and rice wasn't exactly a *normal* breakfast to eat here, but Emily was keen to welcome home comforts for him, when she could.

"Of course, I think this one came from my grandma," Theo replied, sliding the fish onto a plate in front of Emily. "What was all the drama out there about?"

Emily glanced up, wishing she didn't have to tell him. His eyes remained fixed on her waiting for an answer. "They found a body in the lake. Apparently, it's been there for years."

"Damn. I wonder who it is?" Theo muttered, sitting beside Emily, who pushed the rice around her plate with her fork. "Not hungry?"

She placed her fork down and stared out the window. "I am. It's just been one of those mornings." She shifted in her seat to face Theo. "I wasn't sure if I should tell you or not. I know how much the past few months have affected you, and you've been doing so well recently, getting back to normal."

Theo finished chewing his mouthful and set his chopsticks down. He cleared his throat, wiped the corners of his mouth and straightened his back. He attempted to look grown up, serious, as his face matched his posture. "Is this about the stalker?" Emily sighed. When Theo arrived last month, he was a wreck.

One by one, members of their friend group from university had been systematically followed and attacked. Cassandra had lost the most, with her life. The thought of it tormented Emily most nights since she'd found out. Theo had arrived in Beechwood to ensure Emily was safe. But now, with this letter burning in her pocket, she couldn't help but feel that she—or Theo—could be the next targets. She placed the letter on the table, and Theo leaned over to read it.

"Do you think it's the same person? It must be, right?" Emily asked.

His eyes fixated on the note as he pushed his breakfast away. "When did you receive this?"

"This morning. It came in the mail. Maybe I should just throw it away and forget about it." Emily picked up the note and crumpled it into a ball.

"Wait!" Theo exclaimed, jumping from his chair. "Keep it. You might need it as evidence." Emily froze. He was right, although she didn't want to entertain the idea that this was a credible threat. Keeping the note as potential evidence meant accepting this was real. It meant acknowledging that there truly was someone out there hunting them down. She didn't want her life here to be destroyed. She needed to discover who was behind this note and the one sent to Rose. Perhaps they were the same person. Either way, Emily needed to keep the police out of it for as long as possible.

Emily turned back to face Theo and forced a smile. "You're right. I'll keep it safely tucked away." She walked towards him and nestled into his shoulder as he wrapped his arm around her. "We have to find out who's behind this, Theo. I don't want to involve the police until we're certain. I can't afford to take any risks, especially with the fraud investigation still ongoing."

"I understand," Theo murmured. "Whoever this person is, they're clearly dangerous. Cassandra has already paid with her life. I can't risk losing you, too."

Theo held Emily tightly in his arms, and she felt a mix of emotions swirling inside her. So much had been lost from her friends at University. It had almost felt like a different life, one she had moved on from. But that didn't stop the guilt. It didn't stop the grief of knowing her once friend was now dead. None of this was part of her plan. Theo was only meant to stay a few nights and keep a low profile until things settled down. Now, after years of silence between them, they shared a bed and had fallen into a routine. Emily knew she had to stay focused and keep her wits about her. Anyone could be behind these letters, and if they were as dangerous as Theo believed, she had to act quickly.

CHAPTER FOUR
Family Matters

The mornings always arrived too soon for Florence, who preferred to lie in bed and relish in the precious moments with Regina. Sunlight gently crept in from the curtains, casting a warm glow across the room. On the side, was a photo of them both, hugging, cheeks touching and smiling. To anyone else, it would be a photo of two close friends. Everywhere Florence looked, there was a reminder that Regina was part of this home. A china dove placed on the window seal, Regina's incense stick burning away in the corner. As they lay together, Florence couldn't help but smile, cherishing these stolen hours before the light of dawn revealed their secret.

They hid their romance from Florence's parents, who now lived in the house, too. Every morning, as soon as Florence heard a peep of noise outside their bedroom door,

Florence would softly rouse Regina, urging her to return to her own bed on the opposite side of the corridor. It felt like a teenage affair, sneaking around, hoping not to get caught by her parents. Only this time, it was happening in her own home.

When Florence descended the stairs, she was greeted by her mother, a face she hadn't seen in years until a month ago. The years apart now emphasised every sign of ageing on her mother's face and body: the wrinkles, creases, and white hair.

"Morning, mother. Is there any coffee for me?" Florence asked, trying to sound casual.

Her mother looked up from her tablet with glasses perched on the point of her nose. "If you make another, fill me up, love. You could do with a bigger cafetiere."

Florence playfully narrowed her eyes at her mother, who had already returned to her tablet. She filled the kettle and observed a dishevelled Lucas sluggishly descending the stairs. He hadn't even bothered putting on a shirt as he slumped on the couch. Florence waited, half-expecting her father to scold him again. Sure enough, her father, who sat with his feet propped on the armchair, nudged Lucas and whispered something in his ear, prompting him to leap to his feet. Florence approached him.

"Where are you going?" she asked.

Lucas scratched his messy hair, seeming to contemplate his response. "Just grabbing some stuff for granddad. Need anything, Gran?" he called to her mother.

"Dad, can't you pick it up yourself? I assume you still have something left in your wallet," Florence said, a hint of annoyance in her voice.

Her father's face flushed as he straightened in his seat. Opening his wallet, he handed a note to Lucas, who surprisingly shook his head to refuse the money, pulling a hoodie over his head before leaving the house. Florence found it peculiar that Lucas was going to great lengths to please his grandparents. She couldn't quite figure out why.

Before she could question her father about Lucas's behaviour, Regina's steps could be heard coming down the stairs. She stepped into the kitchen, a few inches away from her mother.

Florence's mother fixed her eyes on Regina; she held her glasses with one hand, tapping a rhythm with her pen in the other. She assessed Regina from head to toe. Florence wanted to intervene to prevent any uncomfortable conversation, but it was too late. Her mother stood, plastering on a smile as she addressed Regina.

"It's absolutely fascinating," her mother cooed. Regina glanced at Florence's mother and smiled.

"What is, Joan?" she asked, cornered against the sink. Her gaze flitted to Florence.

"Isn't it lovely, Gill?" Florence's mother called to her father. "We've known each other for a while now, dear. Would you mind if I touched it?" Without waiting for an answer, Joan ran her fingers along Regina's hair, who recoiled and stepped back.

Sensing the rising tension, Florence stepped forward to position herself between the two women. She observed the anger simmering in Regina's eyes and aimed to defuse the situation before it escalated. "Mum", please don't do that."

"Do what? I was merely admiring her hair," Joan said, an edge in her voice. Florence glared at her father, although she doesn't know why she bothered. He turned his head to focus on anything else he could.

"It's a personal boundary, Joan. I'm sure you wouldn't appreciate someone pulling and tugging at your hair, would you?" said Regina.

Joan rolled her eyes and gave an exasperated huff. "Well, I don't see the problem. You lot are always making a fuss over nothing."

Florence shot Regina a look to keep her from retaliating as her mother walked away towards the lounge. Biting her bottom lip, Regina turned to Florence, her frustration evident.

"Well? Don't you have anything to say to her?" Regina whispered.

"She doesn't mean any harm by it. I'll talk to her later, I promise," Florence said, hoping to ease her concerns.

Regina leaned in closer, whispering into Florence's ear. "You better make sure you do. Otherwise, there might be another body in that lake soon."

Florence felt a shiver crawl down her spine. "Trust me, I'll handle it. No need for any more bodies, alright?"

The salon buzzed with the sound of hairdryers and chitchat. It was the only place where Florence found solace since her home had been invaded. At least at work, she could distract her mind and keep an eye on Olivia. Despite Florence's advice to take time off until the baby arrived, Olivia insisted on staying busy. Florence understood her need to keep occupied, but she couldn't help worrying. Olivia was already struggling to stay on her feet all day, and she was barely three months pregnant. Florence dreaded thinking about the challenges she would face in the next six months.

As Florence flicked through a newspaper, she stumbled upon a small article about the body discovered in Beechwood's lake. The mere reminder of it made her sick. Bodies in water seemed to be a strange re-occurrence in Florence's life. She thought only of Oscar when she found the suitcase floating in the lake with the skull peeking through the fabric. The identity of the deceased remained unknown, though the article speculated it was an adult female. There wasn't much else to go on, but Florence hoped the victim's family or friends would find closure soon.

When Florence glanced up from the reception desk, she locked eyes with Lesley Graham. Lesley's dark hair swayed as she stopped before Florence, wearing a wide smile that contrasted the grief Florence knew hid beneath. The last time Florence saw Lesley was on the night of the fire when her son, Johnny, tragically lost his life. Yet despite her grief, Lesley appeared composed. Her makeup was flawless, and her crisp white clothes were pristine.

Florence offered Lesley a smile, hoping Olivia was occupied with other tasks. Johnny being the father only complicated things further. The one thing Florence wanted to keep secret from Lesley was the fact she would be a grandmother soon. "Lesley, how have you been?" she asked, feeling an immediate sense of regret. It was a question she despised receiving after Oscar's death.

"Well, you know, it's not easy," said Lesley, her voice breaking. "But I've put on a brave face, and well, the news has truly lifted my spirits." Lesley glanced around the salon and leaned in closer. "It's hard to believe we're going to be grandmas, isn't it?"

Florence's stomach twisted into knots. How did Lesley know Olivia was pregnant? She anxiously surveyed the salon as Olivia approached them with a radiant smile. Florence remained silent as Lesley turned to Olivia, arms wide open, pulling her into a heartfelt embrace.

"Olivia, you didn't tell me about Lesley. If I had known, I would have called you," Florence said.

Lesley raised a hand to interrupt. "Don't worry, Flo. I understand. Mothers and their secrets. Olivia has a sensible head on her shoulders." Lesley turned to Olivia. "She visited me and told me everything. My Johnny would have been overjoyed, and knowing that I have a little part of him in there... well, it's given me the strength to face each day again."

Florence offered Olivia a tight-lipped smile. "I always knew my little girl was smart. So, Lesley, are you here for a blow dry?"

Lesley let out a boisterous laugh, momentarily silencing the salon. Florence noticed clients turning their heads, glances at Lesley from the view in their mirrors. "Oh, no, not today. I'm taking Olivia out! Spoiling her and the little one. I would invite you along, Flo, but I brought the convertible. Two seats and only enough room for bags, I'm afraid."

"Sorry, Mum. Maybe another time," said Olivia, linking arms with Lesley. Together they left the salon, leaving Florence with a whirlwind of thoughts. She despised the idea of Lesley worming her way into Olivia's life. This was precisely why she hadn't wanted her to know about the baby. Florence scratched at her wrist, suddenly craving a drink—a sensation she hadn't experienced in months. Deep down, she knew alcohol wasn't the answer. She had to remain focused. Lesley would seize any opportunity to exert control. All Florence needed to do was ensure that Olivia's life ran smoothly until the baby arrived.

Given the events of the past year, Florence desperately hoped that her streak of misfortune had finally come to an end. She glanced at the newspaper once more, the haunting image of the body flashing through her mind. Despite all the hardships, she reminded herself to be grateful for one thing— she was alive, wasn't she? She could be thankful for that.

CHAPTER FIVE
Order Restored

Stacks of cookbooks with her face on it stared back at Rose. Seeing that woman looking back at her pulled Rose away from where she was. The hair pristine, make up neat. That fake smile and empty eyes that no one else could see, but Rose did. Was she still that woman? Or had she changed into something else? Was that something else better or worse? She chewed on her nails, thinking over the unsettling words scrawled onto the note. Snapping her curtains shut, she locked the door, seeking solace in the confines of her home. She did not want to face the world today.

Within the silent, empty house, Rose was acutely aware of her loneliness, the only company being that of her racing thoughts. There was no one to confide in. She placed the letter on the coffee table beside her beloved cookbook, which now seemed tainted after everything that had happened.

When her phone turned on, a notification alerted her to three missed calls from Elisa Thorn—the woman who claimed to be married to Rose's late husband, George. That phone call she received, all hope and expectation about getting a publishing deal to only end with more lies and fabrication from a stranger. Elisa had persistently tried to reach Rose, eager to discuss their complicated connection, but Rose had adamantly refused. She had believed George was out of her life, only to discover his death invited even more trouble. When the phone rang, Rose half expected Elisa's name to appear, but another unfamiliar number flashed instead. With a sigh, Rose answered, waiting for the caller to speak first. If it turned out to be Elisa using a different number, she would simply hang up. The line remained silent. Rose moved to end the call before a man's voice said, "Hello? Ms. Walker?"

Rose, taken aback by the unfamiliar voice, inquired, "Who's speaking?"

"This is Brian from McGerry Solicitors."

Rose's heart skipped. Had Elisa sought help from a solicitor to make claims on George's will? Surveying her surroundings, she realised that technically half of her house belonged to his other wife. Every piece of furniture, necklaces, investments. How much would she need to give up because of this woman? "How can I help?" she asked, determined to keep her voice steady.

"I'm calling on behalf of the late Violet Chansky. Following her instructions in her will, I was tasked to contact you."

The mention of Violet's name made Rose's chest tighten. The devastation of that fateful night still haunted everyone involved. Rose could still see her eyes, the fire dancing in them, the way she gripped onto The Leader. Lit them both up in dancing hot flames. No one deserved to go like that. Rose did not expect Violet to have anything to leave behind, let alone something for her. Rising from her seat, Rose pulled back the curtain. "What is it? What were her instructions?"

"Well, she didn't have any property of her own, but she left explicit instructions that, in the event of her death, you were to collect her belongings, keep what you need, and dispose of the rest."

Rose thought back to the first time she met Violet. She was desperate to be seen, to be heard by anyone and Violet pounced on that vulnerability. Joining The Order, finding out Nick was a member. Katherine being Violets mother. It all mounted up and all the pain drew a line right back to Rose. So much loss. So much death. The weight hung on her shoulders.

"Did she specify anything she wanted me to have?"

"Her will was quite explicit. It stated that all content and belongings were to be left to one Ms. Rose Walker of Beechwood Close." The man paused, seeming to catch his breath. "There's something else. She wrote that *'Rose Walker will know the order of things.'* Does that mean anything to you?"

Rose's spine tingled at the mere mention of those two words: The Order. Violet had deliberately included them. "I understand, sir. Can I get the keys to her flat?"

"Yes, they are available at the office whenever you're ready. You have five days to clear it out."

Rose ended the call and darted upstairs to the spare bedroom, a space she seldom visited nowadays without George's outbursts forcing her to hide. Inside the dressing table lay her mask she once donned while attending meetings at The Order. The memories of that dark cult, which Violet had introduced Rose to, resurfaced like an unwelcome nightmare. Violet's fiery act of destruction had somehow buried those haunting memories, which now clawed their way back into Rose's life. She firmly shut the draw, resolving never to put on that mask again. She kept it only as a stark reminder of her past. While Rose intended to honour Violet's request by sorting through her belongings, she knew she needed someone else with her.

The meticulously trimmed grass felt plush beneath Rose's feet as she made her way toward Ava's back gate after knocking several times. Truthfully, Rose wasn't here for Ava. She wanted Katherine. As she pushed open the wooden gate, Rose stepped aside for a passing gentleman, who flashed her a cheeky grin and combed his hand through his hair. Rose couldn't help but notice that the fly on his jeans was undone and the buttons on his shirt were fastened in the wrong order. Rose darted her eyes away, focusing on the pristine lawn, hoping her flushed cheeks wouldn't betray her. Her heart skipped at the thought that Ava might already be involved with someone new. After all, Nick had only just passed away. Suppressing her judgement, Rose pushed the speculation aside and continued down the path. Assuming Ava was upstairs, busying herself to appear presentable, Rose headed towards the annex on the other side of the garden.

Rose had only caught glimpses of the annex during its construction. It was intended as a space for Nick's mother, who passed away before she could spend a night there. The wooden sage green annex blended with its surroundings; large glass panels adorned the front, acting as a reflective mirror preventing Rose from seeing inside. Knocking gently on the glass, she coyly slid open the door and stepped inside.

In the short time that Katherine had been living here, she had truly made it her own, with framed posters of old Hollywood films and pin up stars of days gone by. Artwork adorning nearly every inch of the walls from modern to abstract. Towards the back of the living space, Katherine brushed her long red hair before a mirror, catching Rose's eye through the glass. Rose smiled warmly as she approached. The neat yet vibrant living area contrasted with the dishevelled bedroom, with clothes strewn across the floor, scattered on cabinets, and sprawled on the bed. Rose gathered a few items of clothing from the bed, meticulously folding them, and then settled into the small, cleared space. Katherine didn't turn to face Rose but continued to gaze at herself in the mirror as she spoke. "Rose, my dear, what brings you to my humble abode? Are you hoping to build a similar one for yourself and secure a fabulous lodger like me? Or perhaps you're seeking some much-needed decorating advice to bypass your sister's terrible taste?" Katherine cast a sly glance around her room. Katherine had done a good job with the place. It exuded a cultured atmosphere that made Rose's home seem like a pristine show home in comparison.

"I'm here to discuss a sensitive matter." Rose glanced at her lap before correcting herself and meeting Katherine's gaze. Katherine's face didn't move. Her entire outlook on the world seemed to solely focus on herself. "I just received a call and wanted to talk to you about it. I thought you should come along."

Katherine raised an eyebrow and set down her brush before turning to face Rose fully. "Forgive me, Rose, but get to the point."

"It's about Violet," Rose said.

Katherine rolled her eyes and turned away dismissively. "I see, and what does that have to do with me?"

Rose took a step closer to Katherine, refusing to back down like she usually would. Although Katherine could be intimidating, Rose couldn't give up. She couldn't live with the regret of not trying. "Well, she was your daughter, Katherine. My visit pertains to her will."

Katherine stood up, leaning against the windowsill. "She has nothing to leave for me. If they called you, then it's all yours."

Rose joined Katherine near the window, sensing the mounting tension. She refused to let it deter her. "I'm going to her flat tomorrow to sort through her belongings and clear out the place. I'll pick you up at ten."

"I have no reason to go there. In my mind, she died over twenty years ago," Katherine retorted.

Rose stood and headed for the door, facing away from Katherine when she said, "I know you don't mean that. I know the pain never truly went away. I'll see you tomorrow. Dress sensibly."

Fumes from Katherine's cigarette filled the annex as she leaned against the window frame. Rose shut the door, leaving her to it. Even though Katherine was stubborn, she'd regret not coming. Honestly, having someone like Katherine by her side would also provide Rose with much-needed support. The thought of what she might uncover while going through Violet's belongings worried her, as though The Order still lurked in the shadows.

Having someone else there to keep an extra eye out was precisely what Rose needed.

CHAPTER SIX
True Motivations

Theo gripped Emily's hand as they strolled along the pavement, enveloped in the symphony of crashing waves and the sea breeze. The cloudless sky stretched above them, transforming the typically grey waters into a brilliant pastel blue. Emily felt a surge of uncertainty when glancing down at their interlaced fingers. Their friendship had so swiftly developed into... whatever it was now. With a gentle tug, she withdrew her hand from Theo's grasp to scratch her head before resting against the strap of her bag.

When they turned the corner, they found Cynthia in the same seat they had left her in, delicately sipping from a cup of tea, while shielded from the sun beneath a large umbrella. "Would you like an ice cream, Cynthia?" Theo asked, his enthusiasm akin to an eager puppy.

Cynthia narrowed her brow and redirected her gaze to

Emily. Returning the smile, Emily nodded. "We'd love one, Theo. Vanilla for Grandma and mint for me." Theo beamed at both of them before turning to enter the nearby cafe.

"So, is there anything you want to tell me about you two?" Cynthia's piercing gaze lingered, her question cutting through the air like a knife.

Emily thought she had retracted her hand from Theo's in time, but Cynthia's sharp observation had caught her yet again. "No, why do you ask?" Emily gave a coy tilt of her head.

"Just making sure, my dear. You must tread carefully. You're not the same person you were when you knew him," Cynthia said, swilling her tea around the cup.

"I haven't changed that much."

"You've got money now. That alone should make you cautious when men suddenly reappear from your past," Cynthia warned.

Emily rolled her eyes, her frustration clear. "He didn't show up out of nowhere. You know why he came back."

"Didn't expect him to stick around for weeks, though," Cynthia continued in a tone that implied there was more to the conversation.

When Theo returned to hand Cynthia her ice cream, Emily anticipated a shift in topic. "Do you mind ordering me a coffee?" Emily asked him sweetly. "There are a few things I need to discuss with Grandma." She caressed Theo's hand, who nodded and hurried off. "Could you please try not to be so difficult?" Emily said to Cynthia once Theo was out of earshot.

"Well, excuse me," Cynthia retorted. "In case you've forgotten, he left you all those years ago and left me to pick up the pieces. So, watch your step." After a thoughtful lick of her ice cream, Cynthia set the treat down on the saucer before wagging her finger in Emily's direction. "All I'm saying is, take it slow. If it's true love, it can wait. You don't need to go a hundred miles an hour just to make him happy. You don't know why he's here or if anything he's said is even true."

Emily fought to compose herself. Dealing with her grandmother was always a struggle, but when she was in a mood, penetrating her defences was practically impossible. "I know he's telling the truth, Gran. Our friends are being followed. One of them has been killed, and all Theo wanted to do was make sure I was safe."

"You don't know if that poor girl's death is connected to you or your friends," Cynthia countered, her gaze drifting past Emily to the sea beyond.

Annoyingly, Cynthia was right, as she so often was. Emily thought about telling her Gran everything. This letter was consuming her mind, what if shes right and Theo isn't being honest. These letters didn't start arriving until he did.

"I received a threatening letter the other day," Emily confessed. Cynthia's tough facade appeared to crack as she locked eyes with her granddaughter. "I believe it's from whoever is after us. They've finally come after me, Gran. And trust me, it's not pretty."

"Why? What have you done?" Cynthia rubber at her wrinkled neck. "Something illegal?"

"No, not exactly. I don't want to delve into the details. Let's just say what happened was for the best. I thought nobody saw, but now I've received a letter suggesting that someone did. They warned me not to trust my friends."

Cynthia pouted, one of her *I told you so*, looks.

"Like Theo, perhaps? Maybe it's not a threat, but a friendly caution about letting people into your life?" Cynthia suggested, a subtle smile dancing on her lips.

Emily's gaze shifted to Theo, who was returning with a

steaming cup of coffee. "Please, let's leave it at that. Be kind. Even if you're right—which I doubt—let me navigate this game at my own pace."

Cynthia nodded as Theo settled into a seat beside her, his eyes darting between the pair. "Is everything okay here?" he asked.

Cynthia slapped his thigh. "As long as you never hurt my granddaughter, then yes. Everything's fine."

Theo had finally succumbed to sleep, and Cynthia's snores echoed through the hallway. Wrapping her dressing gown tightly around herself, Emily descended the stairs, clutching her laptop with one hand. Despite trusting Theo and believing his story, she couldn't escape her grandmother's words and felt an undeniable urge to verify the truth for herself.

Sitting alone in the living room, shrouded in darkness, she began her online search, starting with the article detailing Cassandra's death. Emily had already skimmed the headline in Theo's presence, but now read through the piece with a fine-toothed comb.

In a shocking incident that has left the local community reeling, Cassandra Knight, a resident of 89B Widows Avenue, was found with a critical stab wound in the streets near her home. The 32-year-old woman, who shared the flat with a roommate Theo Kato, succumbed to her injuries three days later at the local hospital.

Emily's heart skipped. The article mentioned Theo as Cassandra's roommate. The address, 89B Widows Avenue, was forever burned into her memory. Unable to resist, she delved into an online exploration of the apartment—the town, street, floor-plan. The apartment block resided in a pleasant neighbourhood, characterised by clean streets and a commendably low crime rate.

The night stretched on and sleep eluded Emily. Tumbling down a rabbit hole of searches, desperate to uncover information about the perpetrator behind these events, Emily eventually turned her focus to their other friend in the group, Rachel. According to Theo, Rachel had been followed home, which is why Theo arrived in Beechwood to check on Emily.

Emily had always been fond of Rachel. They were in the same art class together at university. She was always the sensible one. Always had a keen eye on anything going on. For her to be spooked, it had to have been serious. She found Rachel on one of her old social media platforms, with a green circle displayed beside her name. Emily glanced at the clock, which now read three in the morning. Biting her lip, Emily composed a message. *'Hey Rachel. I know it's been a long time, but I heard about Cassandra and wanted to get in touch.'* With a hesitant click, she pressed send, hoping she wouldn't be swiftly blocked. Anxiety settled in her stomach as she stared at the conversation box, waiting. Yet as time dragged on with no reply, Emily rubbed her eyes and headed to the kitchen for her nighttime medication. She'd forgotten to take it earlier, and her neck was flaring up.

When Emily returned to the laptop, Rachel had not only read her message, but had also replied. *"Hello, stranger. So glad to hear you're doing okay. It was horrible to hear about Cassandra. No one deserved that. Keep in touch. It's nice to know some of the group still get along."* Emily read the end of the message again. Was Rachel trying to hint at something? Who from their group had fallen out? Could she be talking about Theo?

She had to be cautious and avoid prying too deeply. The last thing she wanted was to cause more trouble. *"I'm always here if you want to chat. Have you heard much from any of the others?"* Emily typed, hoping to sound vague.

"Theo stuck around for a while after the attack," Rachel replied, providing a wave of relief that at least this part of Theo's story was true. *"When I reached out to him about being followed, he soon moved out of the flat. Jessie was still there, but she's gone into hiding as far as I know. She was absolutely terrified the last time we spoke. Not that she's ever had much time for me."* Emily's heart raced at the mention of Jessie. Emily and Jessie went back years. On the first day at Uni they had bumped into each other. Emily noticed she was upset. That look and feeling you get when you've lost a parent. Emily noticed it in Jessie the second they locked eyes and that kind of connection created a bond between them instantly. They were never natural friends, once Uni finished and they went their separate ways, Emily didn't really think about her again. Maybe it should have been obvious the others kept in touch with her though. Emily had never been great at keeping friendships going. Theo had never brought up the fact that they lived with Jessie though. In fact, he hadn't mentioned Jessie once.

Emily realised she had yet to respond to Rachel's message. *"It all sounds incredibly messy,"* she finally typed. *"I'm glad I left when I did. I'll make sure to keep in touch."*

Emily couldn't escape the sense of betrayal, knowing Theo had kept Jessie's presence a secret. Her mind churned with questions and doubts. Meeting up with Rachel seemed like the next logical step. *"Maybe we could meet up soon for a proper catch-up. You name the time and place, and I'll be there,"* Emily replied, hoping Rachel's perspective would provide her with some much-needed clarity. Perhaps Cynthia was right. She had let her guard down too quickly, and now Theo was comfortably sleeping under her roof and consuming her food. Emily massaged the tension in her neck.

Sneaking back into her room, she slid into bed beside

Theo, hoping he would remain undisturbed. Emily felt dirty in bed beside him, burdened by these endless thoughts. What if she was jumping to conclusions, and he was genuinely the kind and honest person she believed him to be? After all, he had no apparent reason to lie. He had sought Emily out to warn her, ensuring her safety. However, Emily now recognised the need to maintain some distance until she delved deeper into Jessie's situation. Clearly, there was a fracture within their group, as Rachel had implied. If Emily could unravel the events leading to their fallout, she might uncover the truth behind Cassandra's murder and the sender of the menacing letters targeting her and Rose.

CHAPTER SEVEN
Unpopular Truths

The weather always seemed to favour Ava. She parked her car at The Nebula Health Spa and handed her keys to the valet, flashing the young boy a charming smile from beneath her sun hat. He blushed and couldn't help but cast his gaze downwards whenever Ava arrived. Sensing his bashfulness, she slipped a fifty-pound note into his pocket and strolled towards the entrance.

Ava glided past the white marble reception and entered the foyer, its pristine facade the perfect backdrop to her vibrant red summer dress and jet-black hair. Making her way towards the seating area, Ava couldn't help but notice clusters of women laughing and babbling together, while the gym bustled with energetic young men. The swimming pool on the other side was noticeably vacant, and Ava averted her gaze from it—those waters still haunted her.

Sweeping the room in search of a suitable group to join, she spotted Lesley standing near the reception desk. Ava contemplated slipping by unnoticed, but knew it was an impossible feat, especially with her current appearance. Instead, she positioned herself beside Lesley to face the inevitable awkward encounter head-on. Lesley turned, clutching a new membership card and a welcome leaflet to her chest. The moment she laid eyes on Ava, her expression faltered and her jaw dropped. She scrutinised Ava from head to toe before reluctantly stepping aside. "Well, isn't it nice to see you taking a break from your usual activities?" she sneered, snatching her purse and hurrying back towards the group of women. Ava trailed behind, the click of her heels echoing throughout reception.

Ava grasped Lesley's shoulder before she reached the women. "Can't we try to be civil?" she asked.

Raising an eyebrow, Lesley settled into a vacant seat, while the other women avoided making eye contact with Ava. In the corner of her vision, Ava noticed Olivia sitting at the table, sipping on a green smoothie. Ava couldn't help notice the small bump. *Thank God shes so young*, Ava thought. Her waist will snap back in no time. Lesley's smile widened as she turned to the group. "Gail, why don't you enlighten Ava about what you've heard?"

Gail glanced fleetingly at Ava before returning her gaze to Lesley. "I'd rather not repeat it," she muttered.

Ava crossed her arms, her resolve hardening. "Come on, Gail. Don't be shy. Tell me what you've heard," she pressed, determined to confront the rumour head-on. The idea of becoming the talk of the town unsettled her, particularly after everyone had avoided meeting her eye at the lake—hardly anyone paid her attention when she stood up.

Gail glanced again at Ava and Lesley. "Well, I've heard a

few whispers about your *activities* at home, that's all," she reluctantly revealed, tightening her grip on her coffee mug.

Lesley let out a booming laugh. Olivia stayed focused on her drink. Her eyes never daring to meet Ava's. "Activities? More like never-ending escapades." Lesley said. "People claim they've seen men coming and going from your house day *and* night, Ava. Quite tacky, don't you think? Especially so soon after Nick."

"Not that I owe any of you an explanation, but those men weren't there to see me," Ava retorted, clenching her jaw. She despised being the subject of gossip. The mere thought made her blood boil.

Lesley laughed once more, rising from her seat to face Ava. "Don't even attempt to suggest they were Katherine's conquests. She's already made it clear that she wants no part in your affairs. Absolutely nothing to do with her, she told us."

Ava's mouth fell open. Katherine spreading lies about her? While living in Ava's own *home*? Her gaze flitted towards Olivia, who remained huddled in her chair. "No support from you, Olivia? Nothing else to say about me?" Ava implored, hoping for a semblance of solidarity.

Olivia looked up, and her eyes flitted to the new membership plan Lesley had placed before her on the table. Just as she was about to speak, Lesley positioned herself between them. "Leave now, Ava, while you still have a shred of dignity," Lesley whispered venomously into Ava's ear. "I've heard plenty of stories about you and Florence's husband. Leave quietly without making a scene, and let me continue to cling to what little remains of my Johnny. Or should I expose the incident where you forced a kiss on my young son as well?"

Ava's heart raced as anger surged through her veins. Part

of her yearned to slap Lesley and tell the entire group to go to hell. Yet she maintained a stoic expression, refusing to let them see her falter. With a composed smile, she glanced in turn at the surrounding judgemental faces, knowing they wanted nothing more than to cast her out. There was a time when Ava held sway over groups like this, but Lesley had cunningly devised to seize her place, and succeeded. Casting one last look at Olivia, who stared into her drink, Ava departed, her head high. Lesley's victory wouldn't last long.

Furious, Ava sped home, hastily parked her car at Florence's house, and rushed towards the front door. Banging on the door, she caught a glimpse through the front window of Florence's father in an armchair, engrossed in the television.

Florence's mother turned her head and offered a warm smile when spotting Ava through the window. She made no move to let her inside. After a moment, Ava knocked again, impatient. Finally, Florence appeared at the door, with a tea towel draped over her shoulder. She brushed aside a few loose strands of hair and sighed. "Ava, what can I do for you?" she asked wearily, her shoulders sagging.

"Do you have a moment to talk? You won't believe what Lesley has been saying about me," Ava pleaded.

Florence hesitated and glanced at her watch. Florence's mother called out from the living room, and Ava breathed in the scent of burnt food now floating outside. Florence's gaze shifted toward the commotion before refocusing on Ava, who flashed another pleading smile. And then she saw it—the *look*. It was the look Ava had directed at countless unwanted guests over the years. Despite Florence's efforts to conceal it quickly, Ava recognised the fleeting expression of pity and eyes that conveyed no time for such trivial matters. Other concerns took precedence.

"I can see you're busy, Flo. We can catch up another time," Ava murmured, turning to walk away.

A pause followed until Florence called out, "No, wait!" But before Ava could turn around to offer her another chance, chaos erupted from within the house. Florence mouthed an apology to Ava and abruptly closed the door with a resounding slam.

Ava didn't resent Florence for this. After all, she recalled what it was like having Nick's mother living with them. Ava retraced her steps home, pausing on the path outside of Rose's house along the way. Rose had always been reliable. When Ava approached the front door, she froze at the sound of a revving engine. Rose's car emerged, roof down. Rose wore a headscarf, and Katherine sat beside her, oblivious to everything happening around them, as she focused only on her nails.

"Everything okay, sis?" Rose called, lowering the radio volume. Ava managed to smile and waved for Rose to continue with her day. "Nothing that can't wait," she said. Rose sped off, leaving a trail of exhaust fumes and dust where Ava stood. A stark realisation hit Ava then. She was no longer part of society. Her social status had plummeted. She couldn't find a friend anywhere. No matter where she turned, there was no one willing to spend time with her.

During moments like these, Ava longed for Nick's presence. He had always been dependable, listening to her grievances, and offering solace when he could.

Ava wandered aimlessly along the close. For years now, she had yearned for this kind of freedom—to break free from Nick and the confines of their marriage. Yet, she couldn't help but resent her inner longing for something she had spent years trying to eliminate. When she looked up, she realised she stood before Edna Howard's old bungalow. Reluctantly, her feet carried her toward the front door. She knocked. She knew Larry would be out; he always took his walks along the lake with Cynthia around this time.

When no one answered, Ava pushed open the back gate that dangled from its hinges, holding on for dear life. She stepped into the immaculate garden that boasted the best view in Beechwood. It overlooked an expanse of fields and a glimpse of the lake peeked through the shrubbery at the back of the garden. Ava glanced at the kitchen window and pressed her face against the glass, cupping her eyes to peer in. Spotting Edna's walking stick on the floor, Ava flung open the back door and called out, "Edna, are you in here? Are you okay?"

Her initial concerns were quickly dispelled when she found Edna in the lounge, one leg propped up on the sofa.

As Edna's eyes met Ava's, Edna hunched her shoulders and curved her spine. She gave a weary sigh and clutched her back with aching hands. With a trembling gait, she hobbled towards Ava, extending her bony hand with a quivering lip. "My stick, Ava... *Please*." Ava raised an eyebrow, a flicker of amusement dancing in her eyes. Reluctantly, she handed Edna the walking stick, yet kept a slight distance between them.

Edna grasped for the stick, the trembling of her fingers increasing. Her neck sank into her shoulders before she pleaded, "Please, I'm going to fall!" Ava reached out, holding the walking stick inches from Edna's desperate grasp. Edna expertly played the part of an award-winning actress as she leaned forward. Ava watched, curious to see how far Edna would go before relenting.

With a sudden surge of energy, Edna straightened, moved away from the window, and cast a suspicious glance around the room. "Why are you in my house? I could have you arrested, you know," she said, striding confidently towards Ava and snatching the stick from her grasp.

"One call to the benefits office, and I could have your carer's allowance revoked," Ava fired back, an edge of satisfaction in her voice.

Ignoring Ava's threat, Edna nonchalantly asked, "Cup of tea?" but headed to the kitchen and flicked on the kettle before she could answer.

As the kettle hissed in the background, Ava leaned against the kitchen countertop, gazing out at Edna's garden. "So, you're milking Larry for all he's worth, huh?"

Edna didn't miss a beat. "Don't act self-righteous, Ava. I do what I must to survive. Larry is a man who likes to care for others. I keep him occupied."

Ava smiled as Edna handed her a cup of tea. "Don't worry. Your secret's safe with me. Frankly, I'm impressed. I didn't think you had another marriage left in you, but here we are." She sipped from her drink. "Although faking your own illness and death might not be the most sustainable plan, time-wise."

Edna smiled, a glint of mischief in her eyes. "I've seen off five husbands who all believed they would outlast me. I can do it again."

Ava contemplated Edna's long history with men. She wondered if Edna was the woman Ava would become in the years to come—still living in the same house, on husband number four or five. "Tell me, did you at least love any of them?"

"Some I loved, some I detested. And others, I wasn't bothered either way. Jimmy turned out to be gay, but I loved him. We had quite the wild time," Edna confessed, a hint of nostalgia in her voice.

Ava rolled her eyes. "And what about your first

husband? I've never heard much about him," she asked, leaning forward.

Edna's face grew solemn, and she averted her gaze. "There's a reason for that."

Edna waved her walking stick in the air and changed the subject. "Do you miss Nick?" The question seemed to come from nowhere.

Ava let out a sigh and dropped her guard. Was it Nick she missed, or the attention he brought her? Ava knew people didn't look her way as often now. No letters or cards reached her letterbox the same way they used to. Invites to parties and holidays had vanished. Everything felt so pointless now. "Of course I do. My house feels so empty without him."

Edna shook her head, dismissing Ava's response. "Don't give me that. It's just you and me. No need for pretences."

Ava's shoulders slumped. She glanced out the window, wondering if the view would lighten her mood. "Fine. I can't say I was devastated by the news. It was horrible, though. No one deserves to go like that. But let's be honest... Nick wasn't exactly squeaky clean. Ending the way he did... it was almost inevitable. When you play with fire long enough, you're bound to get burned."

Edna nodded knowingly. "True for a man. But us women, Ava, we know how to survive. You and I, we do what it takes. I've always admired that in you." she declared, placing a hand on her shoulder. "How is it living with Katherine? I know first hand she's enough to push anyone to their limits."

Hearing Katherine's name only boiled Ava's blood more. The bare faced lies she'd told Lesley after all she'd done for her.

"Not good, and it's only getting worse. I was a fool to let

her stay, but I needed the money. She caught me when I wasn't thinking straight. I thought she had changed, but she's still the same," Ava said, her gaze drifting towards the lake through the window. "So, Larry is down at the lake with Cynthia, huh? What do you make of it?"

"Cynthia and Larry are of no concern to me. He would never leave a vulnerable woman like me for her. Not with my diagnosis." Edna shrugged, an edge of possessiveness in her tone.

"I meant the body they found there," Ava murmured. "Such a tragedy. Murdered and stuffed inside a suitcase. Can you even imagine?"

Edna's gaze remained on the lake, her mind seemingly elsewhere. "A terrible way to go. All those years rotting away like that." Edna shuddered and rose from her seat. Brushing her skirt with her hands, she said, "Hopefully, they'll find the culprit. Probably some poor builder who worked on the close's redevelopment—that's the latest theory," she speculated. "Whoever it is, as long as it doesn't lower the house prices around here, I couldn't care less. Now, do you mind leaving? My Larry will be back soon, and I need to look well-rested," Edna concluded, putting an end to their conversation.

Ava froze when she entered her home, closing the door behind her. Footprints marked her carpet, leading up the stairs. She had locked the front door before leaving—she was sure of it. Hurrying to the back door, she found the sliding door was locked as well. She was about to shout at Katherine, letting herself in again, using god knows what in the house but then she remembered, she was out with Rose. "Is anyone here?" she called. "I have a gun!" Ava shouted, feeling foolish. She picked up a knife from the kitchen sink, her grip tightening against the hilt as she cautiously made her way towards the stairs. She closed her eyes for a split second. She wanted to hear something, a creak of the stairs, a door whine, but she heard nothing. The house was in total silence. With trembling hands, she dialled emergency services on her phone, her voice strained. "I'm calling the police!" she yelled before whispering into the receiver. "My home has been broken into, but I don't think anyone is here."

The young woman on the other end of the line instructed Ava to stay outside, and wait for the police to arrive. Ava rushed to the front porch, and minutes felt like hours as she anxiously awaited their arrival. After conducting a thorough search of her home, the police requested a list of any missing items. At first, nothing seemed amiss.

All her valuable possessions remained intact, but the bedroom was the intruder's target. Clothes were strewn across the floor, draped over the drawers in her bedside table; the closet was left open. Ava scanned the room, trying to identify any missing items, but nothing stood out. Realising the intruder must have had a key, she called an emergency locksmith.

That night, sleep eluded Ava. Her entire house felt tainted, as if she had been violated. The unsettling feeling lingered in the morning. The break-in must have been personal. Something must have been taken from her home, but what? She was frightened, but the uncertainty scared her more than anything else.

CHAPTER EIGHT
The Order of Things

They were silent for most of the car ride, and it finally came to an end when Rose parked outside Violet's flat. The same flaked brick and cracked pavement greeted Rose as it did the last time she visited. She had been here once before. She thought—and hoped—she had left this behind when Violet pleaded for her help. Returning seemed even less likely when she made the building go up in flames. Rose thought she could put the entire ordeal of The Order behind her. But now, even in death, Violet controlled the narrative.

Rose turned to Katherine, who hadn't uttered a word during the entire journey. "Shall we get on with it then?" she blurted, getting out and slamming the car door.

As they ascended the grimy concrete stairs leading to the apartment, Rose spared another glance at Katherine, whose expression remained unchanged—stone cold and unmoving.

Rose rummaged through her bag, searching for the keys the solicitor had given her earlier that morning. Katherine sighed and pulled Rose's bag closer, reaching inside and retrieving a brown envelope. With a snarky smile, she handed it to Rose.

With trembling fingers, Rose discovered a key on the key ring and attempted to unlock the door. Her fingers weren't cooperating with her mind. Behind this door could be a hundred different horrors awaiting them. She wanted to get this done and finished, wanted this entire thing put behind her. It didn't fit. Panic surged through her as she felt Katherine's breath on the back of her neck. She tried another key but still had no luck. The door had two locks, and Rose's fingers seemed to have a mind of their own. Katherine rested her hand on Rose's before snatching the keys from her grip.

"Didn't the man show you which key goes in which lock?" Katherine held up one key and shook it, causing the others to fall in line. She deftly inserted the key and turned. Directing another smile at Rose, Katherine placed the lone silver key in the lock above, turned the handle, and pushed the door open. Extending her arm with dramatic flair, she gestured for Rose to enter. "After you," she said, stepping back.

The air was stale inside, suffused with the scent of weeks of sun beating against the windows with no airflow. It wasn't pleasant, but Rose did her best not to react. After all, this was the home of Katherine's child's, and she wanted to show respect.

"I'll crack open a window. Smells like something died in here," Katherine remarked, pulling open the main window—the same one Violet would lean out of while smoking. Katherine settled into the solitary armchair and lit a cigarette. "So, was this all a waste of time? I see no treasure chests overflowing with gold." Katherine exhaled a puff of smoke through the open window.

The flat was in complete disarray. Mouldy bowls and plates were strewn across all surfaces, and Violet had scattered her clothes across the bed and floor. It struck Rose as peculiar that Violet hadn't bothered to tidy up before taking her own life, as she had planned. "Where should we begin?" Rose asked, wafting the smoke from her eyes.

"Why are you asking me?" Katherine snorted. "I'm only here because you wouldn't take no for an answer."

Rose planted her hands on her hips. Katherine was an expert at putting on a front. It would have gone above Rose's head before, but now she knew Katherine better, she could notice her hand shaking, the long drags she'd take on the cigarette. The subtle twitch of her foot. "You don't have to put on a show, Katherine. She was your daughter." She gestured around the room. "This is her entire life—everything about the daughter you never knew is right here. Don't you want to learn about her?"

"My daughter died over twenty years ago, Rose. The woman who lived here..." Katherine paused. "She wasn't my daughter any more than she was yours."

Rose took a deep breath, knowing all too well the experience of having a child whom you know nothing about. "I brought you here as a favour. This is your opportunity to finally learn more about her. Don't you see how fortunate that makes you?"

Katherine rolled her eyes. "Please. You don't have the slightest idea what it's like."

"Really?" Rose perched beside Katherine on the armrest. "I had a child, you know. When I was fifteen. My mother forced me to have him and then give him away to a stranger. So don't tell me I don't know how it feels, because I do."

Katherine spun to face Rose, wide-eyed. She stubbed her

cigarette on the windowsill. "How about we start over there—with those piles of papers and books? Let's get the boring stuff out of the way first." As Katherine rose from the armchair, she brushed her hand along Rose's shoulder.

As they sifted through the papers, they discovered printouts of websites, rumours about a secret cult, and mentions of Violet's father, along with old texts about The Order. Piles and piles of Violet's useless research. Katherine sat cross-legged on the floor, diligently going through each page.

Yet among the papers, Rose stumbled upon a leather-bound box, with a birth certificate stowed inside. She suspected the birth certificate was a fake, given to Violet by whoever had raised her. She handed Katherine the box. Alongside the certificate was a necklace—a golden symbol of The Order—that hung delicately from a fine chain. Rose held it in her palm, the same hand that bore the scar from her initiation. Underneath the necklace, a small black book lay with a note attached by a paperclip.

Rose opened the book and unfolded the note. Rose froze. Reading this letter could mean taking a path. One she wasn't sure she wanted to take. She'd come this far, though, to back away now would be foolish. *'If you are reading this, Rose, then I've failed and The Order is still active, please use this list to put an end to it.'* Rose turned to the other pages in the box. Lists of names. Members, some Rose knew of. Violet's name was there in black ink. She passed the note to Katherine. "Look at this. She's made a complete list. Every member she discovered is documented here."

Page after page of names—members of The Order—seemed to be arranged according to rank. It included old members, those who had passed away, and even the newest recruits. Rose's own name caught her eye. She glanced back at Katherine. "What should we do with it? Violet wanted me to find this."

Katherine snatched the book from Rose's hand and flipped through the pages. Katherine's eyes were alive now. Rose noticed her chest raising with each breath. This was the most animated Rose had seen her. Why was this the thing to awaken Katherine? "She's got every bloody name in here—even people I had no idea were members."

Rose reclaimed the book, considering her options. "Violet left this for me. Shall I take it to the press? There are names in here—politicians, celebrities, even police officers." She turned to examine the contents of the box, finding photographs of the members without their masks. One woman stood out. She was an actress, been in hundreds of films. As she flicked through the images, she stumbled upon one of a group of members encircling a dead body. Each person had their mask off, their hands stained with blood. The MP listed was there. He was in a dark robe, stood above the body of a young man. The Order's symbol carved into his forehead, rib cage ripped open. Rose tried to turn away, to remove the image from her thoughts but it was burned in her mind forever now. "Katherine, look at this. Isn't she an actress? And him, he's a member of parliament." Rose closed the box, her stomach churning. "What should we do?"

Katherine rose to her feet, lighting another cigarette. "It's a dangerous list, Rose. If it falls into the wrong hands, you won't live to see another day." Katherine blew a stream of smoke in Rose's face. "You only scratched the surface of that place. If you go to the press and a member finds out, you'll be gone—no questions asked, no search for your body."

Rose stared at the book, struggling to steady her trembling arms. "Should we burn it? Or send it anonymously to the press or the police? We can't let this continue."

Katherine scanned the book again, then met Rose's gaze. "Give it to me. I can bear the burden."

Rose hugged the book to her chest. "Violet left it for me. I should keep it."

Katherine folded her arms. "You brought me here because she was *my* daughter, Rose. Give me the book. It will be safer for you this way."

Katherine reached for the book, but every instinct in Rose's body forced her to pull back. She couldn't give the book to her. The Order could not resurface, and Rose had to do everything in her power to ensure it didn't. Entrusting Katherine with such power and information seemed like an invitation for trouble. Rose tucked the book securely in her bag and handed the necklace to Katherine. "You can keep anything you want from here, Katherine. Take some time to get to know your daughter. I'll hold onto this information for a while." Rose stooped down to collect the box marked by Violet. "In the meantime, I'll think about what to do with this."

As Rose turned to leave, Katherine stepped forward. "You're playing with fire. You escaped it once, but don't be naïve enough to think you'll escape it again. That place has a way of holding onto you and never letting go." Rose closed the door on Katherine before she could say more.

Once inside her car, Rose no longer held it in. Her knees shook, and tears welled up in her eyes. Her heart pounded in her chest as she rolled down the window for fresh air to calm her panicked breaths. Placing the box beside her, Rose closed her eyes and took a moment to collect herself. Violet had wanted this to end. She had sacrificed her life to ensure it did. Rose had one last task—to expose the members and ensure that The Order could never reform. She only hoped it wouldn't cost her life.

CHAPTER NINE
The Art of Blackmail

As the first to awake, Florence made her way downstairs. Despite the endless problems her parents caused, she appreciated how spotless they left the house, which was no longer littered with the remnants of dirty plates or shoes.

Florence waited for the kettle to boil and ran her hands through her hair, only now realising how long it had grown. After years of sporting a pixie cut, it had grown into more of a bob in recent months. Movement from upstairs caught her attention. While Lucas' car was in the driveway, she hadn't heard Olivia return last night. Florence moved towards the stairs to call up to her, but halted upon spotting an unmarked envelope wedged under the front door. Curiosity piqued, she picked it up and stepped into the lounge.

Inside the envelope was a single note written in blue ink: *'Don't trust new friends.'* Florence glanced up the stairs to check she was alone before flicking through the images hidden within, revealing photos of her and Regina kissing. Black and white photos, taken from a distance, but it was clear what was going on. It showed them both, holding each other at the back of the salon near the exit. One photo taken through a window of them kissing. They had been so careful. How did this happen? Florence's heart sank when she looked up at her mother. Joan stood by the stairs, her immaculate cotton cardigan pulled tight around her

"Mum, I didn't hear you come down," Florence said, swiftly tucking the photos and note into her back pocket. "Let me make you a coffee." She hurried past her mother, forcing the note deeper to ensure nothing would fall out. Her heart raced as she poured her mother a drink.

"No sign of Regina this morning?" Joan asked.

"Regina?" Florence replied, feigning ignorance.

"Yes, you know, the black girl who lives here."

"Mother, please don't say that. It's unnecessary."

"Well, excuse me. I can't say anything anymore without someone jumping down my throat." Joan picked up her coffee and made her way to the lounge. "Did you see how defensive she got when I asked to touch her hair?"

Florence rolled her eyes. With her father now descending the stairs, she knew addressing her mother's habit of invading personal boundaries would prove futile. "Mum, Dad, if touching Regina's hair makes her uncomfortable, please refrain from doing so. I won't say anything more about it. Okay?"

Her parents exchanged a glance before her father shrugged, rubbing Joan's back, who headed over to the sofa to settle in the lounge. Florence desperately wanted to kick them out and regain control of her life. If she was truly heartless, she would. But she knew they had nothing to fall back on, and if she did ask them to leave, then Florence knew she truly wasn't any better than they were. Regina had left early—once again—to avoid her parents. Florence needed to speak with Regina and reassure her she had spoken to them, and things should hopefully improve. But the letter burned into her mind. Someone had seen them.

Lucas joined them at the breakfast bar, scraping his long, tangled hair back from his eyes. Florence smoothed it down and massaged his shoulders. "When are you going to cut that off and leave your travelling days behind? You're such a handsome man underneath all that hair."

Lucas shrugged her off with a disgruntled, "Hey!" He looked up at her. "Dad always liked my hair long. It was only you who never let me grow it out. So, I'm doing it for him."

Florence recalled her arguments with Oscar about who would take Lucas to the barbers. Oscar never allowed Florence to cut his hair. She smiled at Lucas, unable to ignore his resemblance to his father—those same ocean eyes. Leaning closer, she whispered, "You haven't mentioned anything about me and Regina, have you?"

Lucas scrunched up his face. "No, I would never do that," he replied, forgetting to whisper.

Florence bit her lip. "I know, but I just wanted to make sure. You haven't said anything to a friend or a neighbour, have you?"

"No, Mum. I wouldn't. Not even to Dad's grave. What do you take me for?"

Joan turned around from the sofa. "Everything alright in there? Seems a bit early for bickering, doesn't it?" She turned to Florence's father. Glee etched into her faded eyes "We never used to argue like this, did we?

Florence rolled her eyes, refocusing on Lucas. "And what about your sister? Where has she been the past few nights?"

Lucas raised his eyebrows, glancing at the countertop. "I don't know either," he replied with a guarded smile. Florence arched an eyebrow, urging him to continue. "I really don't know."

"Come on, Lucas. She's pregnant! She shouldn't be out at all hours. Please tell me where she is. I won't meddle," Florence said, raising her hands innocently.

"Alright. She's at Lesley's place. She said she'd be staying there for a few days... or weeks."

Florence stood up. "Lesley? Really?"

"Mum, please. You promised you wouldn't do anything."

Florence turned, picked up her coat that was draped across the banister and collected her keys from the side.

"I'm sorry, Lucas. You should know by now that I can't keep every promise."

Florence parked her car opposite the water fountain, joining a row of vehicles lined across the driveway. Gardeners bustled around outside. Adjusting her sunglasses, Florence waved at them and called, "I'm here to check on the orangery!" She waited for their acknowledgement, and when the men nodded and returned her wave. she hurried to the front door, hoping to avoid any interference. Surprisingly, the door was unlocked, and she stepped inside, finding herself in a grand entrance hall adorned with white marble flooring and walls. Before her were two sweeping staircases, each adorned with a regal red carpet leading to different wings of the mansion. Florence possessed some knowledge about Lesley's home, as Ava had gossiped about it during her time working here. She turned right to pass the kitchen and continued straight towards what she hoped was the garden room. According to Ava, that was where Lesley spent most of her time.

In the distance, laughter reached Florence's ears as she

entered the room, distracted momentarily by the scent of chlorine emanating from the pool. Lesley and Olivia appeared from the other entrance. Lesley's blown-out curls bounced as she sashayed beside Olivia, who carried numerous bags of designer items. Florence counted at least ten. Lesley greeted Florence with a smile. "Flo, what a delightful surprise! I thought that car outside looked familiar," she said, turning to Olivia. "Though I initially thought it belonged to one of the gardeners." They laughed as Lesley settled onto the cream and gold-detailed chaise longue. Florence hated seeing what Lesley was already doing. She could see Olivia following her every step and that killed her. Kicking off her shoes, Lesley fanned her feet. "We really made a killing today, Florence. You should have seen Olivia. Even with the baby on board, she shopped non-stop."

"Mum, what are you doing here?" Olivia asked, pensive.

As Florence approached her, Lesley swiftly rose, standing in front of Olivia. "Actually, Flo, you can help us out. For the baby's room, I wanted a sun-yellow theme, but Olivia prefers blue and pink. What do you think?" Lesley smiled, slipping her arm around Olivia's.

"The baby's room? Are you both moving in, then?" Florence asked, fixing Olivia with a look.

"There's no harm in it, is there? The child needs care, and who better than me? I have so many empty rooms and so much money lying around. I might as well spoil my grandchild while I can," Lesley said.

Florence looked at Olivia once again. She at least had the decency to look somewhat embarrassed by the whole thing, that was one thing Florence could be proud of. "Come on. I need you to come home," Florence said, extending her hand. "Come on. Home. Now."

Lesley stepped forward, but Olivia tapped her on the

shoulder. "It's okay, Lesley. I can handle this." Olivia walked toward Florence. "I'm staying here, Mum. Look at what she can offer," she whispered, out of Lesley's earshot. "Just go. I'll be fine. Lesley will take care of me."

Florence leaned toward Olivia, pleading. "You come home now. This woman will suffocate you."

She seized Olivia's wrist, who recoiled and staggered back. "Get off me! Let go, Mum! I'm staying here."

Lesley smiled from behind Olivia. "You can visit whenever you want, Florence."

"Olivia, come with me now," Florence begged.

Olivia stepped closer to Florence. "If you force me to go with you, your secret fling might come out into the open. I'm staying *here*." Olivia stepped back, and Florence's mind raced. Did Olivia send the warning note? Had she told Lesley?

Unable to stop herself, Florence slapped Olivia across the face. The room fell silent, except for Florence's footfall as she staggered back, shocked by what she had done. She looked at her hand, then back at her daughter. She couldn't believe her own actions. She reached for Olivia to apologise, but Lesley stepped forward, embracing Olivia and stroking her cheek. "I'm so sorry, Olivia."

Florence stood there, shocked. Lesley held Olivia and narrowed her eyes at Florence over her shoulder. "Have you been drinking?" she snapped. "What kind of mother are you? Get out! Get out of my house before I call the police. You are not welcome here anymore." Florence watched as Olivia turned her back on her, and Lesley crouched beside her. "It's okay. It's just you and me and the baby now. That's all we need, darling." Lesley rubbed Olivia's back and called out for help. A couple of workmen approached, surveying the scene with raised brows. "Please escort Ms. Foster off the premises. She is no longer welcome in my home."

Florence looked at the men before walking past Olivia and bowing her head. She had just shattered any chance of having a relationship with her grandchild and handed Lesley an easy victory.

CHAPTER TEN
Friendshp Test

Katherine's cheque weighed heavily on Emily's mind, a tiny glimmer of hope during such dire circumstances. A few months ago, Katherine had extended this lifeline to her, a gesture to make up for all the countless wrongdoings against Emily. But now, with her bank accounts frozen and her remaining cash dwindling, Emily needed to entrust someone to safeguard the money and provide her with an allowance. Cynthia's police pension helped fill in some of the gaps, but Emily couldn't rely on her grandmother. It wasn't fair. She set aside her own issues for the moment and made her way to Ava's house.

The police had been there the other night. Just as Emily was about to knock, the front door swung open, revealing a smiling Ava with her hair casually pinned up with a clip. She sported comfortable lounge wear.

"Emily, what brings you here? How can I help?" Ava greeted, welcoming her inside.

"I saw the police were here and thought I'd stop by to make sure everything was alright. It's part of my..." Emily paused. "... duty of care".

Ava rolled her eyes and playfully dragged Emily into the house. Ava walked her into the living room. "Ah, yes. Rose must have sent you to keep an eye on me. *'Poor Ava, the lonely widow struggling to go about her life.'* I suppose all the neighbours and friends must gather round to care for such a delicate flower."

"If you'd rather I leave, just say the word," Emily offered, already turning for the door.

"No!" Ava gasped. "Since you're already here, you might as well share my burden. It's too heavy to carry alone—I'll get wrinkles!" Ava insisted, half-joking.

Emily followed Ava to the garden, where the sun reached its peak in the cloudless sky. She settled into a rattan chair, disturbed momentarily by the buzzing of insects near her ears. "So, what did the police want? An update on the dead body or about Nick and the fire?"

Ava shook her head. "The police did provide an update on the body, but they weren't here for that. They were here to inspect the house."

Emily leaned forward, taking a sharp breath. "The house? Why would they do that?"

Looking around cautiously, Ava lowered her voice. "I didn't want to alarm anyone, but someone broke into my home the other night. I returned to find my belongings strewn about everywhere. The police discovered boot marks and searched for fingerprints but found nothing substantial."

"Oh, Ava, that's terrible! Why didn't you say anything? We all need to watch out for our homes now," Emily exclaimed, reaching for her phone. "I should let Gran know, since she's home alone."

Ava snatched the phone from Emily's hand. "No,. There's a reason I didn't want anyone to know."

Emily retrieved her phone. Ava rolled her eyes, her jaw tight "You better have a good reason for keeping everyone in the dark while there's a thief about."

Ava hesitated, then whispered. "The police asked me to thoroughly check the house and make a list of any missing items. But from what I can tell, nothing of any value was taken."

"Well, that's a relief, isn't it?" Emily remarked.

Ava's expression darkened. "I double-checked the bedroom, and some of Nick's belongings are missing. His ID, important documents, things like that."

Emily was all too familiar with the troublesome circles Nick used to navigate. Only he could cause such chaos even after his death. "Do you think he crossed the wrong person?" she mused.

Ava tapped her nails on the table, contemplating Emily's words. "If I didn't know you better, Emily, I might suspect you. After what Nick and Katherine did to you, I wouldn't blame you for it." Bitterness laced her words. "But this situation has unnerved me. If I report what was taken, it might complicate the life insurance claim. It's been challenging enough to prove that he died with his body burned to a crisp. Adding a theft into the mix will only make it worse."

Emily shrugged. Ava's selfishness to keep this quiet grated at Emily. She had someone threatening her and Rose with letters, and they had no idea what the next step would be. What if this break in was linked with that? Maybe it would be better to keep it from the police, for now. "Then don't report it. Nick is gone, and you can't bring him back. Digging into all this will only cause you more pain. I'd keep quiet, make a list of the missing items, and be done with it."

Ava grasped Emily's hand, her lips parting. Her gaze shifted towards Emily's phone on the table. "And you promise to keep it quiet?"

"Yes, as long as it doesn't put our homes at risk, I'll stay silent." Emily exhaled, and they both settled back in their chairs. The warm sun blared on Emily's shoulders, causing her skin to prickle. "Gran mentioned the lake has been closed off again. They stopped her and Larry during their walk."

Ava turned her face towards the sun, Emily assumed that she had moved on from the horror of finding a body.

"Is she trying to steal Edna's man?" Ava quipped, a mischievous smile forming.

Emily chuckled. "No, Larry just needs some time away from looking after Edna, that's all."

Leaning forward once more, Ava's eyes sparkled. "I never told you about the latest update on that lake, did I? They believe it's a woman: young, around forty years old."

Emily gasped, a pang of sadness settling in her chest. Her father had been no older than that when he passed away—it seemed unfairly young, a life cut short. "Someone must be missing her. Do they have any leads on her identity?"

Ava shook her head. "No idea. They mentioned the body had likely been submerged for decades, and by the time it resurfaced, there wasn't much left. I don't know how they'll ever find out who she was."

Emily slumped into her chair. It seemed there was a constant barrage of disheartening news lately. Just a few weeks ago, she had found some semblance of happiness with Theo, but even that had been shattered by her recent conversation with Rachel. She had found it hard to be close with Theo since. All she wanted was for him to be honest with her.

Taking a sip of her drink, Ava sighed. "Well, I feel sorry for that poor woman. Killed and left to rot at the bottom of a lake, forgotten for years. It makes you wonder what kind of life she had. For no one to miss her, she must have... well... it's no way to live."

A sombre silence settled between them. It hadn't gone unnoticed by Emily that Ava's once-vibrant social connections had faded since Nick's death. She could sense the worry in Ava's gaze, the fear that if she were to vanish one day, no one would bother to search for her either. Emily rose from her chair and lay a hand on Ava's shoulder before saying goodbye. She couldn't afford to dwell on endless gossip. She messaged Rachel again about their meet up. Emily needed to uncover the truth about Theo's living arrangements and why he had lied to her when he reentered her life.

They agreed to meet at Greenfield Park. Despite the long three-hour drive, Emily didn't mind. The solitude of the journey allowed her some much-needed time to clear her head. She waited on a wooden bench, observing children playing on the swings, and families enjoying picnics in the park. The gentle breeze carried the sound of lapping water from the nearby lake. "Emily?"

Emily looked up to see Rachel, wearing a linen jersey blazer and donning dark-framed glasses which accentuated her oval eyes. Emily stood and extended her hand, and although they hadn't spoken in years, it felt too formal for old friends. A smile spread across Rachel's face, who pulled Emily in for a hug instead. "Shall we walk and talk? I need to get my steps in before I'm back to work," said Rachel, glancing at her smartwatch before they set off along the path.

They strolled beside the lake, joined by a flock of ducks bobbing gracefully in the water. "Thank you for agreeing to meet," Emily said. "I know it's been a long time, and I wasn't exactly a great friend to you."

Rachel let out a tut, not one of anger or agreement in how bad Emily had been, but to say it didn't matter "It's okay. People grow apart. I just wish it wasn't such a gruesome event that brought us back together." Emily averted her gaze. "Have you had any trouble?"

Emily shook her head. "No, I was completely clueless about the whole thing. I had sort of disconnected from my old life and everything in it."

"Like Jessie," Rachel interjected.

Jessie was the shy one in the group. When they met at University, Jessie's mother had just died, which was something Emily related to. Being part of that *club* joins people together, even when they have little in common elsewhere.

"It wasn't until Theo showed up, looking as pale as a ghost, that I found out what had happened," Emily explained.

Rachel raised her eyebrows. "Yeah, Cassandra was so gentle and quiet. I can't understand why anyone would want to hurt her, let alone..." Her voice trailed, unable to complete the thought. "At least Theo and Jessie got away, I suppose."

"He mentioned that you've been followed. Have the police done anything about it?" Emily asked.

Rachel let out a humourless laugh and paused to watch the lake. "No. I filed a report, and they advised me not to go out alone, but what can they really do? Nothing happened to me. The person might not have even been following me for all I know." Rachel crouched near the ducks, rummaging through her handbag. "My mind was all over the place after

Cassandra's death and when Jessie disappeared off to who knows where. I was constantly on edge."

"Maybe it was for the best that I didn't know. Nobody knew my whereabouts. It wasn't until a few months ago when I reached out to Theo for help with a book launch that we reconnected."

Rachel broke up a piece of bread in her hand and threw it into the water, watching as the ducks eagerly feasted. Emily was thankful for all the text messages her and Rachel had already sent. She'd filled her in on most of the events and gossip, including her and Theo. "How is Theo? He never really got over you, you know." Curiosity laced her voice.

Emily crouched next to Rachel, while the ducks clamoured for crumbs. "That's one of the reasons I wanted to meet up. You mentioned Jessie lived with him and Cassandra, right?"

Rachel nodded. "Yeah, they all shared a flat. Unfortunately for them, they didn't sell the crypto at the same time as us. They were all broke. I suppose we were lucky."

Emily had always battled with that guilt. It seemed so unfair she walked away with so much. She had a plan for that cash though. It's what brought her to Beechwood in the first place.

"When he came to me, he mentioned Cassandra's death, and that you had been followed. But he never mentioned Jessie living with him. It just seems odd. What do you make of it?"

Rachel brushed off her hands and rose to continue their walk along the path. "Are you worried that something happened between them? Is that why it bothers you?" she asked with a playful nudge. Emily shrugged, feeling uncertain. "I don't know if they had a thing or not. I know he cared deeply for you. When things didn't work out for you both at university, it devastated him."

Emily smiled. "As for us getting back together... I honestly don't know. He's been staying at my place. With everything going on, I thought it would be safer. It's been a few months, and he's still staying at mine, sleeping in my room." Emily sighed. "But knowing he kept his relationship with Jessie a secret makes me worry. Do you have any way to contact her? Maybe I could talk to her and find out what really happened."

Rachel shook her head. "I don't think so. She disappeared somewhere. She was never the most talkative, but after I was stalked and Cassandra passed away, she vanished. Theo claims he has no idea where she went, and he had to leave their flat because he couldn't afford the rent alone."

Emily chewed on her lip, realising she wasn't any closer to discovering why Theo had kept secrets about Jessie. They came to a halt back at the bench where they met, having completed a full lap around the lake. "Thank you for meeting with me, Rachel. It's nice to know that even after all this time, it can still feel like the old days."

"I should get back to work," Rachel said, glancing at her watch. "Let's keep in touch, though. If I come across any leads on Jessie, I'll let you know. But perhaps you should just confront Theo directly. He's never been good at lying, and there might be a perfectly innocent explanation." Rachel leaned in for a final hug before making her way back toward the office buildings adjacent to the park.

Emily remained seated on the bench, focusing on the calm water. Rachel didn't seem to suspect Theo of being the stalker, but if there was one thing Emily had learned since moving to Beechwood, it was that her intuition was usually right when she had a bad feeling about something.

CHAPTER ELEVEN
Unexpected Invite

Incessant ringing snatched Rose from her thoughts. She stared at the number flashing on the screen and noted yet another missed call from Elisa. The fourth one that morning. Instead, Rose peered out of the window at the empty close beyond. Families had already left for work after dropping their children off at school. Rose used to relish these quiet moments at home, when George would leave for work, and she could breathe again. But that was a distant feeling now, overshadowed by the constant presence of The Order—the endless names etched into her heart, her very being, reminding her of the weight she carried. She glanced toward the drawer where the box remained inside, as if it were a restless heart yearning to escape.

Once more, her phone buzzed, indicating Elisa's call. Rose hesitated and her hand hovered over it, but the ringing stopped before she could answer. There was a beep, and then a voice message followed. Rose closed the curtains, unable to escape a sense of guilt, as if she were a criminal awaiting a police raid. She pressed the phone to her ear.

"Rose, you need to speak to me," Elisa pleaded, carrying a hint of breathlessness. "I don't want to leave any traces of this behind, so please, for your own good, call me back now before I'm left with no choice but to take it further."

Rose rubbed her hands together, sweat forming in her palms. Was this message another threat, or a warning? Rose placed the phone back on the table and stood to draw back the curtains again to invite in the sunlight, which flooded the room. She made her way to the kitchen, switching on the oven and dusting the countertop with flour. After rolling the pastry and preparing the baking tray, her gaze drifted back to the lounge, where her phone vibrated once again. Forty minutes had passed since Elisa's last call. Brushing her hands together, a cloud of flour lingered in Rose's wake as she strolled toward the phone, answering Elisa's call with a casual press of the button. "You're on speakerphone. I'm keeping an eye on some croissants, and I really don't want to burn them. What do you want?"

A momentary pause followed on the other end of the line. "Rose, please take me off speaker phone. It's a sensitive matter."

"My hands are full, Elisa, and I've made it clear that I want nothing to do with your lies about my husband. Say what you need to say and then leave me alone."

Elisa sighed, and her next words were strained with a mix of frustration and concern. "I wish I could leave you alone, Rose. Truly, I do. But something has come to my attention—something that I felt you should know about before anyone else."

Rose bit her lip. Eyes focused on the oven. "Go on, then," Rose shouted into the phone, crouching to check on the croissants.

"I received a distressing letter about George..." Rose bolted upright, placing her spare hand on the cool marble side. "It claims he's been murdered. I thought you should hear it from me before the police get involved."

Silence engulfed the house once more. Rose shivered upon recalling the letter she had received a few weeks ago, knowing they had somehow reached Elisa too. Rose had mentioned the call to Emily when it happened after Elisa claimed to be George's other wife. Emily was the only one who knew, yet Rose trusted her completely. Besides, it made no sense for Emily to set her up like this, especially when Emily was the one who actually killed George. Which meant that Elisa might be the mastermind behind the letters. If George had inadvertently let something slip about Rose, Elisa could have known about her for years. "Rose, are you still there?"

"Yes. It's quite the tale you're spinning," Rose said. "First, you appear as George's long-lost widow, and now you claim he was murdered. Some might think you're after something. If you want money, name your price and spare me the theatrics."

Elisa let out a sigh. "Rose, I'm not your enemy here. We both want the truth. I wanted to know if you had received a letter like this. I still don't have a clear picture of what really happened to George."

Rose glided her hands along her flushed cheeks, the burning sensation rising within her. "His death was an accident, Elisa," she finally croaked. "A tragic fall. Please, leave the past alone. Discard the letter and move on."

Rose hung up, her chest pounding. A headache crept in

and throbbed behind her temples. Suddenly, the smell of smoke jolted Rose, and she rushed toward the oven to find fumes billowing from the charred croissants inside. In a panic, she flapped the oven glove around the room to avoid setting off the alarm. Finally, she slumped to the floor and dropped her head between her knees, trying to calm her racing mind.

"Knock, knock." A voice called from the front door, shortly followed by the clicking of heels against the hardwood floor. Rose lifted her heavy head to find Katherine standing before her, a false smile stretched across her face. Rose swore she detected a hint of pity in her eyes. Katherine extended her hand and pouted. "Looks like the baking didn't go so well," she said, pulling Rose to her feet. "You must be meticulous with timings when baking, Rose."

Rose forced a smile and flattened her hair. "If only you had arrived unannounced a few seconds earlier, Katherine. You could have saved the day," she said, turning to brush away the remaining flour from the countertop. Katherine watched Rose's every move, her hands on her hips. Her raised brow didn't go unnoticed as Rose turned away."So, what brings you here?"

"I wanted to talk to you... about the box from Violet's," Katherine said, her tone shifting.

Rose raised an eyebrow. "How did it go at her flat? Did everything go smoothly?"

Katherine gathered a small amount of flour in the palm of her hand and brushed it into the sink. "Oh, that place? I managed to empty it and clean it up. You're welcome, by the way."

"Did you learn anything about her?"

Katherine's usually harsh tone softened. "Actually, I did. Thank you. I know I can be defensive at times, but it was nice to know you thought of me."

"Alright, now why are you really here?" Rose narrowed her eyes.

Katherine turned the bar stool and took a seat, spinning it back to face Rose. "Well, since you went out of your way to do something nice for me, I thought I should give you an early warning, considering how eager you were to keep that box." She swayed slightly as she spoke.

"I'm not giving it to you. I haven't decided what to do with it yet."

Katherine stopped swaying and smiled. "I wouldn't expect anything less. But I need to let you know that I've heard rumours."

"Rumours? About what?" Panic seized Rose again. Had Katherine found out about George's death? Had someone sent her a letter as well?

"The Order. There are whispers in certain... *circles* I'm familiar with. They want to revive and rebuild it. Rise from the ashes, so to speak."

"Who? Who is saying this?"

Katherine stood. "Just people. Surviving members. With the leader gone, the position is up for grabs. I wanted to give you a warning, Rose. Think about what you're doing and the information you hold. If you choose to play the hero, I won't stop you, but powerful people are vying for that leadership role, and if it means getting you out of the way, they'll find a way to do it."

Rose narrowed her eyes, glancing at the sideboard before facing Katherine again. She was so smug, standing tall, chin up high as if nothing could touch her, believing that Rose would bow down and accept every word. Maybe a few months ago, that would be the case, but Rose didn't want to be that woman anymore. She could be more, better. "Are you threatening me, Katherine? If I didn't know any better, I'd think you were planning to take on the role of The Leader."

Katherine let out a cackle. "No, that role wouldn't suit my talents. I just wanted to give you a heads up. Make that box disappear before it's too late." Katherine waved her fingers in the air, "I wanted to thank you for being there for Violet in her final moments and for allowing me to visit her flat and learn about her life." Katherine walked toward the front door. "All I wanted was to repay you. I've done that now. What you choose to do with the information is up to you. I've done my part."

Katherine brushed her floury hands together before flashing a close-lipped smile at Rose and exiting the house.

Rose remained in silence for most of the evening, craving peace and no distractions. Her hands trembled, despite having taken four paracetamols to ease the headache that wouldn't budge. Yet it was like her nerves were reignited, ricocheting through her body like a wounded animal in fight or flight. She had switched off her phone, not wanting any further hassle from Elisa.

She contemplated opening a bottle of wine to calm her frayed nerves and glanced at the clock. Nine-thirty. She decided to retire early and pray for sleep, but just as she started up the stairs, a knock at the front door made her halt. Another three knocks followed, echoing in the hallway. Rose turned, tied her hair up with the band from her wrist, and approached the door.

Standing before her were two men in tight dark suits, emphasising the swell of their biceps and the broadness of their builds. Behind them was a blacked-out, top-of-the-range SUV. Scrunching up her face, Rose asked, "Can I help you?"

The taller man flashed his ID badge. "Are you Ms. Rose

Walker?" he asked.

"Why?" Rose responded, tightening her grip on the door handle as she took a half step back into her home.

"Sir Kenneth Banks MP requires your company," the man said, a slight smile touching his lips. He handed her a letter. "He requests your attendance at his next meeting. You'll find the date inside." He placed a piece of paper across the letter in Rose's hand. "Please sign here to confirm that you will not speak to the press or disclose any information before speaking to Sir Banks." Rose looked up at the man as his partner handed her a pen. "We will arrange to pick you up from this location and transport you to his residence."

Rose looked at the men, the paper, and the men again. She attempted to read through the contract, but it made little sense to her, except for 'non-disclosure agreement' in big, bold letters at the top. "I'm sorry, but what is this for exactly? Why does Mr. Banks want to see me?"

"It involves the last will and testament of Ms. Violet Chansky. He has an offer for you." The man took another step closer to Rose. "Please sign here, and we will collect you on the agreed-upon date."

Rose's eyes widened as she signed the paper. She thought Violet's secrets had ended with the flat. What else could possibly come from her estate? Rose thought of the box, the list of members, Katherine's warning. Powerful people wanted that information. How far were they willing to go to get it? He snatched the letter and pen from her before turning away with his partner and heading for the car. Rose watched until they drove away before hurrying back inside. Retrieving the box from the side table, she opened it and swiftly located the list of named members, and there it was.

Sir Kenneth Banks. MP.

Folding the paper closed, Rose placed it back in the box.

He has an offer for you. This must be the same offer Katherine had warned Rose about earlier.

Rose tore open the letter and skipped to the bottom. Sir Banks had signed the letter himself. He invited Rose to attend an unofficial meeting in London in two days' time.

With Rose's recent troubles—the blackmail letters, George's death, Elisa—perhaps, if she played her cards right, she could leverage the information about The Order for some form of protection. Holding the letter in one hand, Rose glanced at where the box was stowed. By leaking the list, she could eradicate The Order once and for all. Yet if she was to be strategic with this information, it might assist her and Emily in evading a potential murder charge. Overwhelmed by the various outcomes, Rose slumped back onto the sofa and looked at the clock. With a sigh, she leaned over to retrieve a bottle of wine from the rack and placed it on the table. The prospect of having an early night had vanished. She needed to carefully plan her next steps before the upcoming meeting.

CHAPTER TWELVE
A Deadly Surprise

Ava sat alone at her dining table, glued to her phone. She had sent a text to three different people. The anticipation was killing her. Unable to sit still, she got up from her chair and paced the floor, folding her arms tightly across her chest, and glancing at her phone again.

Just as her restlessness peaked, her phone buzzed. She leaned over the table, only to be met with disappointment. Mary had responded. She was occupied today and couldn't meet up. Ava raised an eyebrow and swiftly dismissed the message with a swipe. Then came Lucy's reply. With a heavy sigh, Ava read the words that crushed her hopes—Lucy's child was sick, and she had to cancel their plans.

Frustrated, Ava turned to gaze out the window once more, tapping her foot. It seemed never-ending. Every time Ava tried to arrange a gathering or get-together, fate intervened to thwart her plans. It happened more frequently now, and Ava couldn't help but take it personally.

Once again, her phone buzzed. A message from Angelina. Ava had intentionally asked about a meet-up with the girls, fully aware that no such event had been planned. It was a test, a means to see what excuse Angelina would conjure up. Sure enough, Angelina had crafted a response, claiming she was already meeting Lucy. Ava's frustration grew, how dare she not even consider inviting her along. She reopened Lucy's text, confirming that she had indeed declined because of her sick child.

Ava slammed her phone down on the table and screamed. She felt completely ostracised from the group—excluded from parties and those dreadful lunch dates she never even enjoyed attending. No longer able to contain her fury, she shoved open the back door and stormed towards the annex in the back of the garden.

Katherine had tarnished her reputation, allowing individuals like Lesley Graham, who before the fire and her son dying, had never even been looked at twice. Now she perched right at the top in Ava's place. While simultaneously knocking Ava to the bottom, isolated and alone.

Gusts of wind splayed Ava's hair behind her as she swung open the door, not bothering to wait for an invitation. Katherine's head spun at the intrusion, hastily ending her phone call before she forced a smile. "My darling, here to collect the rent already?"

Ava cut to the chase. "I want you out, Katherine."

"I see," Katherine replied, rising from her seat and heading toward the bedroom. "This was always meant to be a temporary arrangement. I can leave by the end of the week."

Ava pouted. This was too easy. She craved some confrontation. She wanted Katherine to push or shout back, not accept her demand with no resistance. "I want you out in three days," Ava pressed, determined to assert her dominance. "And I expect this place to be exactly as you found it."

Katherine smiled, her eyes glinting as she reached for her phone. "No problem. I can have everything sorted by tomorrow," she said, tapping away on the screen. "Consider it done."

Ava's mind buzzed as she surveyed the room, her eyes landing on the numerous pieces of artwork on the walls and the various clothing items strewn about every available surface. Necklaces and earrings lay scattered across the dressing table. "I thought you claimed to have no money, Katherine," Ava said, her gaze sweeping the room. "It seems you're not as destitute as you made yourself out to be. Where will you go on such short notice?"

A mischievous glimmer danced in Katherine's eyes as she sauntered closer to Ava, lightly brushing her hand against her shoulder. "I don't think I'll leave a forwarding address. Luck has smiled upon me once again, Ava, and I've hit the jackpot."

Ava pulled her jaw tight. How had Katherine found such luck, such wealth so fast?

"You do realise that people believe all those men coming and going from here are visiting me, right?" Ava snapped. "In fact, Lesley whispered in my ear that you supported those rumours."

Katherine shrugged, reaching for Ava's cheek. "They love their gossip here, don't they? Wear it as a badge of honour. Wouldn't it be worse if they weren't talking about you?"

Ava slapped Katherine's hand away. "No. It wouldn't. Especially when everyone believes I'm entertaining multiple men just weeks after my husband died." With that, Ava turned and marched toward the door. "It's been great catching up with you, Katherine. Your return to Beechwood has only made me realise how little I missed you. Enjoy your new life, wherever it may be."

Leaving Katherine to collect her belongings, Ava resisted the urge to dig deeper and inquire about how Katherine had regained her footing so swiftly. She refused to give her the satisfaction.

Ava was surprised at the speed with which Katherine gathered her belongings, leaving later that evening without another word. Once again, Ava was alone. The women in this town had given up on her and she was ousted from their social circles because of Lesley's venomous rumours. The friends she truly cherished were preoccupied with their own troubles. Florence with her secret lover, Emily and the art fraud over her head, no thanks to Nick and Katherine. And her sister Rose was all over the place, keeping things secret but too busy to spend a second in Ava's company.

Ava stumbled upon a bottle of wine that Nick had reserved for a special occasion. She guzzled the entire bottle before cracking open another, contemplating dragging herself upstairs to the empty bed. Instead, she settled back onto the sofa and propped her feet up.

Exhausted, Ava didn't realise she had dozed off until a creak from the kitchen jolted her awake. Despite the lamp switched on beside her, the corners of the room remained shrouded in darkness. She hadn't been asleep for long. Then came another creak, this time from behind.

Slowly, ever so slowly, Ava leaned forward and slid off the couch and onto the floor, using the back of the sofa as a shield. She shut her eyes, attempting to sharpen her senses. She could hear the blood pounding through her body, her ears burnt red hot. Footsteps echoed behind her, seeming to make their way toward the stairs. Ava held her breath to refrain from making a sound. She turned her head and rose to her feet, grasping the nearest object within reach, a small metal lamp. It was a man—tall, broad. Ava crept forward, clutching the lamp, while desperately hoping he was unarmed. When she glanced toward the kitchen for her phone, the man spun. Ava yanked the cord from the socket and swung for him, plunging the room into darkness.

But not before she glimpsed his face.

Overwhelmed by the momentum, Ava couldn't stop herself. The man instinctively raised his hands to shield himself, and Ava released her grip on the lamp, allowing it to crash onto the ground.

In a panic, she stumbled toward the kitchen in the pitch-black, outstretching her hands to seek the counter top. When she did, she fumbled for her phone, and then traced her hand along the wall for the light switch.

When the lights flickered on, the sudden brightness forced Ava to shield her eyes. Her head pounded from the effects of the wine, and as she rubbed her eyes to adjust, she found him again. He pressed his finger against his lips, urging her to remain silent.

She blinked, unable to believe what she was seeing. How could he be standing there? She took a cautious step forward. "Nick, please tell me this isn't real," Ava pleaded.

Yet there he was. Nick stood before her, in dark, ripped trousers marred with stains and an all-black, long-sleeved top. While he appeared dishevelled, it was undeniably him. Clutching her phone, Ava itched to dial the police. "Say something then!" Ava snapped. "What the hell are you doing here in the middle of the night?"

Nick raised his hands in a calming gesture. "Please, don't

shout," he said, moving toward the surviving lamp on the side table to switch it on. He returned to the main light switch and flicked it off. "We need to be discreet, darling."

Anger surged through Ava's mind, fuelling her words. "*Darling*? You think you can stand there and call me darling? What are you doing here? How are you even alive?"

Questions flooded Ava's thoughts; there was so much she wanted to ask him. Who's body was found with his wedding ring on? How did he escape the fire? Did he fake his own death? Was she about to loose the inheritance? Could she go to jail again? She clenched her fist, tempted to strike him. How could he have done this? How did he have the audacity to stand in front of her now?

Nick moved closer to her, his voice low and urgent. "I can explain, but the last thing we need is for anyone to hear you." His gaze darted toward the phone in Ava's hand. "Why don't you do us both a favour and put that down? We need to talk."

"I want you out of here, Nick. Get the hell out of Beechwood. Now!" Ava pressed her back against the countertop, shrinking away from him.

His beady eyes scanned the kitchen, and he stepped back toward the lounge. "There are too many windows in here, love. Come into the lounge, take a seat, and I can explain everything. Time is of the essence."

Still clinging to her phone, Ava followed Nick into the lounge. He swiftly closed the curtains and settled onto the floor, crossing his legs. He patted the space beside him for Ava to join. She forced a smile and sat in the armchair opposite him. Now she'd had a second to breath, to think. To truly believe what she saw in front of her. Her mind wondered. Was she thankful he was alive? Happy to know he didn't die in such a painful and gruesome way? Was she relieved to see him before her?

"Come on then, husband. Tell me whose ashes I spread and who I mourned for. Although, looking at you now, I wish I hadn't bothered."

Nick's face sank to the floor, his cheeks falling, his knees weak.. "I understand your anger. I didn't plan for this," he confessed, his voice laced with sorrow. "I wanted to contact you sooner, but it was too risky. I didn't know where to begin."

Ava lifted her arms and gestured to the room. "Well, here we are now. So, please, why don't you start by enlightening me about whose charred body it was that bore your watch and wedding ring? Oh, and how could I forget your last message of love to me during your dying breath. Let's start there."

"First of all, you must know that I didn't orchestrate this," Nick reiterated, avoiding Ava's gaze. "So much happened that I was forced to follow my instincts."

"You've already mentioned that." Ava interjected. "Get to the point, Nick."

Nick continued to avoid Ava's eyes, yet when he spoke, his voice was tinged with regret. "When the fire broke out, I was in the back room with another member. We were in the middle of an argument, clueless about what was happening outside. Until we noticed the smoke."

Ava crossed her legs as she sat above Nick, her posture poised yet tense. Ava remembered that night, the roof caving in, Emily on the floor desperate to get out with them all. The smoke filling their lungs. "What were you arguing about?"

Nick looked up, meeting Ava's gaze with a hint of sheepishness. "Katherine," he admitted. "The other member knew she had returned to town and wanted to stir up trouble and expose the art sales and money laundering that we were involved in. The argument got heated. He planned to trap

Katherine and me, I had to act. Eventually, the fire spread to the back room, and the smoke got too much for him. It was my chance, so I took it." Nick crawled toward Ava's feet, resting his hand on her knee. "I'm not proud of it, but I had to do it to protect the money. I assume the life insurance payout came through?"

Ava shoved Nick's hand away and rose to her feet. She paced back and forth. Her heart pounding. Money, he faked his death, had a funeral, left her with an empty house all for money that hadn't even come through yet. "It didn't take long for money to enter the equation, did it? You know Emily is under investigation, don't you? You've ruined her life! Katherine has moved on to another wealthy man in no time, and not a single person in Beechwood will even speak to me now you're 'dead'."

Ava moved toward the window, cautiously pulling aside the curtain to peer outside at the close. The close was dead, darkness covering the sky. Cars parked along the street. Silence filling the space. Nick shot to his feet and swiftly closed the curtains. "Ava, please. I did all of this for us. We can be together again, live a life of luxury away from everyone we know, and start afresh."

Ava couldn't bear to be in his presence any longer. She stepped away from him. "We don't have a life anymore, Nick. You died, and I've moved on."

Nick shook his head, his eyes wide as an animal about to be shot. Those words hurt him, and Ava enjoyed delivering them. "You don't mean that. I did everything for you. If I hadn't taken action, the insurance policy would have been voided, and all the money would have stopped."

"I want you to leave, Nick. I can't think straight right now. All of this might be for nothing. The money hasn't even come through yet. You could have *died* for nothing."

"But, love—"

Ava spun to face his unwashed face, pleading with her like a sickly puppy would its owner. "I said get out!" she screamed.

He raised his hands in surrender. "Let me just gather a few things, and then I'll be gone."

Ava flicked her hand dismissively and turned away, refusing to look at him. "Do whatever you need to do." He hurriedly made his way up the stairs.

Leaning against the windowsill, Ava listened to his frantic rummaging. Those heavy steps, the creaking of the floorboards. At least she now knew who'd broken in that night. After a few minutes, he reappeared downstairs. "Are we finished here?" she asked, still refusing to look at him.

"Yes. I left a contact number on the coffee table. It's a burner phone, in case you change your mind or ever want to talk." Nick scraped back his unwashed hair. "I can't do this without you, Ava."

"I highly doubt I will ever contact you again."

He turned to leave, but stopped at the door. "I heard about Gabriel Moulin. He died in the fire as well."

Ava raised an eyebrow, her curiosity piqued. "Yes, they were able to identify his body. He wasn't left burned beyond recognition like your deceased friend was."

"Well, Gabriel's final art piece is in your possession. Seek out Rupert Gullis. A piece like that will set you up for life. Consider it a parting gift from me." Nick smiled, opening the door that led to the garden.

Ava lifted her chin with a smile. The *art* was the dress Katherine wore to Emily's summer art show. The one that was full of fraud. The piece of art she'd commanded Katherine to sell, the one bit of charity work Ava had ever been part of to give Emily something to hold onto. "I would have loved to, Nick, but I already sold it. The money went to Emily."

Nick froze and stepped back inside. "What?"

Ava smiled, relishing in his shock. "Well, you left her in quite a predicament. I thought the neighbourly thing to do would be to help her out."

Nick ran his hands across his face. "Darling. That piece would have been worth a fortune. Who did you sell it to? How much did you give to Emily?"

Ava felt foolish, realising she had trusted Katherine to negotiate the best deal for the artwork and deliver the funds to Emily. She hadn't even questioned the amount at the time. "Katherine handled it. I allowed her to stay here on the condition that she made amends with Emily."

Nick laughed, yet the sound was manic as it echoed through the room. "Well, there you have it. Ava Moore strikes again." He approached her slowly. "You trusted Katherine to give away all that money to Emily?"

"She gave her nearly eight-hundred-thousand pounds."

Nick laughed, an uncontrollable cackle. Ava narrowed her eyes, turning her gaze away from his. "Oh, really? You've been played, love. Katherine would have been sitting on millions for that. She played all of you, and now she's gone." Nick turned to leave once more. "Perhaps I should have stuck with her after all," he muttered, leaving Ava alone in the wake of his departure.

Furious, Ava stormed into the kitchen, her grip tightening around the bottle of wine before smashing it against the ground. She screamed, releasing the pent-up anger that had consumed her. She pounded her fists against the tabletop. How could she have been so blind, so foolish, to be played by everyone around her and unwittingly hand Katherine a fortune? Katherine's smug face ringed in her mind. The acceptance to move out, the new clothes spread around her room. Leaving was no burden to her.

Wallowing in the silence, Ava marched up stairs and noticed the paper Nick had left on the table, his contact number scribbled on it. She held it for a moment before tucking it into her pocket. She needed time to process her options and then determine the best course of action. She had allowed herself to slip, to prioritise others over herself, but now she realised the need to reclaim her own agency, and put herself first once again. From now on, she would be the one pulling the strings.

CHAPTER THIRTEEN
Tough Decisions

Florence continued to seethe as the days went on. Her mother was getting too comfortable. In fact, both her parents were taking advantage of her hospitality. If she had any strength, she'd kick them out. But having them here, made her feel like a child again. Powerless and under their control. On top of that, her attempt to confront Olivia had backfired entirely, leaving her constantly fearing her secret relationship with Regina would be exposed at any moment. Despite her efforts to remain unaffected, Florence had become more cautious around Regina. Even when they were alone, she was constantly glancing over her shoulder, hoping to catch the blackmailer in the act.

Regina had even started working the late shift at the salon to minimise her interaction with Florence's mother. Florence empathised with her. Having grown up around such hurtful comments, she understood the weight of such words. But she also knew her mother thought—and wrongly so—that she was doing nothing wrong.

It was only when Florence anxiously watched the door, waiting for Regina to burst in, that she felt the absence of her family. With Olivia now living with Lesley, and Lucas hardly here, Florence had no one to wait for.

Her mother joined her on the couch, pulling Florence from her thoughts. "You know, staring at the door won't make her come back," she said, and Florence rolled her eyes. "I'm not surprised she's ignoring you. I mean, slapping your pregnant daughter!"

Florence sighed. She still couldn't believe she'd done that. It was like an out of body experience. The fear of being exposed, by someone she loved, trusted took over her mind and she acted without thinking. "I know, Mother. Trust me, I don't need you to remind me how terrible my actions were. I'm far from happy about what I did."

"If you tell me what it was all about, it might help me understand," she suggested with a slight lift of her chin.

Florence glanced at her mother. "I lost my temper over a comment she made. That's all."

"Give me that woman's address. I can go over and sort things out," Joan offered.

Florence turned back to face her mother. Throughout Florence's life, her mother had never been there to lend a hand. In fact, she'd kept her distance throughout Florence's entire childhood. "No. I don't need you interfering." Florence stood to leave her mother behind.

"Before you go, there's one more thing I wanted to mention," Joan added.

"Make it quick. Regina will be back soon, and I need to talk to her." Florence felt the urgency rising within her.

"Now that Olivia has moved out, don't you think it would be better if Regina moved into her room? It's rather unsightly for the two of you to share a room like this," Joan said, raising her eyebrows.

Crushed beneath her words, Florence turned away and fought back tears. She felt the sudden urge to shout and confess to her mother about their secret relationship and how deeply in love they were. But she couldn't bring herself to do it. Instead, Florence simply nodded as the front door swung open and Regina entered, Lucas trailing behind her. Florence immediately strode to her side. "We need to talk. Can we go to the garden?"

Confusion flickered across Regina's face as she looked at Florence, and then her mother. She nodded. "Sure thing," she said, smiling at Joan as they walked past her towards the garden.

The fresh air outside helped clear Florence's mind, yet the letter and photographs burned in her back pocket. She needed someone to confide in, and Regina deserved to know. They sat on a bench in the back of the garden, hidden from view. Florence clasped Regina's hands before releasing them with a quick glance back at the house. Inside, her mother and Lucas appeared to be exchanging serious words, her mother pointing a finger at him. If Florence had time, she'd question what they were arguing about. But her mind needed to focus on herself, for now. She returned her attention back to Regina, who sat there, eagerly waiting. Florence had to act quickly. "We don't have much time," she began, pulling the note and photographs from her pocket and handing them to Regina. "Someone is trying to blackmail me. We can't let anyone see these."

Regina read the note and scrutinised the photographs. She looked up, her mouth agape. "What are we going to do?

Who the hell would do something like this?"

Florence raked her hands through her hair. "I don't know. I received it the other day, and then Olivia threatened to expose us. That's why I slapped her." Florence hung her head.

"Do you think she's told Lesley?" Regina asked, lowering her voice.

"I have no idea. If she has, Lesley wouldn't waste any time spreading rumours. But this feels like someone else — someone with their own agenda."

Regina scanned the house again before placing her hand on Florence's shoulder. "Have you told anyone about us? About you and me?"

"Only Ava. Have you?" Florence countered, and Regina nodded.

"My friend Claire knows, but she wouldn't blackmail me. What about Ava? She's been tight on cash since Nick's death."

"No, it couldn't be her," Florence insisted. Ava had lied before, Florence thought. She had an affair behind her back. Lied for Nick and her upbringing with Rose. Florence shook her head. She didn't like doubting Ava, but something pulled at her even so.

"Could she have mentioned us to someone? Maybe someone around here? Does your mother know?"

Florence smiled and glanced back at the window. "If she did, she wouldn't still be sitting inside."

Regina rubbed Florence's knee. "Well, maybe it's time we told her. Don't let this pathetic person control you. If we come out to everyone, there will be nothing left to hide."

Florence felt her heart pounding in her chest once more. Just the brief discussion they had sent her nerves into overdrive. If she came out, she'd lose her parents forever. Even though they have been absent, they were still there, in a way. All she'd feared growing up was not having them there as an option if she needed them. That small girl inside her was begging for them to stay around, even if they caused harm. The thought of revealing their relationship to her mother was too much. "I don't know. I don't think I can."

Regina's face dropped, her eyes fell to the floor without saying a word. Before Regina could respond, Joan appeared in the garden with Lucas, a fake smile plastered to her face. Florence knew that look all too well from her childhood. "Regina, dear," she called, heading over to them. "We were just discussing your... arrangements. Now that Olivia has moved out, don't you think it's more appropriate for you to stay in her room?"

Regina turned to Florence, her eyes searching for answers. "Were you discussing me? What arrangements are they, Flo?"

Florence couldn't look Regina in the eyes. She darted around the garden, desperately trying to find anything else to focus on. "It was nothing more than a suggestion." Florence said, glaring at her mother. "Please don't jump to conclusions."

Joan furrowed her brow. "Please, someone has to talk some sense into her. I understand you people enjoy cramming ten to a room, but we prefer our own space." She rubbed Regina's back, then looked at Florence and Lucas, as if expecting back-up.

Florence hated the tone and words her mother used. The well meaning was there, she hoped, and she'd let some of it slip by because of her age. But really, was that an excuse? She wasn't sure. Regina bit her lip, widening her eyes at Florence, as if silently urging her to speak up in her defence. But Florence's words were trapped in her throat, and she struggled to summon any sound at all.

Regina leaned in and hissed, "If you don't say something,

Flo..."

Summoning her courage, Florence stood up and forced a smile. "Mother, I believe you've said enough. Why don't you go grab some drinks from inside and bring them out? We can all sit down and have a proper discussion."

Joan nodded, but it was obvious by the way she carried herself, upright and ridged that she thought she was in the right, that she was winning this argument. The moment Joan was out of earshot, Regina stood up. "I won't tolerate this, Flo. Your mother is a racist. Either ask her to leave, or I will."

Lucas stepped forward, his eyes wide. "Regina, please. Let's find a way to work this out. We can't just throw Grandma and Grandpa out on the streets."

"And what do you suggest we do, Lucas?" Regina shot back.

Lucas scratched his neck. "Well, we can find a compromise. We can't let them be homeless." Lucas reasoned.

Florence watched Regina and Lucas continue to argue, their voices rising. Lucas seemed to lose his usual composure in his desperate attempts to ensure his grandparents stayed. While watching Regina, her heart broke at the thought of her leaving. Regina was right—her mother was a racist. And Regina being gay probably didn't help matters. She glanced toward the house, knowing her mother would return soon. "Regina, go inside and let me talk to her."

Regina laughed. "Sure, I'll start packing," she said, walking away. The heaviness of her departure settled in the air.

Florence's hands trembled as she ran them through her hair, turning to Lucas, whose turmoil reflected her own. Leaning closer, she gently brushed his overgrown hair from his eyes and turned his head to meet her gaze, searching for answers. His blue eyes mirrored his father's, and a pang of longing settled in her chest. "What do you think, then? Should I ask her to leave tonight?"

"What? No, Mum, you can't kick Grandma out. Or risk loosing Regina. They both need to stay," Lucas protested.

"I don't see any other options, and I can't bear the thought of losing Regina." Florence choked.

Lucas' shoulders slumped. "Mum, you can't. I..." His words trailed off as he glanced back at the house.

"Why can't I? We've managed without them for years. They've never been there for us," Florence argued, unable to dampen the rising frustration.

"You're wrong." Lucas spoke so quietly Florence could barely hear him. "Granddad was there for me."

Florence felt a knot tighten in her stomach. She had sensed Lucas's unwavering support for her parents since their arrival, but she hadn't fully comprehended the depth of their connection. "What do you mean?"

He looked up at her, his eyes pleading. "Promise you won't get mad?"

"I promise," Florence said, her voice softening.

"When I left after Dad died, I wasn't just travelling or camping. I was in the city, sleeping rough and crashing at friends' places. I got into some trouble and did stupid things." Lucas turned, noticing Joan returning with a tray. "I have to hurry, Mum. I got involved with some dangerous people and racked up a lot of debt. I didn't know who to turn to, and I asked Granddad for help. I owed so much money."

Florence raised her hand, struggling to make sense of the revelation. "Lucas, slow down. What kind of people were they?"

"I need to say this before she gets here. Granddad used up all his savings, everything he had—even the house—to pay off my debt. Grandma knows nothing about it, and

Granddad has been covering for me ever since. If you kick them out, it would be all my fault if they ended up homeless. Please, Mum, don't throw them out."

Joan arrived and placed the drinks on the table. Florence tried to slow the pounding of her heart. "Is Regina not staying around to go through it all, then?"

Florence turned to Lucas, who mouthed the word 'please.' Forcing a smile, she glanced back at her mother, burying what she had learned. "I believe we've reached an agreement. Just give me a moment." She grabbed the letter from the table and crumpled it before heading inside.

Regina stood by the window, watching Joan and Lucas laugh about something together. She turned to face Florence, a small bag by her feet. "I was thinking. Maybe book in to visit Mike in prison. After all, he knew about us. He could be behind that letter. Maybe you can stop it from coming out." Regina turned to sip from a glass of water and then picked up her bag. "I assume you made your choice, then?"

Florence glanced between her mother and Regina, Lucas's plea replaying in her ears. Florence nearly spat out Lucas' secret, the money he owed, what her father did to protect her boy. But she couldn't. He obviously didn't want anyone to know. She couldn't risk loosing another child like she had Olivia. "Lucas has put me in a difficult position," she replied, her voice filled with conflict.

"I suspected as much. I've already called a taxi. I think it's waiting outside. That should make things easier here," Regina stated, moving to the door.

Florence reached out to take hold of Regina's hand. "Please, it's not as simple as that."

Regina pulled away gently. "It's okay, Flo. I understand. Maybe some time apart will be good. Let things settle, let people move on, and we can pick up where we left off," she said, stroking Florence's cheek. Regina walked towards the front door. "I'm serious about Mike. He's delusional enough to do something like this. He was desperate to tear us apart." Florence followed Regina outside towards the taxi. With a bittersweet smile, Regina blew her a kiss as the taxi set off to leave Beechwood. Watching her leave made Florence's heart ache, and she swiped at a tear.

Heading back inside and toward the window, she paused to find her mother laughing with Lucas again—the picture-perfect image of a grandmother. Florence rolled the crumpled letter between her fingers and made her way upstairs to the office, unlocking the desk drawer. Inside, she retrieved the letter she had received a month ago, despite pushing it back to the corners of her mind.

It was a visitor's request from Mike.

She had refused to let him back into her life, but now Regina's words echoed in her mind. Mike could be blackmailing her, but even if it wasn't him, she needed to know who was behind this. She unfolded the slip of paper from the envelope and filled it in, agreeing to meet with Mike.

CHAPTER FOURTEEN
Into the Night

The Terra Cotta Italia offered much-needed solace for Emily's racing mind as she took her seat across from Theo. She breathed in the scent of different cheeses and freshly baked bread. Classic Italian elements adorned the restaurant: murals of the picturesque Italian countryside, charming trinkets of glass bottles, candles, old framed photographs carefully placed throughout the restaurant. Emily traced her fingers along the smooth tablecloth, her gaze wandering to the bustling open kitchen at the back of the room.

She hadn't told Theo about her trip to visit Rachel, or about what she learned about his living arrangements. She wanted him to be relaxed, unguarded, so she could find out the real reason for him withholding the truth.

Yet the secrets tugged at her conscience, reminding Emily of the things she, too, had kept from Theo. She picked at her fingernails, contemplating whether it would be wiser to let sleeping dogs lie and focus instead on the future, rather than unearthing the past. But people had suffered. Cassandra had died, and Emily needed to ascertain whether Theo held more knowledge than he had let on.

Theo lowered the menu, smiling in a way that illuminated his face. "Have you made up your mind yet? I'm going for the lasagne, smothered in extra cheese, and some garlic bread on the side." He placed the menu gently on the table, running his fingers along the smooth surface of his glass of water. "If I could, I'd order one of everything, but perhaps I'll steal a bite from your plate."

Emily looked up at him from the menu with a genuine smile. It felt wonderful to be out, enjoying his company, and experiencing a semblance of normalcy once again. It had been far too long since Emily had indulged in anything solely for her own pleasure. For the past year or so, she had been swept up in a whirlwind of events. She reached out for Theo's hands, finding comfort in the warmth of his palms. "Tell me what you're interested in, and I'll order that for myself."

"No, go ahead and order what you want. This one's on me," Theo insisted.

Emily perused the menu, her appetite overshadowed by her nerves. She glided her fingertip along the array of choices before settling on one.

A waiter appeared at their side. He was trimly built with slicked-back dark hair, his gleaming smile marked by a shadow of stubble. With one hand casually tucked behind his back, he asked, "Are you ready to order, or shall I leave you love birds a while longer?"

Theo blushed, yet the waiter's words earned a small giggle from Emily. "Yes, please. I'll have the Pappardelle al Ragu di Manzo," she said.

"A splendid choice. And for you, sir?"

Theo responded with a discreet smile and pointed to an item on the menu.

The waiter arched an eyebrow. "The Filetto di Manzo con Tartufo Nero. An excellent selection, sir." He leaned in to collect the menus, then left them alone at the table once more.

"I thought you wanted the lasagne with extra cheese?" Emily quizzed.

Theo chuckled and scratched his head sheepishly. "I did, but your choice sounded so posh that I couldn't have something so basic." He puffed out his chest playfully. "I think I made a rather *splendid* decision."

A smile tugged at Emily's lips as she turned her attention to the ambience of the restaurant. The room reverberated with lively conversations, punctuated by the clinking of cutlery on dishes. "So, how are you finding Beechwood? Does it live up to your expectations?"

Theo took a sip from his glass, contemplating her question. "It's a bit pretentious, I must admit." Emily leaned back in the chair. "I initially felt like a fish out of water. Funny, though, because it's what we used to dream about back at uni. Making it big and living in a place like this. And now that we're here, it still feels surreal... I suppose undeserved is the word."

Emily swirled the wine in her glass thoughtfully. "Undeserved may be the right word. I don't believe many who reside in Beechwood truly deserve it. Most who stumble upon Beechwood do so from pure chance, not through genuine talent or hard work."

"It certainly beats the flat I was living in before," Theo admitted, watching Emily. "I thought I had lost you forever until you reached out to me. It felt like a lifeline. I thought I had lost you forever. Thank goodness one of us found success, right?"

"My own success was just as random, Theo. I wrestled with guilt, you know, after selling off my stocks and shares when they were at their peak. We were all advised to hold on and wait for a more substantial sale, but I feared losing it all, so I sold when I did and got lucky."

Theo nodded along to what Emily said. He made all the correct movements in his face, but she couldn't help wonder if he truly felt okay by the result of everything. Her bank was once full, more than she'd ever imagined. Loosing out on that, must have hurt.

"No one blamed you, Emily. Sure, a few of us may have felt envious for a while, but it passed. We all moved on, got jobs, and continued with our lives."

This was it. Emily had to steer the conversation toward her friends. Placing her hand on his, she said, "Thank you. It's comforting to know." But before she could delve further, their food arrived, drawing their attention to the steaming dishes. She released her hand from Theo's, whose eyes lit up with delight. He reached for the plate until the waiter intervened.

"Please do not touch the plate, sir. It's very hot. Enjoy your meal."

Though distracted by Theo's childlike wonder, Emily knew she had to seize the opportunity. They began eating in silence until Emily said, "Theo." Her voice was gentle yet probing. "You never mentioned how you ended up living with Cassandra."

He shifted his gaze from hers, transfixed on his plate. "It just sort of happened. We didn't know many people, so we gravitated toward each other, I suppose."

Emily toyed with her food, prodding it around her plate with her fork. "And what kind of job did she eventually land?"

"Nothing special. She worked at a coffee house." Theo rolled his eyes.

"Oh. Rent and bills must have been challenging." Theo looked at Emily, his eyebrows drawing closer.

"I suppose so. It feels like a lifetime ago now."

Emily's heart sank. She wanted him to open up about Jessie living with him and his failure to mention it. Still, he evaded the issue, his avoidance clear by his darting eyes, looking anywhere but at her. Emily bit her lip, determined to give him another opportunity to speak. Resorting to her next tactic pained her, but she needed to gain his trust if he was to ever tell her the truth—offer something that would tug at his heartstrings and compel him to confess. Retrieving her bag from the back of her chair, she pulled out her purse.

"Emily, it's too early to pay." Theo whispered. "Besides, I insisted on treating you today."

"Theo, there's something I wanted to ask you. Something I can only entrust to someone I genuinely trust."

Theo dabbed the corner of his mouth with the napkin, raising his brows. "Of course. What is it?"

Emily inhaled deeply for dramatic flair. She offered him a closed smile, looking into his eyes with an intensity she hoped would be convincing. Reaching into her purse, she produced the cheque Katherine had given her as an apology a few months ago. "You know my accounts have been frozen, and I have some cash that I need to assign with someone I genuinely trust." She glanced down at the cheque and nudged it toward him, into his hands. "Would you be willing to take it and cash it for me under your name?"

His face turned ashen, drained of all colour as he stared at the cheque, which trembled in his hands. He shook his head, unable to look at her. "I... I can't accept this, Emily. Please don't ask this of me."

"Why not? I trust you. You're the only person in my life whom I can rely on for this." Emily paused, allowing the weight of her words to settle between them. "What's stopping you?" Reaching out, she grasped his hand across the table, finally locking eyes with him. They brimmed with regret. His turmoil felt genuine, and she sensed his internal battle. She took a breath and willed herself to say, "Theo, may I ask you one question? Just one, and I'll accept your answer."

He looked up, searching her eyes. "What is it?"

"The flat you and Cassandra rented... Was it just the two of you?"

He pressed his lips into a tight line and nodded. Pushing the cheque back toward her, he said, "Please, Emily. Don't ask me to do this."

Her eyes welled, and she fought with every fibre of her being to hold them back. How could he deceive her while his face showed such pain? Emily gazed at him, desperately searching for clues in his expression that would unravel the emotions preventing him from speaking the truth. Cassandra, buried six feet under, flashed in her mind and sent a chill down her spine. Her thoughts raced, and all she could envision was Theo standing over Cassandra's lifeless body. Overwhelmed, she rose abruptly, ignoring his outstretched hand and impassioned pleas to stop. She couldn't bring herself to turn back. She needed to leave, to distance herself from him and go home.

The town's dazzling lights temporarily blinded her as she stepped outside, surveying her surroundings. Beechwood Close wasn't far, home was only a short journey. Her car was just a few steps away. Sitting in the driver's seat, Emily pounded her fist against the steering wheel. She just wanted Theo to be honest, but a lingering unease gnawed in the back of her mind. Something didn't add up, and tonight, she had finally glimpsed it in his eyes.

Upon arriving home, Emily glanced at the twelve missed calls and four texts flashing from Theo, inquiring about what had happened. Guilt washed over her for abandoning him in town, but he had the means to find a hotel. If he arrived here tomorrow, she wasn't sure if she would welcome him back or if she even wanted to. Right now, she needed to gather her thoughts. She entered the kitchen to find Cynthia, counting coins on the countertop. Looking up, Cynthia's concentration faltered. "What's happened?" she asked.

Emily stumbled toward a chair and sat across from her Gran, sinking her head into her hands. "I'm not sure. I was trying to test him, and it backfired."

Cynthia chuckled. "Most men fail tests, love. Don't let it eat away at you."

"What are you doing, anyway? Shouldn't you be asleep?"

It was nearly nine o'clock. Cynthia was usually out cold by now, or at least in bed reading or knitting. "Should be, but I couldn't sleep. It's been a while since I've had to count pennies."

Emily's head shot up, startling Cynthia and causing her to drop a coin from her hand. "Oh God," Emily gasped, running her hands through her hair. "I left it with him."

"Left what?" Cynthia pouted. "Emily, sit up and talk to me."

"The cheque. God, I'm so stupid sometimes. I left the cheque with Theo."

Cynthia tapped Emily on the shoulder. "Leaving that amount with a boy as untrustworthy as him?" Cynthia chuckled. "Let's just hope he'll be back soon. Fights don't last forever."

"This one might. He's been lying to me. Well, not exactly

lying, more like *withholding* the truth."

"Sounds like lying to me," Cynthia grumbled.

"It's complicated, Gran. With Cassandra's murder and Rachel being followed, it's messing with my head. That bloody note through the door has caused me nothing but trouble."

Cynthia's puckered lip and furrowed brow melted slightly. "Let me call Clive. We'll get the police involved."

Emily moved her hand forward, wanting to stop her gran. The last thing she needed right now was the police involved, even if they could trust Clive. The risk was too great.

"No, Gran. I need to handle this on my own," she said. "I'm finding it hard to trust anyone, and I gave Theo the chance to tell me, but he clammed up."

Someone knocked on the front door. Emily looked at Cynthia. "Let me handle this. I'll make sure he doesn't come back here again." Cynthia pressed her hands on the table to push herself to her feet.

Emily stood, watching as Cynthia shuffled toward the door. "Gran, let me deal with this. I've learned enough from you to handle my own troubles."

Cynthia paused and raised an eyebrow. Finally, she stepped back. "Fine, but if anything goes wrong, you yell. I'll be right there."

Another knock sounded, and as Emily opened it, she was surprised to find Rose standing there, accompanied by two men in suits. Confused, Emily said, "Rose? What's going on? Who are they? Are you in trouble?"

Rose turned to the men and spoke with a smile. "Give me a moment, please," she said before stepping inside. Leaning closer to Emily, she whispered, "I think I've found a way for us to escape our... situation. They need us to come with them right away. Grab a coat."

"Rose, I need more information than that," Emily pressed, seeking clarity. She looked the men over once again. Crisp expensive suits. Stern faces. What could they want with Rose? How exactly could they help in anyway? Emily bit her lip, hoping Rose hadn't gotten them involved in more trouble or danger.

One of the men called out from behind Rose. "Ma'am, please, we must go. Sir Banks is waiting."

"Who on earth is Sir Banks?" Emily exclaimed.

"Please, Emily, trust me." Rose implored, gripping Emily's hands. "It won't take long, and all our troubles could disappear. The whole issue with George could be resolved. Please? For me?"

Emily glanced back at the two imposing men behind Rose, then glanced back at her. With a sigh, she raised her voice to alert Cynthia. "Gran, it's Rose. I'll be out for a few hours. Don't wait up." She shifted her attention back to Rose, who now wore a radiant smile. Taking hold of Emily's hand, she led her outside.

A darkened Land Rover awaited them, with another suited man inside, midway through a phone call. "Yes, sir. They're on their way now. Taking them to the helicopter. We will be there as soon as possible."

Emily's heart pounded in her chest as she sat in the backseat between the two men. She leaned toward Rose and whispered, "Where are we going?"

"London. We have an appointment with a member of parliament," Rose replied, tightening her grip on Emily's hand. Her smile remained fixed, unyielding.

CHAPTER FIFTEEN
The High Life

Rain pelted against the window, and its assault felt almost personal to Emily, who clutched the armrest, her head spinning in response. The helicopter's vibrations reverberated through her body, accentuated by the powerful winds swirling outside. Peering through the condensation on the small window, she strained to glimpse the city below—a hazy backdrop of distant lights battling their way through the rain, their glow soft and muted. Sat beside her, Rose had her eyes squeezed shut, while the two men remained silent.

As the helicopter adjusted course, Emily's attention returned to the window. The once-familiar town of Beechwood vanished, replaced by a countryside panorama of rolling fields. Through the diminishing rain, a vast country home emerged on the horizon. Her stomach tightened with a mix of anticipation and apprehension as the helicopter descended, landing gently on the ground in an empty space, a lone path leading towards a country house. With a shrug and an encouraging push from Rose, Emily strode alongside her toward the mansion's entrance. The rain lashed at Emily's cheeks as they followed a short gravel path, guided by the men walking ahead of them before ushering the women into a grand kitchen through the mansion's rear.

The heat from the crackling fire inside enveloped Emily, providing a reprieve from the elements. She stole a quick glance at her surroundings and tried to absorb them; Grand halls, bespoke wood finishes on the doors, thick rugs laid across the wooden floors They were quickly handed over to another man donning a similar suit. Emily desperately tried to orient herself, but only knew the little information the men had told her; they were somewhere outside London. There hadn't been an opportunity to speak to Rose or any ask questions about the details of their arrangement.

Silently following the man through the grand hallway, Emily sought to glean whatever information she could about the person she was about to meet. Framed images of family portraits and artwork adorned the walls, and as they turned a corner, Emily's gaze fell upon a small painting hanging above a shelf. She froze, caught off guard by the sight of her own work, a piece that had sold during her recent art show. The painting was of a lush landscape, in full bloom from a long summer. A man cleared his throat, drawing her attention. "Is everything all right, miss?" He tapped his ringed finger against the mantel. Emily nodded, regaining her composure, and resumed following Rose up the staircase. They waited in a narrow hallway. More art littered the walls, the wooden seat was cushioned with royal red velvet. "Sir Banks will see you shortly. Please wait here while he prepares." He nodded to another security member before descending the stairs himself.

This was the first opportunity Emily had to be alone with Rose, a chance to engage in conversation and unravel the mystery surrounding their presence. Jabbing Rose gently, she whispered, "What on earth are we doing here? What's going on?" Attempting to keep her composure, Emily glanced at the man stationed by the door.

Rose clasped her hands in her lap.

"I don't have all the answers, Emily. They came to my door with an invite a few days ago, and I thought it could be an opportunity, so I wanted you to be here too," Rose whispered.

"What kind of opportunity? Who *is* this guy?" Emily's voice dropped, but her inquiries drew the attention of the guard by the door. He pressed a finger to his lips and narrowed his eyes in their direction. Emily sensed the warning to withhold any further discussion until they were inside. "Promise me, Rose, that once we're in there, we won't agree to anything too quickly," she pleaded. The guard coughed, shooting Emily another stern glance. But then he gestured for them to approach the door.

It was time to enter.

The hallway loomed before them, cloaked in darkness. A note of sandalwood accompanied the air as they stood before two towering wooden doors. Rose turned to Emily with a reassuring smile and reached for her hand. Together, they pushed the doors open with a creak that echoed through the room, momentarily blinded by the stark light inside. The walls were painted a regal shade of green, adorned with half-wall panelling that encased the space. A man sat behind a large oak desk, positioned near a bay window that offered a view of the tempestuous weather outside. The dramatic backdrop seemed fitting with the rising tension in the room.

Emily felt rooted to the spot, her feet glued in place.

The man behind the desk glanced up from his array of papers and gestured for the escort to leave the room before the doors closed behind them. With a wide smile, he extended his arms, signalling for them to take the seats opposite his desk. He was striking, Emily realised. Although he was older—potentially old enough to be her father—remnants of his once-youthful features were still discernible. He boasted a full head of hair, and his skin appeared vibrant beneath the light. "Thank you both for joining me here at this late hour on such short notice. I worried it might be too much to ask of you," he said, his smile unwavering. "Can I offer you something to drink?"

"No, thank you. I prefer to keep a clear head," Emily replied. "May I be blunt and ask why you've brought us here?" Suspicion coloured her words, and though she loved Rose dearly, she knew her friend was easily swayed. "I have some questions, sir. I haven't been briefed like Rose has."

"Of course," Kenneth said calmly. "I want you to understand that my offer is quite simple. Rose possesses something I desire, and I am prepared to pull whatever strings necessary to obtain it."

Emily turned to Rose, who squirmed awkwardly in her seat. "And what exactly does Rose have?" Emily noticed Rose squirming awkwardly in her seat.

"What I want is not something you need to know, Emily. But I can offer you the reason why you're here. Rose wouldn't agree to anything until we arranged something involving you. Now, I understand that you're currently under investigation for art fraud," Kenneth stated matter-of-factly.

"That's correct," Emily said.

"Well, I've reached an agreement with Rose. I can ensure that the matter is resolved. Your life can return to normal."

Emily didn't want to believe he held such power. How could one man, no matter how rich, command something so huge to be forgotten? But the way he looked at her, such confidence running through him. He felt familiar to Emily. She'd seen his face before, on the news, or in the papers. She noticed a name plate on the desk. Sir Banks – MP. Could he be telling the truth? Could he really hold that much sway?

"I highly doubt that," Emily muttered. "May I have a moment alone with Rose, please?"

The man nodded and rose from his chair. "You'll have a few minutes, but I expect an answer soon."

As the door slammed shut behind Kenneth, Emily turned her attention to Rose. "What the hell have you gotten us into now?"

"I'm sorry. I didn't anticipate all of this," Rose replied. She smiled, one that showed guilt in her large eyes.

"No, it seems you never anticipate anything," Emily snapped.

"Violet left me something—an entire book of information about The Order and its members and all the nefarious deeds they've committed over the years. Sir Banks contacted me with an offer for that information. He was once a member of The Order and wants what I have."

The words *The Order* made Emily freeze. She had known nothing about the group until just a few months ago, and now it had insidiously seeped into her life like a chronic disease. She had hoped to never hear about it again, but like most cults, once they got you in, it became impossible to get out.

Emily mustered a sympathetic smile for Rose. "Do you truly believe this is wise? Isn't he a bloody MP? We can't get caught up in this!"

"It's a solution to our problems. He has promised to

sweep everything under the rug: your fraud case and any potential *complications* regarding George's death," Rose's tone mirrored the pleading in her eyes. "I know it's a lot to ask, but I can't go to prison because of him, Emily. I simply can't."

The wooden doors swung open behind them, interrupting their conversation as Kenneth returned to his leather chair. "I believe enough time has been given. Now that you're all caught up, can we come to an agreement and proceed with the document exchange?"

Emily narrowed her eyes, placing a hand on Rose to keep her from speaking. "Hold on. You mentioned you knew Rose possessed this information, but how? Who informed you about it?"

Kenneth smiled. "I have a vast network of contacts. Some of us within The Order anticipated the existence of such hidden knowledge, and it's something we cannot allow to become public."

"I suppose having ties to a satanic cult isn't the most favourable image when you're aiming for the highest office," Emily retorted, raising an eyebrow.

Kenneth pinched his fingers at the mention of a cult. His eye twitched, it was only for a second, but Emily spotted it.

"We desire The Order's resurgence—re-imagined. We don't wish to be haunted by our past," Kenneth calmly explained, resting his hands on the desk. "I'm being quite reasonable here, Ms. Lamont. You both find yourselves in troubled waters, as do I. Let us help each other."

Rose turned to Emily with a hopeful smile. "Come on, Emily. Once we've done this, it will be over."

Emily scrutinised Rose, who tightened her grip on her bag. Emily turned to face Kenneth again, who resembled a wolf, poised to pounce. "Are you the one who has been sending us the letters? Are you behind these threats, attempting to scare us?"

He chuckled. "I find that accusation insulting, Ms. Lamont. Either agree to the deal or leave."

"Come on, Emily. Let's not be foolish," Rose urged.

"I can't tell you what to do, Rose. The documents are in your possession, but if you hand them over, that darkness will resurface. Consider that," Emily warned, fixing her gaze on Kenneth.

Kenneth slammed his fists onto the desk, abandoning his previous composure. "I am mere months away from assuming the role of prime minister. If you require more incentive, speak now, and I will provide it."

"I think we need some time to think, Sir," Rose said, wrapping her arms protectively around the documents.

A vein pulsed on Kenneth's forehead. "You've already toyed with me enough. I'm attempting to handle this with as little mess as possible. Don't assume I won't take more serious measures to obtain what I need. There are many members out there desperate to retrieve that information."

Emily stood, tugging Rose up by the wrist. "We don't take kindly to threats, Mr. Banks," she declared. "We're leaving. Come on, Rose."

Rose paused, glancing back at Kenneth before looking at Emily again. "Are you certain about this?" she whispered.

Kenneth turned to face the window, biting his lip. "Once you step out of that door, the offer is no longer on the table."

Emily's heart pounded in her chest. "Give us some time. The information will remain secure, at least for now. We won't do anything to affect your polling numbers."

Kenneth's expression hardened, and he faced them once again. "Don't attempt to deceive me, because you won't emerge victorious."

Emily and Rose walked back to the helicopter in sombre silence, their thoughts tangled in a complex web of emotions. She sensed Rose's anger for having squandered what might be their only chance at freedom. But deep down, she had made the right decision. Allowing The Order to resurface in the wrong hands felt inherently wrong, and she believed Rose understood that too.

The rain continued to pour from the heavens as they took flight. As lightning split the darkened sky, the country house below was momentarily illuminated in a blinding flash, accompanied by the distant rumble of thunder. Emily gazed out of the small window, watching the tumultuous scene unfold. The helicopter sharply turned, briefly bringing them closer to the house before proceeding its intended course back home. Lightning struck again, lighting the house once more. Through the window of Kenneth's office, Emily caught sight of him peering out of the window, and with each subsequent flash, Emily could make out the figure of a woman joining him in the room with distinct crimson hair. Emily was certain it was Katherine standing beside him. She hastily rubbed the steamed-up window, but it was too late. The house disappeared into the fog.

"Did you see that?" she asked Rose, who shook her head, her confusion clear.

"See what?"

"Inside the office, there was a woman with him," Emily explained.

"So?"

Emily grabbed Rose's hand. "It looked like Katherine. She was there."

Rose's brows furrowed. "Katherine? Are you sure?"

"I think so. It happened so quickly, and it was distant, but I'm convinced it was her."

Rose ran her hands through her hair, her expression troubled. "She knew about the documents. She warned me about the lengths people would go to obtain them," Rose recounted.

"Well, it seems she's willing to go to great lengths herself. We need to keep an eye on her and perhaps warn Ava about her, too."

Rose's face fell, as if a sudden realisation had hit her. "Katherine has already left Ava's house. She found a new place to live within hours," she revealed. "Ava said she seemed financially well-off but had no idea how."

"She must be involved in all of this, Rose. Ever since she arrived, there's been nothing but trouble."

CHAPTER SIXTEEN
Visiting Time

Hatfield Prison met Florence's expectations. Strolling through the car park made her question why she had agreed to come here in the first place. Confronting Mike had seemed like the logical choice when she was in the comfort of her own home, but now, surrounded by the cold, unforgiving concrete walls, her decision felt somewhat foolish.

She glanced back at Regina, who had agreed to accompany her but stay in the car. Florence smiled. Despite their recent argument, Regina was still there for her.

A woman barged past Florence, pushing her pram through faded wooden doors, the loose wheel rattling with her steps. Florence paused and stepped aside to watch the young mother navigate the hallway with ease, exchanging smiles with a plump officer, and greeting another visitor like they were old friends.

The yellow-lit waiting room felt stale as Florence waited at reception. Unlike the young mother, the officer behind the desk was nowhere near as welcoming to Florence. Florence felt like the new employee at work or the new girl at school. As she tapped her leg, a voice broke the silence. "Alright, visiting time is starting. Ms. Foster, over here please," called the plump female officer, gesturing for Florence to follow her through a metal gate reminiscent of those at airports. The officer held out her hand to halt Florence's steps. "Arms up, legs apart," she instructed.

Florence complied, offering a smile as she followed the officer's directions. She had no idea why all this was necessary. It felt like she was the one behind bars, being looked at and searched. The officer sighed as she patted her down, blowing the scent of mint and cigarette smoke in her face.

After, they walked through the concrete corridor until entering a small, dimly lit room. Florence scanned the tables, her stomach coiling with anticipation until she finally spotted Mike behind a plastic screen. He sat on a solitary chair, waiting for Florence to occupy the one opposite. She wasn't sure what seeing his face again would do to her. Her chest felt warm, her fingers clenched into a ball. She hated him with a passion. But she didn't want him to know that. If he was behind these letters, then anger wasn't going to be the way to win. Her gaze shifted to where she had entered, and the stern-faced guard watched her with folded arms. Florence forced a smile and made her way toward Mike. The chair screeched as she pulled it out, punctuating the silence. All the other visitors had taken their places in the cubicles, their muffled conversations forming one continuous murmur. She looked up through the glass screen and locked eyes with Mike. A smile spread across his face as he picked up the phone. Seeing him, with no suit, basic wrinkled clothes only made her eyes dance. He was the same man still, but not fully. Florence startled at the phone placed beside her on the table before picking it up with shaky fingers and placing it to her ear.

She encountered some static before hearing Mike's breath on the other end. "Hello, Florence. I'm so glad you agreed to come see me." He paused with an expectant look on his face. His cheeks had sunken and his hair had turned more salt than pepper.

Clearing her throat, Florence felt uncertain about what to say. "I'm not here for you, Mike. I'm only here for some answers."

He nodded, his eyes solemn. "I get it. I've been speaking to Reverend Arnold. He told me to seek forgiveness."

Florence smiled. "Found religion, have you?"

"It has helped me cope," Mike said. "It allows me to escape the horrors of this place. It's dreadful in here. Truly."

Florence's hand trembled as she held the phone to her ear. He hadn't changed at all, still employing the same excuses to ease his own conscience. She refused to pity him. "You asked me to visit, Mike. What did you think you'd gain from it?"

His brow furrowed. "Please don't be so dismissive. I asked you here as part of my program. To warn you."

Her heart raced as thoughts of the threatening letter and unsettling photos resurfaced. Was he behind the letters? "Warn me? That's an interesting choice of words, considering you killed my husband and then tried to kill Regina. I thought my problems would be over once they locked you up in here."

His face dropped to one of remorse, yet it felt forced, like a child caught in a lie. "My actions have been inexcusable, I know that. But I acted with good intentions concerning Oscar. I did it all for you."

Florence refused to take the bait. She wanted to confront Mike about the letter, to uncover the truth, and leave. However, his excuses only fuelled her anger. "Did it for me? Really? And what about my children, who must grow up without a father because of you?"

"He was having an affair and planned to leave you. You would have never gotten over him. You said as much during our therapy sessions. I merely acted on what you shared with me. Then, Regina got in the way," he rationalised. He said her name with a bite. Almost as hateful as Florence felt when uttering his.

There it was—more blame, more excuses. Florence adopted a firmer tone. "You killed him in cold blood. That burden rests solely on you. Until you accept that, you'll never find forgiveness."

His breathing grew heavier, causing mist to form on the glass. "You don't know how far I've come in such a short time, Florence. I acted hastily, even in here, but I regret that now. Let me start anew. I need to warn you, to put my mind at ease."

An officer walked past Florence, glaring at Mike. Florence bit her lip and moderated her voice. "You mentioned warnings. Are you responsible for all of this? Do you have someone watching me?" she blurted.

Mike narrowed his eyes. "What has happened? What have they done?" He pushed his palm against the glass screen.

"They? So, it was you. You're behind all these games?" Florence exclaimed.

Mike slammed his free hand against the table, then took a deep breath as another guard stepped closer to his side. "I need to tell you. When I first arrived here, a prisoner threatened me, wanting information about Ava, about all her friends, and about you."

"Who was he? Is he still here, locked up?" Florence pressed, heart hammering.

"No, he's gone. He was working for someone and was days away from being released. Whoever it was offered him a huge amount of money for information. I was furious with you and Regina at the time, so I told him everything I knew." Mike lowered his head. "I'm sorry, Florence. I shouldn't have divulged anything. What has happened? What have they done to you?" He gently placed his hand against the glass, searching her eyes.

Florence fought to maintain eye contact and tried to conceal her deep-seated hatred for him. He appeared weaker than she had imagined, a pitiful man now trapped in his own personal hell. He was talking, though, and confessing his wrongdoings, and Florence intended to keep that dialogue going if she wanted to glean the most from this visit. It wasn't one she was planning to make again.

"I received a letter with photos of me and Regina, threatening to expose us and warning us about our friends. Do you think it's someone from our inner circle?" Florence asked.

He raised his brows, pushed out his bottom lip. "It could be anyone. There are plenty of people who could be behind this," Mike replied.

"I thought it was you. Part of me still does..." Florence's voice trailed off.

Mike chuckled. "I'm behind these bars. The obstacle standing in your way is gone, but if you are so certain about Regina, then why not come out and live a happy, open life with her?"

Mike reclined in his chair, crossing his leg over his knee.

"Maybe I will," Florence retorted.

"What's stopping you? If you did, the threat would prove irrelevant," Mike prodded.

Florence gritted her teeth, feeling a surge of frustration. Regina had suggested the same thing, saying it out loud as if it was nothing. But when you've kept a secret for so long, hidden a part of yourself for years. It isn't easy to say it. Maybe the burden wasn't heavy, but it had weighed Florence down since childhood. "I'm not ready yet. But when I am, I will."

Mike tapped his chin with his finger. "You will never do it, Florence. You will never fully commit."

"I will. I love her," Florence asserted, lowering her voice on the word *love*.

"Don't forget, I know you. I know every thought and fear you've had. You confided in me for years. I know you will never come out publicly, even though the power to end this issue lies entirely in your hands," Mike concluded. Something sinister tinged his words, and a smirk crept across his lips.

Florence noted his relaxed demeanour, like he were back in his office during one of their therapy sessions. She suppressed the intense urge to smash through the plastic screen and strangle him. Instead, she glared, realising she had extracted all the information he possessed—information that was mostly useless, but at least it shed some light on a part of the puzzle. Mike may have provided some insights, but he wasn't the mastermind behind all this.

Florence glanced back at the officer, which seemed to catch Mike off guard, prompting him to straighten and place his hand against the partition. "Florence, you're not leaving, are you?"

"I have nothing more to say to you," she stated, rising to

her feet before addressing the female officer. "I'm ready to go now."

"Wait. Tell me!" Mike pleaded, his eyes widening. "Have you forgiven me? I've told you what I know. I've explained why it had to happen."

Florence looked back at the man who killed her husband, desperately awaiting her response. She despised him and harboured hatred for everything he'd done. "Goodbye, Mike," she said.

Without giving him the opportunity to say another word, she turned her back on him and strode through the hallways back to the car park. Not once did she look back at him—no, she found solace in the knowledge he would never see her face again.

After dropping Regina off at her friends' place, Florence returned to an almost empty house. She assumed Olivia was still at Lesley's, whereas Lucas could be anywhere. The thought of spending the evening alone with her parents made her heart sink. As she strode into the living room, the glow of the television outlined the door frame. The sound was on low, which meant her mother was elsewhere. She'd never admit it, but her hearing was going. Her father greeted her with a tired smile as he sat up. "How was your day, love?" he asked.

Florence hadn't told her father where she'd been. "It was okay. Got a splitting headache," Florence said, sitting down beside him. "Is Mum not home?"

He shook his head. "She went to visit a neighbour, I think. I try to enjoy the peace while I can," he said, a hint of relief in his tone.

Florence smiled. She cherished the sight of her father being relaxed—a rarity whilst growing up. He turned his attention back to the television, where an old comedy from the eighties played.

Mike's taunts had lingered in Florence's mind ever since leaving the prison. His arrogant certainty that she would never come out or openly express her feelings for Regina. It felt like an impossible obstacle. Before her parents had arrived, she was certain of the path to take. "Dad, do you mind if we have a chat?" she asked.

Her father turned to her, his focus divided between his daughter and the television. "Of course."

Florence searched for the remote control and switched off the television. "I need your full attention, Dad," she stressed. "Lucas told me about what you did for him."

He raised an eyebrow. "I don't know what you mean, dear."

Florence took hold of his hand and patted it gently. "Thank you. I know it couldn't have been easy. It means a lot to me to know that you kept him safe when I couldn't."

His kind, clouded eyes looked back at her. He was so proud of Lucas, so happy to have been able to help, and that feeling swelled in Florence's heart. To know he truly loved his grandson, that helping him in a way, also meant he must love her too.

"It's what any grandfather would do," he murmured, leaning forward to reach for the remote control. Florence picked up the remote and placed it beside her.

"There's something else I need to tell you." Her throat felt dry, but she knew she had to have this conversation. "I dropped Regina off at her friend's place, but I don't think she's enjoying being away from here."

"I don't understand why she left," her father said. "There was plenty of room for all of us here. She seems like a nice girl."

"Yeah, she is. But do you know *why* she left?"

A smile formed on her father's lips. "Your mother?" he guessed.

Florence laughed. "Mostly, yeah. She made Regina feel uncomfortable."

"Well, remember, your mother and I aren't used to change. We know the world as it was. Not that I'm excusing her; she says some silly things sometimes."

"She's a special friend to me, Dad. I hate the house without her here," Florence confessed.

"Please give us a bit more time," he pleaded. "We have nowhere else to go, not yet. I spent everything I had to get Lucas out of trouble." Genuine sincerity marked his words.

"I know, Dad. I know. But I want this rare opportunity of time we have so close together to mean something, and that means being honest with each other."

He turned his gaze toward the blank television. "I should have told you when he showed up. I know that now, but Oscar had just died, and the boy needed some space."

"It's not about that, Dad. This is about *me*," Florence clarified, clearing her throat. "Did Mum ever tell you about Clem? The *friend* I had at school?"

"Florence, I don't think this is appropriate. Why don't we leave this conversation for another time?" He shifted in his seat and reached for the remote again.

She knew that this might happen, but her relationship with Regina was too important to let this slide. "No, Dad. I want to talk about it now. Mum told you, didn't she?"

He tugged at his collar, visibly uneasy. "Oh, I can't remember. It was all those years ago, Florence."

"I told Mum that I kissed her. She told me not to mention it again, and I didn't. But she told you, didn't she?" Florence pressed, determined to get the truth out of him.

He pursed his lips. "Yes, I remember her saying something, but you were just a little girl."

"I was old enough to know what I was doing," Florence asserted.

"Please, Florence. Let's drop it."

"I can't, Dad. Regina has been there for me through so much. I don't want her to be some big secret anymore."

His eyes flicked around the room. They settled onto the blank tv screen "If she means something to you, love, I won't step in your way."

Florence couldn't fully comprehend his reaction. Years feeling like her parents kept her at arm's length, and like she could never open up to them for fear of rejection, had built up this moment, only for it to fizzle with less than a spark. "Should I call Mum? Tell her and say that Regina is moving back?"

"No, you shouldn't mention this to your mother," he blurted, eyes widening. "She wouldn't understand."

That was the reaction she had expected. Her mother was the one with the problem, and all this time Florence had mistakenly blamed them both. "Okay. For now, I'll leave it. But in a few weeks, I'm going to invite Regina back here. If Mum doesn't want to know, then you'll have to move out. I refuse to put my life on hold any longer."

He leaned in closer to his daughter. "I won't pretend that I don't struggle with it, Florence. When you met Oscar and married him, I was genuinely happy for you. We both were. I thought it was just a phase," he admitted, his eyes dropping to the floor. "But I can see now that it's more complicated than that. I won't say anything to your mother for now, but let me have some time to plan a few things out."

Tears blurred Florence's vision. "Do you think she will ever accept it? Or am I going to lose both of you for good?"

He fidgeted with his collar and planted a kiss on her forehead. Stretching for the remote, he turned the television back on, and though he didn't reply to Florence's question, she somehow knew the answer.

CHAPTER SEVENTEEN
New Horizons

Knowing Nick was alive, the world was once again bleak. So much of her life, her friendships, and her power had been in his hands, and it became increasingly clear to Ava that ever since Nick's 'death,' her own social status had disintegrated into nothingness. In a way, it was a fitting punishment for all the times she had pushed women away in the past, exploiting the influence—influence she gained from Nick—to manipulate situations for her own benefit.

It had only been a week since she'd seen her *husband* again, but it truly felt like he'd never left her life. Ava strolled through the grounds of Beechwood Close. Even on a cloudless summer day, the grass and sky felt faded, devoid of the typical buzz of life and excitement. Most of the spark left Ava's life when Oscar died. It wasn't only the sneaking around and the sex that excited her with Oscar. But the moments between. The friendship they had gained, their shared concern for Florence at the height of her drinking. The stolen moments they had together, to speak of music, to dance in each others arms. So much life came from being around him. While being free from Nick had lightened her burden of being around a man she no longer loved. A man she could no longer look at with pride or desire, her every waking second was haunted by the possibility of him reappearing and forcing himself back into her orbit.

The police had left their mark on the lake, leaving boot prints in the mud and scattered, trampled flowers in their wake as they combed the area for evidence. Ava got as close as she could to the lake before being forced to turn back. It had been cordoned off once again with yellow tape.

Ava had entertained the idea of making a fuss and rallying the neighbourhood to demand the council restore the area to its once pristine state, but the thought soon faded when she looked around, knowing she was on her own yet again.

She slowly made her way back to the close and contemplated how to enjoy her evening. Rose was home, but she had been a bundle of nerves lately, likely overwhelmed by the impending launch of her new book. That's when Ava spotted Katherine casually strolling out of her garden with another bag on her shoulder. The audacity, Ava thought. She roamed about the close as if she owned the place. Ava narrowed her eyes as their gazes met. Katherine flashed a smile, swaying her blown-out hair in the wind. She approached Ava, who glanced around, searching for someone she could talk to as an excuse to walk away. After spotting Edna on her porch, cupping a mug to her chest, Ava decided to confront Katherine instead.

"So, you're still on my property, are you?" she snapped.

Katherine swung her long hair to one side, clearly unconcerned. "I just have a few remaining bits to collect, and then I'll be out of your hair and gone for good. Things are really looking up," she said, punctuating her sentence with a smile.

"I've been thinking about Nick a lot lately." Ava said, studying Katherine closely. "The house just isn't the same without him here." Nick had said Katherine was unaware of his survival, but Ava didn't trust either of them.

Katherine patted Ava on the shoulder before glancing at her old home, where Emily now lived. "I know all too well how quickly a home can turn into a mere house," she said with a hint of sadness, studying Emily's house with watery eyes. For a moment, Ava couldn't help but feel sorry for her. "I noticed you've just come back from the lake. It's been shut off again, hasn't it?"

"Yes, police tape everywhere, and the whole area is in ruins from the cars and machinery." Ava grumbled. "God knows what they're doing with the body, but they keep coming back."

Katherine blinked, a faint glow appearing on her cheeks. "I've heard a few things," she admitted, capturing Ava's attention. "Some of my contacts keep me informed." She glanced around, noticing Edna observing them from her porch. Katherine adjusted her body, prompting Ava to turn as they walked back towards Ava's house. "You know, Ava, I've been terrible to you. I never intended for our living arrangement to end the way it did. I've never been good at maintaining friendships with women."

"No, you make me look like Goldilocks in comparison," Ava retorted with a touch of sarcasm.

Katherine maintained a slight distance from Ava while clutching her bag under her arm. "Listen. Let's go inside.

There's something I need to tell you."

Ava didn't trust Katherine one bit. But she allowed her the space to gossip. Maybe she was about to admit she knew about Nick, that his death was faked and she couldn't hold onto the secret any longer. Or maybe, she knew who the body was, or the killer. Once inside, Katherine took a few steps away from Ava, tightening her grip on the bag. "Well, what is it? Do you have some sort of wise motherly advice for me?"

"Well, if you're going to be snippy, I might reconsider telling you," Katherine warned, crossing her arms.

Ava was done with Katherine's games. "Fine. Apologies. Blame Nick for my mood."

Katherine's shoulder slumped at the mention of Nick. "I miss him, you know. He was a dear friend who got entangled in things he shouldn't have," Katherine said. "But anyway, I need to give you some advice—advice that I suggest you keep to yourself."

Ava stepped forward, her pulse quickening. "Oh? Enlighten me."

"It's about the lake. I've heard through the grapevine that there's more to it than what they're revealing, and I'm *not* referring to the murder," Katherine said.

What could be more important than the murder of a woman? Ava thought. "Go on," Ava pressed, unable to contain her curiosity. Katherine's fingers danced along her fine necklace as she leaned over, her breath a whisper.

"Well, let's just say we're both women with little to no connections here now. Maybe you should follow in my footsteps and move on from Beechwood Close. This place will sell in seconds."

Ava scrunched up her face. "Sell? Why would I sell this place?" She gestured at the impeccable décor and structure of her home, unable to fathom the suggestion.

Katherine sighed. "Ava, trust me. Take my advice. Put this place on the market. Get it lined up and go with the cash. I've heard rumours that the body in the lake emerged because of some underground movement. The moment all this becomes public, the house prices around here will plummet, if they haven't already. Take my advice. Sell up and leave before you lose out on even more."

"What about everyone else? Shouldn't I warn them too?" Ava asked.

"No!" Katherine yelled, eyes wide. She leaned forward to hiss, "If this gets out, you can say goodbye to your money. Sell your place first. Once you've left, let the others know and let them fight it out." Katherine stepped towards the door. "Do something for yourself, Ava. You must know by now that no one else around here will do anything for you, and while it's been great having you back in my life, it's time for both of us to move on." With that, Katherine turned to leave, and Ava followed her retreating figure through the window.

Ava glanced at the surrounding homes until her eyes found the lake in the distance. She imagined the houses sinking and cracks forming. Katherine was right; if the rumours about the lake were true, they were all sitting on ticking financial time bombs. Determined, Ava reached for her phone and dialled the estate agent they had worked with when she and Nick purchased the house. "Hello? A woman answered. "Yes. I'd like to get my home listed for sale as soon as possible," she said, her voice resolute.

Ava made her way towards the front door, noticing the letters that had been wedged in the letterbox. As she remained on hold, she pulled out the letters to sort through bills and junk mail. Among them was a hand-written letter addressed to her with no sender's address. Intrigued, she tore it open. *'We know Nick is alive, and you are involved. Don't trust the people around you, especially new friends.'*

"Miss, would tomorrow be okay for the valuation, or do you need more time?" interrupted the voice on the phone, yanking Ava back to the present.

Ava read the note repeatedly as her legs weakened beneath her. "Sorry, yes. Tomorrow is fine for the valuation. I'll message you the address now." She hung up and clutched the note tightly in her trembling fingers before rushing towards the window to face the empty close. She scanned the houses, desperately trying to figure out who could be behind the ominous message. How could anyone know Nick was alive? Overwhelmed, she ran her hands through her hair and sank to the ground.

The thought of returning to prison made her sick. It wasn't an option. She needed to heed Katherine's advice: sell the house, gather as much cash as possible, and disappear. She refused to let anyone from Beechwood Close bring her down.

CHAPTER EIGHTEEN
Two Wives

It was only the aroma of freshly brewed coffee that kept Rose awake. She tapped her nails along the smooth wooden table, anxiously awaiting Elisa's arrival. The Surf-side café was a cosy place, adorned with charming seaside trinkets, such as ropes, seashells, and surfboards. Rose's gaze flitted between the decor and the entrance, waiting for Elisa to appear. The flurry of messages from her had only added to Rose's already burdened mind, ever since Emily declined Sir Banks' offer.

Elisa had demanded they meet, and Rose's stomach twisted in knots at the thought of facing George's 'other' wife and uncovering the secret life he had hid from her for years.

Under normal circumstances, Rose would have flat-out refused Elisa's demands, but when she mentioned a letter arriving at her desk, Rose's heart had plummeted. Whoever was behind the blackmail had contacted Elisa, too, revealing that George's death was no accident. The sole flicker of hope—the only thing that kept Rose going—was the absence of the police at her doorstep. Elisa might not be planning to hand her over for the murder of George after all. Not yet, anyway.

Rose glanced at her watch; Elisa was five minutes late. She breathed in the scent of freshly baked pastries, and although they smelled heavenly, she couldn't help but think she would have done a better job herself.

A man approached the table with a notepad. "Can I get you anything while you wait, miss?"

Rose glanced at him before redirecting her attention to the door. Still no sign of Elisa. "The coffee does smell wonderful. Maybe I'll have another cup, if you don't mind." Her right foot tapped against the floorboards.

"Hold on a second—are you Rose Walker? The home cook?" asked the man, lips parting.

Rose looked up to meet his gaze. He appeared ordinary enough, with kind eyes and peppered hair. Maybe a few years older than Rose, but she'd always enjoyed the company of older gentlemen. She couldn't quite place him, but there was a faint sense of familiarity. "Sorry, but do I know you? I can't seem to place you."

He pulled out the chair beside her and sat, a broad smile stretching across his face. "My apologies. My name is Benny. Benny Roach. We met briefly during the summer."

"We did?" Rose furrowed her brow, desperately trying to match his face and voice to anything that could jog her memory. Her heart sank momentarily as she wondered if he was a member of The Order, sent by Sir Banks to track her down.

"It was at the art event for Emily Lamont. You catered for the event, if I remember correctly. You made some exquisite smoked salmon canapes," Benny explained.

Emily's art event felt like a lifetime ago. But Rose remembered it well. Katherine making her grand entrance. The food she prepared being a renowned success, and then the kind man who forgot his ticket.

"Yes, I remember now. You were the man who lost his ticket," Rose recalled, chuckling. "And the man with impeccable taste in food." She smiled, and a sense of relief washed over her. She eased her shoulders.

"You know what? I haven't been able to forget the flavours," Benny whispered conspiratorially. He scribbled a number on a piece of paper and handed it to her. "Perhaps we could have some of your food here at the cafe." Rose beamed and tucked the note into her bag. Benny leaned in then, a hint of intrigue in his voice. "I heard about the body found in the lake. Do you know much about it?"

Rose's brow furrowed in curiosity. News of a body was bound to spread around the area like wild fire. "Lake? Well, not really. My sister was the one who found it, but besides it being a young woman, I don't really know much about it." She swirled the coffee in her cup. "Why do you ask?"

"No particular reason," Benny replied, shrugging. "I've had quite a few people in here lately, discussing it. Seems like it's gone viral online. True crime fanatics are going crazy over it. I've had visitors stopping by on their way to Beechwood, hoping to find out more about what happened. Some even wanted to set up podcast recordings right here in the cafe. It's great for business, I suppose, but some of their theories are enough to make your toes curl."

Rose's eyes darted towards the entrance, hoping Elisa wouldn't walk in yet, as she hoped to learn more from Benny. "Oh? And what theories are they?" she inquired, her curiosity piqued.

"Well, one group claims that Beechwood Close was built on an ancient burial site," Benny shared with a chuckle. "That one sounds rather far-fetched, but then there's another group of lads who believe a theory that the woman was killed by her partner to facilitate the sale of the house for redevelopment, allowing him to pocket all the money."

Rose rolled her eyes. "That's ridiculous. Nothing like that happens there."

Benny nodded, though his expression became thoughtful. "Well, people have pointed out that the date of the redevelopment aligns with the woman's death. I even looked it up myself. Banks & Son Industries purchased the land over forty years ago."

Just then, a short woman with a blonde bob strolled in, donning a grey business suit. Rose's relaxed mood quickly shifted as she realised it had to be Elisa. During her conversation with Benny, she had allowed herself to forget her worries. "Ah, this must be your friend. I'll leave you two alone," Benny said kindly. "I'll be right over with the coffees." He bowed his head to Rose with a playful wink before departing, leaving Rose and Elisa alone.

She studied Elisa for a moment, noting her clear complexion, the faint lines around her eyes, and the powdery appearance of makeup on her cheeks. Had George treated Elisa in the same controlling manner he had treated her? Did he dictate what she wore and when she could go out? Or did he view Elisa as an equal, the *real* wife in their relationship, while Rose was nothing more than a plaything? An unsettling thought crossed Rose's mind. Perhaps *she* had been the other woman all along. She shook her head to dispel such intrusive thoughts. The will was written in her favour, and she had inherited all of George's belongings. She was his wife, and Elisa was the spare.

Elisa smoothed out her clothes and took a seat. Her voice trembled as she said, "Hello, Rose. I recognised you immediately from your book cover. Thank you for agreeing to meet me." Rose sensed her own nervousness mirrored Elisa's. "Although I must admit, I was surprised you chose such a... *public* place to meet."

Before Rose could ask why, Benny returned with two steaming cups of coffee. Rose instinctively moved hers closer to her chest, feeling the warmth radiate from the mug into her trembling fingers, the coffee sloshing in her grip. "Well, I haven't felt safe lately. I've been trying not to be alone, especially when meeting new acquaintances."

Rose's hands continued to shake as she replayed the events of the past few weeks—the blackmail letters, the items Violet had left her, the threats from Sir Kenneth Banks, and her decision to decline his offer. Worst of all was the persistent fear of being implicated in George's murder. Elisa reached for Rose's hand. "Rose, I can see you're panicking. I didn't mean to frighten you with my call. It's just... well, we have so much to go through. George kept so many secrets from both of us. When I got that letter about his death... well, I thought it was best for us to talk."

Rose pulled her hand from Elisa's touch and clutched her coffee cup. "What did you want to say? Are you here to accuse me?" Rose asked.

Elisa shook her head, seeming to stifle a laugh. "No," she whispered. "I grew accustomed to him disappearing for long periods of time. Deep down, I always knew something was wrong, but I never questioned it." Elisa's eyes met Rose's, the spark from their greeting having faded. Then, she glanced around the cafe, as if ensuring no one could overhear their conversation. She pulled out a note, printed in a similar fashion to the one Rose had received. It was sent by the same author. "*This* is what frightened me."

She slid the note across the table, and Rose unfolded it. She felt immediately sick. *'Your husband's death has gone unpunished. The woman you have found has the answers.'*

Rose shrugged. She tried to look past the guilt, the truth. She let her lips sit naturally. Made sure not to blink too fast. Tried to control her breathing. "I don't know what to say. George slipped and fell down the stairs. The impact broke his neck. There's nothing more to it." Elisa's lips curled into a sceptical smile. She didn't believe her; that much was clear. Rose glanced at the note again. "Who do you think sent this? How could anyone know about you?"

Elisa shrugged and retrieved the note, tucking it back in her bag. "That's why I came here. To find out the truth. I assumed you might have confided in someone?"

Rose shook her head. "No. No one. Not even my closest friends know about... you."

"Well, believe me, I haven't told anyone either. It's embarrassing enough as it is." Elisa took a sip of her coffee. "Listen, there are things we need to discuss, Rose. Whoever sent this letter is trying to stir up trouble." Elisa dipped her head, and lowering her voice, she said, "My relationship with George wasn't exactly picture-perfect. When I saw your dedication in the cookbook with the mention of women's aid, it was easy for me to put two and two together."

Rose felt her cheeks flush. The realisation of how obvious it must have been, what she endured at George's hands, made her sick. That this stranger knew made her feel even more humiliated. Rose thought George's torment was for her only. The idea that there was another woman out there who went through the same broke her. She thought of all the places she hid in the house, all the times she tried to escape his touch. Had Elisa had to do the same?

"He wasn't perfect to me either," Rose replied, mustering a small smile.

Elisa's eyes darted around the cafe. "Do you think he might have told anyone else about me? About us?"

Rose contemplated mentioning her own letter, but didn't trust Elisa—not yet. For all she knew, this meeting could be a ploy, and Elisa could be the one behind it all.

"Maybe. Despite being married for so long, I believe now that there were things he hid from me. Seeing as I didn't know about you, there must be countless other things he kept from me. Perhaps he confided in a friend, although I wasn't aware he had any."

"Me neither. He always seemed to keep his distance from others, and when he went away for work, I never questioned it. To be honest with you, Rose, I actually enjoyed the times he was gone," Elisa confessed; her own hands trembled as she clutched her coffee mug. "I'm going to ask you something, Rose. Something that I hope will help ease my mind."

Rose nodded, holding her breath. Of course she knew what was coming; she saw it in Elisa's eyes the second she sat down.

"This letter says my husband was murdered, but he wasn't a kind man to me. When he disappeared without a word, I didn't try to find him. I didn't pine over his return. He did the same to you, didn't he?" Elisa rubbed her wrist, and Rose nodded. She couldn't bring herself to admit it out loud, but a deep connection seemed to forge with Elisa then—a bond shaped through shared experiences and the tragic life they had both lived with George as their husband.

Rose surveyed the café again, but no one was close enough to hear them. "He was a terrible man, Elisa, but I did not go out of my way to kill him. I promise you that is true." Rose gestured towards Elisa's bag. "Whoever sent that letter is trying to cause trouble, but they don't have all the facts." She tightened her grip on her necklace, finding solace in its presence. Rose felt a lump form in her throat. Her bodies reaction, a warning to think about what she was about to do. "He attacked me. A friend witnessed it and pulled him away. That's when he tripped and fell." A single tear escaped Rose's eye, and she swiped it away. She was determined not to waste any more tears on him.

Elisa reached forward, resting her hand in the middle of the table. Lowering her voice, she said, "It's okay. I understand. There were so many times where I wanted to do the same thing. When I saw his picture in your book and learned that he was dead, I felt relieved. I know it makes me a horrible person, but I understand why you did what you did."

"Thank you. It was a shock to discover your existence, and even more shocking to learn he treated you like he treated me," Rose confessed, glancing towards the café ceiling and blinking back tears. She focused on the grinding of the coffee machine in the background, willing her eyes to remain dry as the hiss of hot milk resonated from the counter. "What will you do about the letter? About his death? He left you with nothing."

Elisa let out a short laugh. "I'm not here for money, possessions, or property. I've made my own way in life, and I don't want to take anything from you. As for the letter, I won't let it go any further—at least on my end. I have no clue who sent it. If you haven't told anyone, and neither have I, then it must be someone who was close to him or someone who knew about both of us."

How could Rose ever work out who sent these letters. She clearly didn't know her husband as well as she once thought. He kept an entire life hidden from her. Had he told anyone else? Was there a neighbour or friend she hadn't thought of who could yield the answers she so desperately needed?

"Thank you," Rose said, inching her hand closer to Elisa's. Though their encounter had been brief, she felt an inexplicable bond with the woman before her, almost as if they had been friends for years. "I won't be so hostile the next time you call," Rose promised, a genuine smile gracing her lips. Benny passed by, tending to more customers.

"Let's stay in touch, Rose. I still have your book at the office. Maybe we can talk and get it on the shelves," Elisa proposed. The thought of her cookbook had slipped from Rose's mind amidst the whirlwind of blackmail and death surrounding her. She was meant to be her answer to getting the book out there. Elisa, the publicist. But now it was the last thing on her mind. "Perhaps we can omit the dedication to George, though," she added with a wink.

After Elisa left, Rose remained in the café for a while longer, lost in her thoughts. She replayed the years she spent with George—both the painful moments and the rare instances of happiness. Seeming to sense her contemplation, Benny eventually came to sit beside her, and together they shared another cup of coffee. They laughed together during discussions on trivial matters, like food and travel—simple, normal things that had been scarce in her previous life.

However, Rose's respite from her problems was abruptly interrupted when the radio cut to breaking news. "In a stunning turn of events, Sir Kenneth Banks has officially announced his intention to run for Prime Minister of the United Kingdom. The announcement was made this morning during a live broadcast, where Sir Kenneth expressed his vision for the nation's future." Rose shivered, remembering his warning. Knowing he was now vying for the highest position in the country as he stood outside his country home—the very one she and Emily had recently visited—to wave alongside his friends and family, made The Order feel more potent than ever. If Sir Kenneth was positioning himself for the most powerful job in the nation, he would want to settle his past demons sooner rather than later.

CHAPTER NINETEEN
Trust No One

Another text arrived from Rose while Emily watched the news, asking whether they should be concerned and consider his deal again. Emily understood her panic. Seeing Sir Banks on television worried Emily too. She had never paid much attention to politics before and had known little about him, but knowing now what he was like behind closed doors, she feared not only for herself but also for her country. She responded to Rose, urging her not to discuss such matters over text. She promptly deleted the entire thread.

Ever since returning from their trip to his country home a week ago, a persistent headache had plagued Emily. She felt trapped. Rose's desperate desire to resolve everything made sense to Emily, who knew accepting his offer would rid their lives of this constant stress. However, she couldn't help but consider the dire consequences that would follow if they allowed The Order to continue its reign.

Her phone chimed again, this time with an incoming call. Turning it over, she half-expected to see Rose's name flashing on the screen, but to her surprise, it was Rachel. Emily hadn't spoken to her friend since their encounter in the park several weeks ago—an encounter that now felt like a lifetime ago. "Hey, Emily, I had to call you," Rachel said softly.

Emily surveyed her empty living room. Cynthia had already retired for the night, a pattern that happening more frequently. "What's going on? Is everything alright?" Emily asked, hoping Rachel's problem was something trivial and didn't involve a dead body or a cover-up by a secretive organisation.

"I heard about you and Theo and about your breakup," Rachel said.

Emily rolled her eyes. "Well, we weren't exactly together. How did you find out, anyway?"

There was a momentary pause on the other end of the line. "Alright, fine. Theo told me. But I had to pry the information out of him. He's really upset, Emily."

Emily thought it was amazing how one minute someone is out of your life for years, and the next, they are calling up to sort out your love life. Theo had been absent since their date. He'd tried to call and text but Emily didn't want to see him. He'd put the cheque back through the door, although Cynthia didn't let him in to see Emily.

"I tried to give him more than one opportunity to be honest with me, but he lied to me about Jessie and who he was living with. Can you blame me for being scared? Especially considering everything that's been happening with our group."

"I think you should meet up and talk to him. Give him one last chance to explain himself." She exclaimed.

"Has he said something to you, Rachel? Why are you so eager for us to get back together?"

Rachel let out a slight giggle. Her friend had never been good at concealing the truth. A laugh always escaped her when she was caught off guard. "Listen, we all know Jessie was intense. She struggled to understand boundaries, and when you stepped back, she jumped at the chance to latch onto Theo. But nothing ever happened between them. He always held out for you. I just want you two to give it another shot, that's all."

Emily never questioned who Theo had been with romantically since University. She didn't own him, anymore than he did her. Who he was with wasn't the problem. It was keeping it a secret that hurt her. Emily yearned to have Theo back in her life. She secretly cherished the moments they had shared over the past few months. Theo's presence had brought her joy, even if she hadn't been willing to admit it then. She thought she could gain trust with him, handing him the cheque. To be in charge of her life's worth should have prompted him to stand up and speak the truth. However, Rachel's description of Jessie struck a chord within her, even if she didn't want it to bother her.

"Are you suggesting that Jessie had a thing for Theo?" Emily probed.

"I don't want to get too involved, but let's just say she got quite jealous. Invite Theo over, talk to him about it, and hear his side of the story," Rachel said, her voice carrying a hint of caution. "I never questioned Jessie before, but things feel different now. That's all I'll say. Speak to Theo, and then we can figure out our next steps."

Rachel ended the call, leaving Emily even more perplexed than before. Why did Rachel suddenly seem so suspicious of Jessie? And why was she pushing so hard for

Emily and Theo to reconcile? Emily was determined to gather the scattered puzzle pieces, hoping they would eventually form a coherent picture.

The howling wind whipped against Emily's ears, and she tugged the hood of her coat higher around her neck. The waves crashed below, the volume completely contrasting the quiet streets that once bustled with activity but now lay deserted, with empty seats and abandoned tables outside closed establishments. Emily sat outside the shuttered ice cream shop; she had arrived early to clear her head before facing Theo once again.

She turned her head at the sound of footsteps, instantly recognising the owner's brisk pace. Rising to her feet, she tightened her coat around her and walked towards Theo, the anticipation building in her chest. His eyes flickered at the sight of her, the light from the streetlamp overhead glistening on his glasses. He quickened his steps, mirroring the warmth that surged within her.

Theo greeted Emily with a closed-lip smile as if unsure of how to act. Yet Emily returned the smile and glanced at her boots before tucking a loose strand of hair behind her ear. "Shall we go down by the wall?" she yelled above the wind. "It'll be easier to talk there."

Theo smiled and nodded. His hood slipped off his head as Emily led the way down the stone steps that descended from the street towards the pebble beach. Beach houses stood along the wall, supported by metal railings; the wall protected the town from flooding and acted as a shield against the gusts, muffling the noise that comes with the lashing of wind.

The sudden tranquillity enveloped them. Emily pressed her hands to her ears to warm them, while Theo shivered, his knees trembling. She smiled and lay her hand on his arm. "Are you nervous or just cold?" She crouched down, pulling her knees up to her chest.

"A bit of both, I suppose." He pushed his glasses up his nose and crouched beside her. "Thanks for meeting me. When you stormed off from the restaurant, I had no idea what was going on."

Emily shook her head, trying to force the smile off her face.

"Didn't you? I gave you plenty of chances to come clean."

He lowered his head. "So, you knew all along?"

"No, I met up with Rachel for a chat. She mentioned Jessie was living with you guys. It made me worried and suspicious that you hadn't told me."

Theo smacked his palm against his forehead. "I'm such an idiot, Emily. I had something incredible with you, and I didn't want to jeopardise it."

Emily shifted slightly to allow herself room to escape if necessary. Even being with someone she trusted so dearly. The lies he so easily told made her wary of being trapped. She knew all too well how men could hide who they truly were. "What do you mean jeopardise? Theo, is there something you need to tell me?"

Emily's mind raced around the note she had received. Could Theo have been involved in it all along? He averted his gaze, focusing on the turbulent sea. "Jessie wasn't significant," he began, his frustration clear. "Not after we reconnected. I never imagined we would regain our old connection so quickly." He turned to face her. His wet eyes reflecting the world around him "I never got over us, you know. I always wanted us to be together again. When you left and started a new life, it felt like we were left behind. I never thought you'd want to see me, but you were still the same, Emily."

"Then why did you lie about Jessie living with you?" Emily asked, searching his eyes.

"I don't know. She started acting strangely and tried to insinuate there was something between me and her, but there never was. I made it clear to her I still thought of you, but she persisted. Then everything started happening: Cassandra was found dead, and before I knew it, Jessie became an afterthought."

Emily studied his face. His eyes shimmered with tears, silver beneath the moonlight, and his bottom lip trembled, revealing his regret—something Emily hadn't witnessed until now. She reached for Theo and turned him to face her. She felt safe in his presence. He would not harm her.

"There's something more, isn't there?" she whispered.

He arched his eyebrows. "More?"

"Please, Theo," Emily pleaded. "I want us to work through this as much as you do, but I know you're withholding something from me. I could read it on your face at the restaurant, and I can sense it here, now. If we're going to figure out who's behind all of this, we need to be completely honest with each other." Emily clasped his hand. "Even if it means sharing something difficult."

He looked back at her, a broken man burdened by his secrets. "But what if it means our relationship ends?"

"Try me. You might be surprised."

Theo lowered his hood and ran a hand through his hair. "This is going to be hard to say, Emily, and even harder for you to hear." Theo paused, biting his lip. "I've been lying to you, not just about Jessie, but about something much greater." Emily continued to hold his hand, determined to support him now that he was opening up. "When you first reached out to me to help Rose with her book, I was thrilled. But things went wrong. Cassandra was murdered, and I started receiving threats—letters demanding I take certain actions."

Her heart pounded in her chest. Letters. Theo had been receiving letters even before he arrived here. She wanted to share her own experience with the letter, yet something held her back. Instead, she squeezed his hand, and asked, "What letters? Who were they from?"

He shifted his focus away from the ground and into Emily's eyes. "I don't know, or at least I'm not entirely sure who sent them. But *what* was written in those letters is what matters most."

Emily wondered what could be in those letters. Did Theo know the truth about George? Maybe he's been upset at her keeping secrets from him this whole time. Maybe she was as bad as him for lying. Or maybe they would hold answers to figuring everything out.

"And it could be the key to uncovering who's behind all of this," Emily whispered.

Theo squeezed her hand. "Please, let me say what I need to, and then you can decide if you want us to work this out," he whispered, his voice heavy with regret. He took a deep breath. "This is going to sound terrible—well, because it is—but the letter arrived, and whoever sent it knew that we had reconnected. I have no idea how they found out, but they did."

Emily hadn't told anyone about Theo. No one but Cynthia, and Rose. She knew the gossip around the close wouldn't have been worth it.

"What did the letter say? What did they ask of you?"

Tears streamed down Theo's cheeks yet he wiped them away. "They wanted me to come to you, to your new home," he confessed, his cheeks flushed with embarrassment. "Honestly, it's what I wanted to do anyway—to find you and have another chance, but I only did because of that letter."

Emily stiffened, overcome by a mix of emotions. The realisation that Theo's arrival was driven by blackmail hit her hard. Had he not genuinely cared for her at all? She bit her lip, silencing the multitude of questions and words she wanted to unleash. Yet she remained silent. He was hurting, which she hoped meant his feelings for her were genuine.

"Tell me, what did the letter say? What compelled you to act on it?" she implored.

"It involved my parents. The letter came with photographs of them in Tokyo, in their home, and also pictures of my father's business. The letter accused him of embezzlement within the company. He became the CEO last year and inherited everything, but an accusation like that becoming public would ruin him and destroy my entire family," Theo explained, his voice quivering.

Emily leaned forward, enveloping him in her arms. "Theo, my god, I'm so sorry," she whispered.

As she rested her head against his chest, she pieced together the fragments of information she knew. She heard his heart rate increase as he leaned his head on top of hers. Whoever was behind these threats had a wide-reaching influence, spanning from Tokyo to the night George died.

Gently withdrawing from their embrace, Emily said, "I don't blame you, Theo. It hurts to know that the beginning of our relationship was built on a lie, but I believe your feelings for me are genuine."

He grasped her arms, his eyes pleading. "They are. It's all true. I've wanted nothing more than to find you again. That it had to happen under these circumstances hurts me deeply, but what has transpired ever since means so much more."

"Have your family received any threats? Have you spoken to them about this?" Emily asked, concern etching her features.

He chuckled bitterly. "No, I would never burden my father with such questions. As far as I know, they are oblivious to all of this. The letters were addressed to only me, specifically demanding I come to your home."

"And you've received no further communication?" Emily pressed, her mind racing.

"No, not yet. I've been waiting every morning, expecting something, but nothing has come."

"So, the person orchestrating all of this wanted you near me and nothing else?" Emily pondered aloud, furrowing her brow. "Who could it be? And who would have knowledge of your father's business?"

"No one. I only communicate with him through my personal email. One of my old school friends works at the company, and he mentioned the previous bosses before, but I don't think it's him."

"And no one had access to your email?"

"No. It was either my home laptop or my phone. Cassandra was always clueless about technology," Theo explained.

It struck Emily then—the answer seemed so obvious.

"Wait. Jessie was always up to date with coding. She's the one who set up the NFTs for us. She lived with you guys and worked from home," Emily pointed out.

"But she didn't know my password," Theo interjected.

"Perhaps she didn't have to. You mentioned she always came on to you and refused to take no for an answer, and the next thing we know, she's commanding you to come visit me," Emily reasoned.

"You think Jessie killed Cassandra too?" Theo asked, as the realisation sunk in.

Emily shrugged, acknowledging the craziness of her own words. "Maybe."

The wind intensified above the wall that provided them with shelter. Emily edged closer to Theo, seeking further solace in his warmth.

He tapped his chin. "What if it was her? She completely disappeared when everything started happening. That's when Rachel started feeling like she was being followed."

"The letter that was sent to you... Do you still have it?"

Theo pulled out his phone and frantically scrolled through his images. "I took a photo of it. It must be here somewhere," he muttered, sticking his tongue out in concentration. "Ah, here it is."

Emily examined the letter. The paper was the same off-white colour, and the words were written in the same dark blue ink. She pulled out her own phone to compare the two letters and examine the handwriting. The letter 'b' stood out the most, with its curve at the end identical to the one in Theo's letter.

She raised her eyes to meet Theo's, determined. "The letter that was sent to me. They must be from the same person," Emily confessed. "Rose also received a letter with a warning about me. Whoever is behind all this, it's connected to me."

"Rose had one as well? Why did you not tell me?"
Emily raised a brow. "Like you told me about yours?"

"Okay, point made, but who could be doing all this?" Theo encircled her shoulder with his arm, tucking her in close. "Jessie?" he suggested, and Emily nodded.

"I'll text Rachel. Let her know about Jessie and find out if she has any information on where she's been staying." Emily's fingers flew across the screen as she typed out her message to Rachel, her heart racing. When she clicked send, a brief sense of calm washed over her as she glanced back at Theo, who gave a reassuring smile. However, her attention quickly returned to her phone when she noticed a missed call from Rachel.

Without hesitation, Emily dialled Rachel's number, the wind picking up around her and sending shivers down her neck. Pressing a hand over her exposed ear, she closed her eyes to focus on the call. The phone rang and rang, but Rachel didn't answer. Emily anxiously waited, the icy grip of fear tightening around her chest. Finally, Rachel's heavy breathing. Rushed footsteps. Panting.

"Rachel, are you there? Are you okay?" Emily asked.

Silence. More footsteps. And then a scream.

Emily spun to Theo, her eyes wide. "Rachel. Find somewhere safe. Where are you?" she pleaded, gripping onto Theo's coat as the weight of powerlessness kept her rooted to the ground.

Emily strained to listen, but all she heard were more footsteps and then a crashing in the distance. The phone fell to the floor, and Rachel's voice became distorted. "Please, please don't," she screamed through the line. And then the call abruptly ended, leaving Emily staring at her phone in disbelief.

She dialled Rachel's number again, her desperation mounting, but the call wouldn't connect. Whoever was after Rachel had either turned off her phone or damaged it beyond use. Panic welled up within Emily, and together, she and Theo sat in shocked silence, drained of colour.

"What do we do?" Emily finally croaked as they both grappled with the terrifying reality that their friend was in grave danger.

CHAPTER TWENTY
Unfinished Revenge

The closest thing to Regina's presence was the lingering scent of her perfume at home. All Florence yearned for was a chance to live her life without restrictions. Glancing across the kitchen, Florence observed her mother's face—sharper than ever before and shadowed by resentment. She appeared cold and rigid, mirroring Florence's father, who couldn't bear to maintain eye contact for more than a fleeting moment ever since she revealed the truth.

Still, the question remained about who had sent the incriminating photos. Regina was worried too, not for her own sake, but for Florence and her family. Part of Florence wished to forget the incident, destroy the photos, and prove Mike wrong by embracing her new life of freedom. However, the looming presence of someone out there, eager to inflict harm upon Florence and her family, prevented her from simply letting go. After all she had been through, she couldn't allow that to happen.

Breakfast with her parents held no appeal, so Florence slipped out into the close. She had grown accustomed to checking her phone, hoping for a call or message from Olivia. Still, nothing came. Yet when her mother appeared in the doorway, arms folded, and tapping her wedding ring with her finger, Florence forced a smile and asked, "Everything okay?"

"I didn't want to upset you, but your father thought I should tell you."

Confused, Florence glanced through the window at her father on the sofa. She bit her lip, wondering if he had exposed her secret, and if she no longer needed to carry the weight of her worry alone.

"Olivia called." Her mother stepped closer and raised her hands. "It's all right. I spoke to her calmly, and I'm going to see her." Florence opened her mouth to speak, but her mother's raised finger silenced her. "Before you explode, she didn't want me to tell you. I did this against her wishes. I won't disclose anything further. Understand?" A raised eyebrow was all her mother needed to silence Florence, like she were still a child. Florence nodded, eager to conclude this conversation. She turned away and sent a message on her phone to Olivia, checking in. She didn't expect a response, but she wanted Olivia to know she was thinking of her.

Florence wandered towards Ava's house, the only person who knew about her relationship with Regina. She needed advice. As she strolled along the path leading to the lake, she paused and peered closer at a crack running along the pavement, extending towards the road. She snapped a photo. She was frustrated by the police and their negligence, and complaining to the council about the cracked path seemed like a good outlet for her anger. But she decided it was a fight for another day and closed her phone.

Florence yelled for Ava as she knocked on the door. Her friend's voice floated from the garden, and so Florence entered through the back gate, where Ava's head poked out from the lounge chair. A brochure for Prime Estates with the tagline 'Sell your house and find your forever home', lay on the glass table.

Florence wondered if Ava was having more trouble than she let on, especially after losing Nick. She tapped her gently on the shoulder, momentarily blinded by the sunlight reflecting from her glasses. "Seems like you're managing fine without Katherine," Florence quipped.

Ava raised her sunglasses and tilted her head. "It's surprising how quickly one can adapt to solitude," she said, sitting up. "What brings you here so early? Aren't you working at the salon today?"

"I noticed the brochure inside," Florence said, changing the subject. "Are you thinking of selling this place?"

Ava's eyebrows shot up. "No, just exploring my options, that's all." Ava leaned closer to Florence. "What's troubling you, Flo? I can always sense when something's on your mind. Your right eye does that thing."

"What thing?" Florence rubbed the eye in question.

"The twitch thing. I could always tell when you were bluffing during our card games. Oscar and I used to laugh about it..." Ava's voice trailed. Florence bit her tongue. She knew about her giveaway, her awful talent at hiding an irritation, but she didn't expect Ava and Oscar to have shared joy in the fact.

"I actually came here for some advice," Florence interjected, placing a hand on her hip. "Given that I'm apparently so transparent, I might as well just say it. It's about Regina."

Ava grabbed Florence's arms and pulled her closer. "Spilt up? Already?" she gasped. "I've heard rumours about lesbians moving too fast: breaking up one minute, and then getting back together the next. You'll be married within a week, just you wait."

Seeking respite from the heat, Florence moved towards the kitchen, and Ava followed her inside. "No, we haven't broken up. It's... it's more serious than that."

"Well, what is it? If you two need some alone time, you can use the annex. I had it fumigated since Katherine left, so you should be okay. I'm sure you won't catch anything." Ava took a sip of her drink before whispering, "God knows what she brought into that bed." Seeming to sense Florence's discomfort, she straightened. "Oh, Flo, come on. I was only joking." Ava shook her head. "Okay, I'm here. Let's be serious now. Tell me what's going on. We can fix anything."

Florence hesitated before finally confessing, "I think I'm being blackmailed."

Ava slammed her glass onto the counter, spilling the contents onto the marble surface. "Blackmailed? About what? You and Regina?"

Florence nodded. "I know it doesn't sound that serious, but the idea of someone out there toying with me unsettles me." She grabbed some kitchen towel and started cleaning up the spilled drink. "I visited Mike, thinking it might be related to him."

"Mike? God, it must be serious," Ava muttered.

"He told me that someone questioned him, demanding information about me... and about you," Florence revealed, searching Ava's expression for any telltale signs. When her throat tightened, Florence knew Ava was hiding something. It was a familiar sight she knew too well.

"What did they want to know? I have nothing left to hide for Mike to reveal," Ava said, flicking her hair from her shoulder. Ava had many secrets in the past, Florence knew that much to be true. She hoped she could believe her friend now.

"I'm not sure. Mike wasn't very forthcoming, but he did talk. There's someone out there watching me—possibly you as well." Florence winced as Ava's nails dug into her arm.

"What was sent to you? A letter? Photos? What?"

"Both—photos and a short, handwritten note," Florence said, showing Ava her phone. She had taken pictures of everything. Ava scanned the images.

Ava sighed. "I don't know if I should say this..."

"What? You can say it to me," Florence said, searching her eyes.

Ava scratched her nose, seeming to contemplate her following words. "These tactics—photos, blackmail, and reaching out to Mike for information—it's happened before."

Florence's mind flashed back to that night when Cynthia had manipulated her with alcohol and planted dark thoughts in her mind, leading her to act against Ava. "You don't think?" Florence gasped upon realising her insinuation. "No! Emily and Cynthia have moved on from all that nonsense."

Ava rolled her eyes. "None of this trouble started until they moved in. Cynthia sent photos of me to Mike to drive me away. The photos are eerily similar to the ones you have right there." Ava tapped Florence's phone. "I received a note, too, and a photo. I must admit, my mind instinctively went to them. I don't want it to be true, but it's the only thing that seems to make any sense."

Florence had grown close to Emily since she moved to Beechwood. She had always been there for her, for all the woman in the close. Could she or Cynthia really be behind these letters and threats? Florence tried to picture it from Emily's side. She'd lost all access to her money. Police were investigating her for fraud. Maybe the idea of being back to her old life scared Emily. Maybe it would be enough to push them back to their old ways.

"Should I ask what your note was about?"

Ava glared at Florence. "No, it's not an easy subject to discuss. The fewer people who know, the better." Ava wiped her eyes. "The less you know, the safer it is for you. Trust me."

Florence suppressed the urge to dig deeper and inquire about Ava's new secret, but she lacked the strength. She needed to stay focused on her own problems and entertain the notion that Emily might still be playing games with them, even after all this time.

CHAPTER TWENTY-ONE
Direct Message

Rose locked the door to 39-C and took a deep breath. Clutching the key in her palm, Rose made her way to the reception to sign the necessary paperwork before heading to her car. In that moment, she was struck by a surge of empowerment— after months of uncertainty, she finally felt in control.

The announcement of Sir Banks' campaign for Prime Minister had stirred something within her. Rose wasn't stupid. She was aware of his power and extensive influence, but she still possessed crucial information—documents that *he* needed. She had secured three separate lock-up locations to ensure that each contained a copy. At least if anything were to happen to her, this offered some measure of protection. The truth would be exposed and released for the world to see. It was a small source of comfort, knowing that she still held some control.

Her phone buzzed, and a text message appeared on the car dashboard. It was from Elisa. *'Hello Rose, I hope you are keeping well. I wanted to let you know I've had no more bother my end. I hope the same can be said for you. It was great to finally meet you. I look forward to the next one.'* Another message appeared from Benny then, asking Rose to visit the café to discuss some food options to add to the menu. Life seemed to regain a sense of normalcy—a positive outlook for the future. Although, the present still needed work.

During many a sleepless night, Rose still questioned whether she and Emily had made the right decision in refusing Sir Banks' request. While her life was looking up, brighter than it ever had before, her past demons still loomed large. Rose parked outside her home and unlocked her phone, dialling Emily's number. The phone rang, but no one answered.

She glanced down the street. Emily's car was parked outside her house. Perhaps she was deliberately ignoring Rose, blissfully unaware that the problem they faced hadn't' disappeared.

Through the car's wing mirror, Rose spotted Katherine's distinctive flame-coloured hair as she made her way towards Edna's house. To avoid detection, Rose quickly lowered into her seat. Emily thought she'd seen her at Sir Banks' country home the night they were there, and although Rose couldn't be sure, she didn't want to risk speaking to Katherine about The Order or what she'd done with the list. If Emily was right, the risk would be too great.

Rose found a pair of sunglasses and a silk scarf in the glove compartment. Wrapping the scarf over her head, she readjusted her position to monitor Katherine walking into Edna's backyard. She stepped out of the car and tripped, dropping her house keys and bag onto the street. Glancing around to ensure no neighbours were watching, she swiftly gathered her belongings and tucked the lock-up key safely in her pocket.

With another cautious glance at Edna's house, Rose noticed Katherine crossing the street, having left Edna's already. Feeling a sudden sense of urgency, Rose pushed against her front door, twiddling the key in the lock. It didn't budge. She twisted it again, accidentally kicking the corner of the door. "Rose, darling," Katherine called out from behind. Rose finally swung it open, dropping her bag to the floor before turning to close it. Only she couldn't, because a pretty red-heeled shoe was wedged in the door. Slowly lifting her gaze, Rose found Katherine before her, brushing her bouncy hair away from her face. "You almost took my leg off, Rose. Didn't you hear me calling?" Katherine asked, leaning into Rose's home. "Mind if I come in?"

Rose patted herself down and removed her sunglasses. "I'm sorry; I have a hundred and one things to do. Can we catch up another time?" She looked down, only to realise Katherine hadn't moved her foot.

"It won't take long." Katherine flashed a sickly-sweet smile and stepped inside, surveying Rose's impeccably clean home. While Rose hadn't expected guests—least of all Katherine—she knew her home wouldn't draw any criticism. Before Rose could react, Katherine casually swiped a look at the lock-up leaflet Rose had left on the sideboard. Rose swiftly folded it up, hoping Katherine hadn't had enough time to read the name.

Trying to maintain composure, Rose wiped the already spotless surface of the kitchen counter and asked, "So, what brings you to Beechwood today, Katherine? Ava mentioned that you found somewhere better to live."

"Edna needed someone to house-sit while she went to a hospital appointment," Katherine said, taking a seat on the sofa and kicking off her heels. "Well, she actually wanted me to accompany her, but I declined. I've always detested hospitals. Watching over her place is much easier."

Rose frowned. "So, you made poor Larry take her? Didn't you want to give him a break from her?"

Katherine shrugged.

"Don't give me that look. I received enough flak from Edna when I asked Larry to take her. I don't know what her problem is."

"Shouldn't you be over there then?"

Katherine leaned over to grab a sweet from Rose's sweet bowl. "I can see her place from here, don't worry," she said, leaning back on the sofa to glance out the window. Katherine's idea of not staying long clearly meant taking off her shoes, lounging on the sofa and eating Rose out of house and home. Although Rose still managed to smile. She was still a guest, after all.

"You said you had something to say? I'm quite busy," Rose interjected.

Katherine sat up and laughed, briefly scanning the room. "Oh yeah, you look *swamped*," she remarked, standing up to grab another sweet. "I wanted to check in on you to make sure you're okay with everything." She leaned in closer. "With such a burden to carry, I thought you would need a friend to look after you. Have you faced any trouble from any members?"

"You mean aside from yourself? No, nothing." Rose cleared her throat. If Emily was right and Katherine was at Kenneth's home that night, she wasn't an ally Rose needed.

"Wonderful news, although not unexpected. There's talk of a dossier circulating among some of the more *colourful* members, if you catch my drift. I've been asked about it countless times."

Rose briefly glanced at the front door, silently hoping for Katherine's departure. "Perhaps you should surround yourself with better company," she said. "But I don't want to dwell on that place, and the fact you're still so involved doesn't exactly earn my admiration."

Katherine placed an open hand onto her chest.

"I'm doing it for you, Rose. You need someone on the inside to ensure things don't get out of hand. I warned you about that document when you got it. Those warnings still hold," Katherine said. She seemed to enjoy word games.

Frustration seized Rose. She despised these manipulative tactics Katherine employed and wished she would just come out and say it. "Come on then. What's being said? What's going to happen to me? If you genuinely have my best interests at heart, then tell me," Rose urged, but Katherine pouted, as if disappointed by her bluntness.

"Like I said, it's just gossip "or now. But you saw those photos. You heard the story straight from Violet's mouth. That place deals with things in dangerous ways. If you end up on the wrong side of this, you're toast."

Rose yearned to confide in Katherine about Sir Banks and his offer, and how Emily spotted her in his office. However, she remained silent, knowing that a fleeting moment of satisfaction wasn't worth revealing all her cards.

"The documents are gone. I made copies and sent them to multiple locations. I don't have them here, nor do I have access to them. I've instructed my solicitor that if anything happens to me, they will immediately be released to the press." This time, it was Rose who leaned over to pluck a sweet from the bowl. "I refuse to live in fear of them, and certainly not of you." She poked Katherine's chest, whose eyes sparked. She glared at Rose, her fury uncontained. Instead of retaliating, Katherine rose from the seat and stepped back. She smoothed her hair and plastered on a smile.

"I'm not your enemy, Rose. I'm merely a messenger. There are individuals with a lot to lose if that document sees the light of day—people far more powerful than both of us. Although, I suspect you already know that."

Rose shifted her gaze beyond Katherine towards Edna's home, where a man stood at the door with a parcel. "There's work for you at Edna's," she said. "Please leave my house, and if our paths must cross again, let's keep the conversation light. I no longer want to hear about The Order or any of its members," Rose said, walking towards the door and opening it. Katherine gave Rose a fleeting smile, a silent mark of respect for finally standing up to her. Rose couldn't help feel like Katherine respected her more for it.

Slamming the door shut behind her, Rose collapsed onto her knees and buried her face in her hands. Her heart thudded in her chest, while the persistent buzzing of her phone demanded her attention. She fumbled through her bag and retrieved it. Emily had sent a text. *'Rose, did you receive a text too?'* it read. Leaning against the wall, Rose opened her phone, only to find another message from an unknown number.

'We have been waiting. If nothing materialises soon, we will be forced to take action. Your loved ones will suffer if you refuse.'

With trembling hands, Rose tapped on the number to dial it. It beeped before a voice said, "This number is not recognised. Please hang up and try again." Sweat trickled down her forehead as she attempted to call the number again, only to hear the same automated response.

Rising to her feet, Rose peered through the small window

in her door. There stood Katherine outside of Edna's home, conversing with the mailman with no phone in sight. Running her fingers through her hair, Rose flung her phone to the ground. It was obvious who was behind these messages. He had warned her, and Katherine had warned her too. The list held immense power—a burden she believed she could overcome. But when the threats extended to her family and friends, it became a risk too great to bear.

She retrieved her cracked phone from the floor and messaged Emily. *'We need to accept his offer. There's too much at stake. I'm going to do it, with or without you. X'*

CHAPTER TWENTY-TWO
Old Company

Katherine sprinted toward the mailman, struggling with her high heels as she wobbled toward Edna's house. She couldn't help but notice the impressive breadth of the man's shoulders. Slowing her pace, she shook her head to ensure her hair looked bouncy and effortless in the breeze. She pouted and waved at him. "Darling, give me a second!"

She sauntered up the steps of Edna's wooden porch and leaned on the rail, which creaked under her weight. "I'm watching the place for the old bat." Her smile grew as she scrutinised the mailman from head to toe. "I suppose I'll have to take your delivery."

He returned her smile, briefly meeting her gaze before jotting something down on his tablet. She positioned herself before him. "No time for a chat, then? They must really work you to the bone."

"Sorry, Miss. We're tracked and timed," he replied, looking back towards his van.

"That's no fun, is it? How can these lonely women ever dream of having an affair in this day and age?" She chuckled as he descended the porch steps toward his van without looking back. Rolling her eyes, she lit a cigarette and exhaled a cloud of smoke into the air before setting the parcel down on the bench and taking a seat. The wood creaked beneath her. From her vantage point, she could see Cynthia hobbling over from her home. Katherine quickly stubbed out her cigarette and darted inside Edna's home with the parcel, just as Cynthia reached the porch.

Inside the dark living room, Katherine watched Cynthia limp toward the porch, glancing around before heading over toward the garden gate, clutching sandwiches wrapped in clingfilm. Crossing her legs, Katherine lit another cigarette, fixing her eyes on the back door of the kitchen. She observed Cynthia turning the doorknob and carefully pocketing a small key.

Katherine chuckled. The old bat expected to find Larry here, who was supposed to stay home while Katherine accompanied Edna to the appointment.

She tapped her ash into the tray, staying silent. "Larry, are you here? I've got a mix of brown and white today," Cynthia called. Katherine stood and made her way across the lounge, heading toward the alternate entrance to the kitchen just as Cynthia entered the room from the other side. "Larry? Get down here. I hope you're not stuck on the loo again." Cynthia collapsed onto the sofa, a cloud of dust erupting and swirling in the air. She sniffed and waved her hand.

Katherine stepped forward and blew a puff of smoke in her direction. "You sly old dog," she remarked.

Cynthia jumped, another cloud of dust erupting from her

movements. "What the bloody hell are you doing here? You nearly killed me!" Cynthia exclaimed, narrowing her eyes at the redhead. "Where's Larry? Aren't you supposed to be out with Edna?"

Katherine smiled and approached. "I switched. In fact, Larry practically begged me to stay here so he could be with Edna."

"You're lying," Cynthia retorted, raising her nose.

Katherine shrugged. "Believe what you want. I'm here, and Larry is with *his* lady."

Cynthia laughed and slapped her leg. "Lady? Please." She sized up Katherine and wafted the smoke from her face. "So... What brings you here? It's not like you to carry out a good deed. I heard you'd moved on."

"Everyone seems to say the same thing to me. It's quite amusing, really. I'm just here to help an old friend."

Cynthia groaned and then prodded the parcel. "What's this?"

Katherine picked up the box, examining it for the first time. A company named VitaPharm was printed across the top, with an old-fashioned logo underneath—Herbert's Old Pharmaceuticals. "No idea, just some package for Edna," Katherine said, giving the box a gentle shake. It felt light. She scanned the address and the name. Edna Cracken. Edna's maiden name. "Any idea what VitaPharm is?"

Cynthia shrugged and averted her gaze. "Probably a pharmacy, I'd guess."

Katherine rolled her eyes. "Well, duh. There's another name underneath it—Herbert's Old Pharmaceuticals."

"Sounds old," Cynthia replied, her voice monotone.

Katherine cast a sidelong glance at Cynthia and rose from her seat. "So very helpful," she muttered, placing the parcel on the table. "So, are you having an affair?"

Cynthia coughed, pounding her chest. She looked up at Katherine with red cheeks. "You what?"

"Come on. It's not uncommon around here. Many wives, and even husbands, are involved in such things. I find it all rather thrilling. Even at your age, it means there's still hope for me," Katherine teased.

"No, I am not." Cynthia crossed her arms "Larry is a dear friend, and when he needs support away from Edna, I'm here to help," Cynthia said.

"Oh, I bet you are," Katherine quipped, stepping toward the window. "Shall I let Edna know you paid her a visit, then?"

"No!" Cynthia shouted. "There's no need for any of that. I'll leave now, anyway. This place is uncomfortable at the best of times."

Katherine sat in Edna's garden, tapping her ash onto the tray while admiring the picturesque view of the lake peeking through the trees. She had stowed the parcel in her bag, eager to investigate the unfamiliar name. She'd been secretly helping herself with Edna's pills and medication for years. This parcel seemed like a great way to thank Katherine for watching the house.

The rumble of Larry's car pulling into the driveway reached her ears, accompanied by a heated exchange. Edna stormed into the garden, slamming the gate against the brick wall. Edna speed soon slowed when she noticed Katherine. With a raised brow, Katherine watched as she hunched over and started to hobble. Katherine turned and flashed a smile, and Edna's sour expression transformed into one of delight. She nudged a chair with her foot. "Take a load off. You look utterly pissed off."

"Hospital visits and Larry do not mix," Edna grumbled. "I

could have killed him when he came with me."

Katherine flicked her ash onto the tray. "I don't understand why it was such a problem. You only have a handful of days left together. The time you spend together is so... precious."

Edna cackled. "I'm counting down to the next husband, I think."

Katherine let out a small chuckle. She only hoped she could be half the woman Edna was in her later years.

"So, what happened? Why was it awful? Not bad news, was it?" Katherine glanced toward the kitchen where Larry stood, his cheeks flushed, filling the kettle.

"No. He got upset because I made him stay in the car."

Katherine raised an eyebrow. She knew Edna's knack for manipulation. "Why didn't he come in with you?"

"Because that's private—it's my business. It would have been the same if you accompanied me."

"Remind me never to offer then," Katherine said, watching a bird perched by the water fountain. "So, a charming mailman paid a visit while you were out."

"The attractive dark-haired one? You lucky devil," Edna mused.

"He had a parcel for this place."

Edna's eyes widened. "Oh, where is it? Must be Larry buying more junk online."

"No, I don't think so. I handed it back. It wasn't a name I recognised. Well, not entirely."

Edna leaned back in her chair and placed her walking stick across her lap. "You sent it back? Why? I could have had whatever was inside. Whose name was it? You know, Florence from across the street had a parcel sent here by mistake about a month ago, and when I opened it, my teeth nearly fell out. I had no idea she was so... experimental in the bedroom."

"The name on the parcel was for Miss Cracken," Katherine said carefully.

Edna's eyes widened. "So, it was for me! That's my maiden name, you know."

Katherine leaned closer, intrigued. "Yes, I do. But why would they use your maiden name?" She took another drag from her cigarette. "It's rather peculiar. Been centuries since you used it, no?"

Edna turned her head away, seeming to avoid Katherine's eyes. "I have no idea. It must be a printing mistake or something."

"It didn't seem like a mistake to me. Is there something you're not telling me?"

"Don't be ridiculous. With my condition, I can make mistakes. Perhaps I used the wrong name," Edna replied.

Katherine studied Edna closely. For a woman supposedly on her deathbed, she had a surprising vibrancy to her.

"I should get going, but as always, it's been a pleasure." Katherine stood and brushed down her dress from any ash that had fallen onto her lap. "Oh, by the way, you might want to keep an eye on Larry. Cynthia was snooping around here earlier, expecting a warm welcome from him, but encountered me instead." Katherine warned.

"I hope you sent her packing," Edna grumbled.

"Of course."

"Good girl. Now, let's not discuss my hospital visits any further," Edna said, rising from her seat. Her legs and arms trembled, and she dropped her walking stick. Neck twitching, she sat back down. "Be a dear and hand it to me," she asked, extending her bony arm.

Katherine couldn't help but smirk. "I might just give you an Oscar one of these days."

Katherine closed the curtains, shutting out the city lights that cast a stark-white glow in the hotel room. She despised staying in hotels, but it was her only option for the time being. At least it was a five-star establishment, and the bill was fully covered. She reached into the mini bar to pluck a small bottle of champagne from the shelf. Settling onto the plush silk sheets, she opened her laptop. Kenneth had sent her three emails requesting updates, but she decided to make him wait a little longer before giving him her attention.

Her mind was elsewhere. She had opened Edna's parcel, expecting to find some pills to take or sell. Instead, there were several tiny bottles of insulin. Alongside the address, she searched for the company name VitaPharm. The search yielded results showing that VitaPharm was a massive multinational corporation, operating from many countries. Katherine drummed her fingers against the champagne bottle, taking a sip as she continued searching.

She examined the box again. Edna had never used insulin when Katherine stayed in her home. Katherine tapped the box before conducting a search for Herbert's Old Pharmaceuticals. The search results were limited, which meant the company had likely ceased operations decades ago. However, when she searched the names together, a few more hits appeared. She clicked on an article. *'The historic Herbert's Old Pharmaceuticals was acquired by the industry giant VitaPharm, marking the end of an era for the century-old company. The acquisition, finalised two months ago, was orchestrated by the grandson of the founder, Thomas Herbert, who decided to sell the family business.'*

Katherine's lingering doubts intensified. Why would Edna use the surname 'Cracken'? Even if it were a mistake related to her maiden name, she wouldn't have been called

Cracken for decades.

On the VitaPharm website was a contact number. Katherine dialled it and then patiently navigated the various options until finally finding a human voice on the other end.

"Hello, Miss. I understand you are confused about a recent order."

"That's correct," Katherine confirmed. "I recently received an order under the name of my mother. I was wondering if you could advise on how this happened. You see, she passed away years ago, and seeing her name was quite triggering for me. I want to ensure it doesn't happen again."

"I understand, Miss Cracken."

Katherine twirled her hair around her finger. She created a backstory, a sob story to truly get her heart racing. If she wanted answers, she needed to create a full scene. "My son saw it and has been crying ever since, asking for his grandmother. I really want to get to the bottom of this."

"Of course. Give me a few minutes to look into this. Do you have the ID track number on the receipt?"

After reading the code aloud, they put her on hold. She opened the mini bar again, popping open a bag of popcorn and retrieving another bottle of champagne.

After twenty minutes, the woman returned. "Miss Cracken, are you still there?"

Katherine hurried back to the bed. "Yes, I'm here. Just putting the little one to bed."

"I think I have tracked down the problem. It appears that after VitaPharm acquired Herbert's Old Pharmaceuticals, we also acquired their entire client base, including records of old customers."

"How did my mother's personal items end up being sent to an address, then?"

"Well, Miss Edna Cracken was a customer of Herbert's

Old Pharmaceuticals dating back to the sixties. Does that sound correct?"

Katherine contemplated Edna's history. She was around eighty years old and had been living in Beechwood for years. "Yes, that is correct."

"When we transferred the physical records to digital, it seems an error was made. All the old customer prescriptions were sent out to their last known addresses."

"I see." Katherine reached for a cigarette and pushed open a window.

"What I don't understand is why your mother's account stopped in 1984. If your son knows about her, I'm assuming she lived long after that. But with her type of diabetes, she would have been taking prescriptions years after that. In fact, she would have needed a daily insulin shot." Katherine paused then. She'd lived with Edna years ago, briefly. She knew all her pills and medication, but never once had she mentioned insulin. "Also, her final bill was never paid."

"You're not going to charge me for it, are you? After all the memories you've brought up for me and my family?" Katherine forced a hint of anxiety in her voice.

"No, we won't expect any payment. But I can't comprehend why she suddenly stopped. Did she live at 74 Beechwood Close until her death?"

"Yes, family home. We loved her dearly." Katherine paused, to add a dramatic flair to her sorrow. "Listen my son has woken up. I need to go. You have been such a help."

She took a long drag of her cigarette and tapped the ash into the wind. Her mind raced as she pondered Edna's secrets. Edna had never needed insulin before, and she had never mentioned having diabetes either. Something didn't add up. If Edna didn't need the insulin, then who did?

CHAPTER TWENTY-THREE
Hunted

Emily's fourth message to Rachel also received no reply. Since Rachel's last phone call, she had only replied to Emily to reveal she was in the hospital and didn't want to speak further on the matter. That was all they knew—Rachel wasn't willing to share any additional information about what happened to her.

Glancing over at Theo, Emily found him engrossed in Jessie's social media pages, desperately searching for any clue regarding her whereabouts. Cynthia approached the pair of them and placed a mug of tea by Emily's side. She gently stroked her shoulder. "Are you sure there isn't anything I can do? I'm just wandering around this house with no one to talk to."

Emily clutched the mug and set her phone aside. "No, Gran. Shouldn't you be at Larry's place, anyway?" She glanced at her watch, aware of Cynthia's usual routine. It was a Wednesday. Every week Cynthia would meet Larry before lunch for a walk.

Cynthia pursed her wrinkled lips. "No, I don't live in his pocket," she snapped, shuffling toward her chair. "Besides, he's got Edna to worry about. I don't need to add to the chaos. She expects most of his attention." Cynthia let out an exasperated huff and picked up a magazine she had already read to aimlessly flip through its pages.

"Hey, Em, check this out!" Theo called. Emily hurried over to the table, leaning across his shoulder to see what had caught his interest.

Cynthia turned her head to face them. "Oh, finally tearing yourself away from that screen?"

Emily focused on Theo's laptop, which displayed multiple open tabs at the top—over twenty, she realised. "I was going through Jessie's Instagram page. It took forever but look." He tapped on a photo, showing Jessie wearing a yellow life jacket. The image showed Jessie, a short bob, full fringe. She looked happy, smiling at the camera.

Perplexed, Emily looked at Theo. "What's so significant about this? She's just on a boat. She looks about twelve. This was taken years ago."

Theo clicked on another tab on the screen. "Ah but look here. While going through her Facebook friends, I stumbled upon an uncle of hers. Check it out. He owns a holiday cabin."

Emily peered over Theo's shoulder once again. The next photo depicted a man with brown hair standing before a wooden cabin, smiling with two young boys. "So? It's a family cabin from a distant uncle. I don't understand the connection. We can't be certain she'd be there."

All the features on his face lifted. Hope shimmered in his

eyes as he looked at them both.

"Jessie captioned the photo of her in her life jacket as her 'special place.' And look, in the background, along the lake shore, there's a cabin," Theo explained. He saved both photos and displayed them side by side. "See? The pitch of the roof, the pattern of the logs—it's the same place."

Emily sighed, torn between wanting it to be that easy and not wanting to embark on a journey, only to find nothing there. Cynthia sighed and made her way toward the table.

"Cynthia, you tell her. This adds up, right?" Theo urged.

Squinting at the screen, Cynthia said, "It's the same place, Em."

Emily rolled her eyes. "But we don't know if that's where she would go to hide."

Cynthia glanced at Theo and winked. "Why not?" she challenged. "She's been feeling nostalgic about the place, seeking safety in familiar memories. Where better to retreat than to a cherished place from happier times?"

Emily glanced back at both of them, a faint smile gracing her lips. She feigned a cough to avoid getting sentimental. It was a relief to see them finally getting along, even if it meant they were ganging up on her. "Fine. So where is this cabin? Can we find its location from the clouds in the sky?" she quipped.

"Now, now, Emily, no need to get grouchy," Cynthia chided, pulling a chair to sit beside Theo.

"She always gets like this midweek," Theo whispered into Cynthia's ear, who responded with a nod before patting his knee.

Emily bit her lip and squeezed herself in between them, while Theo resumed scrolling through Jessie's Instagram. He froze at one image, having stumbled upon a photo of the entire gang, smiling at the camera during their university days—the last time they were all together. It was taken a few months before Emily cashed in the money, and she and Cynthia hatched the plan of moving to Beechwood Close. It felt like ancient history now. Theo swiftly moved on to another photo of Jessie, taken during a hike in a forest about a year ago. "Look, she's tagged the location," he pointed out. The location tag indicated The Lake District.

"How can you be sure it's the same place as the cabin?" Emily questioned.

"It's easy." Cynthia turned the laptop toward herself. "See, her uncle commented underneath. It's the same name listed on Facebook, right?"

Surprised that Cynthia possessed the knowledge to navigate a social media post, Theo and Emily exchanged glances. "She's right," Theo exclaimed, clicking back and forth between the Facebook page and the Instagram photo. "It's the same guy. Cynthia, you're a genius!"

Cynthia narrowed her eyes. "Course I bloody am."

"So, we're looking for a cabin in or around The Lake District then? It narrows it down a bit, I suppose," Emily concluded, while Cynthia rose, tea in hand, and headed toward her bedroom.

Emily reached for Theo's hand, her voice tinged with uncertainty. "So, are we sure about this? Should we go and confront Jessie?"

He nodded, a slow smile spreading across his face. "It makes sense, doesn't it? It's a shame we can't reach out to Rachel, though. She must still be shaken up."

Emily desperately wanted to hear from Rachel again. Both her and Theo had tried to contact her, but they received nothing but silence in return. All she could think about was the scream they heard on the phone. The way Cassandra died, in such pain and fear. Emily rubbed her wrist, only hoping Rachel didn't go through the same thing.

"I just hope she's okay. Losing Cassandra was devastating, but if we can sort this out, maybe it'll all stop."

Emily tightened her grip on Theo's hand, a surge of determination coursing through her. She desperately wanted everything to stop and to find a resolution for all this. However, the ominous text message sent to her and Rose haunted her every waking moment, lingering as a reminder of the potential danger not only she was in but also Theo and Cynthia—people she held dear.

Loss had followed Emily since she was a child. Loosing not one but both parents changed her, more than she cared to admit. Her biggest fear was going through that loss again. If she lost Cynthia or Theo, due to her own stupidity, she'd never be able to forgive herself.

Cynthia's bedroom door swung open, jolting Emily back into the present. Cynthia marched over and placed a piece of paper on the table before them. It contained an address for a place in Ulverston. "What's this?" Emily asked, unable to take her eyes off it.

"It's an address, just south of The Lake District," Theo explained, typing something into his laptop. A chuckle escaped his lips. "I could hug you," he exclaimed, beaming at Cynthia.

"You better bloody not," she retorted. "Look, Em. This is it. The uncle passed away two years ago, and guess who inherited the place? Can't say for certain if you'll find her there, but you won't know until you try."

Emily looked at Cynthia, whose eyes glinted like a Cheshire cat's. "How did you get this information?"

"I called in a favour with Clive down at the police station. He's got his uses," Cynthia revealed, a hint of pride in her voice. "That's the place. Now, whether you'll find Jessie there or not remains to be seen. But sometimes, you've got to take a chance, love."

Emily jumped to her feet and rushed toward Cynthia, enveloping her tightly. Cynthia stiffened and groaned. Appearing to sense the moment, Theo joined in, wrapping his arms around both of them. "Oh, you two! Get off!" Cynthia grumbled though she couldn't hide the amusement in her words. Emily paid no attention. She clung to Cynthia and expressed her heartfelt thanks for the unexpected support.

Emily's back ached from the long car journey. The initial rush of adrenaline had long since faded, and now she felt exhausted, having driven for the first three hours of the journey before Theo took over for the final two. Needing reassurance, she sent another text to Florence, asking her to check on Cynthia while they were gone. She felt a bit silly making such a request, but her grandmother's wellbeing was her main priority.

Glancing at the navigation system, Emily realised they were close to their destination. "Are you ready for this?" she asked Theo.

Theo shrugged, seeming somewhat apprehensive. "I don't know what to expect. We're venturing into the unknown here," he said, glancing at Emily before refocusing on the road. "It's not too late to turn back."

Emily gazed out of the window. The sky was ablaze, a fiery orange hue, yet the air conditioning provided some respite from the heat. "No, we have to do this. It's now or never," she declared.

"Any word from Rachel?" asked Theo.

Emily checked her phone once more. "No," she sighed. "I texted her before we left to tell her our suspicions about Jessie. I urged her to keep an eye out."

"Did you mention the cabin?" Theo pressed, his voice desperately trying to sound strong, but Emily could hear the cracks forming.

"Yeah, I said we had a hunch," Emily said. "I guess I wanted to make her feel like she could trust us, so I told her everything." She turned to look out of the car window. The silence worried Emily. Rachel had replied to her instantly when she got in touch last month. They had met up, formed a friendship again. Could she blame Emily for the attack happening? Emily seemed to invite trouble everywhere she turned. Perhaps Rachel saw her as a bad omen "I'm sorry. I wasn't thinking clearly."

"No need to apologise. It's been a long day," Theo said, his voice softening.

As the car slowed down, they approached a gravel path. "And it's about to be a long night," she whispered as the log cabin came into view. The structure itself was magnificent, constructed from dark logs with a wide, pitched roof. The front showcased a deck with a long table, a Jacuzzi, a fire pit, and an outdoor kitchen. The surroundings were calm. Tall tress and a large lake near by. It was the sole cabin in the area, truly isolated.

Emily stretched before stepping out of the car. She shook her legs to rouse her sleepy feet. An eerie stillness surrounded them both, punctuated only by the faint sounds of water lapping against the lake and the gentle rustling of trees. "Emily, look!" Theo whispered, pointing toward a group of trees next to the cabin. "Beechwood trees. It must be a sign."

They proceeded with caution and crept toward the cabin.

Taking a deep breath, Emily clasped Theo's hand. This was it. The threats, letters, the attacks on her friends, the blackmail—the weight of such pressure bore down on her as they prepared to confront Jessie, demanding an explanation for her actions and searching for a way to put an end to it.

They walked toward the large glass door. "There's no lights on or cars outside. Are we sure someone is here?" Emily whispered, scanning the surroundings. No boots were left hanging outside, no furniture or towels drying. The place looked like it was once alive, but somehow now seemed cold. Unloved.

"Maybe we just knock and act natural. Let her confess on her own. Do you have any signal?" Theo asked, checking his phone.

'Act natural', Emily thought. What exactly was natural about two friends from years ago turning up in the dead of night? Emily knew this was mad. That the plan was dangerous at the least. But they were out of ideas. She needed to move things forward, and this seemed like the only way.

"Just a single bar. Not much, but better than nothing," Emily replied, sliding her phone back into her pocket. She rapped her knuckles against the glass door, the sound echoing through the stillness. Leaning closer, she cupped her hands around her eyes to peer inside.

"Anything?" Theo asked from behind her.

"No, I can't see much. There's something there, but I'm not sure," Emily responded, narrowing her eyes to adjust to the darkness beyond. She then turned her attention to the door handle and pulled it toward her before sliding it open. Her heart raced as she braced for the sound of an alarm or the scream of an unsuspecting person, but silence greeted her instead. She glanced at Theo, whose cheeks reddened slightly. He tapped his foot and scratched his head. Taking a deep breath, Emily stepped inside. "Jessie? Are you here?" she called out.

They entered the open-plan lounge and kitchen, and

Emily's gaze fell upon broken glass strewn across the floor. Her eyes followed the trail until she froze. Turning to grab Theo's arm, she whispered, "Look! Down there." He looked to where she pointed, and then their eyes met again. They rushed toward the sofa, crunching over shards of glass. Blood soaked the cushions, and Jessie lay motionless on the floor. "Don't touch her. She could be injured. I'll call an ambulance." Emily grabbed her phone from her pocket, but dropped it onto the floor. Reaching for the phone again, she sliced her hand on the broken glass littering the wooden surface. "Get some towels and cold water, or something!" she yelled.

The hospital waiting room sucked all of Emily's energy from her weary body. She paced along the corridor, fixing her gaze on the tiled floor as she mechanically counted each step. The wait for the ambulance was bad enough. It had felt like hours she was kept on the phone. Theo pressing down on Jessie's wound, stopping the blood from flowing. At least Jessie was alive, and at least now, they could gather information to help the police unravel the mystery behind all this.

Emily's former conviction that Jessie was the mastermind behind everything wavered. A nagging uncertainty had taken its place. Who could be behind it all? While pondering this, a doctor entered the room, interrupting her thoughts. "Jessie is awake now. She can have visitors, although she may still be drowsy from the anaesthetic," said the doctor.

Emily glanced at Theo, who had been nursing a cup of weak coffee since their arrival. With a sigh, he pushed himself to his feet and clasped Emily's hand. Together, they made their way to Jessie's recovery room. The surgeons had to stitch up the wound in her side, and now she lay in bed, a slight smile gracing her face upon seeing them enter. It had been years since Emily had seen Jessie. She still sported the same haircut, her fluffy wavy hair hung lank. The mousy brown colour that matched her eyes. Her skin was smooth, no signs of ageing or stress, even after being stabbed. It always was her best feature.

Tears welled up in Jessie's eyes when they sat beside her. "I don't know what you two were doing there, but you saved my life," she whispered. "You were like guardian angels, appearing just at the right moment."

"I'm relieved to see you're okay, Jessie. When I found you on the floor, the worst thoughts crossed my mind," Emily confessed.

"Like Cassandra and Rachel? Yeah, I was fortunate. If you hadn't shown up, I would be like them," Jessie admitted, a shudder passing through her. Emily gasped. She didn't expect the sound to come out but she couldn't stop it. Was Rachel dead?

Theo's grip on Emily's hand tightened. "Rachel? She's not dead. She's in the hospital," he interjected.

Jessie's eyes widened. "Oh, I guess you didn't hear. She was attacked."

"Yes, we knew about that." Emily explained, checking her phone to ensure she wasn't mistaken. "But she sent me a message when she woke up,"

"Oh. Well, maybe I don't know what I'm saying. These drugs must be strong, but I know she died. It's all online. Her mother even made a post about it," Jessie revealed. The colour drained from Theo's face as he absorbed the news. Emily's stomach churned as pain flooded her body. Another death. Another friend gone. "I didn't mean to shock you both. Oh, gosh, I'm sorry. I thought you knew. I thought that's why you came to see me," Jessie apologised.

"It's okay. We're just taken aback, that's all. The important thing is that you're safe," Emily said, wiping away a tear. She clung to Theo's hand, unwilling to let go.

CHAPTER TWENTY-FOUR
A Test of Loyalty

Ava clicked 'send' on the confirmation e-mail. The decision was made. She had officially put the house up for sale. But this wasn't your typical real estate transaction. Ava's one condition was utmost secrecy. No 'For Sale' signs in the front garden, no public listings to attract prying eyes. She wanted only private buyers with deep pockets, who were eager to swiftly seal the deal. Ava was surprised at her sudden sense of relief after finalising her plan. Perhaps, against all odds, Katherine's advice had hit the mark this time, though it likely never would again. Yet guilt crept in, gnawing at her conscience as she thought of her loyal friends trapped in this sinking neighbourhood. But Ava could no longer sacrifice her life for the sake of others. She had to put her own well-being first. Escaping those who knew the truth about Nick's existence—and acquiring a bit of extra cash—seemed the best way to do it.

As soon as she sold the house, Ava would reveal everything to her friends. There was still hope for them, a chance to escape this sinking ship. Yet, she couldn't help but doubt Emily, and if Emily and Cynthia were indeed the masterminds behind these letters, then Ava had no qualms about watching them sink along with the rest of Beechwood.

Ava closed her laptop and reached for the bottle of whisky, pouring herself a generous shot to steel her nerves. Just as she downed the drink, the doorbell chimed, interrupting her moment of reflection. She grabbed her red coat and headed towards the door, finding Florence standing on the other side, clad entirely in black, with her hair slicked back behind her ears. Ava noticed her eyes shift, as Florence's hand rubbed against her arm.

"You know, we're not about to rob a bank, Flo," Ava quipped, closing the door behind her. "What's the rush, anyway?"

"Come on, Ava, it's not like you have a busy schedule anymore," Florence said, linking her arm through Ava's and crossing the road. "Emily texted me. She'll be out all night with Theo, leaving Cynthia home alone."

Ava raised an eyebrow. She couldn't be upset or jealous over Emily. It was nice, in the typical boring Emily kind of way, that she'd found someone to be with. "Ah, perfect timing for us to check up on her then." Their laughter reverberated through the narrow streets.

"Ava! Flo!" a voice called from behind. They both spun to find Rose waving at them from across the road. She was frantically waving as she walked towards them.

"Rose, what's going on? Is everything all right?" Ava inquired.

Rose strode toward them, her hair tucked back. "I was

wondering if the police had reached out to you?"

Ava's spine stiffened. Had news about Nick leaked? Had they run out of time? "The police? About what?"

"The woman's body found in the lake. The police released an updated report after the post-mortem. They're reluctantly revealing more information to generate interest. It's all over the news. I was going to go see Edna and Larry and watch the report with them."

"Why would the police contact me about it?" Ava snapped.

Rose's glow quickly faded at Ava's reply.

"Sorry, I thought they might have kept you informed since you both found it. She'd have been over eighty years old if she was alive today."

Ava bit her lip, her gaze shifting towards Emily's house. "Well, why don't you go talk to Edna and Larry about it? The old cronies might have known her."

Florence playfully slapped Ava's arm. "You know what? They just might. They've been around here for ages. Even looking at Edna's house will transport you back in time."

Rose nodded. "One of my friends mentioned that the murder and the redevelopment coincided, you know."

Ava scrutinised Rose from head to toe. She was well dress tonight. Rose had suddenly became more... confidant, Ava thought. Her clothes were ever so slightly tighter. She'd pulled her shoulders up, less slouched. Not so much like a mouse anymore. Like the little sister she used to be. "Since when did you have friends?"

Rose narrowed her eyes. "I have plenty, thank you. Besides, Benny is a special friend. He mentioned that a company bought this place, and people online think the murder was to do with their profit-making."

"You know, it could be true." Florence interjected.

"Wasn't that dreadful politician's father the owner of the company that acquired this place? I recall Oscar complaining endlessly about the land issues when he wanted to expand the garage."

Ava regarded her friends with a puzzled expression. She couldn't even remember the last time she gave the news any attention. As for politics, well, as long as her earnings weren't being taxed, she didn't care what was going on in the world. "Hold on a second. Who is this dreadful man you're referring to?"

"Oh, you know," Florence replied. "That Sir Banks guy campaigning to become the Prime Minister. His father is the one who bought this entire area, evicted all the residents, and constructed these houses instead. Well, everyone except for Edna, of course." Florence leaned closer to Rose, grinning. "Your 'special friend' might actually be onto something."

Rose's face flushed crimson, betraying her embarrassment. To spare Rose from any further awkwardness, Ava turned towards Emily's house.

"Well, have a lovely time testing that theory, Rose. We're off to check up on Cynthia's well-being. One can never be too cautious when it comes to someone of her age," Ava said, flashing a smile as she tugged Florence along. She had matters to attend to and preferred to avoid any more distractions.

Ava swung the front door open without bothering to knock or wait for Cynthia to answer. She stormed inside, having replayed each word she planned to say on the walk over. Darkness enveloped the kitchen, save for a solitary lamp illuminating Cynthia's chair. Even at nighttime, she was clearly trying to save on the electricity bill. Florence grasped Ava's wrist, urging her to slow down, pointing towards

Cynthia in her chair. They approached cautiously, Cynthia's head drooped, sinking into her chin. Ava exchanged a wide-eyed glance with Florence and leaned closer to Cynthia. She noticed the absence of any visible chest movements or the sound of her breathing. Taking a step back, Ava accidentally bumped into a coffee table and clutched Florence's arm to steady herself. "Is she..." Ava whispered, her voice barely audible.

The coffee table wobbled, causing an empty mug to crash onto the floor, shattering the silence. Suddenly, Cynthia's face brightened, her eyes widening as she looked at Ava. "What in blazes is going on?" she grumbled, struggling to her feet. "What the bloody hell are you two doing here?" Cynthia glanced around the darkened kitchen and rubbed her eyes. She hobbled to the wall to switch on the main lights.

Florence raised her hands in a conciliatory gesture. "Apologies, Cynthia. Emily asked me to check up on you."

"We thought you might have... passed away," Ava admitted, absently inspecting her nails.

Cynthia huffed before settling back into her chair. "Nearly bloody did, waking up to you two gawking at me like that. Well, now that you've confirmed I'm alive, you can bugger off."

She leaned over and reached for a magazine, which Ava swiftly snatched from her fingers. "No, we're not quite finished yet. There are a few things we need to discuss with you."

Cynthia raised an eyebrow, her mouth falling open as Ava dangled the magazine in front of her. "Get on with it, then."

Ava glanced at Florence, who appeared to be checking the location of every exit in the house. Ava turned her attention to the window before pulling a chair closer to

Cynthia. "We want answers, Cynthia. No nonsense, just the unadulterated truth."

A smile played on her thin lips. "My, my, very serious."

"Florence and I have received some threats. Notes, letters, some photographs. I don't need to remind you about your past experiences using these forms of... *intimidation*, do I?"

Cynthia dropped her gaze to the floor. "I ain't proud of what we did—of what *I* did— but I thought we put all of that behind us."

Florence stepped forward, adopting a bold stance. "We believed the past was behind us until those letters arrived. Ava told me how you used the same tactics with her when you manipulated Doctor Mike into pushing her away, and then used me to set your plan in motion." Florence positioned herself behind Cynthia. "All we want to know is why. Why are you and Emily trying to harm us?"

Cynthia's face contorted as she rose to her feet, eyes wide. "Hold on a second. We haven't done a damn thing. I know nothing about any letter. What do they say, anyway?" she asked with a defiant lift of her chin.

Ava stood, raising her hand to keep Florence from responding. "Don't say a word, Flo. She's trying to gather information." Ava leaned closer until their faces were inches apart. "You already know what those letters say because you're the one behind the poison pen."

Cynthia erupted into laughter, every chuckle only fuelling Ava's anger. Ava clenched her hands into fists. "This isn't a joke!" she screamed.

"I told you; it has nothing to do with me. I thought we were well beyond this nonsense. Emily and I made a mistake, more so me than her. We're *friends*, and Emily genuinely cares for both of you. Whoever sent those letters, it certainly wasn't anyone in this house, I can assure you."

"How do you know Emily isn't orchestrating this behind your back?" Florence asked, bending down to collect the shards of the broken mug. Cynthia glared daggers at Florence. Ava assumed the mere mention of Emily doing any wrong was a line not to cross with her.

With a heavy sigh, she turned to Ava. "Because Emily received a letter too. So did your sister."

Ava searched Cynthia's eyes for any flicker of deception. "Rose? What letters?"

"I don't know. Emily thinks she's managed to hide it from me, but I overhear things—things I shouldn't. They've been discussing letters," Cynthia explained, shuffling toward the kitchen and switching on the kettle. "By my count, that's one letter for each of you."

Ava furrowed her brow, searching for a reason why Rose would have received a letter too. At first, Ava thought she was special. Now it turns out all four of them had received a letter, all living on the same street. Who could be behind it? And what is the reason behind it all? The only link she could think of was everything that went down with The Order a few months ago. "We need to figure this out. Why would all four of us receive these letters? There must be a connection."

Cynthia poured herself a cup of tea, contemplating the question. "There's only one person who's been causing trouble around here lately."

"Who?" Florence asked, leaning against the kitchen counter.

"That red-haired vixen who was staying with you a few weeks ago. I caught her snooping around Edna's house, chatting with all sorts of people in the neighbourhood. Why is she still lingering around here?"

Ava's mind raced, recalling her own encounter with Katherine, who warned her of the plummeting prices of their homes once news of the murder got out. Katherine never disclosed how she came to know such details and left Ava with more questions than answers. She thought about Rose and her involvement with The Order. Katherine had been a part of it, too. Ava looked at Florence, contemplating the potential knowledge Katherine might possess about her and Regina. Ava knew she was in contact with Lesley, having spread false rumours about Ava's promiscuity. It was possible that Olivia had told Lesley about Florence and Regina, who, in turn, told Katherine.

Ava nibbled on her lip. All these questions seemed to converge on one person. She glanced around the room. Cynthia's face stayed stern. Florence on the other hand had clear doubt laid across hers. "It makes sense, Flo. Katherine has mentioned nothing about receiving a letter. She's been parading around with money from who knows where. I think she might be involved."

Florence stared at them both, her expression blank. "But what would she gain from it? Why would she seek to hurt us after everything we've done for her?"

Cynthia cleared her throat, as if to re-assume control of the conversation. She slowly sipped her tea. "Katherine looks out for one person above all else. We all know the lengths she would go to in order to fulfil her own desires. If it means trampling over everyone she knows to get what she wants, she'll do it."

"When is Emily due back? Do you know?" asked Florence.

"Sometime tomorrow, as far as I know."

"Okay. Ava, text Rose and ask her to come here tomorrow. I'll inform Emily. All four of us need to sit down and work this out once and for all. No more excuses, no more lies, and no more secrets," Florence declared with determination.

CHAPTER TWENTY-FIVE
Out in the Open

Emily tapped her nails along the table, staring at Florence's text, requesting a meeting with Rose, Ava, and herself. She'd not been called to a meeting like this for awhile. If the request came from Rose, she might have some idea of what it was all about. But right now, she felt clueless in her own home.

When Emily returned home with Theo, her grandmother insisted she attend and refused to let her get out of it. It wasn't unusual for Cynthia to be forceful with others but never with Emily. Experiencing this side of her grandmother made Emily understand for the very first time why everyone who crossed paths with her fell in line.

Cynthia sent Theo to his room, and Emily longed to join him. She yearned to go over the events of the past few days, after learning that Rachel had passed away. While they had discussed nothing else during the entire ride home, it felt like there was still more to say on the matter.

Glancing at the clock, Emily turned to her gran. "Are you going to give me a warning before they arrive, or am I going in blind?"

Cynthia seemed to force a smile. "Just be honest. Tell them everything, and work together. Tonight is bigger than just you, Emily."

Emily turned away from her gran, finding no solace in her words. If her comment was intended to comfort her, it had the opposite effect.

The first to arrive was Rose, who was a bundle of nerves as she greeted Emily. Placing a jar full of biscuits on the table before Cynthia, she asked, "Is everyone okay? Any idea what this is about?"

Emily shot a pointed glance at Cynthia. "Ask her, although I doubt you'll get any answers." She plucked a biscuit from the jar, breathing in the smell of nutmeg, and taking a bite with a satisfying crunch. "How have things been? Anything to report before the others arrive?" Emily inquired, her mouth half full.

Rose shook her head. "No. It's been radio silent on all fronts. What do you think of the biscuit?"

Emily wiped her hands. "It's wonderful, just as I expected it would be coming from you."

"Benny has asked for a few to sell in his cafe. I've been playing around with the recipe, but I'll mark that as a pass," Rose smiled, closing the jar. "How was your trip to the Lake District?"

Emily mustered a half-smile. What could she say? The truth would only worry Rose more than she already was. Emily had hoped the trip to see Jessie would result in the identity of the person harassing her being exposed. That it would have put an end to it all. Instead it ended up with a crime scene and another of her friends dead. "It was fine. I'm just glad to be home."

A knock came from the door, and Ava waltzed into the room with Florence behind her. Ava placed a bottle of wine on the table to mark her entrance and removed her coat to reveal yet another stunning red dress beneath. "I see everyone is here. We really have perfected our timing, haven't we?"

"We come at your command, Ava. Please, take a seat," Emily said, patting the sofa.

"Cynthia, so nice to see you awake at this late hour," Ava greeted, extending her hand.

Cynthia shook it with a polite nod. "Phones," she requested. Ava retrieved her phone from her bag and handed it over, and Cynthia's stern gaze scanned the room. Florence surrendered her phone, and then Rose, despite seeming puzzled about the demand.

"What's going on, Gran?" Emily asked.

"Just taking precautions. I'll hold onto the phones while you talk. Now, hand it over," Cynthia instructed. She glanced around, confusion on her face, but understanding on Ava and Florence's. Emily retrieved her phone and checked it one last time before handing it over. "Right, I'm off," Cynthia declared with a sigh, hobbling towards her bedroom.

The atmosphere shifted as soon as Cynthia left, the tension growing. This gathering was not like their usual get-togethers. Florence and Ava had orchestrated this meeting without Rose or Emily having any prior knowledge.

"Alright, let's lay our cards on the table tonight, my loves." Ava declared, remaining standing. "We have a problem, and I, for one, refuse to stand idly by while someone takes advantage of us. So here we are, all four of us together as dear friends. Some new and some old." Ava glanced at Emily, and then Florence, "and some who are family." Ava stepped closer to Rose. Emily tried not to roll her eyes at Ava taking any opportunity for adding a spark of drama. "Now, we've all had our share of secrets in the past, but I believe I speak for all of us when I say we won't tolerate blackmail or threats to our lives." Ava paused, taking a breath. "So, we've all received letters. Cynthia has already confirmed she knows something about you two."

Emily stared at Rose, whose hands trembled in her lap. How did Cynthia know about Rose's letter? Yet Emily was more intrigued that Ava and Florence had received similar ones. Suddenly, everything Emily thought she knew crumbled to ashes, and her theories about who might be behind it all instantly vanished.

"Letters?" Rose stuttered, gripping the fabric of her skirt. "What were your letters about?" Her eyes widened as she glanced at Emily.

Florence reached for Ava's hand, bringing it closer. "This is why Ava and I felt the need to gather us all here. I believe we can trust each other. We must share our secrets, one by one. We need to understand our letters , so we can work together to figure this out."

Emily took a breath. Talking about secrets was fine, but she doubted the others would end in prison time for murder if they got out. Rose's voice quivered as she spoke, "But what if some of the letters are worse than others?"

"No judgement here." Ava said. "Whatever is said tonight remains strictly between us. Deal?" Ava proposed, scanning her eyes across the group.

Emily looked around the room. She glanced at Rose for a split second. Was she about to tell the room that they left George to die? What would Florence think of them if she knew the truth? Emily gave a quick smile at Ava. Maybe she would finally see Emily as an equal, if she knew what she had done to help her sister. Everyone nodded in agreement. As Emily looked around the room of her newfound friends, she was transported back to the first time they were all together in this very house, occupying the same seats. The only thing missing now was their husbands by their sides. Emily could never forget how nervous she had been that night, carrying the guilt of her impending betrayal while building a web of lies to befriend these women. But now, all this time later, she considered them her closest allies. She was afraid to admit the truth and reveal the secrets she had kept, but deep down, she knew she could trust them. It was the only way to unravel the mystery and get to the bottom of it.

"So, who wants to go first?" Ava asked, raising an eyebrow.

Florence raised her hand and took a sip of her water. "I will," she said, a vulnerable edge to her voice. "It might sound silly and insignificant, but whoever is behind this has been following me and taking photos of me in private." Ava reached for Florence's hand. "It's something I've struggled with my whole life, and I've always made choices to hide away from it. But in the past year, things have changed, and I found someone. Someone I truly love." Florence wiped a tear from her cheek. Emily leaned closer. "It's Regina. We've been seeing each other in secret. I was just about to come out and tell everyone when my parents arrived, and, well, it turned into my worst nightmare." Another tear fell, and Emily could see Florence's cheeks flushed with emotion. "Someone took photos of us and threatened to expose our relationship before we were ready. Having my control taken away made me want to hide it for longer."

Emily and Rose got up from their seats and moved to sit beside Florence. Emily knelt on the ground, holding the hand that Ava clasped tightly. She hated that anyone could be made to feel this way. Emily imagined the years that Florence had kept this part of her hidden. The hurt she must have felt. She wiped a tear as she got closer to her friend. "It's okay, Flo. You're safe here, and you can say whatever you need to."

Rose nodded, wiping a tear from Florence's cheek. "Of course. We're genuinely happy for you, you know. All of us," Rose looked at Ava and Emily. "We'll find a way to work through this."

Florence wiped her nose with her sleeve and sniffled. "Thank you. I know it may not sound like much, but I need to find out who the person behind this is. I need to feel safe again." She exhaled. "God, it feels good to get that off my chest. I feel lighter already."

"Okay, who's next?" Ava asked, breaking the silence.

Emily looked at Rose. They both nodded at each other. An unspoken contract between them, that tonight, they were willing to let their guard down. "Ours are linked, we believe." Emily stood and walked toward the side table, retrieving the letter from the drawer. "Mine was more of a warning, telling me not to trust the people around me. I'm not entirely sure, but I think whoever sent it was trying to make me push people away. Rose received a letter at the same time." Emily turned to Rose to give her the space to express it in her own words.

Rose took a deep breath and began, "Well, all of you helped me when George died. You all backed up the story I wanted to tell the police, and I suppose some of you might have guessed that things weren't what they seemed that night." She looked at Emily. "George attacked me, and if it wasn't for Emily, I don't know what he would have done."

Ava's eyes widened and she brought her hand to her mouth. "Emily, you were there?"

Emily nodded.

"She came to speak to me," Rose continued, "Yet found George on top of me and pulled him away. He fell down the stairs, and, well... I asked something of her that has haunted me since."

Ava smiled, a touch of understanding in her expression. "You left him there to die, didn't you? Can't say I blame you."

Florence nodded in agreement. "We all know the lengths some men can go to. There's no blame here, Rose."

Rose slumped down. Her face lowering towards the floor.

"But someone does blame me because they know. They know I killed him," Rose confessed, looking at Emily. "Someone else received a letter too. I'm sorry I didn't tell you, Emily, but it's a secret I had to keep for a while. George had another wife."

Emily recoiled. She couldn't believe what she was hearing. She thought Rose had shared everything with her. "Another *wife*?"

"Yes. Whoever this is, they sent a letter to her and informed her that George was murdered."

Emily panicked then. More than ever before. She knew the person behind this reached far, knowing the threats to Theo's family in Japan. But now there were others. A stranger with the power to send her to prison for murder, or to at least involve the police to start asking questions. How far could one person's power reach?

Ava crossed her arms, deep in thought. "Who else knew about her?"

Rose shrugged. "I don't know. As far as I'm aware, no one else knew. I've spoken to her, and we've sorted everything out. She won't say anything."

"So, it's not her?" Ava scanned the room. Emily noticed

Florence's eyes widen. "What? She could be behind all of this."

"It must be someone who knew George, someone who knew about his secret," Emily pondered, turning to Rose. "Any idea who it could be?"

Rose shook her head, and then Florence raised her hand, a flicker of uncertainty crossing her features. "Wait, this might be a long shot. But both you and George saw Doctor Mike for therapy sessions in the past, right?"

"Yes," Rose confirmed. "Only one or two sessions before George put a stop to it. I think he was afraid I'd reveal too much to him."

Florence tapped her fingers along her chin. With a sigh, she continued.

"I paid a visit to him in prison, thinking he might be behind my letters before I found out that all of you had received them too," Florence continued. "He told me that someone in the prison had paid an inmate to gather information on all of us—someone who wanted answers from Mike for information only he'd know from us being his clients for all those years."

Emily wasn't sure what she preferred. When it was only her and Rose with letters, she could attempt to make things add up. With Theo's involvement, she knew it had to be personal to her. But now so many more people were at risk. It seemed like every person she's ever cared about was now on the edge of being ruined.

Ava turned her gaze toward Florence, perplexed. "Well, that doesn't explain my letter. It happened after Mike was already in prison."

"Come on, then, Ava. You're the final piece of the puzzle. What was your letter about?" asked Emily.

Ava gave a nervous chuckle. "You know, I thought it

would be easier sitting here and listening to all of you, but now that it's my turn, I feel a little tense." She glanced around the room, her shoulders raised.

Emily rose and walked over to the kitchen, returning with a bottle of whisky from Cynthia's liquor cabinet. She uncorked it and poured a shot, handing it to Ava. "Something to loosen you up."

Ava downed it in one gulp, coughing slightly to clear her throat. "I'm just going to come out and say it." Ava paused. "Nick's alive." Emily heard Rose gasp, clutching her hand to her mouth. Ava's gaze drifted across the room. "I had no idea. To be honest, I was a little taken aback when I found him at home. It turns out someone else was surprised too. They took a photo of me inside the house with him, just before I closed the curtains."

Emily struggled to hide her reaction. She had secretly relished the thought that Nick had been punished for what he'd done, not only what he'd done to her, but to her father. Knowing he may have suffered until his last breath was a thought she had held on to. But knowing he was alive pained her deeply, but she concealed her disappointment from Ava, not wanting her to notice the betrayal in her eyes upon discovering that monstrous man was still out there.

"How can he be alive?" Emily whispered. "They found his body in the fire, and he left a message to you, dying." Images of the fire remained vivid in Emily's memory—the smell of burning flesh, the chaos, and destruction.

"He tried to explain it away. He claimed he was protecting Katherine. People within The Order wanted to expose them for the art scam and punish her for what she did all those years ago," Ava explained, her eyes flashing with anger. "I told him to leave and never come back. But whoever saw us together wants to see me in prison, and that's not an option for me. Not again."

Florence leaned forward. Her face was hard, serious. "Katherine's name keeps coming up. We suspect it's her."

Emily and Rose exchanged a guilty look when Ava said, "Why are you two looking at each other like that?"

Emily averted her gaze to the floor, holding her breath. Tonight's meeting was difficult. So many hidden secrets had piled between them all. She looked up, giving Rose a slight nod. "Katherine is still involved with The Order, or at least a faction of it. We both witnessed her staying in the same manor house as another member from higher up. Violet left Rose a list of its members when she died, and Katherine wanted it. When Rose refused to give it up, we suddenly received an offer from a man, who I'm sure you have all heard of by now, named Sir Kenneth Banks." Emily let out a sigh. "He promised to eliminate our troubles in exchange for the information. We think Katherine is working alongside him."

"I can't believe it," Florence murmured. "He's been all over the news. He's running for bloody prime minister, and yet he's mixed up in this? Really?"

Emily nodded, feeling a cold chill run down her spine. The idea that a man so prominent in politics could be entwined in their darkest secrets was almost too much to bear. "We've got to be careful," Emily added, her face pale. "This changes everything."

Florence looked at the woman. "So, what are we saying here? Has Katherine used the money from The Order to investigate our lives and threaten us to retrieve the list from Rose?"

"It's possible," Emily said. "It depends on how much Mike knew and if he shared any information. But George died before Katherine even returned to Beechwood."

Ava poured herself another shot, seeming to be deep in contemplation. "The police could have suspected something. We were always told The Order had influential members. Katherine makes sense. She has a motive and stands to gain the most. It all adds up."

Florence tapped her fingers on the coffee table. She clicked her fingers as her eyes lit up. "Wait, you mentioned Sir Kenneth Banks, right?" Rose nodded. "He's related to the 'Banks' who owned the company that helped to build this place, right?"

"Banks & Son Industries," Rose confirmed. Emily watched as Rose's eyes darted in all direction. Her lips slightly apart as she worked everything out. "Of course! The Banks family played a part in funding the construction. My friend Benny mentioned it to me, but I never connected the dots until now."

Emily stood abruptly. "Theo!" she called.

Ava grabbed her shoulder, yanking her back into her seat. "What are you doing?"

Theo's head appeared at the top of the stairs. "Can I help with something?"

Emily nodded. "Can you do a search? Look up anything related to Sir Kenneth Banks, his family, their building business, and Beechwood Close."

Theo nodded and pressed his glasses up the bridge of his nose. "I'll see what I can find."

Ava rolled her eyes. "Why are we looking into him? We have the answer—Katherine. Let's expose her and run her out of town."

"We have to be smarter than that," Emily replied. "There's a connection here, something linking everything together. If we find that connection, we can use it to stop Katherine. Ask yourself this: why would Katherine send me a letter, warning me about not trusting the friends I've made?"

Ava shrugged, reclining on the sofa. "Maybe she's just crazy. I don't know."

Theo hurried downstairs, balancing his laptop in one hand. "I found something. Banks & Son Industries purchased the plot here for redevelopment. They were funded by a private source."

"That would be The Order, I bet," Rose chimed in.

Theo continued, "There's an article here where Sir Banks Sr. allowed his son to plan and manage the construction of Beechwood Close. It was his first major opportunity."

Ava swirled her whisky around her glass, seeming to grow more disinterested by the minute. "So what? That's not a big deal. Rich daddy gives son a job."

"But there was another article years later, claiming that the building's conditions were poor and mismanaged," Theo explained. "Builders and workers complained about loss of wages, but nothing came of it. The trail just disappeared, and the articles stopped."

Ava bolted upright. "The body!" she exclaimed. "The lake was filled in towards the end of the construction, right? It's always the last thing to be done on site. What if a worker or someone tried to expose Kenneth, and he hid the evidence?"

"But how did he manage to erase all records of it from the press?" asked Florence.

"It's The Order." Rose said. "He's a member, and his father must have been too."

Theo turned to Emily. "Am I missing something?"

Ava leaned forward, stroking Theo's chin. Emily watched Ava's every move. She wasn't worried, but you could never be too careful when Ava and men were concerned. "Oh, love, you're missing out on so much. Best not to worry."

Emily's head spun from the influx of information. The

complexity of it all clouded even the simplest of thoughts. "I'm still uncertain about Katherine," she confessed. "But something is happening here, and we're closer to the truth than we were half an hour ago. I think I know someone who might have more information."

"Who?" Florence asked, intrigued.

"Let Gran and me work on that. I'll keep all of you updated."

CHAPTER TWENTY-SIX
Living a Lie

Florence clung to Regina's hand to draw strength from her presence before facing the daunting conversation ahead. With a soft smile, Florence met Regina's kind almond eyes, their warmth steadying her racing pulse.

She paused before her mother, who remained absorbed in her book. She didn't even look up. Florence tried to ignore the pang of sadness at her mother's obliviousness to the fact her daughter stood just two feet away, holding hands with her partner. Florence had anticipated this moment her entire life and now had to find the courage to share the news with one of her parents.

When Florence introduced Oscar to them in the past, she had hoped that would be the end of it. She believed those cherished moments she had dreamt of were meant for another lifetime, a path she would never have to tread. But circumstances had brought her to this point, and now she stood tall and proud, ready to face the truth with Regina by her side.

The letters, pictures, and threats no longer held power over her. Florence found the strength to face this conversation thanks to the love and support of her friends. No matter how it ended, she had nothing to fear. She was determined to stand beside Regina, be true to herself, and live her life on her own terms.

Regina leaned closer to Florence and whispered, "Are you ready?" Florence nodded and took a deep breath, stepping forward toward her mother. Her mother's gaze shifted from the book to meet Florence's eyes before returning to the pages. Florence felt her chest flush. Yet there was a subtle change in her mother as she slightly raised her head. Florence knew she noticed their entwined hands. The room stilled, the air thick with unspoken tension.

Her mother placed the book on the coffee table with deliberate care before resting her hands on her lap. Slowly, she turned her head to meet Florence's gaze, her eyes vacant and devoid of emotion.

"We have something we need to say," Florence finally said, her voice steady, yet tinged with apprehension. She smiled at her father, who sank deeper into the sofa by the window. He brought his shoulders up around his neck as he braced himself.

Joan's next words dripped with disdain. "I can see that. But what on earth do you think you're doing?" She turned her body away, so she faced the wall, as if shielding herself from Florence's presence. "Silly girl," she tutted.

Regina leaned forward instinctively to speak, but Florence gently placed a hand on her shoulder, pulling her back. "Regina makes me happy, Mum," Florence asserted, with a slight quiver in her voice. She despised the idea of seeming vulnerable before her mother and quickly cleared her throat, attempting to mask any hint of distress. "I'm not going to stand here and let you pretend this is news. You've known for as long as I have."

"I knew nothing of the sort." She pursed her lips and narrowed her gaze to scrutinise Regina further. "Is this your new habit? Preying on a grieving widow and turning her into... *this*?"

Regina bit her lip and her eyes widened. Standing beside her, Florence felt strength she'd never noticed before. What she had here, now. It felt right. "I have brought happiness to your daughter, Joan. And she has shown me what real love feels like," she replied.

Florence pulled Regina's hand gently towards her in a silent plea to hold back. Meanwhile, her mother's cheeks turned a violent shade of red.

"This is her home," Regina continued, her voice growing stronger. "This is the life you missed out on for all these years. You weren't here when she lost Oscar, when she fought for her life, when she resorted to alcohol to numb the pain caused by *your* absence. You were nowhere to be seen!" Regina now leaned over Joan and pointed her finger directly at her chest. Florence glanced towards her father in the background. He hadn't moved an inch.

Joan turned away from Regina and walked toward the window to join her husband. "Flo, it was just a phase. You were young and attention seeking. I understand that now, and I know you're looking for attention again. You want our love," Joan stated, stroking Gill's shoulder in what would be an affectionate gesture, if Florence didn't see it for what it was. Her asserting control. Joan glared at Regina. "I think it would be best if you left. You lot are nothing but trouble, and you can't fool me. You would never fit into this family. Leave us to talk."

Florence clung onto Regina's hand, her grip steady and resolute. She felt Regina's warm breath on her neck, a grounding presence amidst the rising tension. Her mother was playing the same manipulative games she always did, just like Florence had anticipated.

Before Florence could retaliate, Lucas stormed down the stairs, his anger swelling in his eyes. He positioned himself between them, confronting his grandmother with a clenched jaw. "Regina has been a rock for all of us, Gran. She stood by us through everything. You take back what you just said!" he shouted. Florence instinctively stepped forward. Joan's body stiffened. She clearly didn't expect anyone to argue back, especially her grandson.

"Lucas, you don't have to," Regina interjected, but Lucas turned to his granddad, his frustration evident.

"Are you going to say anything? Are you going to stand up for your daughter? For my *mother*?" he demanded.

Florence's father squirmed in his seat, seemingly torn between loyalty to his wife and the desire to support his daughter. She loved her father dearly, yet recognised his kindness for weakness. His eyes shifted from Joan's piercing gaze to the floor, and that simple gesture alone dissipated Florence's hope that he would finally stand up for her.

"Are you going to say anything, Florence?" Joan turned her attention to her daughter, her voice biting. "Will you let your son speak to your father like that? Get a backbone, girl, and sort out this mess of a family."

Stepping forward, Florence wrapped her arm around Lucas, pulling him closer to her and Regina. "The family I need is right here, the ones I've had in this home all along. If you won't accept this, then you are not welcome here,"

Florence declared, lifting her chin.

Joan laughed without humour, her gaze lingering on Regina, before refocusing on Florence. "Silly, silly girl. You're throwing everything away for something that won't last a year," she scoffed before turning to Gill. "We're staying. We'll work things out."

Lucas shifted his attention to his grandfather, and the sharpness in his next words cut through the tension. "Such a strong marriage, Granddad, built on trust and honesty... Maybe it's time to speak up?" His piercing gaze bore into Gill, like a spotlight exposing hidden truths.

Florence watched the gears turning in her father's mind as the furrows on his forehead deepened. She knew his secrets and the sacrifices he had made to protect Lucas. It pained her to witness Lucas using this knowledge against his own grandfather in such a manner. But she allowed it to happen. She'd learnt over the past year that no relationship can live with secrets being kept.

Gill rose from his seat and faced his wife. "Come on. I think it's best we go."

Joan scrunched up her face, her eyes flitting between Florence and Gill. "No, Gill. I won't go."

"We are going. Pack a bag, and we can collect the rest later. No questions," Gill asserted, shouldering past Lucas and giving Florence one last look before forcefully slamming the door behind him. She caught a glimmer of sadness in Lucas' eyes. His grandfather had saved him not long ago. It couldn't have been easy to do what he did. But Florence knew she would be forever grateful.

Joan followed in his footsteps, and passing her daughter, she snarled, "Your family will never be complete. One day, you'll find yourself in the exact same place I am now." She scowled at Regina.

"Your daughter is better off where she is, away from you and out of this home."

With the resounding slam of the door, Florence stood frozen, the weight of the moment sinking in. Her body trembled, not enough for others to notice, but she could feel it. Every bit of blood in her body pounded in her head as her mothers words echoed. *'Your family will never be complete.'* Lucas and Regina embraced Florence, enveloping her in their love. Deep down, she couldn't deny her mother was right. Her family had not been complete for a long time, and the ache of that absence remained.

Florence's footsteps echoed as she rushed past the front gates, kicking up white stones with every hurried stride. Beyond the splashing fountain were the imposing wooden doors marking the entrance to Lesley's mansion. Olivia was here, and Florence desperately needed to find her daughter. Missed calls and unanswered messages were no longer enough. Florence had shattered their family, and she was determined to bring them back together again.

Silence enveloped the once vibrant halls of the mansion. The walls and rooms served as silent witnesses to a life that had become a mere memory. Florence thought of Johnny, and the tragic loss he suffered in the fire, leaving Lesley alone. A grandchild was the only glimmer of hope that kept Lesley moving forward. Florence paused, debating whether to intervene and take away the only thing Lesley had left. But Lesley wasn't the only one losing something in this situation. Florence had lost her daughter to the allure of money and an easier life.

Soft music reached Florence's ears as she navigated her way to the kitchen. To her surprise, Olivia was the only one there, with her back to Florence as she held a glass of wine in one hand and gripped the counter with the other. She sipped slowly, lost in thought. A bottle of wine sat beside her. Olivia hadn't noticed her mother's presence until Florence was right there, close enough to catch the scent of grapes and alcohol emanating from her daughter's breath. Florence gently tapped her on the shoulder. "Is Lesley around?"

Startled, Olivia gasped and straightened, her eyes widening at the sight of her mother. "Mum?"

Florence folded her arms, shifting her gaze from the wine to Olivia. Olivia's lips formed a slight pout, reminiscent of her younger days whenever she was caught in a mischievous act. "It's not what it looks like."

"I think I know the smell of wine. I've had enough practice hiding the stuff," said Florence, reaching for the bottle. "What on earth do you think you're doing, drinking in your condition? Does Lesley know about this? Has she given you permission? Because it isn't okay."

"I know. I shouldn't have done it, but I needed a little release," Olivia admitted.

Florence shook her head, unable to hide her disappointment. "Come on. I'm here to bring you back. We need you home, love."

"I can't. I... I don't want to move back home," Olivia protested, running her hands through her hair.

"What's going on? Talk to me," Florence pleaded.

Olivia's voice quivered as she replied, exposing her vulnerability. "So you can slap me again?"

Florence's heart clenched as she listened to Olivia's words. She pulled a stool closer and sat down, the weight of guilt heavy on her shoulders. "I'm sorry. Truly. I lost my temper. I was under a lot of stress that day, but that's no excuse. I shouldn't have done it. I regret it, I really do, and I miss you so much. Regina misses you too."

Olivia sighed, her tears flowing freely. She pulled the sleeves of her hoodie around her wrists and hid her face in her arms. "I miss you guys too. But I can't go, I can't leave her."

"Lesley?" Olivia nodded. "She will understand. I can speak to her. Maybe we can come to an arrangement when the baby arrives."

Olivia burst into tears then, burying her face in her arms. Florence lifted her daughter's chin to meet her gaze. "Come on, what's the matter?" Florence urged. "Talk to me. I'm here now. Share with me what's been going on."

With tear-filled eyes, Olivia mumbled, "You won't like it."

"Try me. I'm in a very forgiving mood," Florence assured her, rubbing Olivia's back gently. "I told Gran about Regina. She and Granddad stormed off. There's plenty of room at home now."

Olivia lifted her head from her arms. "Gran's gone? Really?"

Florence chuckled. "You don't have to sound too happy about it. She cared for you. Wasn't she the one you called a while back, anyway? She certainly enjoyed rubbing that in my face."

Olivia pulled at her sleeves. Florence watched as she scratched at her wrist. She wasn't the only one in the family who had such an obvious tell.

"I wanted to speak to you, but she answered. I didn't have my phone at the time, and the only number I could remember was home."

Florence's mind had been all over the place recently. She remembered her mother saying Olivia had called. How she'd asked to see only her. Florence didn't think anything of it at the time, but now, with clarity, it was painfully obvious something was wrong with that story. "She made it out like you specifically requested her. I should have known better, really," Florence said, looking into Olivia's eyes, who peeked at Florence from between her arms. "What was it all about? I'm here now."

"It's too late. Now I'm in an even bigger mess because of Gran, and she's left!" Olivia cried.

Florence gently held Olivia's chin and lifted her upright, urging her to face the truth. "What happened?" she asked, ignoring the pounding in her heart.

Olivia's eyes darted around the room, avoiding Florence's gaze. "When I called, I was in the hospital," she admitted, her voice barely above a whisper.

Florence's heart sank. "Hospital?"

"It was the baby. I had pains. Lesley had left me here alone for days, while she went to see some man. I didn't think anything of it, and then I started bleeding. I left my phone at home, and Gran said she would come meet me."

"Liv, is..." Florence's voice trailed off, the question lingering in the air. She looked at Olivia again then—truly looked at her—taking in the wine glass, the baggy jumper, and the emptiness in her daughter's eyes. The answer became painfully clear. Florence pulled Olivia close, wrapping her arms tightly around her as tears streamed down both their faces.

"Lesley doesn't know," Olivia whispered, her voice muffled against Florence's chest.

"What? Has she not returned since?"

"Gran had an idea. She told me to keep the thought of a grandchild going while Lesley was still paying me," Olivia explained, her head sinking in shame. "I didn't know what to do. I had left home. Lesley had given me everything, and I had taken it all. She talked about Johnny and how happy she was to have a grandchild. I shouldn't have done it. I shouldn't have listened to Gran, but she was desperate. Lucas had told me about Granddad; I knew they had lost all their money, and I wanted to help, to find a way for them to leave you, so things could return to normal."

Tears continued to stream down Florence's face as she listened to Olivia's confession. "I'm so sorry, Liv. I'm sorry I wasn't there. I'm sorry that she put that burden on you," Florence whispered. She stood then and wiped away her tears. "Get your things. Pack up and come home."

Olivia hesitated. "What about Lesley? She's going to be furious when she finds out."

Florence held Olivia's hands and gave them a gentle squeeze. "We'll deal with her. Together. We'll face the consequences, but we'll face them as a family."

CHAPTER TWENTY-SEVEN
Tight Lipped

Emily sat beside Cynthia and tapped the scorching radiator beside them on the sofa, despite the blazing sun outside. Edna's house was like living in a different climate. Emily understood the elderly often felt the cold more intensely, but Emily was perspiring in just a simple t-shirt.

Shifting uncomfortably, Emily leaned over to retrieve the glass of ice water she had requested, wrapping her hands against the cool surface. The fleeting sensation brought her a momentary relief from the stuffiness indoors.

Larry sat across from Emily, his eyes shadowed by the weight of caring for Edna in recent months. Emily offered him a reassuring smile. "Is she all right in there?" Emily asked, glancing toward the kitchen. "If you need assistance, Edna, I'm here to help!" she called.

A loud crash echoed from the kitchen, accompanied by

the sound of shattered glass. Emily sprang to her feet and gestured towards Cynthia and Larry to stay put. "I'll go check. Gran, please keep Larry company."

As Emily entered the kitchen, she discovered Edna on her knees, clutching a drawer handle with a trembling hand. A small broken glass lay scattered on the floor with a few sizeable shards at Edna's feet. Her overly large eyes pleaded for Emily to help. She knelt to swiftly clear the shards away before extending her hand towards Edna. Just as she anticipated, Edna extended her thin, trembling hand, and Emily firmly grasped it, helping her to her feet.

"Thank you, love. I'm not as steady on my feet these days," Edna murmured before turning to the kettle. Leaning against the counter, she sighed. "Do you mind pouring? I'd hate to create any more mess. I don't want my Larry to witness me like this."

Emily smiled, playing along with Edna's charade. Ava's quiet word in Emily's ear had come in handy. Things become so clear when you've been told the truth. Emily turned towards the window and rinsed her hand under the sink, glancing outside at the serene view of the lake peeking between the trees and bushes. "You're incredibly fortunate, to have the best view in the neighbourhood," Emily remarked.

Emily glanced at Edna, who rolled her eyes. "Should we return to the living room? I don't always trust my Larry around a woman like your grandmother."

"Did you ever consider it?" Emily leaned against the counter, gazing again at the breathtaking panorama of rolling treetops and the glistening lake peering through.

"Consider what? What are you talking about, girl?"

"When the redevelopment happened, were you ever tempted to accept the offer and move out?" Emily clarified. Edna's face wrinkled at the mention of moving.

Edna chuckled. "No chance. I made it clear to those builders from day one that I wasn't budging, and I didn't. This old place might seem like decaying wood to all of you, but to me, it's home. I intended to die here back then, and I still do now."

Emily turned to face Edna, the distant murmurs of Cynthia and Larry's conversation floating in from the other room. "Have you heard anything about the body they found down there?" she asked, lowering her voice.

Edna stumbled, her hand instinctively reaching towards her head. Emily tried her best to conceal a smile, although she feared her acting wasn't on par with Edna's. "Sorry, dear. Feeling a bit faint," she murmured. Slowly, she walked towards the lounge. "Are you coming?"

Emily trailed behind Edna as they entered the living room, grateful for the opportunity to ask further questions.

Larry extended his hand towards Edna as she settled beside him. "What were you two chatting about in there? Are you feeling alright, dear?"

"Just reminiscing about old memories," Emily interjected smoothly. Edna nodded along. "I was quizzing Edna about the history of this place—the close and the bungalow."

Larry chuckled. "My, my. Edna has always been stubborn, even back then. Who would have thought the original property would still be standing here?"

Edna pursed her lips, a flicker of annoyance crossing her face.

Passing a cup of tea to Cynthia, Emily continued, "I was just curious about the building work that took place around here. It must have been quite a nightmare to live through all of it. Were you around at the time, Larry?"

Larry placed a hand under his chin. "In the area, yes, but nowhere near Beechwood. Although I do recall the council facing quite a challenge to get it all approved. But as always, they emerged victorious in the end," Larry replied with a chuckle.

"Not here. I put my foot down," Edna interjected. Cynthia's eyes darted to meet Emily's. She was practically beaming as a smile raced along her face.

"I wanted to ask you about the builders, Edna. Did you ever hear of any issues? Reports of mistreatment, accidents, or injuries involving the builders or contractors?" Emily asked.

Edna shuffled in her seat with a small groan. "No, can't say I do," she said, taking a sip of her tea. "Shall we discuss something else?"

Emily exchanged a brief glance with Cynthia, communicating their understanding. "I was speaking with Ava the other day, Edna. She mentioned an incident when she walked in on you while Larry was out." Emily's smile thinned as Edna's face contorted; she cried out to Larry, clutching her head.

Concerned, Larry stood up and leaned over. "Darling, what's wrong?"

"Ouch! Oh, the pain is unbearable! Love, please fetch my headache pills. They're in the bathroom in our bedroom," Edna exclaimed with a dismissive wave of her hand. "Cynthia, go with him. He might bring back the wrong ones."

Cynthia huffed. "Come on, let's go get the poison instead." She prodded Larry and left the room.

Edna opened one eye, waiting until Larry and Cynthia had left. When they were gone, she straightened and faced Emily with a look of alertness. "Alright, what do you want?" she snapped.

Emily smiled and took a sip of her tea. "Ava suggested using that ploy if necessary. Consider yourself lucky that I haven't informed Gran about your fabricated illness," she whispered, leaning closer. "And *poor* Larry... It's truly heartbreaking to witness what you're putting him through."

"What do you want to know?" Edna said defiantly, raising an eyebrow.

"About the construction work. I want to know about the body found in the lake. Was it true that the lake was the last thing to be completed around here?"

Edna shrugged. "How in blazes would I know? It's been forty odd years. I have no recollection."

"It's important, Edna. Do you remember any of the staff? The person in charge, Kenneth Banks?"

Edna turned to face Emily, folding her arms. "No idea."

Edna was hiding something and intentionally avoided answering the questions.

"Tell me, Edna," Emily said, "Otherwise, I'll go over there right now and reveal the truth to Larry. You will lose him!"

Edna cackled, yet it was an eerie sound devoid of amusement. "Please. I have him under control. I don't appreciate threats, Miss, and I certainly don't appreciate you dredging up the past. This place has already been ruined enough by the likes of you moving in, changing everything, and disrupting the status quo." Edna pointed a bony finger in Emily's direction. "Leave the past where it belongs, or you'll witness a side of me you wish you hadn't awakened. Understood?"

Emily nodded, and with that, Edna rose from her seat, called out to Larry, and hobbled away towards the back bedroom. Emily was left even more bewildered than before. Edna's abrupt change in mood felt like a personal attack.

Cynthia poked her head around the corner to break the silence. "The old bat said she needs to sleep. Did you learn anything?" she asked.

Emily shook her head in frustration. "No, nothing we didn't already know. But she exploded when I asked about the lake and the builders here. She went off the rails. What could that be about?"

"She's just a bitter old woman. Who knows?" Cynthia shrugged, running her finger along the dusty mantle. "Look at this, though." She gestured toward a series of framed photographs displayed on a wooden unit. "The many husbands of Edna Howard," Cynthia declared with a hint of morbid curiosity.

Emily pushed herself up from the uncomfortable sofa and examined the photos lined along two shelves. Each frame depicted a different man, captured on their wedding day or within the confines of their home. Emily picked up one photo, captivated by the strikingly handsome young man. The couple posed in a dancing large hall, arms entwined with each other as blurred couples danced behind them. Emily had never seen Edna so happy before. "Look at this," she exclaimed, turning the photo around to reveal the inscription, *'Rupert and Edna, First Date - 1973.'*

Beside that photo, three others of Rupert were prominently displayed—far more than any of the other husbands. "I suppose he must have been her first husband," Cynthia said.

Emily reached for another photo, her eyes widening when she had a closer look "Gran," she beckoned, tapping on the glass. "He must have been a builder." The photo captured Rupert, clad in overalls, smiling at the camera. It seemed to have been taken on the porch. Emily examined the image, noting the yellowed signs of ageing and creases. Turning it over, she discovered the year marked as 1984. Cynthia leaned in, squinting to examine the details more closely. "That bag next to him, it's a plastic builder's sack—the kind they use to carry dirt and rubble. And there's a logo!" Cynthia pointed out.

Emily adjusted the photo and tilted it away from the light. "B-S-I," she chuckled. "He must have been a builder involved in the renovation. B-S-I. Banks & Sons Industries."

Cynthia's eyes widened. "Well, no wonder she didn't want us prying if her first husband worked on the bloody thing."

Setting the photo down, Emily felt a sudden sense of urgency. "We should leave," she suggested.

As they passed through the hallway, Emily glanced back into the kitchen, staring out the window at the glistening reflection of the lake beyond. A shiver ran down her spine as she turned towards the front door. This old house held secrets and lies that Edna desperately wanted to keep hidden. Closing the front door behind her, Emily caught sight of Edna standing at her bedroom window. A warning glint in her eye cautioned Emily against probing further.

CHAPTER TWENTY-EIGHT
Escape Plan

The pill fizzed, creating tiny bubbles in her glass of water. Sleep had eluded Emily for what felt like an eternity now, burdened by the weight of her troubles piling up. There seemed to be no respite. Misfortune laced her every decision, and just when she thought she was making progress, another hurdle emerged to mock her efforts. She massaged her temples and downed the water in one swift motion.

Wiping a stray droplet from her chin, she shifted her gaze to Theo, who was hunched over Cynthia's shoulder, attempting to learn the skill of knitting. Emily smiled, capturing a precious and seldom-seen moment of tranquillity.

The pride swelled within her as she regarded Theo. He had returned to Emily's life with no inkling of the mess he was stepping into or the dark secrets unravelling within their community. It would send most people fleeing, yet Theo stayed, striving to mend the broken pieces and become an integral part of the peculiar little family Emily had forged with Cynthia.

Theo withdrew his phone and looked at Emily. Her heart skipped when he approached, as if the world slowed in those few seconds. Her head throbbed. "It's Rachel's Mum. She messaged me on Facebook," Theo said. "Rachel's funeral is in a few weeks' time. She's asking if we know where Jessie has gone."

Emily had sent Jessie a couple of messages but hadn't heard back. "So, she's out of the hospital then?"

Theo didn't look up from his phone. "Seems like it. Rachel's mum can't get hold of her to inform her about the date." He sighed.

"What's wrong?" Emily placed a hand on his shoulder.

"I don't know what to say. The poor woman must be so upset, losing her daughter. It can't be easy." Theo replied. Emily watched as tears formed in the corners of his eyes. To truly see him this vulnerable, to see how much he'd grown and matured since University. It helped remind her, how much he meant to her.

Emily looked at Cynthia, who caught Emily's eyes but averted her gaze. "Tell her we'll be there, and if there's anything she needs, let us know."

"She shared a post by the police, asking if anyone knows anything. I'll share it too. It's the least we could do," Theo said with a sad smile, continuing to read the post. He raised his eyebrows.

"What?" Emily's anxiety surged once again. "What?"

"The information about her time of death… it's peculiar," said Theo.

Emily placed her hand on his shoulder, but he didn't look up. "How? Theo, my head is pounding. Please don't tell me there's more."

"Remember, she sent you a text? After she was attacked?" Theo asked.

Emily nodded. The relief she felt when that message came through. Emily couldn't forget it. "Yeah, only to say she was awake and not to bother her. That was the only thing she sent."

"But the report states she died in the morning after the attack."

Emily scratched her neck, trying to recall that chaotic day. So many different things had happened all at once. She couldn't remember if she had spoken to Rachel or if they had only exchanged that single message. "Wait. We didn't know Rachel had died until..." Emily's memory flashed back to her conversation with Jessie in the hospital, where she learned about Rachel's death. "What time was the death? Have they included that?"

Theo nodded. "Yep. 11:42 a.m."

Emily scrolled through her phone to find Rachel's texts. She looked at the last one Rachel had sent. Her heart dropped. "Look," she said, turning the phone to Theo. "3:28 PM. That was sent hours after she died. Why haven't the police checked her phone records?"

"Do you think it could have been sent with a delay?"

"Considering Rachel's condition, I doubt she was in any state to schedule text messages, Theo. This might be our clue—"

Just then, Emily's phone rang and slipped from her hand to the table. "Sorry," she apologised. It was Rose calling.

"Emily, can you come to mine?" Rose said. "I think there's someone here, trying to break in."

Emily jumped to her feet and turned to Theo. "I'll be right there. Theo, we have to go." She looked at Cynthia. "Gran, I'll only be a few minutes. If I take any longer than an hour, call the police."

Cynthia twisted to face them, dropping her knitting needles to the ground. "Hold on a second. What's happening?"

"Maybe nothing, but Rose is panicked. We'll be right back."

Emily pulled Theo to his feet and they burst out of the door into the deserted close. Only the distant sound of a long owl accompanied them as they rushed across the road toward Rose's home. "No one out front!" Emily yelled to Theo.

"You going to tell me what happened?" Theo asked, gripping Emily's hand. The ran across the road, hand in hand.

"Rose thinks someone is at her place, but if we make some noise, we might scare them off." Emily released her hand from his and began clapping. "Come on!" she shouted.

Theo looked around with a puzzled expression before he started screaming, his voice echoing through the close. The screech made Emily jump. She only hoped the same worked on whoever was at Rose's.

They stopped outside Rose's door, and Emily laughed. "I wasn't expecting that."

Theo shrugged. "You wanted noise."

Emily knocked on the door and heard someone on the other side unbolting the lock. "Come in," Rose whispered.

"Is everything okay, Ms. Walker?" Theo asked, scanning the surroundings as he stepped inside. Rose's home looked as it always did. Picture perfect. Not a thing out of place.

"Thanks for coming. I saw someone in the front window while I was in the kitchen. When I got closer, they were gone, and then I heard a crash in the garden," Rose babbled, wringing her wrists.

"What was it?" Theo inquired.

"I don't know. I phoned you the second it happened. I can't bring myself to go out there, and Ava has gone out for the day, so I didn't know who else to call."

Emily leaned across the kitchen sink, trying to catch a glimpse of the garden in the darkness. "Do you think it's a warning from Sir Banks?" Rose asked.

Emily shook her head, not wanting to worry Rose further. Theo looked towards Emily, his face contorted in confusion. "Sir Banks?" She smiled back at him and mouthed *'never mind'*. She approached the back door and pushed it open, determined not to be frightened. Theo followed Emily as they stepped into the garden, turning on the outside light. The air was calm, devoid of wind, and the lawn looked perfectly maintained. Near the wall was an overturned metal bin, the lid having rolled a few feet away. She turned back to Rose and grasped her shoulders to reassure her. "The bin must have fallen over. I think we're okay." She smiled and met Rose's eyes, which were like deep wells of fear

"Thank you for coming. I was certain I saw a person at the window."

"Maybe my yelling scared them off?" Theo chuckled, readjusting his glasses.

Rose looked at them both with a puzzled expression, her face reddening as she forced a laugh. "What are we like, eh? I feel so foolish."

"Anytime. We better get back to Gran, though. She'll have the police here if we're not back soon," Emily said, lacing her fingers with Theo's as they strolled back toward their home.

He slowed his pace until Emily matched his steps. "Is everything okay?" she asked him.

Theo paused in the middle of the road, the moonlight

framing his short stature. He ran his fingers through his hair, creating a dishevelled look. "I've been thinking... Jessie went into hiding to escape all this madness. She was attacked, Rachel is dead, and Cassandra..." He bowed his head. "I don't want us to meet the same fate."

Emily rubbed his arm and pulled him closer. She had thought the same, but had never dared utter it into existence. "That's why we need to figure this out and uncover who's behind all this."

"But it's so much more than that. You have the fraud case hanging over you. All that stuff the other night with the girls. The letters. It's a lot, Emily."

Emily lowered her head, loathing the fact she had dragged Theo into this mess. She despised the wasted time they had spent apart, given how effortless it was when they came back together.

Theo drew his shoulders up, hands in his pockets. He kicked a stone with his foot. "I wish it could all disappear. I want us to start fresh, with no lies or secrets. Just you and me somewhere off-grid."

Emily sighed. There was an answer to this, a way to make it all go away. Smiling, she looked up at him. "I had an offer," she said. "A way to make the art fraud disappear. Some influential people who can make it happen."

His head shot up, eyes wide. "What? How?"

"It's best not to ask. I turned them down. It goes against all my principles," she explained.

"Can you tell me more? If we have a future, I want to explore every possibility."

Emily glanced around the close as they approached her house, contemplating the heavy weight of death that haunted these homes. So many secrets intertwined within the bricks and picket fences. She wondered if she could find true happiness here, if the handful of beautiful moments outweighed the multitude of hardships. She smiled at Theo, his cheeks still flushed from their rush to Rose's house. Adrenaline coursed through her own chest as well.

Before Emily could speak to Theo and share more about The Order and Sir Banks' offer, she froze. The front door was left wide open, gently swaying. Gripping Theo's hand, they both rushed inside. She spotted the small droplets of blood first. Panic surged through them, and their faces drained of colour.

"Gran?" Emily yelled, frantically scanning the room. They followed the trail of blood to Cynthia's cherished armchair. A ball of wool lay by her feet. As Emily's gaze followed the thread of wool, her legs trembled and her heart pounded as she processed the shocking sight before her. Cynthia lay slumped in her chair, head tilted back. Blood seeped from her chest, where the knitting needles protruded from her body.

CHAPTER TWENTY-NINE
Hidden Ending

Ava double-checked the pin on her maps to confirm she had arrived at the right location. Looking up from her phone, she surveyed the Mossbrook Junction Train Station, where the weathered concrete steps led her towards a weather-beaten blue door. She revisited the text message. *'Meet here. Tell no one. I will be inside, behind the blue door.'*

Bypassing the overgrown weeds, she gingerly pushed open the flaked door just enough to slide through sideways. This was uncharted territory for her; the place had been abandoned and left untouched for years—perhaps decades. Ava couldn't help but wonder why Nick had chosen such a peculiar meeting spot.

Inside, the air felt stagnant, and its staleness clung to her senses. The floor was covered in shards of glass and crumpled leaflets. Light barely managed to penetrate the gloom. And there he was, right in front of her. Nick. He sat on a rusty bench, waiting patiently as Ava approached, the clicking of her heels echoing through the desolate space.

Ava paused before him and assessed his appearance. He seemed noticeably better than their last encounter. He had shaved, trimmed his hair, and shed some weight. She smoothed down her top, holding her bag protectively against her chest. As Nick's beady eyes met hers, a glimmer of hope sparked within them. He tapped the empty seat beside him, a silent invitation.

Ava glanced at the accumulation of rust and debris on the seat, remnants of years gone by. She shook her head. "I'll remain standing, thank you." Her gaze swept across the dreary room. "You're fortunate I decided to come at all. This place is—"

"Empty. Safe. It's the only location I could think of that was nearby," Nick interjected. His eyes danced over her body. "Thank you for coming. I wasn't certain you would."

"Nor was I, but here I am," Ava replied. "I made sure I wasn't followed. We need to make this quick, Nick. I can't risk being seen here."

Nick chuckled. "It's not as terrible as it seems, is it? With you, any place can feel like paradise."

Years ago, those kind of words would have meant something to Ava. She would gaze back into Nick's eyes, see the world he could offer her and fall from her feet at such devotion and love. Now, it only made her stomach retch.

"I wasn't commenting on the surroundings, dear. I was referring to being seen with *you*." She crossed her arms, and when he reached out to touch her, Ava swiftly pulled away. She stepped back, crushing glass beneath her heel. "I'm not your wife anymore. I'm your widow. What do you want?"

His eyes narrowed slightly, only a second. "I wanted to

see you, to check about how you're coping with our... situation."

"I told you I wanted nothing to do with you. You crossed a line, and even I have boundaries. I can't live a life on the run with you, constantly watching my back. I *won't*."

Nick rose from the bench and approached her slowly. "I understand," he murmured, dropping his gaze to the floor. "I thought I was doing right by the people I loved, but tell me this: am I doing right by you, even in death?" He gave a hollow chuckle, and Ava sidestepped him, needing to keep the distance between them.

"For now," she said. "Your insurance payout finally came through. Who would have thought it was so easy to fake a death?"

His dopey expression turned more calculating, the look he once wore when closing a deal. A sinking feeling gnawed at her stomach. She didn't want him back but witnessing how quickly he gave up on trying to win her over stung. At the mere mention of money, she could see his mind already whirring, calculating the details of the transaction.

He coughed into his hand, as if trying to regain his composure. "We need to discuss our future."

"You're a free man now. Go to some tropical country and swindle your way into a life of luxury. I'm sure you'll do just fine."

Nick hesitated. "I have something potentially lined up, but I need some capital. Cash."

Ava couldn't help but laugh. "Coming to me for money? How times have changed. The bank's closed, love." She finished with a sly smile.

"Don't be absurd. You have the insurance money, the savings, the house. It's only fair that I get half."

Ava feigned surprise, raising an eyebrow. "Half? How

can I give half to a dead man?"

Nick's expression hardened. "I can cause you trouble too, my love. You know I'm alive."

"You wouldn't risk your own freedom just to hurt me."

"If I'm left with nothing, I might have to," Nick retorted, narrowing his eyes.

Ava turned away, gazing at the dilapidated reception desk, barely visible through the shards of broken glass. Ava had only managed to survive prison the first time. She was so much younger than, had nothing to loose. But now, prison wasn't an option. Going down to protect her sister, that was admirable. Being behind bars because of Nick. That was a fate worse than death. "You can have twenty grand."

"Twenty? *Please*. I need at least five-hundred thousand."

Ava kicked a broken bottle with her shoe and spun to face Nick. "Half a million? In cash? Handed over to you in a deserted train station? Nick, get real. I'm the one in control here."

He lifted his head, though a smirk played on the edges of his lips. "Babe, it's a negotiation. It's what I do. Two-fifty, and I'll walk away."

She ran her hands through her hair, contemplating. "It's complicated, Nick. I'm considering selling the house, I'm worried about the market."

"The house? Moving somewhere nice?" Nick leaned toward her but settled back into his seat at the look she gave him. "The property value in Beechwood will never go down. It's not that kind of area." He crossed his leg and chuckled. "Even with Cynthia moving in across the road, it didn't affect the market."

"Well, Beechwood might not be as stable as you think. Our mutual friend, Katherine, actually gave me some interesting advice."

"Oh?" Nick's head lifted at the mention of her. His eyes grew wide as he leaned closer.

"Did you hear about the body found in the lake? Wrapped up and stuffed in a suitcase?" Nick nodded. "Well, Katherine mentioned rumours of underground movement, which caused the body to resurface. She thinks there might be unstable foundations in the homes and warned me to sell quickly before it's too late."

Nick rose to his feet, his tone suddenly urgent. "Well, is it up for sale?"

"Not yet," Ava lied, crossing her arms.

"Well, bloody hurry up. If you lose that house, we're screwed."

"We?" Ava questioned, raising an eyebrow. They hadn't been a team, a *we*, in a long time.

"Yes, *we*. Get it sold and make sure none of the neighbours find out."

Ava rolled her eyes. Nick sounded just like Katherine. "Anyway, I've been doing some background checks. It turns out the man behind the project of the illustrious Beechwood Close may have been a friend of yours. Sir Kenneth Banks. Does that ring any alarms?"

Nick huffed. "It rings plenty, none of them good. You're not involved with him, are you?"

"No, I'm not *involved* with anyone, but is there anything I should know about him?"

Nick sighed, shrugging his shoulders. "I wouldn't even know where to begin. He was a member of The Order and always considered himself a big shot. He's pulled off some deals in the past that make me look like an amateur. You need to stay far away from him, Ava."

"I will," she said.

Nick tightened his grip on Ava's arms. "I mean it. He's

dangerous, volatile, and wealthy. A deadly combination."

Ava glanced at her phone after it vibrated, and gasped. *'Gran's been attacked. At hospital with her now. X – Emily.'*

Ava shook free from Nick's grasp. "I'm well aware of what a man like him is capable of, Nick." She turned away, desperate to create distance between them. Their relationship was over, and she needed him to understand that. "I'll sell the house quickly, inform the girls once I have the money, and then we'll meet one last time. We'll say our goodbyes. You'll get your share, and I'll get mine."

She turned to leave.

"So, that's it? Nothing more after all these years? It's truly over between us?" Nick's voice held a tinge of desperation. His head sank, legs weak. Ava looked at him then, truly looked at the man she'd married. He stood there, with the face of a child who'd been told no for the first time.

Ava paused, a few steps away from the door. Nick remained hidden in the shadows. "It was a wild ride, love, but it had to come to an end eventually." She headed over to him and brushed her finger lightly under his chin. "We were brilliant, weren't we? Unstoppable, fearless, and charged, but now it's over. It's time to let someone else take the reins." With those words, she turned towards the exit and pushed the door open, allowing the rays of light to flood into Nick's teary eyes. The door closed behind her, leaving Nick alone in the shadows, while Ava stepped into the outside, ready to begin a new chapter.

CHAPTER THIRTY
Giving In

Once again, Emily found herself surrounded by sterile white hospital walls. Nurses and doctors scurried through the corridors, their urgent footsteps mingling with blaring alarms. All Emily craved in that moment was a semblance of tranquillity—a reassurance that her grandmother was safe, and for the police to uncover the identity of the person who had viciously attacked her.

The doctor had informed Emily that her grandmother's condition was stable, though she remained in an induced coma to aid her recovery. The knitting needles had pierced through her chest, but thankfully she'd survived. It truly was a miracle. But the torrent of thoughts continued to race through Emily's mind. Rachel was once said to be stable in hospital, but never had the chance to leave it.

Emily glanced at Theo, who approached her with three

steaming cups of coffee in hand. She rushed over to relieve him of one cup before it spilled and scalded his legs. "Thank you," she murmured. "Ava popped off to stretch her legs. It's so unlike her to be the first one here, you know." Emily blew gently on the steaming cup of coffee, feeling the warmth envelop her hands.

"Do you have any updates?" Theo asked, frowning.

Emily shook her head and glanced at her watch. As the door to the waiting room creaked open behind her, Emily held her breath, and braced for the potentially distressing news. Except it was Regina who stood before them, dressed in a casual jumper and jeans, with her hair tied back. "Emily, how are you holding up? Flo asked me to come down." Regina outstretched her arms and embraced Emily, who quickly withdrew her arm to steady the coffee. "Flo would have come herself, but... well, Olivia is home, and things are a bit complicated between them. Honestly, it's a relief to have a change of scenery and step out of the house for a bit." Regina's eyes widened as she seemed to note the sombre surroundings. "I'm sorry. I didn't mean to sound insensitive. I understand this isn't a day at the park for you guys."

"It's okay. Don't worry," Emily said. "Gran is stable. She's in an induced coma, and she's been stitched up, but she lost a lot of blood."

"Any idea on who might have done this?"

Emily shook her head. "Rose mentioned seeing someone at her place. It could be the same person, but once Gran wakes up, we might learn more."

Emily heard the distinct click-clack of Ava's heels even before she appeared at the doorway. "She'll pull through, no doubt about it. That battleaxe doesn't miss a beat. She's a tough, stubborn woman, Emily. She'll be up and about before you know it," Ava reassured her, exuding confidence. "Rose is on her way. I told her it wasn't necessary, but she insisted. And Regina, how delightful to see you without Florence by your side." Ava circled around Regina with a mischievous glint in her eyes. "What a perfect chance to ask you anything we please."

Regina smirked and leaned in, her voice low. "My lips are sealed, Ava. You won't get anything out of me."

"So uptight," Ava said, raising her eyebrows. "I thought you were the fun one, you've certainly made Flo less... uppity." She approached Theo, who blushed slightly in her presence as he handed her the cup of coffee.

Regina pouted. "Well, she's been through a lot in the past year or so. It's not over yet."

"Her parents are out of the picture, right? That's a huge silver lining. Trust me, Regina, the number one passion killer is an overbearing mother-in-law overstaying her welcome," Ava quipped, turning her attention to Emily. "I'll head off now. I'll swing by your place and make sure everything is locked up and secure." With an airy kiss, Ava strode to the exit until the sound of her high heels were no longer.

Emily glanced at Theo and chuckled. "You can look up from the floor now. She's gone."

Theo sheepishly straightened, finally looking at Emily. "Oh, stop it. Was I really that obvious? She intimidates me."

Regina joined in the laughter and lay a comforting arm on Theo's shoulder. "Don't worry, mate. She scared the shit out of us when we first met her too. You'll get used to her."

Each passing moment in the waiting room felt suffocating and stretched into agonising seconds. Regina impatiently flipped through a magazine, tapping her foot against the floor, while Theo sought solace in a game on his phone. There was nothing any of them could do to hasten Cynthia's recovery. It was pointless. "Want to head back home for a bit?

I can stay here tonight if you need a bed," Emily offered, her voice weary.

Theo tore his gaze away from the game on his phone before shifting his attention to Emily. "No, I'll stay here. I want to keep you safe." He reached for her hand and tenderly rubbed it.

"More like you're too scared to go back to the house alone." Emily playfully poked him on the nose. "I can understand why, though. Nowhere feels safe anymore."

Emily looked towards Regina. Her head was buried into the magazine, oblivious to what they were saying.

"Maybe Jessie had the right idea," Theo mused. "To vanish and escape from all this."

Emily let out a tired laugh. "If only it were that simple. You and I, we could do whatever we wanted."

Theo leaned towards Emily with a whisper.

"It *could* be that simple. Maybe it's the answer. Once your gran is better, of course. Start fresh somewhere new. Build a new life again."

A new life felt so easy last time. She had a plan, her grandmother beside her. Emily never planned to make real relationships here. But now, a new life seemed impossible to imagine. "I've already done that, remember? I've forged connections here," Emily replied.

She glanced at her phone, watching as the minutes ticked away. Flicking through her emails, she stumbled upon one in her junk folder. Intrigued, she tapped it, expecting some promotion, but what she found instead were a series of hashtags and cryptic symbols obscuring the content. The headline caught her attention: 'WARNING.'

Urgently, she tapped Theo's arm to capture his attention before opening the email. "Look at this," she whispered.

'She may live for now, but she won't forever.'

Emily quickly closed her phone, her heart pounding in her chest. Anxiety surged through her veins. She turned to Theo, gripping tightly to his arm, digging into his skin. The threats would never cease targeting her family or loved ones. She could bear it when only she was in danger, but now it involved others—people she cherished.

Theo wrapped an arm across her shoulder. Emily knew it had to end. She wiped away an escaped tear and nodded at Theo. "We'll do it. Let's get out of here. Fresh start."

Emily quickly called Rose to see if she had left home yet. Turning back to Theo, she asked, "Can you investigate this email? Find out where it came from and who sent it?"

Theo scratched his head, uncertainty clouding his expression. "I'm not sure..."

"Theo, please. We need to get to the bottom of this. Please!"

Theo bit at his lip.

"Okay. I'll try to reach out to a few people, but encryption was always Jessie's speciality. Leave it with me. I'll give it my best shot."

Emily stood. "Regina, are you okay staying here with Theo for a while? If Gran wakes up, I want someone here."

Regina glanced up from her magazine. "Sure. Are you heading somewhere?"

Nodding, Emily grabbed her bag. "Yes, off to close a deal."

Rose clasped Emily's hand as they stood in the elevator, both watching the numbers on the screen go up. Emily attempted to steady her breathing; she never felt at ease in office buildings. She preferred the solace of her home, where she could create art—*real* art—on paper or canvas, not confined to a screen while hunched over a desk.

From the reflection in the elevator mirror, Rose seemed to assess Emily, biting her lip. "Are you absolutely sure about this?" Rose's free hand clutched the folder to her chest.

Emily nodded. "It's the only way. He threatened us, we called his bluff, and now my grandmother is in hospital."

Emily remembered Rose's panic, thinking someone was at her home. The texts, the threats he'd given. He would do anything for this information and hurting Cynthia had to have been the last warning shot. The elevator came to a halt, and the doors slid open. Together, they stepped out into a dimly lit hallway. "So, you believe this is down to him?" Rose asked as they strode forward, their steps muffled by the carpeted floor.

"I don't know for certain, but I'd rather eliminate one potential threat," Emily said, fixing her gaze ahead on the glass walls and doors lining their path. The office at the end belonged to him, and faint light emanated from a slither beneath the door. Silence enveloped the office block as they approached.

Sir Banks insisted they met at his workplace, alone. Emily couldn't escape the guilt for giving in to his demands. Surrendering this information could enable numerous individuals to escape justice for years to come, but Emily had to prioritise herself, her friends, and her family. Unlike the people listed in the documents, her family weren't faceless entities, and Emily had to place her loved ones above all else—a truth she despised. Rose hadn't opposed her suggestion. The moment Emily broached the subject, Rose readily agreed, seeming eager to finally end this ordeal.

They stood before his office door and exchanged one last look. They were doing the right thing, Emily thought, and with a shared look, they opened the door.

As soon as they entered the office, Emily was struck by

the scent of cigar smoke. Kenneth turned; he had slicked back his thinning hair, and his top button was undone. He greeted them with a tight smile and placed the cigar onto a tray. "Girls, so wonderful that we can finally come to an arrangement," he said, immediately looking at the folder clutched in Rose's arms. "Shall we proceed? I'd like to leave as soon as this is over." Emily held out her hand, signalling for him to wait, and Kenneth sighed. "I don't have time for games."

"No games, Kenneth. You'll get what you want, but before we proceed, I have a few questions," Emily said. Kenneth narrowed his eyes and reached for his cigar, motioning for Emily to continue. "Firstly, I want to know if it was you or your team behind the attack on my grandmother."

He raised his bushy eyebrows in surprise. "What?"

Kenneth was never one to show his cards, but Emily couldn't help notice the genuine shock in his eyes.

"My grandmother was stabbed through the chest with her own knitting needles. She nearly died. I need to know if you were responsible."

Kenneth turned away to face the window behind him. "No. Don't be absurd. If I wanted to send a warning, I would have done it differently. Anything else?"

Emily was conflicted. Kenneth's threats had felt real, and a part of her hoped he'd orchestrated the attack. He wasn't a bullshitter. Emily had gathered that much about him in the few times they'd met. He would revel in the fact of scaring them. That must mean he's telling the truth. Ending their connection would have given her some sense of relief, but this only confirmed that Kenneth wasn't after her—someone else was.

"The folder, Miss Walker," Kenneth interjected, reaching for Rose. She nodded and handed it over with trembling hands.

"Everything you need is in there, sir. Everything Violet left me. All the copies have been destroyed," Rose assured him.

"If you're lying, Miss Walker, I will find out." A menacing undertone permeated Kenneth's words.

Rose glanced at Emily with a worried smile. "Of course, sir."

"One more thing, if I may," Emily interjected as Kenneth placed the folder on his desk and settled into his leather chair. "It's about Katherine West. I understand she has been assisting you, and I saw her at your country house when we last met."

A thin smile crept across his face. "Very observant. What about her?"

"Her name is mentioned in these documents. She played a significant role in The Order years ago and likely wants to continue her involvement in the future," Emily said. She had given Katherine every opportunity in the past to seek forgiveness for what she'd done, but she'd thrown it in Emily's face with every turn. This time, she wanted to make sure Katherine had to face up to her choices.

Kenneth took a drag from his cigar. "Yes."

"Can I request that you remove her from The Order? Erase her future with the group, and sever all ties?" Emily locked her eyes on Kenneth, ignoring Rose who turned to Emily with wide eyes. Kenneth seemed to ponder the request for a moment.

"Has she harmed you in the past?"

Ignoring him, Emily asked, "My fraud case will be dropped, correct?" He nodded. "Then please, drop Katherine as well. Do that, and I'll even vote for you at the next election." A smile tugged at the corners of Emily's lips.

"That's the easiest vote I've ever secured." Kenneth leaned back in his chair, a smile gracing his face. "Consider Katherine West cut from The Order. I no longer have any use for her anyway."

Emily knew it was petty, betraying Katherine. But after what Katherine had done to her—and what she had done behind Rose's back—Emily believed it was deserved. "It seems like you two aren't as strong as I first thought."

Kenneth chuckled. "It was always strictly business. Besides, the new woman in my life can't stand her. You've actually done me a favour."

Rose stepped forward, looking Kenneth dead in the eye. "You won't disclose our deal, will you? About what we've discussed here? I want to put all of this behind me."

Kenneth leaned in, sliding a round sticker toward Rose. "If I have your vote, Miss Walker, then my lips are sealed."

CHAPTER THIRTY-ONE
A Powerful Woman

Florence stood in the reception, clutching her bag to her chest. The white marbled floors and scent of chlorine from the swimming pool sparked a vivid memory. The image of a pool brimming with blood flashed before her, and only the lingering fragrance of Regina's perfume tethered her to reality. The receptionist behind the desk offered her a sympathetic smile, as if privy to the horrors that unfolded within these walls.

Florence tapped her toes on the cool marble, silently urging Olivia to return soon. Turning her head, she strained to catch a glimpse of the cafe, thankful for Lesley's absence.

The woman behind the reception rose from her seat. "If you'd like to hurry things along, you can go in and find your daughter," she suggested. Florence managed to smile but shook her head. She was only reassured by Regina's touch, who stroked her back. The last thing Florence desired was to set foot in that place again. Olivia merely needed to gather a few belongings before she handed in her membership—the one Lesley paid for.

Flushed cheeks betrayed her embarrassment. "Shall we wait outside?" Regina asked, gripping her hand as they headed towards the exit.

Outside, Florence leaned against the glass and relished the fresh air. She closed her eyes, soothed by the gentle caress of the breeze on her face, allowing her a short moment of reprieve. Olivia tapped Florence's arm with a wide smile. "All done. Membership returned. One less thing Lesley can hold over me," Olivia said, already leading the way towards the car park.

Florence knew Olivia wasn't totally in the right here. She had accepted gifts from Lesley, thousands of pounds worth of clothes, for her and the baby. They had returned what they could, given what they couldn't to charity. Still, there were things they couldn't take back. Used make-up, expensive jewellery with no proof of purchase. Those are the things Lesley would hold over Olivia. The idea that Olivia purposefully lied about the baby to gain these things.

They strolled past freshly-trimmed bushes, the sound of their footfall accompanied by the soft patter of running water from the fountain. "When would you like to meet with her? To explain what happened?" asked Florence.

Olivia shrugged, pausing to run her hand through the cool stream. The sun's rays danced upon her cheeks, highlighting the youthfulness that still lingered in her daughter's face. "I'm afraid of what she'll say," Olivia admitted.

Florence pulled Olivia closer and buried her head in the cascade of blonde hair. Behind them, the screech of tires and billowing smoke disrupted their moment as a white sports car skidded to an abrupt halt. The world seemed to crumble within Olivia's eyes when she realised it was Lesley. "Everything will be okay," she whispered, holding Olivia tightly.

Lesley's flowing linen dress billowed around her as she stormed toward them, with her oversized sunglasses perched atop her head, and her golden bracelets clinking, as if announcing her arrival. Florence tightened her grip on Regina's hand, concealing her panic.

Lesley's face contorted as she halted, flailing her arms in the air. "Darling Liv, where have you been? I've been so worried," she exclaimed, pinching Olivia's cheeks. Florence sensed Regina stepping forward, poised and ready, as Olivia stepped back, away from Lesley. "What's happened?" Lesley looked at Florence, and then Regina. "Should've known you'd poison her again eventually. Typical of you, Flo. Let the girl live and make up her own mind about where she lives, who she stays with."

Regina shook her head, attempting to diffuse the tension as Olivia backed away further. "Lesley, please calm down," Regina implored, raising her hands in a conciliatory gesture. "Olivia doesn't want to go back with you."

Lesley turned her head and brushed Regina's hands aside, directing her attention toward Olivia. "Liv, darling, come on. You can come back with me. I promise not to say another word about this little escapade." Lesley attempted to encircle Olivia with her arm, but Florence instinctively stepped between them, pulling her arm away to shield Olivia, who had stared only at the floor since Lesley's arrival.

Lesley chuckled. "Oh, come now. You two are being utterly pathetic—so overbearing and controlling. What have you said to the girl? We were perfectly fine until you barged into my home, Florence," Lesley taunted.

"Last I heard, you were off gallivanting and leaving Olivia alone in an empty mansion," Regina retorted. "You did the same thing to Johnny no doubt and quickly treated Olivia the same. You know what? You would've repeated the pattern with your grandchild too, if given the chance."

Lesley scrutinised Regina, pursing her lips. "I don't recall you ever caring this much," she sneered. She paused upon noticing Regina and Florence's entwined hands. "Ah, I see. Building yourself a new little family, are we? No wonder Oscar went off in search of something else."

Florence tightened her grip on Regina, preventing her from escalating the situation further. All she wanted was to bring Olivia home and untangle this mess, but before she could ponder her next move, Olivia brushed Florence's arm from her shoulder, and stood beside Lesley. Florence held a breath. Was her daughter really going to change sides again, so easily? Lesley's eyes brimmed with newfound joy. "That's my girl. Come on. I have so much to tell you at home," Lesley declared, reaching for Olivia's hand. "I think our future just got so much brighter."

Olivia swiftly pulled away.

"Don't you dare speak about my mother or my father like that. They may not have been perfect parents, but they were miles better than you could ever hope to be!" Lesley's smile faltered as Olivia continued. "Johnny despised living with you, did you know that? He hated his entire childhood. You forced him into that cult, made him believe it was right to be part of that evil place. You know, he tried to get me to join too! That night of the fire, he brought me there to sign up and follow in his father's footsteps. All those twisted ideas came from you and your despicable group."

Lesley's face flushed red and desperation crept into her

voice as she pleaded, "Liv, it's just the hormones talking. You don't mean any of this. Let's go home, please."

Olivia pushed Lesley away. "I'm not going back with you," she declared, shifting her gaze to Florence before refocusing on Lesley. "The baby is gone, Lesley. There is no grandchild."

Lesley's eyes dropped, her entire demeanour crumbling until only a shell of a woman remained. Florence stepped forward to be closer to Olivia. Pain swelled within Lesley's eyes, seeming to realise that her son was gone, as was his bloodline.

"Gone? What on earth do you mean gone?" Her eyes narrowed as she frantically looked around. "What did you do, you stupid little girl. That was my grandchild. The only link left to my precious boy."

"It wasn't my fault. There was a complication." Olivia's face dropped to the ground. "I wanted that child more than anything. That much is true, I promise."

Lesley's sorrow quickly morphed into something else. She straightened and surveyed the onlookers who had gathered to witness their argument. With an embarrassed shake of her head, she swept her hair away from her face. "This is all your fault," she hissed, jabbing her finger into Florence's shoulder. "All the stress you've caused this girl. Running off with a woman at your age, divorcing your husband, drowning yourself in alcohol. Don't think we didn't all know, Florence. It's a miracle Olivia made it this far with you as her mother."

Florence bit her lip, struggling to contain her anger as every fibre of her being screamed at her to pounce on Lesley, to force her to retract every venomous word. But before she could make a move, Olivia shoved Lesley. In the blink of an eye, Lesley was submerged in the water, emerging with her hair clinging to her face as the fountain spouted water into the air, further soaking her.

Regina swiftly reacted, leaping toward the fountain and pulling Lesley out by her arm. Her earrings had fallen out, her makeup washed away by the water. Black steaks of mascara ran down her cheeks. Her eyes blazed as her face sharpened with anger. "I warned you not to speak about my mother like that!" Olivia screamed. Florence took a half step forward, a gentle hand on Olivia's should.

Lesley attempted to compose herself as strands of wet hair obscured her face. The remaining streaks of mascara trailed in rivulets down her neck. "You ungrateful little bitch. I bet there was no baby in the first place. You probably made the whole thing up just to squeeze money out of me," Lesley spat, shaking her arms to rid herself of some water as she strode toward her car. Olivia recoiled, touching her stomach. "This isn't over. I was going to tell you privately, Olivia. My new man asked me to move in with him. He even made a room for you and the baby. But now... well, you've lost it all."

Regina walked toward Lesley's car and opened the door. "It's time for you to leave," she said, seeming to suppress a smile.

"Don't think I'll let this slide. My Kenneth knows people—people who can make your life a living hell," Lesley threatened.

Regina held the door open yet slammed it shut once Lesley climbed inside. As Lesley drove away, leaving a cloud of dust in her wake, the crowd lingered, watching Florence. She kept her head high. She wasn't that little girl anymore. She was a mother, here to protect her child. She'd had enough of cowering away, hiding herself. "Show's over. Move along," Regina clapped, gesturing for them to disperse. She turned to Olivia. "Are you alright?" Regina redirected her attention to their car.

Florence inhaled deeply. She had thought things were returning to normal. Her family finally together, secrets laid bare—no more troubles. However, Lesley had a new man. Kenneth. She knew all too well, how powerful he could be, Florence ran her hand through the water, cooling her wrist, and hoped against hope that their family could remain united through whatever lay ahead.

CHAPTER THIRTY-TWO
Uncoverd Bodies

Katherine's eyes gleamed while perusing the documents, dancing across the pages to absorb the names of members that hailed from every corner of the country. A flick of her hand turned the photographs—past leaders frozen in time, moments of arcane rituals, and the horrifying spectre of blood sacrifices. One sacrifice that Katherine made sure didn't happen was the one planned for her own child. Looking at these images now, showed how truly dark that was. A shiver ran down her spine, and she hurriedly flipped the page, eager to banish the haunting memories of her involvement with The Order from her mind.

Katherine sat in the opulent room of the grand country house, a place she had only dreamed of having, somewhere which would have been impossible without The Order. She contemplated her life—memories of her ill-fated affair with

Graham and the daughter he had callously snatched away. It was that very daughter who held the key to exposing The Order's dark secrets. Times had changed. The Order had been granted an opportunity to reinvent itself, evolving into an entity that could be transformed into something more advantageous. She would bring in more women, chop away the stuffy business men and suits. Stop the pain and debauchery that had fallen it in the past. She could see herself. The one to bring it from ancient ritual, to a modern club with all the advantages that comes with money and influence. Something from which Katherine could reap significant benefits.

Footsteps echoed down the hallway. Swiftly, she gathered the papers and neatly tucked them back into the envelope. She swept her hair behind her ear and settled into a plush leather chair, absently toying with an unlit cigarette between her fingers. Just then, Kenneth barged in and took his seat behind the desk. Katherine leaned forward, a sly smile tugging at her lips as she traced the tip of her finger along the dormant cigarette. "See? I told you she would cave in," she said.

Kenneth nodded, fixated on the paperwork before him. "She did exactly as you predicted. You did an exceptional job, Katherine. I take it everything she had has been supplied here?"

Drawing herself up to full height, Katherine shook free her lustrous mane and nodded, relishing the sensation of the hairs brushing against her back. "We're there, Kenneth. We can finally relaunch this and shape it into what we've desired for so long."

Katherine walked towards the window, gazing at the sprawling expanse of lush green fields. Her mind wandered to the future, envisioning the inaugural meeting of the revamped group, with her proudly taking the podium alongside the new leader. She would help to craft new regulations, finally putting an end to the ghastly practices of death and sacrifice. Instead, the power amassed within those hallowed walls would become her tool, granting her unfathomable wealth and control, giving her everything at her fingertips. She dropped the cigarette into the bin and spun to find Kenneth shuffling the paperwork.

When she placed her hand on his shoulder, he tensed. "Is everything okay? We have what we need, right?" Katherine asked, slinking to the side of him.

"People have their doubts. About you and your need to control." Kenneth said.

"Really? Who?" Katherine forced a smile, one tinged with veiled intrigue. She peered into the bin to search for the discarded cigarette.

Kenneth cleared his throat. "Well, a few individuals have voiced concerns."

Katherine's smile wavered, and she plucked the cigarette from the bin. "Tell me their names. I'll contact them myself to address their reservations. The members need to understand that things are about to change significantly around here. Might as well prepare them for it."

She watched as he leaned forward, his fingers entwined together. This meeting had transformed into a business transaction.

"I'm not sure how to put this, Katherine. Some of them want you completely removed from the equation," Kenneth admitted, with an uncomfortable cough.

Katherine slammed her fists onto the desk. "No!" she shrieked. "You must have gotten things wrong. Everyone involved is ecstatic that I'm back."

Kenneth shrugged, continuing to flip through the

paperwork. Katherine snatched the documents from his grip and flung them to the floor. "You're not playing games with me, are you?"

Smirking, he glanced up at her and licked the tip of his finger before flicking through the paperwork again. "I have allies on the other side of that door, Katherine. Don't you dare forget that. Now, please, gather your belongings. We're done."

Before Katherine could snap back, a man emerged from the doorway. "Sir, Lesley Graham has arrived. She's waiting for you in the drawing room."

Katherine locked eyes with Kenneth, but his expression remained unaffected by Lesley's name. Her arms tensed, longing for a lit cigarette. "Lesley? Care to explain this meeting?"

"We've grown close recently," Kenneth explained. "I spoke to her about her late husband, his leadership, and our discussions naturally progressed towards the future and what we could learn together."

Katherine slammed her fists onto the desk once more. "Bloody hell, Kenneth! *We* were already doing that. I provided you with the list, guided you on how to navigate it, and kept everything hidden from the media." She gestured emphatically with the cigarette in her hand. "And this is how you repay me? By stealing my idea and dismissing me for some desperate widow?"

Kenneth rose from his seat and approached Katherine, shoving her against the wall. She caught a whiff of his breath as he hissed, "She's far easier to control than you ever were. She has resources, more time than you can imagine, and an innate desire to please. She's a woman I can work with publicly *and* privately. Now, leave. Use whatever money you took from me and go."

Katherine moved to strike him, but he caught her wrist and forced her arm to her side. "Leave," he snarled.

"You've made a grave mistake today," Katherine warned. "If you wanted a woman to manipulate and dominate, you should have never chosen me. I know all about your past, and don't think for a second that I won't go to the press. I'll expose you before your campaign even takes flight."

Katherine shoved Kenneth back and headed toward the door. She turned back one last time, igniting the cigarette held between her teeth. "That woman is cursed, you know. No man associated with her ever lasts long."

"Don't do anything foolish, Katherine. There are more people who remember your early days than you realise," Kenneth cautioned. He tried to hide it from her, with his glance towards the desk, the paperwork. But Katherine knew how tall she stood. She knew that was scared of her.

Katherine wanted to leave, yet something held her back. She had spent years living without the most precious part of her life—her child. If she had fought harder then, she could have spent precious years with Violet, and her life would be vastly different to what it is now. Walking away from this room meant leaving with only half the story, and she might never have another chance to hear it.

"What do you mean? Who could be after me?" Katherine asked.

Kenneth chuckled, sinking into his leather chair. "Members of The Order. They were aware of your return to town and wanted you to be taken care of. On the night of the fire, a plan was already in motion. Your dear Nick tried to intervene."

"Nick?" Katherine echoed, bewildered. There was no way Kenneth could truly know what happened to Nick that night. "Who told you all this?"

His smile grew wider, his eyes patronising. "He told me himself." Katherine froze, her cigarette dangling from her lips. "What's the matter? Your best friend didn't tell you he faked his death? He had nowhere else to go, so he turned to The Order. He wants to establish himself abroad and become a Leader of his own group elsewhere."

Katherine clenched her fists until her knuckles grew white. Nick was alive? How did she not know this? They were so close, practically best friends for decades. Did she really mean so little to him, after the loyalty she'd shown. "Why is he being rewarded while I'm being punished?" Katherine questioned.

"Who can say? Maybe he's just more likeable than you. Regardless, your time here is up," Kenneth said, propping his feet up on the desk. "You know, even your neighbours despise you. That young brunette was itching to betray you as soon as she handed over this folder. She practically begged me to oust you from The Order and cast you aside. Leave you with nothing. It didn't take much persuasion, of course, but I must admit, it gave me great satisfaction to say yes."

Katherine dropped her lit cigarette to burn a hole into his carpet, and with one last glare at Kenneth's smug face, she left the room. Storming past the guards, she barked, "Prepare the helicopter immediately! I'm leaving."

Rummaging through her bag, she searched for her new pack of cigarettes.

Katherine slammed the taxi door shut and sprinted towards the entrance of the hospital, balancing her small handbag above her head to shield from the rain. She scanned the reception area and approached the desk. "Can you tell me where Cynthia Lamont is staying, please?" she demanded, impatiently tapping her nails on the side of the desk.

"Quickly. This is a matter of life and death."

"Are you family, ma'am?" the receptionist asked.

Katherine nodded with feigned certainty. "Of course I am. I'm her niece. Please, it's crucial that I be with her."

The woman quickly tapped on her computer. "She's on the third floor, room 45B."

Without thanking her, Katherine swiftly turned and took the stairs two at a time. She needed to confront Emily, to shout and scream and demand an explanation for what she had done. Anger consumed every part of her being. All her hard work, all the obstacles she had overcome to live and create a good life for herself, had been snatched away.

Katherine composed herself while approaching the room, not wanting to attract attention. Slowly opening the door, she found Cynthia peacefully sleeping, with a visitor at her side. It wasn't Emily. "Edna, you were the last person I expected to see visiting Cynthia," Katherine muttered, closing the door and standing beside Edna.

Edna turned her head, lips parted. "Didn't expect to see you either."

"How is the old bat?" Katherine asked with disdain. She pulled a chair closer to the bed.

"Still breathing."

"I wouldn't expect anything less," Katherine said. Edna watched Cynthia. Her eyes large, full of unexpected respect. "So why are you here? Hiding from Larry?"

Edna shrugged. Her face blank. "Don't really know. Just came to check if she was still alive. She may be an old bat, but I wouldn't wish this upon her."

"Yeah, sure," Katherine snorted.

Edna narrowed her eyes, dropping her voice to a whisper. "I wouldn't! I wouldn't," she insisted, clearing her throat. "Did you come here alone?" Katherine nodded. "The police have been interviewing everyone about when Cynthia was attacked. Have they spoken to you yet?"

"Edna, I left Beechwood Close weeks ago. They can't pin this on me," Katherine said.

"Well, I told them I was with you that evening. If they ask, you need to go along with it," Edna said.

Katherine smiled, suddenly intrigued. More secrets. "Why should I?"

Edna leaned forward, whispering again. "I covered for you when the police searched for you on the night you disappeared. Now, it's your turn to repay the favour."

Rolling her eyes, Katherine said, "Fine, whatever. I don't owe Emily anything, but why would they suspect you in the first place?"

"No reason, really. I may have just threatened her and Emily, that's all. Next thing I know, she's been stabbed. I don't want the police adding things up and getting it wrong, that's all. Besides, what did Emily do to you?"

"She messed with my plans. I had so much to look forward to. I could have been the wife of the next Prime Minister if I played my cards right, but oh well," Katherine sighed, unable to hide the bitterness in her voice.

Edna chuckled. "God, not that bloody Sir Kenneth Banks again. I hear his name everywhere I turn."

"His father must have despised you," Katherine said. "Why did you want to stay so badly anyway? Everyone you knew must have moved away or sold their homes. Why bother to stay?"

Edna's response was simple. "Just did."

Katherine watched as Edna picked at her nails. Her knee trembling up and down. "There is more to it, though. I looked into the package that arrived for you. Insulin shots under your maiden name. Supposed to be taken multiple times a day. You've had diabetes since you were a young girl. Quite peculiar, don't you think?" Katherine leaned back in the chair, watching Edna closely.

Her expression hardened. "You said you turned that parcel away. Who have you been talking to about my private business?"

Katherine shrugged. "A few people. Type two diabetes. It's odd how you've never had to take a shot before and how you've never wanted to leave your home. Is there anything you'd like to confess?"

"That's enough. I don't like all this talk."

Katherine studied her fingers, peering over her nails at Edna. "Well, if you can't trust me, then maybe I won't provide you with an alibi."

"It's not about trusting you. It's just that there's nothing interesting to say," Edna muttered, glancing at Cynthia again.

"Then tell me," Katherine insisted, leaning closer. "What was it? Did you eliminate one of your husbands? Bury him in the basement?"

"I'd never. Loved all my men. Even Larry, sometimes. Truth be told."

Katherine gestured towards Cynthia between them. "Come on. It's just us. Tell me. You know everything about me. Otherwise, say goodbye to that alibi. Old Cynthia here's looking grey. Might turn into a murder charge before you know it."

Edna's eyes locked with Katherine's. Then she turned her gaze to the window with a weary sigh. "It's been so long since I even thought about it. My Rupert was the only one who knew. My first... bloody foolish things you do for love."

CHAPTER THIRTY-THREE
Deep History

38 Years Ago

Edna hurried along the path beneath the pouring rain. She trotted along the newly torn-up road, which transformed the pathway into a muddy mess. Pausing for a moment, she struggled to shield her face from the relentless downpour, clutching tightly onto the shopping bag. The builders had long since abandoned their work—deterred by the rain, Edna assumed. Their absence meant Rupert would be home earlier than expected. This gave a spring to her step as she approached the house.

She continued her trek along the broken concrete and scattered debris marring the landscape of the newly developed properties. Characterless buildings loomed before her, reserved only for the wealthy elite. The thought of selling the house had crossed her mind once before. After Rupert completed his construction work and unfamiliar faces took residence, she would either have to face isolation or endure a lifetime of trying to fit into a world she had no desire to be a part of. All she craved in her world was Rupert—no one else.

As she approached her porch, she frowned at the cracked second step and the pile of builder bags huddled beside the door, collecting rainwater in small pools. She slowly opened the creaking front door—yet another annoyance of this house. Maybe selling was the answer. She decided then that her best option was to speak with Sir Banks' son in the morning and settle for the best price. Perhaps they could live a solitary existence in the woods. Just her, Rupert, and nature. A smile crept across Edna's face as she indulged in the fantasy, imagining a carefree life with a healthy bank account to be shared with the love of her life.

The lights were off in the lounge, except for a faint glow emanating from a lamp in the kitchen. Edna set the bag of groceries down and shook off her coat, hanging it up on a peg in the hallway. The air carried the scent of freshly cooked stew—the one her mother used to make, the only recipe her sister Hillary could faithfully replicate. Once, that aroma would have evoked a warm, comforting feeling within Edna, but now it only reminded her of her sister. Always returning to town, seeking free room and board, and shamelessly flirting with any man who dared glance her way.

In the hallway was Hillary's leather jacket carelessly tossed onto the floor, alongside a smoke-tinged scarf. "Rupert, darling?" She made her way towards the kitchen, gathering Hillary's discarded clothing one piece at a time. "Bloody hell, is my sister here again?" she asked, swinging open the kitchen door.

Edna froze at the shocking sight of her sister and Rupert

locked in each other's arms. Hillary had her leg draped over the side of his body, her bare cheeks pressed against the kitchen countertop. Romantic candlelight lit the room, evidence of a long-winded passion, not an act of spontaneity. Utterly frozen, Edna could not comprehend what she was witnessing. She scanned their dishevelled appearances as they frantically tried to dress, seeking to hide their immodesty.

"What... What in the world are the two of you doing?" Edna's voice trembled. "Hillary, how... how could you?" She took a step toward them, gripping the countertop for support, her head spinning. "Rupert, get yourself dressed and get out of this kitchen now. Hillary and I need a word." She ushered him out with his leg still trapped in one of his trousers. Turning her attention to her sister, Hillary's hair was significantly shorter than when she last saw her and dyed at the ends. "You not only look like a slut, Hillary, but you've become one too," Edna blurted, her words driven by a surge of anger. They had been close once, when little girls. Ever since puberty reared its ugly head, the sister she once knew vanished, and a monster was created in the wake All she felt in that moment was an overwhelming sense of betrayal and heartache. "You're my sister. How could you lead my Rupert astray like this?"

Hillary raised her hands, though her lips twitched, as if trying to conceal a smile. Edna was pleased no one in the area knew about her absent sister. The amount of men and sleaze that filled her life was embarrassment enough. At least she had the decency to stay out of town most of the year. Her visits had become more regular though, Edna now knew why.

"I'm sorry, sis. The game's up. I admit it."

Edna narrowed her eyes, her grip tightening on the edge

of the kitchen counter. "Why? Why have you always tried to take everything away from me?" Tears welled in Edna's eyes, but she refused to let them fall. She wanted to wipe them away and smear them across her sister's face, to make her feel something for once.

"We never meant for it to happen. It wasn't planned," Hillary said, taking a step back. "Maybe it's for the best that it's out in the open now."

"Out? What do you mean *out*? This is just another one of your reckless acts. My promiscuous sister, always proving she can't be trusted around any man." Edna took a shaky step forward, yet her legs felt unsteady beneath her. Her mind raced. "You did the same thing to Mum. You never let her be happy. You tore Dad away from us and shattered our family, forcing yourself onto him, filling the home with your lies about what he did to you."

Hillary bit her lip. Edna knew any mention of their father was a stab to Hillary's heart, forcing memories she wanted to forget. "Edna. Do not go there." Hillary raised one hand, her fingertips stained yellow from smoke.

"It's true. Mother never recovered from what you made our father do. All you do is seduce, seduce, and seduce, only to turn on the waterworks when you're caught out," Edna spat, her words hitting the floor just shy of Hillary's feet. "Get out. Leave this place and never show your face around me again. You're an embarrassment to me and my life."

Hillary laughed, a bitter sound that echoed through the kitchen. "Your life? What life, Edna? You don't have a life. You've never had a friend besides Mum. You never talk to anyone. I'm surprised Rupert didn't move on quicker, considering the little affection you give him. No wonder he wanted me instead."

Edna surveyed her sister from head to toe. Despite being

twins, she hardly recognised her. The hair, the makeup, even the way she carried herself—everything about Hillary was the antithesis of Edna. When Edna tried to take a step forward, her leg gave way. Hillary instinctively reached to catch her, but Edna shoved her sister aside. "Don't you dare touch me. I'm fine," she snapped, turning to open the drawer. She retrieved an insulin syringe and pressed it into her leg, ignoring Hillary's grimace.

Edna turned toward the door, where Rupert stood, now fully dressed, with a bag by his side. She scanned his appearance. "Bit late to sneak off to work. Trying to avoid the consequences of your actions?" Edna shook her head, sensing the weakness in her arms. She hadn't eaten all day. Instead, she'd focused on getting home to avoid the bad weather. The insulin wasn't taking effect quickly enough. "Look what you've done. You've made my head all fuzzy. Throw her out, Rupert, and then we can talk."

Edna leaned against the counter, waiting for Rupert to move. He stood beside Hillary and draped his arm around her lower back. "Really? You're choosing her?" Edna gave a bitter laugh. "You're choosing her over me? She'll use you, tear you apart, and ruin you. That's her speciality. Only thing she knows how to do."

Rupert stepped forward, extending his hand to calm Edna down. "Edna, please. This has gone on for long enough. I've wanted this for some time now. I think it's best you found out the truth."

Edna peered past Rupert at her sister. Hillary's eyes were bloodshot and tears streamed down her face. Not a single thought seemed to cross her mind about the havoc she had wreaked in Edna's life. She was only shedding tears because she'd been caught in the act.

Furious, Edna spun, and the room spun with her.

Clenching her jaw, she pounded her fists against the counter. All she had ever yearned for was a quiet life, just her and Rupert. And now, it had been cruelly snatched away from her. Stolen.

Her eyes lifted to the butcher knife on the kitchen counter, resting beside the fragmented pieces of meat. It reminded Edna of herself: discarded, used, and ready to be cast aside. Seizing the knife, she whirled to the two figures before her. She wanted her sister dead, but if Rupert stood in the way, she would not hesitate to strike him, too.

She lunged forward, and Hillary screamed as Edna advanced. Rupert instinctively thrust his arm out, pushing Hillary backward, but the blade found its mark in his arm. Blood welled and trickled down him, falling onto the floor and staining Edna's fist. She glanced up to find the fear in her sister's eyes and took another step forward. Her legs felt numb, and her entire body was weak as the room spun. She had made a grievous error, but it was too late to stop now. Everything was set in motion.

Yet her weakened legs propelled her forward. She kept her eyes fixed on her sister and thrust the knife once again, but this time, it cut through nothing but empty air. Rupert swiftly positioned himself between the two women, attempting to wrestle the knife from Edna's grip. More of his blood spattered onto the floor, splashing into Edna's mouth, who screamed and relentlessly advanced toward her sister. Rupert held her back and spun her away from Hillary, while Edna jabbed his stomach with her elbows, desperate to break free.

Turning her attention back to her sister, Edna's face contorted as she clenched her teeth and swung again. Hillary shoved Edna back, and Edna collapsed to the ground. The knife slipped from her hand. Her vision faded, yet pain exploded in her head. Light. Shouts. The lingering taste of her lover's blood in the depths of her throat.

Hillary crouched beside her sister, cradling Edna's lifeless head in her hands. Blood pooled on the floor around them. Hillary glanced up at Rupert, who had turned towards the sink, retching. "Edna. Edna, please wake up," Hillary pleaded, lifting her sister's arm to search for a pulse. Hillary struggled to her feet, staining the countertop with blood.

"What have you done?" Rupert whispered.

Hillary scanned the room and noticed a piece of skull on the floor, with blood dripping from it. "I saved you. She was going to kill both of us."

"You can't know that. Not my Edna."

"Your Edna, is it?" Hillary asked. Even when dead, her sister was still able to control the narrative. Shape the future. She looked towards Rupert, wondering if now the choice was taken from him, if he would be with her.

"You know what I mean. God, what were we thinking?"

Pausing beside Rupert, they gazed down at Edna's lifeless body. "She's dead. What do we do now?" asked Hillary.

Rupert ran his hands over his head, staining his hair crimson. "Are you sure she's dead? Can't we get some help?"

"And say what? A bloody piece of her skull is sitting two feet away from her head. I always said that the corner of the counter was dangerous," Hillary replied.

Rupert looked at Hillary, deadpan. "This isn't the time for jokes."

Hillary glanced towards the window. "I know. Tonight was supposed to be so different. I don't know what we're going to do. It's all over now, isn't it?"

Rupert's eyes remained on Edna's lifeless face. "She's

gone, and we're left. I suppose we have to do something. Keep living. Keep moving forward. Somehow."

The fragility of life was staring her in the face. Her twin sister, gone. They shared so much, entered the world together. Had the same eyes, nose, hair texture. So similar, yet so different. Could she keep moving forward? Was there still a future for her with this hanging over her? Could they make it work, together as a couple? Hillary held onto Rupert's arm. "The entire neighbourhood is deserted. There's no one around. No one lives here." She paused, thinking. "We could get rid of her. Hide the evidence."

"What if someone finds her?" Rupert asked.

"We'll make sure they don't," Hillary said, peering outside again. "What about the lake they've been digging? They're filling it in a few days, right?"

Rupert returned from the hallway to lay a blanket over Edna's body. "Yeah, some of the guys are doing it on-site."

"What if we bury her there? We'll keep this place. We have the perfect view." Hillary rubbed Rupert's arm. "After all, we're twins. She was a reclusive woman. The only person she knew around here was you. Everyone else she knew has either moved away or passed on."

Rupert sighed and leaned in to kiss Hillary on the cheek before heading towards the door to drag in a builder's bag from the porch. "We'll wrap her in this, line it with stones, rocks, and anything heavy. Go upstairs and find a sturdy suitcase. One that won't deteriorate easily."

Hillary cleared her throat. "We're putting her in a suitcase?" She glanced down at her sister's lifeless body, the blanket around her head now soaked red. Hillary suppressed her cry, the scream that wanted to come out.

"We have to do this now. Get her wrapped up. I'll take her to the lake. You clean up here," Rupert said.

After what felt like hours, the kitchen was devoid of blood. Rupert returned with dirty, blood-covered hands. His face had lost its innocence, adopting a hollow appearance. Hillary pulled him close, embracing him, finally free from the worry of being discovered by her sister. Finally, she was in the arms of a man who would protect and do anything for her. She looked up at him and smiled at his dirt-smeared face. "So, do you think the name Edna suits me?" she asked, resting her head on his shoulder.

The heavy beat of his heart pulsated through her ear as she closed her eyes.

CHAPTER THIRTY-FOUR
Secret Deals

A stray tear made its way down Edna's sunken cheek. Katherine's gaze momentarily shifted to Cynthia, still peacefully sleeping. She felt at a loss for words, yet she couldn't pretend to be above it all. After all, she had committed terrible acts in the past to protect herself and those she cared about.

"So, you stayed in your sister's home for all these years? Why?"

Edna nodded, her voice breaking as she said, "We were in love. Once she died, there was no turning back. We had to make do with the hand we were dealt. No one moved into Beechwood for a year after the construction was completed. New neighbours came in, and I kept to myself, avoiding any need for explanations." Edna wiped her teary eyes. "My sister was a loner and formed no meaningful connections outside of

Rupert and me. I couldn't risk selling the place. We simply lived. We had a long and happy marriage."

"As Edna. You took your sister's identity and left your own behind?" Katherine whispered. "Did no one miss you, Hillary?"

Edna rolled her eyes. "Well, I was a wanderer, a lost soul. A biker chick, once. I never stayed in one place for more than a month or so. I would visit my sister, and every time I did, Rupert and I grew closer. It led to a happy outcome for us." She leaned across Cynthia, closer to Katherine. "We never intended for any of that to happen, you know. But when you cross a certain line, sometimes there's no going back, only forward."

Katherine lowered her head, all too familiar with crossing lines you shouldn't.

"Now that you know, will you keep your word? Will you tell the police I was with you that night?" Edna asked, absently scratching her arm.

Katherine recounted the night she killed Violets father. How Edna had turned the police away, allowed her to stay in her home and get away. Kept her secret for decades. Katherine nodded. "I understand the reasons behind your actions, and believe it or not, I'm not here to reopen old wounds." Katherine pushed herself to her feet. "Watch over the old bat for me. There are a few loose ends I need to tie up."

"Are you still going after Emily then?"

Katherine reminisced about the choices she had made throughout her life and the individuals she'd trusted—people who had only used her. She shook her head at Edna, her anger having somewhat dissipated. She realised then that she wasn't angry with Emily or Rose. She was angry at the man who had wronged her, and he needed to understand the consequences of his actions.

Classical music played in the kitchen as Rose chatted with Benny over the phone. He had called over forty minutes ago to discuss food arrangements for his café and to request some recipes from Rose. Yet gradually, their conversation shifted from business to more casual topics, laughing together. Rose was getting to know Benny, learning about his ex-wife and the circumstances that brought him to the area. After closing herself off for so long, she hadn't felt free enough to welcome another man into her world—even with George gone. Despite the comfort Benny provided, she couldn't help but worry about what he might be like behind closed doors, afraid of repeating past mistakes.

A knock resounded from the front door, followed by a loud bang. Recently, Rose had bolted the door even when she was at home. "Benny, I have to go. I'll call you later," she said before hanging up.

Rose stepped cautiously to the front door before pulling it open. "Katherine?" she said, slightly surprised as Katherine barged past into her home. Rose glanced out onto the close, yet no one else lingered outside. She bolted the door again.

"My darling Rose, I can always count on you being home, can't I?" Katherine said, pulling a chair from the dining table and sitting down. Her gaze briefly fell upon the menus Rose had prepared for Benny's cafe. "My sources tell me you've been quite busy," she said. A wide smile gracing her lips. "Tell me, why do you believe you're the only one deserving of happiness? Is it too much to allow others a taste of joy as well?"

Rose scrutinised Katherine from head to toe, and their eyes locked until Rose couldn't bear it, looking away and biting her lip. "What do you want?" she finally asked.

"I'm not entirely sure. I've recently discovered that the past few months have been utterly pointless. I've been abandoned like a sack of garbage, and it appears it was all because of you and Emily," Katherine said, frustration seeping into her voice.

"I understand," Rose replied. She pulled out a chair and took a seat. "Have you spoken to Emily?" When Katherine shook her head, Rose added, "There's nothing I can do, Katherine. We had no choice. We gave up everything to him and sacrificed it all for our freedom."

"I had plans for The Order, Rose. I wanted to bring about change and secure a brighter future. And now, I don't have a single connection left." Katherine slammed her fist onto the table. Rose couldn't help but jump at the anger spilling from Katherine. She was fearsome at the best of times, but today she was like a new woman.

"It wasn't what we wanted to do. But he threatened us, and after Cynthia's attack, we knew we had to do something. We were terrified," Rose explained.

"And Emily wanted to betray me as well?"

"He was planning to get rid of you, regardless. He made it clear he had found someone else, and you had served your purpose. He was never going to let you have what you wanted."

Katherine clasped her hands together and leaned back, crossing her legs. "I know what the both of you did to your husband. Kenneth told me as much after your first visit to him. I could expose both of you."

Rose folded her arms.

"And perhaps Emily can expose what you did to Lesley's husband at the same time?" Rose said. Though she was reluctant to use Katherine's past against her, she was determined to protect herself and Emily.

Katherine smiled and reclined even further in her chair. Rose knew the best way to gain respect from Katherine, was to stand your ground with her. To not show fear, but to face her head on. "Fair enough. I suppose we all have our secrets. I'm still furious, though. He's going to get everything he wants. I could have transformed the group, Rose. I could have allowed more women in, given them more power, and eliminated all the grotesque rituals from before."

Rose tucked a strand of hair behind her ear. She wanted to believe in everything Katherine said. But she also knew the inner working of The Order. That place did not change, not for anyone. She doubted Katherine would have been the one to bring any meaningful change even if she'd had the chance. "It would have been a tough battle."

"One that would have been worth it."

"Perhaps," Rose mused, her gaze darting away from Katherine to the photos hanging on the walls of her dining room—remnants of the past. "I agree with you, though. Kenneth shouldn't get away with what he's done. If he gains power, this country will be doomed."

Katherine tapped the sturdy oak table with a mischievous smile . "What if there's a way to bring him down? Something he couldn't escape from."

Rose's mind was blank. What on earth could any of them do to bring about Kenneth's downfall. He was on track to becoming the most powerful man in the United Kingdom.

"What do you mean? How dangerous is it?"

"Don't worry, Rose. You won't have to take on much risk. You'll simply be a supporter. I came across some information today, a potential story to spin. It won't be the whole truth but enough to implicate him."

Rose wanted to ask for more details about Katherine's plan, but she had learned from her past experiences some things were better left unsaid. Sometimes, it was best to continue on in blissful ignorance. "If we can bring him down, expose him for the cruel man he is, then I'll help. But only if it's not too risky. I can't handle any more threats."

Katherine's eyes shone with new vigour. "Does that mean you won't want to be a part of my version of The Order? With him out of the picture, I can make it my own. You're free to join Rose. You understand what it once was and what it could become," Katherine offered, her eyes glimmering.

Rose shook her head, filled by thoughts of The Order—Violet and all the dark memories that came with her. She despised that place, and she was glad to see it burn to the ground. Even if Katherine believed she could change it, Rose wanted no part. If more blood was to be spilled, she wanted to keep her hands clean.

CHAPTER THIRTY-FIVE
Take Down Plan

"How is she doing?" Regina asked, extending her hand to Florence, who descended the stairs. Florence felt a desperate urge to return upstairs and stand guard outside her daughter's room.

"She's okay. She's shaken up and worried about everything. Lucas is in there with her," Florence said, stepping past Regina to glance into the now empty lounge. The absence of her father's presence hung heavy in the air, along with the lavender perfume her mother had worn her entire childhood. Everything had changed once again, forcing Florence to search for a new equilibrium—a new normal.

"She'll be fine, babe. Lesley's all talk. All mouth," Regina said, attempting to lighten the mood.

Florence couldn't help but stifle a laugh. "Sounds like you," she quipped. "But I can't shake off this feeling. We should be focusing on Olivia. She has lost a child, and all Lesley can think of is getting one up on her." Florence ran her hands through her unkempt hair, suddenly aware of how long it had grown. The last time she'd had it cut was when Olivia had just had her first scan. So much had passed her by since then. "I can't even be angry at Lesley, not really. She's hurting too, in her own twisted way."

Regina rubbed Florence's back. On the television screen, Sir Kenneth Banks appeared in a news segment, announcing his plans to introduce thousands of more food banks across the country. Lesley stood beside him, with her bouncy, exaggerated hair, and her usual attire of pristine white linen.

Florence shook her head. "Turn that crap off. Honestly, it sickens me. That bloody man is going to ruin this country."

Sinking into the sofa, Florence occupied the space that had become her mother's in recent times. "I'm surprised one of the neighbours hasn't had a run-in with him in the past and got some terrible story to tell about him?"

"Why would you think that?" Florence asked, a bit too soon. Memories of that night flooded her mind. All four women had promised to keep each other's secrets. It pained Florence to withhold anything from Regina, but she had no choice.

"I heard on the radio the other week about how his first big job was getting this close built. Some fluff piece to make us see him as some young business minded man. Maybe you could speak to one of the girls, get some info or gossip—work something out together. A man like him is bound to have secrets he doesn't want out in the open. Why not play Lesley at her own game?"

Florence rose to her feet, peering out of the front window. "You know, I saw Katherine arrive earlier. She went to visit Rose." Emily and Ava both suspected Katherine and said she was somehow involved with Kenneth. Maybe this was her chance to beat Lesley at her own tricks.

"I'll be right back." Florence strode purposefully toward the door, grinning. "You're a genius, do you know that?"

Florence pounded on Rose's door until the sound of locks clicked from the other side. "Rose, can I come in, please? It's urgent!" she shouted through the letterbox.

Rose opened the door, her cheeks flushed and hair dishevelled. "I have company, Katherine is..."

Ignoring Rose, Florence walked in. "Yeah, I know. I need you both here."

Katherine turned from the kitchen counter, holding a glass of wine. The sunlight accentuated the royal green of her dress, a radiant glow with her sun-kissed hair. "Florence," Katherine greeted, raising her glass. "Long time."

Florence nodded. She still doubted Katherine, and definitely didn't trust her. She had discovered so much about the red-head during the conversations with the girls the other night. Yet Katherine visiting Rose so openly indicated that something might have changed, and Florence intended to exploit that.

"I'm not going to beat around the bush, girls," Florence said. "That MP, Kenneth Banks. I assume you know he's involved with Lesley?"

"Oh, I've been very much informed about *that* development." Katherine took a sip of her wine.

"Well, she's threatening my family. My daughter. And I won't just stand by and let that happen, not after everything she's been through this past year," Florence declared, lifting her chin. "I believe we're all on the same page."

Katherine stood, a smile curling her lips up as she studied Florence from head to toe. "You should have come out years ago, darling. It suits you. Listen, we can do something about him, but it will require some planning. That body from the lake—I think we can pin it on him, or at least create enough doubt to turn the press against him. Enough to ruin any plans he may have and, in turn, ruin Lesley's plan of an easy life."

"The body?" Rose stepped forward. "What do you know about the body?" Florence tried to stay calm. Was Katherine behind the murder of the woman? Was she about to be mixed up in a crime.

"Don't worry. I had no hand in it. It was Edna. She told me a story about her first husband. He was a contractor on site during the construction. All we need to do is plant those rumours of shoddy labour and poor conditions to get to Kenneth. It was his first project, and a body found under his watch will be enough to bring him down," Katherine said confidently.

Katherine wasn't revealing the complete truth, that much was clear, but at this point, Florence didn't care. If it meant stripping Lesley of her power, she was willing to go along with whatever plan Katherine had in mind. "So, what's our next step? I want this resolved as soon as possible. Do you have any evidence of his involvement?"

Katherine leaned in with a conspiratorial look on her face. "The body was wrapped in material used during the construction. This stays strictly between us, understood?" She pointed at both Florence and Rose. "Edna's husband confessed on his deathbed. He admitted to knowing about it for years, burdened by the guilt. I can convince Edna to provide a statement and share what her husband revealed. Even if it's not enough to convict Kenneth, it's enough for the press to create negative publicity around him. Enough to make Lesley lose interest."

Florence wrapped her arms around herself while listening to Katherine's story. The words fell so freely from her lips. It was far too easy and convenient. She still wasn't being truthful.

Rose nodded. "Katherine's right. The online community is obsessed with this case. If we feed them information about it, it will go viral."

A wicked grin spread across Florence's face, and she rubbed her hands together. Hearing Lesley's smug words as she threatened Florence's family felt so bitter. Knowing that she could be a part of taking her down. It was too good of an opportunity good to miss. "With the election just around the corner, it'll be pure gold. Headlines for weeks." Turning to Katherine, she asked, "But will Edna truly go along with this? After keeping it quiet all this time?"

Katherine raised her glass. "Oh, don't worry. Edna will do exactly what I ask. You can trust me on that."

CHAPTER THIRTY-SIX
Forged Friendship

Emily returned home from the hospital, the burden of daily visits to Cynthia weighing heavily on her. The doctors had given her no new updates. She'd heard people say no news is good, but she wasn't so sure she believed that. As she entered the house, Theo greeted Emily with a half-hearted smile, peeking at her over the edge of his laptop screen.

"Any luck?" Emily almost didn't bother asking, knowing his usual response—a nonchalant shrug, or a deflated shake of his head.

"I think I might be onto something. Well, almost," Theo replied, beaming. "Although it might seem rather obvious."

Sinking into Cynthia's armchair, Emily inhaled the lingering scent of her Gran's perfume embedded in the fabric. "Have you discovered who sent the email?" she blurted, unlocking her phone to revisit the menacing words once more. *'She may live for now, but she won't forever.'* She turned to face Theo, awaiting his response. He scratched his head, hesitating. All Emily yearned for was closure—to track down the person behind these threats and put an end to this ordeal. "Theo, please. Give me something."

Theo replied, offering her a closed smile before typing on his keyboard once more. "Alright, can you do me a favour? Gather the letters that were sent to Ava, Rose, and Florence. Bring the letters here with the others. I should be finished by then."

Emily rose from the chair, her feet heavy as she mentally prepared to cross the neighbourhood. In another life, she'd be busy preparing dinner. Spending time with Theo, taking a walk with no thoughts of death, murder, or obsession. Her life had changed, into a mess of a drama and right now, she didn't have the energy to do anything about it. The smell of antiseptic clung to her fingertips while weariness clung to her clothes and skin. Surveying her home, her gaze lingered on the stairs and the bathroom. All she longed for was to turn on the heating, dim the lights, and immerse herself in a steaming hot bath for hours.

While waiting by the lake, Emily sent a text message. The police had concluded their investigation weeks ago, yet their presence lingered in the upturned grass and the tire tracks marking the soil. As Emily turned to observe the ducks bobbing in the pond, it felt like an eternity had passed since she had met Rachel by that lake a few hours away, reuniting after years apart, and reminiscing about old times—a friendship now lost in the abyss of time.

A rustling sound emerged from behind her. Ava, Rose, and Florence approached with linked arms, yet their laughter faded as they neared Emily. "Thank you for coming so quickly," Emily said, her voice lacking its usual vivacity. She wanted to rise and greet them, but her energy didn't allow it.

Ava brushed away dried leaves before settling beside her on the bench and handing over a bundle of folded letters. "What's the plan, then? Have you made any progress in finding out who's behind this?" Ava leaned back, fixing her gaze on Emily. "I know you two have resolved your issues, but not me. Mine are still lurking."

Emily rolled her eyes, weighed by fatigue. "I'm not entirely sure yet. Theo mentioned he might have a lead, and he said these letters would be useful for when I'm back home. That's all I know for now."

"How's Cynthia holding up?" Florence placed a comforting hand on Emily's shoulder, and a bittersweet smile tugged at Emily's lips.

"She's... stable," she croaked. "And what about you all? Any updates? It feels like ages since we last caught up."

Rose and Florence exchanged a look, and Florence cleared her throat before speaking. "Nothing new from us. Although, Ava, when were you planning to share your news about moving?"

Ava's posture stiffened and she glared at Florence. Emily swung her head towards Ava. "How did you know?"

"Regina's friend mentioned a house for sale in the close—quick cash deal," Florence explained, crossing her arms. "I told Regina it didn't sound like something you would do, but she was adamant that was your place and showed me a picture of your house with 'For Sale' written all over it." Florence squeezed between Ava and Rose. "Why didn't you say anything?"

"You're moving?" Rose asked, crouching down before her sister. "When were you planning to tell us? When the moving trucks arrived?"

Ava turned her head, pouting. "I was going to tell you all,

but the right moment never presented itself," she explained, flicking her hair. "It's been incredibly stressful, you know? Dealing with all the arrangements and constantly feeling like Nick's waiting for me around every corner." Ava shot Florence a stern look. "And the agent was supposed to keep it quiet, so I'm not pleased with Regina blabbing her mouth, either."

Curiosity tugged at Emily, who broke the heavy silence that followed. "Where will you go?"

Ava sighed, and her demeanour seemed to soften. "I don't know yet. When the time is right, I'll be the one to share the news with all of you. You can relay that message to Regina." She narrowed her eyes at Florence, sighing. "To be honest, I had concerns about the close even before all this. There were rumours about the roads and houses sinking from the lake," she admitted, slowly turning to face Rose and Florence, whose mouths dropped. "Don't worry, it was all a load of nothing in the end. You can thank Katherine for that, but I have found a buyer, and I want to move on, start somewhere new. So, I accepted it."

Rose stood now. "But your life is here, Ava. *We're* here."

Ava clasped her sister's hand, offering reassurance. Emily knew how vulnerable Rose could be. The little sister. She'd always wondered what it felt like to have a sibling. Wondered if she was in Ava's shoes, if she would have the heart to leave. "I know. I understand it will be tough not having me around, but I need to do this. I have nothing keeping me here anymore, not like you guys do." She smoothed down her top. Attempted to stop her lip from quivering. "Anyway, I'm not here to steal the spotlight. Are these letters all you need, Em?"

Emily was taken aback by her own emotions to Ava's revelation. Ava had always meant little to her, or at least that's what she'd thought, yet her chest felt strangely empty at the thought of Ava leaving. She looked up at Rose, whose eyes mirrored her own emptiness.

"No, these should be fine. Hopefully, we'll uncover the truth and can move forward," Emily said. She turned to face Ava directly, chocking out her next words. "You were the glue that held our friendships together, Ava, even during moments when I wanted to slap you. You're so important to all of us, but I understand your desire to leave. I'm happy for you. Truly." Emily offered a sincere smile to Ava and locked eyes with her for a moment that seemed to last forever. A newfound understanding passed between them, yet guilt lingered within Emily, who desperately desired to escape with Theo. She glanced at Rose, weighed down by the pain of potentially losing two friends. She then smiled at Florence, too, feeling a sense of sadness at not being there to support her in her new relationship and life with Regina. Emily bit her bottom lip. "We must all get together again, just the four of us—at least once before you go, Ava."

Ava nodded. "Sure. I mean, I'd expect a bit more than just the four of us, but it's a start." She linked arms with Rose, preparing to leave. "Come on, take me back to your place, and show me some of those cakes you've been working on to impress your new man." Ava winked at Emily before the two sisters walked away.

Florence raised an eyebrow. "Are you absolutely sure you're alright, Em? If you need anything, anything at all, just let me know."

"I will. Thank you," Emily replied, her voice filled with gratitude. "You were the first person to extend a warm welcome to me and Gran when we arrived. Your kindness meant the world to us." She lowered her head, thinking of the false pretences in which their friendships had formed. "You girls have truly changed my life."

Florence chuckled, a warm smile spreading across her face. "Oh, Emily. I've never seen you so sentimental before. One would think it's you who's moving. Now, go home to your man. Get some rest. Regina and I will handle the hospital visit for you tomorrow, alright?"

Emily nodded, appreciating the support. "Okay. Thank you."

Yet Emily stayed at the lake until she was alone. Her thoughts drifted to the woman who had been found here—all those years, unnoticed and unmissed. It stirred a sense of sadness within her, knowing people disappeared without anyone wondering where they'd gone. She pushed herself up, shivering and wrapping her arms around herself as the sun set. She strolled through the empty close, passing houses buzzing with life and families. The warm glow of the streetlamps guided her back home, to a place that had long since changed but still held that familiar warmth.

Theo handed Emily a cup of coffee as she stepped inside. His hair stuck up in all directions, his cheeks flushed, and his glasses askew. "Okay. You got the letters?"

Emily nodded and handed them over to him. He spread them out on the table, scanning each one. "All the same handwriting, would you agree?" Emily couldn't help but chuckle. "How much coffee have you had?"

"Emily, come on. I'm being serious." Theo tapped his finger impatiently on the table. "These were written by the same person, right?"

"Yes, from what I can see. Why?" asked Emily.

"The email. I couldn't find a name or address, but I narrowed down a location. Not exact, but... well, I think you'll understand when you see it," Theo said carefully.

Emily's heart pounded in her chest. "Just tell me already."

She'd waited for this moment. To finally put an end to the horrors of the past few months. Theo looked at her, his cheeks flushed. Names swelled around her mind. Katherine, Nick, Lesley, Mike, Kenneth. Who had been behind all this torture? "I believe it's Jessie," Theo revealed.

Emily's brow furrowed. "Jessie? She was attacked a few days after Rachel. We both thought her at first, but then Katherine and Kenneth's names were thrown around, and..." Emily sighed. "I guess we didn't want it to be true. Are you sure?"

"I know. I didn't want it to be true either. But the location showed The Lake District."

"The same place as her uncle's cabin," Emily realised, connecting the dots.

Theo nodded. "Exactly. Her uncle passed away and left the cabin—and presumably a significant amount of cash—to her."

"So, why did you want the letters if you already thought it was her?"

"We don't have concrete proof, not yet. I thought if we could somehow match the letters to her, it would provide us with more evidence, more for us to divulge," Theo explained, his eyes searching the screen for any shred of validation.

Emily pulled the laptop closer with one hand while holding her coffee in the other. "Jessie used to be quite active on social media until recently. We've found useful information there before. Perhaps we can do it again."

Theo sighed, giving Emily a look. "What, is she going to post her blackmail letters there for all to see?"

Emily playfully slapped Theo's wrist. "No, not like that. But look here. I remember scrolling past this before." She opened Jessie's Facebook account and scrolled to a post from twelve years ago. Tapping the screen, she pointed at a particular entry. "See, a diary entry? Look closely. The letters, the handwriting. The 'b' matches up with this," Emily exclaimed, leaning over to retrieve Rose's letter. She pressed it against the screen, aligning the two. "Look at the swirl in the letter 'b.' It's unique and consistent. She's been doing that since she was young."

Emily sighed. That friend she made at the beginning of University. A new world, a new adventure they were both on taking the same path. How could someone like that from her life do so much damage, cause so much death and hate and fear? How could she not have seen it before, in the hospital.

"It's really her, isn't it? It's really her behind all this," Emily whispered.

Theo sank into his chair, narrowing his eyes. "She was behind the blackmail and the things involving my father. She nearly tore my entire family apart, Emily. Why? Why would she do this?"

Noticing his clenched fists, Emily wrapped her arm around his shoulder. "I don't know why. We don't know the extent of her actions yet, but we need to find out."

Theo stood. "We need to go to the police. Show them the letters, the handwriting, everything about the cabin. We have to expose her. She's clearly crazy. She must have stabbed herself that night we found her."

Maybe she should have done that when the letters arrived. It would have saved lives. But it would have also altered so many too. Emily thought of Rose. She needed her friends now more than ever. The police would only invite questions, questions she wouldn't be able to answer. Emily's face tightened with worry. "We can't. These letters contain information, things we can't afford to have exposed. It's exactly why she sent them."

Theo lowered his head into his hands. "You're right. She must also have information about my father's business. Something like that, over in Japan. It wouldn't just ruin my fathers life, but for generations our family would be looked down upon. She had enough to intimidate me, but if this gets back to my family, it would be devastating." He prodded his glasses back up the bridge of his nose, searching for a solution. "So, what do we do now?"

Emily stood and grabbed her keys. "Get a coat and pack a bag. We're going to the cabin."

"What? Emily, it'll be nearly eleven at night by the time we get there!"

"I don't care, Theo. We know the truth and now we need to confront her about why she did all this. If you don't want to come, I'll go alone," Emily declared.

Theo let out a laugh. "Oh, you're so quick to play the hero. But don't think for one second I'll let you face this alone. Come on. I'll make some food while you pack."

CHAPTER THIRTY-SEVEN
Motives Exposed

Theo slammed on the brakes, sending pebbles flying. Emily stretched her neck and took a sip of coffee from the flask before reaching for his hand. "The lights are off," Emily said. "What if we're too late? What if she's gone?"

Theo opened the car door. "Haven't we already had this conversation the last time we were here? Come on." He slammed the door shut, yet Emily gripped the door handle, her chest pounding as she scanned the surroundings. Theo stood outside, his breath visible in the frosty night. She was the reason they had come here—the reason they came alone. Emily took a deep breath and pushed open the car door, a whirl of cold air dancing around her ankles as she strode towards the cabin. The sounds echoing from the lake reminded her of the last time they were here, finding Jessie in a pool of her own blood.

Approaching the door, the same one as before, Emily whispered, "It's unlocked. God, why won't my feet let me step inside?" She turned to Theo. "We can turn back and call the police."

Theo shook his head and held her spare hand. "Come on. We can do this together." Gripping the handle together, their hands intertwined, they opened the door. Stepping inside, he turned to his right and flicked on the lights. "Jessie? Are you in here?" he shouted, his voice echoing against the pointed wooden roof. "We want to talk and sort things out between us." He glanced at Emily. "Shall we check the bedrooms?"

Emily shook her head and made her way through the open-plan lounge, heading towards the kitchen. "There's washing up in the sink. Someone's been here recently," she said, with slow steps towards the stairs leading to the rooms. Emily noticed one of her paintings on the wall—a piece that had sold during her art show in the summer. Her art show in the summer had so much to answer for. Nick hadn't only embezzled huge amounts of money under her nose, but sales to Kenneth and Jessie went totally unnoticed by her as well. She couldn't blame Nick for everything. She'd let her eye off the ball too. If only she'd seen the sale. All of this could have been avoided, or at least figured out sooner. "Keep your guard up," she whispered, creeping down the short hallway. To her left was an undisturbed bedroom, and to her right, a closed door. She pressed a finger to her lips and slowly pushed it open. The door creaked as they entered the darkness, but Emily could discern a double bed. She patted the wall beside her and flicked on a switch to illuminate the room. Empty. Her heart-rate slowed as she stepped inside, growing more confident with every step.

As she scanned the room, her gaze fell upon a long wooden desk in the corner. "Theo, check this out!" She stepped towards it and reached for his hand, seeking the familiar comfort only he provided. His fingers entwined with hers, and she relished his warmth, gripping his fingers. "Look. Paperwork and printouts." Emily leaned across the desk, picking up the first piece of paper she laid eyes on—a business sheet detailing bank accounts from Tokyo. She passed the paper to Theo and continued searching. Printed photographs of Regina and Florence caught her attention, which she quickly flicked aside. Beneath them, she discovered letters and handwritten notes, reminiscent of the ones she had received. She read through them, noting the same threats with a few variations and some words crossed out. *'Friends come and go, but enemy's will get you in the end.' 'I know what you did, it makes me sick.' 'Watch your step, you never know who might trip you up.'*

"God, she had everything, Emily." Theo sat on the bed, staring at the pile of paperwork. "All the business accounts, photos of my family—everything."

Emily picked up a letter addressed to Hatfield Prison and quickly scanned its contents. Her breath caught as she realised that Jessie had been in contact with a prisoner. She offered a substantial sum of money in exchange for information from Doctor Mike Thornson.

Curiosity piqued, Emily's heart raced as she pulled out a black tape recorder. She lifted it and pressed play to find only static, so she rewound the tape and pressed play again, hoping for more. Amidst the static was a familiar sound—the clinking of knitting needles, the ticking of a clock. She rewound further and pressed play again. This time, she heard her grandmother's voice and then her own. They were chatting at home about trivial matters. Emily placed the recorder back on the desk and stepped back. "She was listening to us. Recording inside the house." Emily fell back onto the bed, her feet throbbing. "How did she manage all this?"

Theo glanced up from the paper on the drawer. "I don't know, Em. She's got things scattered everywhere in here—papers, photos, private information."

Emily looked down at her hands, feeling dirty and violated. She took a deep breath, counted to five, and exhaled. Theo stood up and opened his backpack. "Grab it all. Put everything in here," he said, pushing the papers into his bag and collecting the evidence strewn across the desk. A photo of Nick and Ava inside their home compelled Emily to intervene.

"Stop," she said, stepping forward and pulling a notebook from Theo's bag. Her gaze fixed on a photo sticking out—a snapshot of her and Cynthia in their old flat from years ago. She peered up at Theo, eyes wide with realisation. "She's been doing this for years. We moved out of that flat ages ago." Emily flipped through the notebook, skimming through the detailed notes about her life—past jobs, previous residences, ex-boyfriends—and even a leaflet about Beechwood Close and her current home. "Theo, she made an offer on my house when it was up for sale. I had to increase my offer to secure it. What kind of twisted person is she?"

From outside the room, a door closed, and Emily's legs turned to jelly. Theo froze, his eyes locked on the desk and his bag. He swiftly took the notebook from Emily's grip and zipped up the bag. "Come on," he said, clasping her hand as he pulled her from the room. Emily scanned her surroundings for a weapon or anything to defend herself, but her legs seemed beyond her control as Theo guided her out of the room and into the lounge, where Jessie was waiting for them, standing by the door. Her curly hair was limp from the damp, her cheeks were flushed red, and her boots were muddy and wet. Emily tried to speak—to move—but her throat felt dry as she laid eyes on Jessie.

Emily cautiously raised her hands, hoping to defuse the situation and bring a sense of calm. "What are you two doing here?" Jessie asked.

"We wanted to talk to you about everything that has happened," Emily said, taking a tentative step forward. She smiled, attempting to connect with Jessie like she did when they first met. "We don't want any harm to come to any of us."

Jessie chuckled. "Last time I knew you two were coming, I could prepare things. Thought I did the job, or at least enough to keep you two from asking questions."

Theo stepped forward, with his bag slung over his shoulder. "Why did you do it, Jessie? Why?" Emily placed her hand on his shoulder in an attempt to calm him.

Jessie narrowed her eyes. "I tried so hard to let it go."

Emily and Theo locked eyes before returning back to face Jessie

"What were you trying to let go of?" Emily asked, keeping a watchful eye between on both of them.

"You," Jessie spat. "Your perfect life, Emily. No bastard alive has the luck you do. Going from having nothing to having it all. You don't even know what you threw away, do you?"

Emily tightened her grip on Theo's hand, trying to prevent him from stepping forward again. Jessie's eyes narrowed again, looking pained as she saw Emily holding Theo's hand. "All of this, it's not because of Theo and me, is it?" Emily asked. "Please tell me that's not true."

Her head shook, hand tapping against her leg. Emily noticed her hands growing tighter. A smile threatening to appear on the edges of her mouth.

"You've never known how to appreciate what you have, Emily. You never could, not even back at uni. Making all that profit from our hard work, while we got screwed over... you landed on a bed of roses!" Jessie accused.

"Emily did nothing to you, you crazy bitch." Theo stepped forward again, and Emily closed her eyes, fearing how Jessie would react. "Why did you kill our friends if they meant so much to you? Emily didn't do those things. You did!" he yelled, his words reverberating around the cabin.

Jessie dropped her gaze to the floor. "I didn't mean for that to happen. Not to Cassandra. She got too close and found out things, looking through my laptop. I had to take action to shut her up."

Emily's grip on Theo's hand tightened. "What things? How long have you been spying on me? I saw the notebook. It goes back years, long before Theo and I reconnected."

"Do you remember why we became such close friends, Emily? What brought us together all those years ago?" Jessie's question stirred memories of their time at uni. Their paths crossed on the very first day. Emily instinctively reached for her necklace, the one Cynthia said belonged to her mother. She wiped at a stray tear and nodded.

"Of course."

A smile tugged at Jessie's lips. Not one of happiness, or peace or relief. But one that showed only danger and darkness. "Exactly. We both experienced the loss of our parents, and we found solace in each other's company. I had no one, just like you, until we had each other."

"Then why have you done all these things against me? Why cause so much heartache for others?" Emily's voice trembled.

"Because you left me, Emily. You dumped me repeatedly for Theo, a romance doomed from the start." Jessie pounded her chest with her fist as she said, "We had a bond, a connection. We were members of the 'club.' It was me and you, and you abandoned me." She covered her mouth with her hand, struggling to hold back tears. "I played you at your own game; I grew close to the people you left behind for your new life. I kept you at arm's length and made sure they tried to forget about you, while I kept watch to see how long it would take for you to ditch your newfound friends." Jessie paused. "I watched you all to see what things you got up to in the close. How could I ever had imagined how exciting it all was. I couldn't look away. When I got the cash from my uncle, well, what better way to spend it than collecting every bit of information I could. I saw how friendly you all were getting, and then I remembered what you are truly like Emily. I wanted to push them away and let them know how unreliable you are as a friend. I got close to Theo." Jessie brought her thumb and finger together, bringing it before her narrowed eye. "I was *this* close to winning him over, and then you showed up again, demanding attention and forcing his focus away from me."

Theo's eyes widened as he looked at Emily and silently mouthed, "She's crazy."

Emily scanned the room, yet Jessie inched closer. Behind her was a hallway leading to more rooms. Their only known exit was the door they had entered through. "Jessie, please. listen," Emily pleaded, raising her hands in defeat. But Jessie showed no sign of stopping. "We don't have to involve the police. We can work this out together in private."

A chilling smile spread across Jessie's face. "Work it out? Really? Maybe we should both call the police and share a cell," Jessie said. "You have so many secrets, Emily. So many lies. It's hard to choose which one to tell first."

Theo's hand was against Emily's back.

"We'll let you go if you let us take the evidence you've collected," Emily proposed, a desperate edge creeping into her voice.

Theo turned his head toward Emily. "What are you suggesting? We can't let this hang over us for the rest of our lives."

Jessie halted near the kitchen counter. "It's gone too far, Emily. I messed up. Poor Rachel. She believed I was her friend, but you were getting too close. She worked me out quicker than even you. She had to be silenced. After that, I had to act. I had to hurt myself. Do you understand the pain I was in?" Jessie's voice echoed through the room, her hair falling over her face.

Jessie moved closer, tucking her right hand into her coat pocket. Emily tightened her grip on Theo's hand before releasing it. They shared a look, fear reflecting in their eyes as they braced themselves, uncertain of Jessie's first target. Emily tensed, ready to defend herself, until Theo stepped forward, positioning her behind him and out of harm's way.

Jessie lunged.

Barging past Theo, Jessie collided with Emily, and they crashed to the floor. Before Emily could comprehend what was happening, Jessie was on top of her, pummelling Emily's body with her fists. A loud crash broke through the screams as Jessie's body went limp, her weight bearing down on Emily. Struggling for breath, the pain in Emily's side and neck bloomed, reminiscent of the agony she experienced as a young girl in the car beside her dying mother. She desperately wanted to push Jessie away, to free herself from the crushing weight of her body.

Blinking, Emily attempted to regain her focus. Theo was there, reaching to pull Jessie off her. "Are you okay? Are you hurt?" he asked, gently patting Emily down when she managed to sit up.

Rubbing her head, Emily replied, "I'm fine. I think I'm okay." She checked herself for any signs of blood, yet only her shoes were black and wet. "Is Jessie all right?"

Theo glanced down at the floor. "I don't know. I'm not thinking about her right now. She had a knife. She intended to kill one of us. I had to do something."

Emily turned her attention to the shattered glass strewn around Jessie's frame. Theo had no choice. He had to pull her away, Emily had him to thank for her still breathing. Jessie laid flat on the floor, her face towards the floor, blood spilling, but no sign of a knife or weapon in her hand. Emily rolled Jessie onto her back with a nudge of her foot and jolted at the sound of breaking glass beneath her body, as a breath escaped Jessie's lips as a shard entered the back of her head.

They both froze when Jessie let out a final groan.

CHAPTER THIRTY-EIGHT
Changing History

Rose placed the slices of cake on the coffee table and arranged them in a neat row. Sunlight streamed through the kitchen window, casting a gentle glow on the coffee and walnut cake. Everyone's anticipation seemed to grow, especially Edna, who licked her lips.

Despite the excitement of having Florence, Katherine, and Edna in her home, Rose couldn't shake an odd feeling in her chest. She longed to invite Ava over, to cherish every remaining moment before her departure, yet Katherine had insisted on keeping the gathering exclusive to only them. Rose absently rubbed her hands together, a nervous habit of hers, as she rejoined the company.

"Is there anything else you need?" Rose asked, glancing at each of her guests. They all shook their heads, and Rose sat beside Florence with a smile, relishing the familiarity of their proximity.

"Well, I've had a little chat with Edna," Katherine announced, affectionately patting Edna's knee. "And she's graciously agreed to make a statement. Isn't that right, Edna?"

Edna wiped the cake crumbs from her mouth and nodded solemnly. "It's my duty."

Confusion furrowed Rose's brow, and she exchanged a look with Florence. Who folded her arms with a tut. "Edna, could you please explain what exactly happened?"

Edna sighed. "My Rupert knew about everything that went on during the build, and he told me the same story most nights—a story that kept him awake for most of his later years. That man, Kenneth... what's his name?"

"Banks. Sir Banks." Katherine interrupted.

"Yes. That's the one. He was the boss, in charge of the labour and all that. On his watch, one of the contractors died. She hit her head and he got a few of the boys to bury the secret."

Florence interjected. "A woman contractor? Back then?" Florence interjected. "That's rather unusual, isn't it?"

Katherine scrutinised Florence, her lips forming a disapproving pout. "Florence, I never expected you to be the one belittling women. What's next? Questioning female doctors too?"

Florence's eyes widened at Katherine's raised eyebrow. "No, not at all. It's just uncommon, that's all. I'm merely surprised that no one questioned her absence or inquired about her whereabouts. Wouldn't all the tradesmen from the local area ask where she was?"

Before Edna could reply, Katherine leaned forward, preventing further discussion. "Florence, haven't we heard enough of your outdated views for one afternoon? As a proud lesbian, I expected better from you." Katherine redirected her attention to Edna. "Apologies for the interruption. Please continue, Edna."

Edna shifted uncomfortably, her gaze shifting to Rose, who smoothed down her cardigan. "Well, I've always wanted to inform the police. I yearned for that poor, desperate soul to be found, and for the person responsible to face justice. I believe now is the time to reveal the truth and disclose everything to the police."

Rose glanced at Florence, who chewed on her lip, visibly hesitant to question them further. Picking at her nail, Rose's mind swirled with numerous unanswered questions, yet a stern look from Katherine served as a warning to remain silent. Clearing her throat, Rose mustered the courage to speak up.

"Edna, do you have any evidence to support what Rupert said? Any tangible proof—a name, a signed confession, anything?" Rose stammered, glancing between Edna and Florence.

Rising to her feet, Katherine interjected, "Listen, girls. We understand this isn't foolproof, but there's enough truth in this story to ignite discussions and raise doubts. We want people to question things, and we want Kenneth to end up in all the wrong headlines." Katherine directed her attention to Edna. "Head home, wipe off that makeup, and make yourself look as ill and feeble as possible. Call the police and request they come to take your statement. Understand?" Edna nodded and used her stick to steady herself, grabbing another slice of cake before leaving.

Florence nudged Rose with her knee, her eyes darting between the two women. "Are you sure this plan will work? We can already see through it."

Katherine beamed. "Of course it will. The police haven't done a damn thing, especially when the answer is right in front of them. That's why we're taking matters into our own hands while Edna plays her part across the road."

"Will this be enough to make Lesley question staying with him?" Florence asked.

Katherine settled into Edna's vacant seat and leaned in closer. "I've already reached out to a few trusted contacts. By now, the information should have reached all the right people—except Kenneth, of course."

Rose gripped the edge of her seat and leaned forward. She wanted nothing more than this to be over. But that didn't stop the fear. Kenneth could ruin their lives with one phone call if he so wished. "So, what do we need to do?"

Katherine retrieved her phone, composed an email, and sent it to Rose. "I need you to get in touch with that friend of yours, the cafe owner. You mentioned people visiting the cafe, searching for clues and information about the lake. Tell him everything Edna just revealed." Katherine paused before adding, "We need to play this up to the online fanatics. Every blog, social media page, podcast—spread the word far and wide. Copy the email and send it to them. They won't care about fact-checking; they'll report it."

Florence sank back onto the sofa. Her eyebrows raised as she shook her head. "And you believe this online gossip from a bunch of nobodies will be enough to bring an end to his political career and involvement with The Order?" Florence's brow furrowed with doubt. "Rose, are you buying into all this? I think we need more than that."

"Social media is a powerful tool." Katherine interjected. "Let the rumours spread. I've already sent some information to those wretched news channels. They've been itching for something to bring him down. Nothing sells more than a murder cover-up. Trust me, Florence, this will be enough."

Rose faced the window and spotted two parked cars

outside Edna's home. "That was quick. Edna must have really convinced them over the phone."

Katherine sprang into action. "Right. Send those emails, Rose. Today, we bring Kenneth down.

After Katherine left, Florence reached out and touched Rose's knee. "Are you sure about all this? Katherine has bulldozed her way through without giving us a second to think. Someone is getting away with murder here. Katherine wants to resurrect that dreadful group. Is this truly what you want to be a part of?"

Rose met Florence's gaze, the determination clear in her eyes. Florence possessed a strength and resilience she herself had always lacked. From the car accident years ago to burying the truth of George's death, Rose had always taken the easy way out: giving up her son without searching for him, allowing Ava to go to prison for a crime she didn't commit. While Rose may never know the truth about the woman from the lake, she could do something about Katherine and The Order—the group that had set this entire mess in motion. Violet's dying wish had been to provide Rose with enough information to expose the truth.

"I know what I should do," Rose admitted, her voice weary. "What I *can* do. I still have the list, the information, and all the photos safely tucked away."

Florence's eyes widened. "The stuff you and Emily gave to Kenneth?"

Rose nodded. She had a copy left, safely stored in her spare room, sitting beside the mask she once used that started this whole thing. "I made copies. I got rid of all of them, except for one. Just in case. The only thing is, my name is on that list. What if Kenneth discovers it came from me and brings back Emily's fraud case?" Rose sighed deeply. Emily had saved her life last year. The one person who was there when she needed to be, even after finding out Rose was the one behind her mothers death. She owed her everything. "Perhaps we should play along with Katherine's plan, at least for now. Let it happen, and then we can get on with our lives."

Florence drummed her fingers on the table. She leaned closer towards Rose. "Ask yourself, Rose. Do you truly trust Katherine? Will she uphold her word and genuinely work towards improving The Order?"

Rose turned her head, her gaze fixed on Katherine striding towards Edna's house. Could The Order ever change? Was even one percent of doubt worth risking. That cult had been around for so long. Years and decades it had survived. If this was the one chance, the one moment in time to cripple it from existence. Could Rose truly risk not taking that chance? She shook her head. "No, I don't trust her. She's done so many terrible things, kept countless secrets, and manipulated all of them to her advantage."

Florence gently rubbed Rose's knee. "Then you know what you need to do."

Rose switched on her phone and contacted Benny, asking him if he could provide a list of customers he remembered from the café inquiring about the body. She began scouring the internet, requesting Florence to compile a list of every blog, website, or platform that had ever mentioned the murder. "Look up The Order too. I remember there were rumours about it when I first joined. I want to include those sites, too."

As the sky darkened outside, Florence and Rose compiled a list of over two hundred email addresses associated with The Order, cult groups, and online murder enthusiasts. Rose uploaded every document, scanned every photo that Violet had left for her. She examined the list once again, where

Rose's own name was etched in black ink. She could cross it out, redact a few names to protect the people she knew, but it wouldn't be fair. It wouldn't be the true story. Fuelled by determination, she attached the files to the email list and clicked send.

Rose watched the tiny spinning circle on her computer screen indicating the emails were being sent.

"It's done. It's out there. Every secret of The Order," Rose said. Her body loosened. For the first time since she was a child, she actually felt free. Free from stress, grief, pain and worry. The relief was instant. "Photos of Kenneth's sacrificial acts, the list of members: police, politicians, celebrities, and every naïve soul like me who fell into their trap."

Rose had left nothing out, and there was nothing redacted. She'd laid everything bare for the world to judge.

CHAPTER THIRTY-NINE
A Living Lie

Ava gently placed the burner phone onto the table after sending the text, the weight of its significance hanging heavy in the air. With a quick swipe, she removed the battery and slammed it onto the floor before retrieving a pair of scissors to cut the SIM card in half. Ava's final message to Nick, finally closing this chapter of her life. It felt bittersweet, mainly bitter with how it ended. She'd wanted to leave him for years, but never found the way to do it. His death, though tragic, did allow her freedom. Having Nick back on the table. It complicated things more than Ava wanted to admit.

She cranked up the volume on the television to drown out her racing thoughts. A breaking news report started. Ava settled onto the sofa and crossed her legs. The dark haired, chiselled jaw of a news anchor began.

"We interrupt your regular programming for this urgent

update on the upcoming election and the shocking revelations surrounding a prominent Member of Parliament, Sir Kenneth Banks. Let's go live with our seasoned reporter, Melissa Anderson, who is currently outside his home. Melissa, what can you share with us?"

Ava leaned forward, reaching for the crystal glass of champagne on her coffee table.

"Earlier today, it was confirmed that Sir Kenneth Banks, a well-known figure in Parliament, has withdrawn from the election following the release of deeply disturbing information to the press. Startling allegations have surfaced, linking Sir Kenneth to a long-standing murder investigation and even hinting at his involvement with a satanic cult!"

Ava instinctively grabbed her phone to open the group chat with Rose, Florence, and Emily. Her fingers flew across her phone, urging them to tune in to the news. Tossing her phone onto the sofa, she returned her attention back to the screen.

"According to reports, the leaked information connects Sir Kenneth Banks to a chilling murder that transpired over four decades ago. Though the exact details have not been disclosed, sources claim that the evidence against Sir Kenneth is substantial. Moreover, shocking revelations of his association with a satanic cult have sent shock waves through the community, with a list of alleged members now circulating on social media, implicating several high-profile celebrities and politicians."

A wicked grin stretched across Ava's face as she absorbed the news. The entire list had become a viral sensation that had spread like wildfire across social media platforms. She scrolled through the posts to find Nick and Katherine's names displayed among the others.

"Presently, Sir Kenneth Banks has remained tight-lipped

about these grave allegations." The news anchor cleared his throat. "His campaign team has issued a brief statement acknowledging the situation, but refrained from providing further comments. Disturbing photographs are circulating online, purporting to show a young Sir Banks engaging in blood rituals. Our news channel is diligently working to verify the authenticity of these images, but even so, it is clear to all that Sir Kenneth Banks' once-promising career has met its demise this morning."

Ava rose from her seat and peered outside the window, seeking a familiar sight—a wave from Emily or a hopeful sprint down the lane from Florence. Yet the close was empty. She had no idea where her friends were. No clue about what was transpiring in their lives. Just then, the sound of the doorbell jolted Ava from her thoughts. She took one last sip of champagne, wiped her mouth, and hurried to the door, swinging it open to find Rose, her smile infectious.

"Rose, you did it! You bloody did it!" Ava exclaimed, pulling her sister into a tight embrace. "I'm so proud of you. So, so, *so* proud." Ava turned back to the lounge to pour a drink for Rose as she squealed in place, her hands shacking with excitement. "Have you heard from Katherine?" she asked, passing the glass over.

"No, no one. I saw the report and came straight to you," Rose said, downing the champagne in one gulp. "I'm worried and scared, but I have no regrets. It's over, Ava. The Order is finally finished, and no matter what happens now, at least I can say I did something."

Ava wrapped her arm around Rose and refilled her glass. Her little, coy, shy sister had done it. She'd finally, after all these years moved on from the sixteen year old Ava left. Her sister had fought harder than she had ever imagined to become the woman she is now. Ava knew that it would be okay. That Rose would continue to flourish, even without Ava beside her. "I always knew you had it in you, sis. You're going to be okay, you know. Once I'm gone."

"No second thoughts, then?" Rose asked with a pleading smile.

She'd done nothing but second guess it. She wanted to be here for Rose, to make sure her life turns out well. Florence had moved on, began a new chapter, a new family. Ava knew deep down, that there was nothing keeping her here. Not anymore. Not once she'd finished her last job. Ava shook her head. "No. I've made up my mind. I just have one more thing to do." She glanced at her watch before handing Rose her half-empty glass. "Here, finish this for me. I have a meeting." Just one more meeting left, she thought determinedly.

As she drove out of her driveway, Emily and Theo pulled up outside of Emily's home. It had been days since Ava had last seen them, so she spun her car and honked the horn. "Em!" She waved her hand and lowered the car's roof. "Why do you look so glum? Haven't you seen the news?"

Emily slowly approached Ava's car, signalling for Theo to go inside. Ava couldn't help but notice Emily's dishevelled appearance. While Emily's fashion sense was more minimalist, she wore a baggy jumper today, marred by dried stains on the sleeves. "Are you okay? Is he treating you okay? You can tell me, Emily. You know that."

Emily scrunched up her face and ran her hand through her hair. "Everything is fine, Ava. It's just been a tough few days. I've barely slept. What were you going on about?"

Ava narrowed her eyes, observing the dark bags under her eyes and chapped lips. Had the honeymoon ended between her and Theo? Ava thought. "Kenneth Banks. The Order. The body from the lake. It's all come out. Everything Rose had on that dreadful group is now public knowledge."

Emily's jaw dropped. "Rose?"

Ava nodded. "She kept a file, sent it off, and exposed the entire group."

A smile slowly crept onto Emily's face, and her cheeks flushed with colour. "That's fantastic news."

Just then, Emily's phone rang. Emily peered at her phone, before focusing on Ava again. "You should answer it. It might be important," Ava suggested.

"I don't know if I can handle anything else right now," Emily murmured, glancing at the caller ID. "It's the hospital."

Ava took the phone from Emily's grip and answered it. "Yes, this is Ava Shaw, a friend of Emily's." She nodded while listening intently, and when she looked up at Emily, her expression was one of defeat. "Cynthia Lamont, yes. That's correct. Her grandmother." Ava relayed the information to calm a nervous Emily, who nervously bit her lip. "I understand. I'll pass her over." Ava handed the phone back to Emily, beaming. "I suppose it's a good day for all of us. Cynthia is awake." Ava winked at Emily as her face lit up with relief.

Ava glanced down at her phone, noticing an email from her estate agent. The money had been transferred. Now all she needed to do was accept the moving date. Turning her attention back to Emily, Ava asked, "Everything okay?"

Emily ended the call and said, "Yeah, she's awake and talking. It'll be a few more days until she can come home, but God, I feel so relieved."

Ava glanced behind Emily at Theo, standing her doorway. His fashion sense mirrored Emily's plain appearance. A beige hoodie hung from him, loose fitting pants. Their lack of fashion pulled at Ava's heart, in an odd way. They truly were suited. "You've got a good man there. I think he'd do anything to keep you happy," Ava said, nodding at Theo.

Emily glanced back at Theo, who blew her a kiss and smiled. As Ava watched Emily, she realised how much more of the world there was. She'd been here for years longer than intended. Emily arrived with a plan to seek revenge on Ava for what happened to her mother. She accepted that. In a way, she respected Emily for carrying it out. But now, there was no hate left here, no plans to meet. She needed to guide Emily. For the first time in years, Ava had some advice to share..

"Now that you know Cynthia is okay and all the art business is behind you, it's time for you to move on with your life," Ava said.

"What do you mean?"

"You came here to uncover the truth. And you did just that. Take some time now to pursue your own desires. Don't dwell on the past and no more seeking revenge or holding onto secrets. You've sacrificed enough." Ava glanced at her phone again as another message came through from her agent, requiring her attention. "Look at me. Oscar and I waited so long to be together, only to have our dreams shattered. Don't let the same happen to you and Theo."

Emily raised her chin. Her bottom lip shaking. "Ava, I've never heard you be so... kind before."

Quickly replying to the message on her phone, Ava agreed to the moving date. "Well, maybe I'm done pretending. The life I built here, the walls I built around myself and my friendships—it was all for nothing. All a facade. I see that now—I can see how terrible I was," Ava admitted, putting the car into gear. "I've sold the house, Emily. I'm moving on. I want you to promise me you'll do the same." Ava didn't wait for Emily's response. She sped off, leaving a trail of dust in her rear-view mirror as she focused straight ahead on her final meeting—the last connection she needed to sever before she could truly let go.

Ava parked her car at the deserted train station to watch the dilapidated building. She glanced at her watch; she had a few minutes less than expected. Stepping onto the gravel path, Ava surveyed her surroundings, but saw no sign of him yet.

She slipped through the gap where the door once stood before waiting in the dark and overgrown reception. The sound of cracking glass reverberated through the air, accompanied by her husband's heavy footsteps. "Nick, you're late," she said. He looked well, almost too well for a man who was suppose to be dead. His outfit hung on him, his stomach no longer bulging. The stubble he now wore helped frame his round face.

"Sorry. I wasn't expecting your message. I had some business to attend to," Nick said, his tone defensive.

Ava purposely turned, wearing the perfume he had gifted her—the scent that always aroused his senses—and slowly, she walked toward him, subtly wafting the fragrance in his direction. "You look awful, dear," she purred, stepping back when he turned to face her. "How's business? Even in death, you work too much."

Nick narrowed his eyes. "Things haven't gone well. All my plans are collapsing, but it's okay. I have a Plan B."

"Plan B?" Ava asked, her interest piqued. Nick let his smile take control of his face as it beamed.

"You, the house, the savings. It may not take me as far as I had hoped, but I can make a fresh start. Rebuild something," Nick said, though a hint of desperation entered his voice. "Has the house sold? I assume that's the reason for our meeting?"

Ava smiled, relishing the moment and savouring each

second. However, she knew time was running out. "Yes, the house has sold—sold for a high price, too."

Nick stepped closer. "The money. Is it in the bag?"

When he reached for it, Ava swung it out of reach. "Now, now. It's not that simple," she teased, inspecting her nails with her free hand. "I saw the news this morning. Doesn't look good for all your contacts, does it?"

"It's already on the news?" Nick's voice quivered.

"Sure is. I think nothing will keep those secrets safe anymore, Nick, not even yours." Ava's tone dripped with satisfaction. Triumph.

"Well then, it's lucky I'm dead." Nick advanced, attempting to snatch the bag once more, but Ava stepped back, keeping her distance. "Hand the money over, Ava. I thought you said you were done playing games."

Ava tossed the bag onto the floor with a mischievous grin. "Oh, I am. I just wanted to relish this a little longer. After all, it's our final meeting."

"You can come with me. It's not too late for us," Nick said, a glimmer of hope in his eyes. Nick stepped forward with confidence. As he crouched down and lifted the bag, Ava watched as his face dropped.

Ava laughed, the sound cold and mocking. "Even now, you think there's hope, don't you? How utterly pathetic. It's over, Nick. All your power has vanished. I'm leaving, and I'll ensure you can never again harm another person."

Nick peered into the bag, and his expression turned to one of disbelief. "It's empty. What the hell are you playing at, Ava?"

Ava grinned. "I've already told the police. I've spilled everything."

Nick stepped toward her, clenching his fists. "You *bitch*. You wouldn't dare!"

"They're outside right now. It's time you faced the consequences, darling," Ava calmly said, closing the distance between them. She gently took the empty bag from his grasp and whispered in his ear. "This is for Emily and her father. You'll pay for faking your death, Nick. Do it quietly, and I'll stay silent about your hitman arrangement and all the years of art fraud." Ava kissed him on the cheek. "Do you understand?"

Nick's face contorted with rage. "You're only keeping quiet because of the money *I* gave you. You were more than happy to spend it, knowing where it came from. Give me one reason to stay silent."

Brushing her fingers against his chin, she chuckled, "Because you're selfish and will want the shortest possible sentence. Now, if you don't mind, I have to pack."

"I'll find you, Ava. I gave you this life. Don't think I won't track you down when I'm free," Nick threatened.

Ava stepped aside as the sound of police footsteps came from outside. The loose door fell from its hinge as the officers marched in. Ava moved away and raised her hands, watching as her husband fell to his knees. A smile tugged at the corners of her lips, chuckling at the sight of his face buried in the dirt. Ava refused to look away from him as they handcuffed and forced him into the police van outside.

Relief washed over her as the tension built from before dissipated from her shoulders. She stretched her neck, reviling in the newfound freedom.

Pulling out her phone, Ava opened a photo of her and Oscar, a snapshot they had taken in a motel room—the night they had spent planning their future. His flushed cheeks, unkempt hair. Those ocean eyes she always became lost in. She missed him dearly. She swiped along to a picture of the Scottish highlands: lush green hills and endless blue skies.

Closing her eyes, she imagined a cottage nestled in those serene landscapes and pictured bitter winter nights spent by the fire, with Oscar by her side. They had dreamed of a future together, plans that would forever remain unfulfilled, but Ava knew she could forge a new life there, a life where she could finally find happiness again.

CHAPTER FORTY
A New Life

Florence surveyed her home and trailed her fingers through her hair. "Are you sure you're up for this, love? It's not too late to cancel."

"Mum, I'm fine. You're not getting out of this party," replied Olivia, her voice firm.

Florence brushed a strand of hair away from her daughter's face; her birthday had snuck up on her with all the chaos from the last few weeks. She glanced at Regina, who meticulously arranged glasses on the table and polished them with a cloth. Florence marvelled at how Regina had orchestrated all of this in a time where everything had spiralled out of control. "Is there anything I can do?" Florence asked her, standing in the middle of the room, feeling somewhat useless. Regina planted a kiss on Florence's cheek.

"Relax and enjoy your day," she said, before focusing

again on the table.

Olivia's smile lit up her face when she glanced at her phone. "Mum, have you heard about Lesley? She's selling her house and moving to Spain. The whole gym chat is buzzing with gossip about it."

Florence looked at her daughter puzzled. Olivia had never been keen on the gym, but then she remembered. The women at the club. Lesley's gossiping friends. "You're still part of that group?" Florence raised an eyebrow. "They're all older than me, Liv."

Olivia grinned. "I know, but I get so much entertainment from them. I can't leave it."

Florence stepped into the garden, where the cloudless sky promised a perfect day for the party. Lucas lay on the grass, gazing up at it, yet Florence's shadow fell across him and likely obscured his view. "Everything alright?"

Lucas shielded his eyes from the sun and sat up. "Yeah, just enjoying the peace. It's rare to have the house so quiet. It feels strange." He crossed his legs and turned fully to face Florence. "Have you heard from grandma and granddad?" Florence shook her head. She hadn't heard from her parents since they left. Admittedly, she'd never bothered to check on them either, but in this instant, she wanted to leave the ball in their court. If they wanted to be a part of her life. Then they would let her know. "Sorry. If you don't want me to talk about them, I won't."

"You can talk about them if you want," Florence said. "I know you didn't have much time for them, but they care about you kids."

"Granddad really looked after me when I went away last year, Mum. I don't think you realise how low I had gotten." Lucas lowered his head. Florence stepped towards him, placing a hand along his shoulder. "With Dad being killed, and you turning to drink again, things seemed hopeless here. I needed some time away and thought I could handle whatever the world threw at me." He wiped a tear from his cheek. "With Dad gone, I thought nothing else could hurt me, but I was wrong. I was stupid to get involved with drugs and end up owing all that money."

Florence had battled her own demons with alcohol throughout her life, always in pursuit of that bitter, numbing taste. It was a struggle she had lived with throughout all her life, a cycle of recovery and relapse. The fear that her children might inherit her destructive habits lingered in the recesses of her mind, and as she looked at Lucas now, she could truly appreciate how much he'd grown. "It's okay. I understand the grip that those things can have on you," Florence said, gently stroking Lucas's shoulder. "I'll never be able to thank my father enough for what he did for you." She gripped Lucas's hand. "I'll always be here for you, Lucas. If you ever need help, know that I won't judge. Know that there's always a place for you here."

The house hummed with activity as guests arrived, spilling out of the garden and into the close. Florence went inside; she recognised some faces, but others were unfamiliar. They were all here to celebrate her birthday. Across the room, Rose stood with a man. She burst out laughing and patted his chest. On the other side of the room, Regina engaged in animated conversation with a friend, shifting from left to right. Ava tapped Florence on the shoulder, fashionably late yet dripping in glamour from head to toe. She enveloped Florence in a warm embrace and handed her a small, wrapped present. "Just a little something. Happy birthday."

"I'm glad you made it. So, the house is sold?" asked Florence.

"Yeah. I'm ready. Leaving everything behind and starting fresh," Ava said.

"I'm going to miss you, you know. We all will."

Ava raised an eyebrow. Casting an eye over every member in attendance. "You don't have to lie, Flo. I don't think everyone will miss me." She picked up a glass of champagne from a passing server Regina had hired. "So, what's up with Regina? She seems all over the place."

Florence glanced at Regina again. She couldn't seem to keep still, constantly fidgeting and scratching her arm as she talked. "Yeah, she's been a bit scattered since this morning. I don't think she's used to organising such a big event."

"Well, when she found out I was coming, it probably added to the pressure. And who's that with our Rose?" Ava gestured toward the man. Seeing Rose with Benny warmed Florence's heart. She knew it was stupid to get so emotional over a simple pairing. But now knowing what Rose has been through. It seemed fitting that she would find such a gentle man.

"That's Benny, her new best friend. He offered her a food contract for his cafe, and they've been talking non-stop on the phone ever since. It's quite sweet, really."

"Yeah, I guess so." Ava raised her glass, sipping her drink. "Any more gossip before I leave?"

"Not much. Things have quieted down. Katherine has vanished, and I've heard Lesley has too. Have you heard anything from Emily? She seems to have locked herself away these past few days." Florence scanned the room, checking to see if Emily had arrived. "Olivia mentioned that she and Cynthia might try to make an appearance today. Regina was quite insistent."

"Well, Regina called me too. She said even though I've already sold the house, I had to come today. It's impossible to say no to your woman, really. You two are quite the match," Ava raised her glass in a silent toast.

Regina rushed to the front door as Emily and Cynthia entered the lounge. Guests parted to make way for Cynthia, who sat on the nearest armchair, resting her walking stick on her lap. "Emily! Cynthia! Oh, I'm so glad you made it!" Florence exclaimed, rushing over to greet them. Cynthia was like a battle worn tank. All her parts were still intact and she'd lost none of her spirit. But Florence was sure she saw a slightly softer side to her smile.

"Waiter, bring me one of each food item," Cynthia called.

"I see you've quickly regained your strength," Ava said. "Emily, you're looking better too. So, Regina, we're all here."

Regina bit her lip and smiled at Florence. She wiped her brow and then brushed her hands along her trousers. "Right. I guess it's time then." Regina turned towards Olivia, who smiled and switched off the lights. Lucas emerged from the kitchen, carrying a cake. Florence tried to battle away any tears. She realised now, that everyone was here, together in her home. That small thing, meant the world.

Rose stepped forward. "It's my special lemon and raspberry sponge with white chocolate," she whispered in Florence's ear, yet she had no time to reply as Regina took hold of Florence's hands. The room fell silent, all eyes turning towards them. Florence's cheeks flushed. This was their first public display of affection, she realised, in front of friends and strangers alike.

Florence's chest tightened as Regina looked at her, teary-eyed. "What's gotten into you, Regina? It's my birthday, not yours."

Regina swallowed and took a deep breath. "Florence, you have shown me what a strong woman looks like. You welcomed me into your life and into your family." Florence glanced around the room, Regina's grip loosening on her hands. Stepping back, Regina dropped to one knee and pulled a small box from her pocket. The room gasped as Florence looked down at Regina's ring, beaming. "Will you do me the honour of being my wife?"

The room froze, the air charged with anticipation. Florence glanced around while a smile she couldn't contain bloomed across her face. She glanced at Ava, who nodded approvingly. Then Florence turned back to Regina. "Of course I will." The room erupted in cheers and applause. Florence pulled Regina up and crushed her lips against hers in a passionate kiss. She held Regina tightly, unable to believe this moment had finally arrived. Her thoughts drifted back to the little girl she once was—the one whose mother had instructed her to keep her feelings a secret, the teenager who had never dared to follow her heart. She thought of the woman who sought solace in alcohol as escapism, to fit into a world that she didn't think would accept her. She had said yes, not just for the love she had for Regina, but for the little girl who never believed this was possible. Regina slipped the ring onto Florence's finger, then turned to find Ava reaching towards the happy couple, eager to congratulate them.

"Well done, girl," Cynthia chimed in, already diving into a plate of food.

"What did I tell you?" Ava leaned into inspect the ring. "I said she'd move fast." With her free hand, Ava pulled Regina closer. "You take care of her, you hear me? I'll be back to check up on you."

Florence finally found a seat to rest her aching feet. Ava stood beside her, her eyes widening at something on her phone. "Ava, what is it?" Florence asked, concerned.

Ava looked up, and her mouth fell open. She glanced at

Emily and then Rose. "It's Doctor Mike."

"Mike? What happened? He hasn't escaped, has he?" Cynthia leaned forward, anger lacing her words. "That bloody bastard better not show his face around here."

"No, there's been a report. He was found dead in his cell." Florence felt the earth shift. Those words. They didn't feel real. "Mike... he's dead."

Regina gripped Florence's shoulder. "Dead?" All eyes turned to Florence for the second time that evening.

Olivia and Lucas rushed into the room then. "Mum! Mum, have you heard?" Olivia exclaimed.

Florence took a deep breath.

"Are you alright, Flo?" Emily asked.

Florence nodded, her mind racing. "I need some fresh air." She pushed herself up, manoeuvring through the crowd of people gathered in the hallway to step out into the close.

Ava followed behind her. "He's gone, Flo."

Florence nodded, peering up at the sky. "Yeah, I... I know I should feel relieved. Grateful that he's gone, but..."

Ava wrapped her arm around Florence's shoulder. "I understand. I wanted him to suffer in there, too. He had years ahead of him to rot in that place."

"And now he's gotten off early." Florence turned to Ava, her expression a reflection of the conflicting emotions whirring inside. "Oscar is gone from our lives forever, and Mike only was punished for... what? A few months."

Ava gently grabbed Florence's chin, tilting her head up to meet her eyes. "Hey. Don't you dare shed a tear for that man. Don't let him have any power over you." Ava said, her eyes burning. "Do you hear me? He's gone. He can't hurt anyone else. Not ever."

Florence turned and glanced through the window at the entire world inside her home—everyone she cared about was there, except for Oscar. She glanced at Ava, knowing how much she missed him. She knew the exact feelings running through her mind. "I'm going to miss you so much. Everything that happened between us with Oscar... I understand it all now. I was a terrible wife to him. We were friends, but never lovers. I was living a lie, and I took it out on him the most." Florence wiped away a tear.

"Hey, don't cry," Ava whispered.

"I just wish you had more time with him, you know?"

Ava wiped away a tear streaming down her own cheek. "We have each other. You have that beautiful family inside to remind you of him. I have plans to carry out the future we had envisioned together." Ava turned. "Come on. It's my last night in Beechwood. Let's not spend it dwelling on the past." Florence watched as Ava went back inside. When her phone buzzed, she looked down to see a text from her father.

'Congratulations, darling. I'm so proud.'

CHAPTER FORTY-ONE
Opening Up

Rose sat at her table, idly swirling the coffee around her mug, lost in thought. The world bustled around her. The customers perused the menu, selecting their desired cakes, while Benny dutifully fulfilled their orders. Leaning on her elbows, she eagerly awaited Elisa's arrival, yet was drawn to a solitary figure occupying the window seat. The young girl wore a leather jacket, her pale complexion and faded blue hair adding to her air of rebellion. The girl was a haunting reminder of what she imagined Violet's life was like before falling under The Order's control, before her obsession consumed her.

The girl slumped, staring into her glass of water. Rose felt a surge of empathy and yearned to approach and check she was alright—the very questions she had longed for strangers to ask her when she desperately sought an escape from her marriage. As Benny passed by with a tray, Rose took the opportunity. She hastily scribbled her number and name on a piece of paper and added a message that read, *'If you need to talk, I'm here.'* She handed the note to Benny. "Could you kindly pass this along to that girl when you bring her the bill?"

Benny folded the note with a mischievous wink. Perhaps the girl didn't need help and would simply discard the message, but the act felt right—a small gesture.

The tinkling cafe bell announced Elisa's arrival. Spotting Rose instantly, George's other wife placed her hefty bag on the table and said, "Sorry I'm late, Rose, but you're looking as charming as ever. Thank you for agreeing to meet me again."

Rose smiled and brushed stray crumbs from the table. "Well, my life has settled quite a bit since our last meeting. Dare I say, my troubles are over, and my pastries have sold exceptionally well here. So when you mentioned the cookbook, it felt like the perfect time to start things up again."

Elisa extracted a folder from her bag. "Yes, the cookbook is nearly complete, right? Just a few adjustments left."

"Adjustments?" Rose asked. With everything going on, Rose had agreed to the suggestions on the cook book without registering them fully. Her life had felt like it'd been on autopilot for weeks.

"Well, for one, that dedication to George needs to go. We both know what a monster he was. Let's keep him far away from the book." Rose couldn't be happier at removing George for her life, the book included. She'd added him as a preface. A way to dodge speculation about herself, but really she shouldn't have bothered. She'd given up caring what other thought of her.

Rose absentmindedly swirled her drink. "I also wanted to change the charity donation. I want one hundred percent of the profits to go to Women's Aid. I want nothing for myself from the sales."

A warm smile spread across Elisa's face. "We can certainly arrange that."

Rose nodded and flipped through the menu. "So, you wanted to meet in person? How come?"

Elisa chuckled, tucking a strand of hair behind her ear. Benny placed Elisa's latte and one of Rose's almond croissant on the table. "I'd like to discuss a proposition with you, Rose. It's about that dreadful cult Sir Kenneth Banks was involved in. It's quite the hot topic these days."

Rose shifted in her seat. She had left her name on that list. Although no one had yet said anything to her. There were hundreds of names on that list after all, all far more important and well known than a Rose Walker. But she was sure that day would come, where she'd be asked about it. "The Order, right?" Rose murmured, unable to stop herself from recoiling. She had vowed never to speak of that place again and bury the memories of the unspeakable evil she had witnessed. Yet every night, those haunting thoughts invaded her mind—the first thing to greet her upon waking.

Elisa opened her folder on the table and scanned its contents. "Now, the list of members. I noticed your name there. You joined fairly recently, right? Many people are now coming forward, sharing stories of being deceived into joining and being threatened when they asked to leave." Leaning closer, she added, "Rose, I believe there's a story within you. A story the world needs to hear."

"I-I really don't. I barely know anything about it." Rose shook her head, prompting Elisa to roll her eyes.

"You knew Violet Chansky. In fact, rumour has it she left something for you in her will." She grabbed hold of Rose's hands. "This cookbook is exceptional—there's no doubt about that. But you have an extraordinary opportunity here." Taking a sip of her drink, she added, "We've both endured hell with George, but this is your chance to shape your own narrative. Not a tragic tale of a battered housewife, but a story of a woman who defied an organisation and emerged victorious."

Rose cleared her throat, grappling with the conflicting emotions. "I... I'm really nobody. I was foolish and allowed terrible things to happen in The Order. I witnessed so much, I'm no hero."

Elisa firmly clasped Rose's hands, her eyes brimming with conviction. "I refuse to believe that. You possess a unique perspective on all of this. The leaked photos, the membership list—it all originated from Violet's home and found its way to you, didn't it? *Do* something with that. Show the world your strength."

Rose felt an overwhelming urge to flee and leave all this behind her, to never confront those haunting memories again. "I don't want to relive those memories every day. I don't want to go back to that dark place. It still haunts me."

"Then take control. Embrace them, put them into words, and transfer them from your mind onto paper." Elisa gripped Rose's hands tighter. "Rose, this could be your defining moment. Please consider it. I'll pour everything I have into making it a success, a story we can share to help others. Something that can offer hope to women like you and me, who once believed there was no way out."

Rose surveyed the cafe, her gaze lingering on Benny, who smiled warmly at her. A smile George had never given her the dignity of. There would have been a time where Rose tried to gain affection from George. She would do her hair, or make up to please him. Wear clothes he'd chosen or commented on, no matter how she felt in them. That life was gone now. She wore her hair how she wanted to, and Benny had only ever complimented her. Never once spoken down to her. The girl in the window glanced at the note before scanning the cafe with wide, hopeful eyes. Memories flooded back to Rose, reminders of her past weaknesses when life seemed utterly bleak and helpless. Elisa's unwavering gaze met hers. "If I say yes, I want it done right. I want to make a difference and to shed light on the truth. I won't portray myself as a saint. I've made mistakes."

Elisa's smile widened. "So, you'll do it?"

Rose nodded, and Elisa leaned closer to shake her hand. As the girl sitting in the window left the cafe, Rose's phone buzzed.

A simple act that held the power to change so much.

Rose's heart raced, overwhelmed by the weight of Elisa's offer. This was her chance to rectify the mistakes she had made throughout her life. The bustling café had since calmed, and Benny joined Rose at the table. "Did your meeting go well, then?" he asked.

Rose nodded, unable to hide the excitement in her eyes. "I believe so. I'm genuinely excited about what the future holds."

Benny beamed. "Me too. I'm grateful that you came here all those months ago. You're a remarkable woman, Rose."

Rose wanted to pinch Benny's cheeks and hold his hand under the table. She yearned to spend the evening with him. But she wasn't ready. She couldn't allow another man into her life, not yet. She desired it, craved to wake up to share breakfasts with him, but even with George gone, that lingering *'what if'* persisted, tugging at her heartstrings. She needed to keep her guard.

"I have an evening off next week and a spare ticket to a

show. I was wondering if you'd like to join me?" Benny's smile widened as he unbuttoned his collar. "Oh God, listen to me. I sound like such an amateur. It's been such a long time. You can say no if you want."

Rose smiled, though her heart ached. "It's been a long time for me, too." She longed to cry. She mourned her old self, who would have eagerly said yes. She longed to laugh, touch, and experience love once more. In her mind, she said yes on repeat, though her lips remained motionless. Benny looked at her, his eyes expectant. After months of becoming friends, he had mustered the courage to ask, and yet she couldn't bring herself to respond.

She smoothed down her hair and nodded. "I would be honoured to."

Benny beamed with joy. They sat together, watching the world pass by in silence. It was a silence that felt right—one that felt safe.

CHAPTER FORTY-TWO
Secrets and Lies

The leaves shimmered like golden confetti as the sun rose, lighting up the horizon. Emily's footsteps echoed in the silence that enveloped the sleeping neighbourhood as she embarked on her last walk along the familiar path. Each step carried a memory. The tranquil lake, the neatly lined houses, the desolate park, and manicured lawns. Her gaze drifted toward Ava's old home, now vacant and eagerly awaiting a new family to breathe life into it. It was this very house, the catalyst that had drawn her here, that had ignited the fires of revenge within her.

In her mind, she retraced the tragic scene that had unfolded on the porch—a haunting gunman's stray bullet aimed at Nick but wounding Mike instead. It was a twist of fate that had allowed that vile man to slither his way into Florence's life, forever altering the course of her world and her family's. Emily wondered how different things might have been if she had let go of the past and left it alone.

Her gaze shifted to Edna's home, who now lived alone. After throwing Larry out, she had become a recluse and refused any visitors. It brought a smile to Emily's face, knowing Cynthia had finally let her guard down. Larry now spent more time at their house by Cynthia's side, caring for her every need.

Emily took her time to pass each house, counting the slabs on the pavement and the bricks in the road. She remembered the anxiety she had felt when she first drove into the close. Arriving in a world where she didn't belong. Where the rich, wealthy, and fabulous lived. It wasn't her world, but over time, she allowed herself to be present here. Realised the people in this close, the community was the best life she'd ever had, even if she had to look past so much pain to get here. From across the street, Theo emerged from the doorway, the scent of his cooking wafting towards her. She smiled and called, "Just five more minutes!"

She yearned for a little extra time, desperate to remember this place. She glanced at her phone, refreshing Jessic's profile, but there was still no activity—no comments, no posts about her absence. Nothing. She closed her phone when Cynthia hobbled from the door to meet her.

"You're getting faster every day, Gran," Emily said.

Cynthia squinted and said, "Can't keep an old bird like me down, love. Are you coming inside or what?"

"Sorry, I'm just taking it all in," Emily replied, her gaze drifting across the surroundings.

"You're being sentimental when you should be thrilled, shouting from the rooftops," Cynthia teased.

Emily approached Cynthia and guided her toward a bench. "You need to rest. Are you sure you'll be okay here?"

Cynthia plopped down on the bench with a thud. "Of course I will. You've told me everything has been sorted, and I believe you. No questions asked." Cynthia gave Emily a stern, knowing look, but didn't comment further. "Larry has had enough practice dealing with that old bag Edna. I'm a piece of cake compared to her."

"I don't know how long we'll be gone. We'll come back and visit," Emily assured her.

"Love, take as much time as you need. They'll be plenty here to keep my eye on, don't you worry. Go out and have some fun. Live your life. You deserve it."

Emily nodded, knowing she had lied to Cynthia about her and Theo going away. It wasn't just a trip; they were escaping while they still could. But if the truth came out, she might not be able to return. It pained her to deceive her grandmother, like a blade piercing her chest. But she believed it was for the best—at least for now. Cynthia was safe, as were her friends.

"I have a confession, love." Cynthia pulled something from her pocket. "Promise you won't be mad, but Larry broke this when tidying up." In Cynthia's hand was a small blue jar, cracked along the glass. It used to hold a candle.

"This thing?" Emily held it. It had been a welcoming gift from when they moved in. She couldn't remember who brought it over. Emily looked closer at the candle. On the bottom was a small black plastic casing with a wire. She looked at her gran. "You found it like this? Can you remember who gave us this?"

Cynthia scratched her head. "No idea. One of the neighbours. It was just in the pile of gifts when we got here. Why?"

Emily turned the device in between her fingers. It was a bug. Clearly another item Jessie had planted to listen to their conversations. The thought of it made Emily sick, yet also satisfied, knowing how things had ended for her. She looked at her Gran, not wanting to explain. Instead, she held her hand. "I was so worried when you were in the hospital, Gran. Leaving you now, the timing is..."

"Listen to me," Cynthia interjected. "Don't you dare think I'm some helpless case that needs looking after. I'm fine: always have been, always will be. Now, enough of that. Let's go have breakfast and check up on the men."

Inside, Theo had placed their backpacks near the door, while their passports waited on the kitchen table. Larry sat beside Cynthia, engrossed in reading the newspaper. Emily silently approached Theo from behind and wrapped her arms around his waist. Her voice trembled with excitement as she whispered, "Are you truly ready?"

He turned to face her and gently nudged his glasses up his nose. "Absolutely. The taxi will be arriving any moment now. Did you say your goodbyes?"

Emily nodded, her eyes welling with tears. "Well, I said what I could. You know what gran can be like. Guarded till the end."

The honk of a car outside ended the bittersweet moment. "Okay, this is us," Theo murmured, reaching for Emily's hand. He picked up her bag and placed it in her trembling grip.

Outside, Florence and Rose stood with sorrowful expression. Florence enveloped Emily in a tight embrace. "Have a great time, won't you?" Florence said, pulling Emily in for a hug.

"I'll keep Cynthia fed. Message me every day. Let me know where you are all the time," Rose implored with a tender smile. "And, of course, you will return for the wedding, won't you?"

Emily glanced at Regina, standing on the other side of the road. Their eyes connected briefly. "As soon as you set the date, Flo, I'll be there," she replied, a touch of longing in her voice.

Rose stepped forward, a wistful gleam in her eyes. "Oh, Ava mentioned that if you find yourself in Scotland, let her know. She has a cabin available on her land, free of charge."

Emily smiled. Staying with Ava? She wasn't sure Theo would be able to cope. She wondered if she would too. But the offer was there, if they ever needed it. That at least brought some comfort.

"Any news on the new neighbour at Ava's place?" Emily asked. "I can't help but dig for a bit of last-minute gossip before I go."

Florence patted Emily gently on the shoulder. "They're actually moving in today. A few cars have been coming and going throughout the morning," she shared. "You need to get going. Remember, we will always be here. Have a great time, Theo. You look after her, okay?"

Emily placed her bag on her lap and closed the taxi door. She looked at her gran, whose face reddened as she wiped away a tear. Emily felt Theo's hand reach for hers, and as the taxi pulled away from the close, they passed a car with a family inside—a couple with two kids. They were neighbours Emily feared she would never get to know, people she would never meet. "Do you think we'll be safe?" Emily asked, her thoughts drifting back to that fateful night and the mess they had found themselves in at the cabin.

Theo wrapped an arm around Emily's shoulder. "We'll be fine. No one will ever find out what happened that night."

Emily smiled and leaned her head onto his chest, sensing his heart rate quicken as he spoke. She hoped he was telling the truth.

A Word From The Author

Thank you for reading Secrets, Lies & Obsession. I truly hope you have enjoyed the series and all the mysteries, twists and turns along the way.

It has been such a blast to create the neighbourhood of Beechwood Close and to explore all the residents that lived there.

If you enjoyed the book, it would mean so much to me if you were able to post a review. Each review is paramount at getting the word out about the Secrets & Lies series, and get as many eyes on this series as possible.

If you are looking for more work from me, you can find it at www.benandrewsauthor.co.uk and subscribe to my newsletter so you never miss and of my future projects.

Printed in Great Britain
by Amazon